SINKING TERROR

Jodi's shocked, gasping breath fought with a sob of denial. Near the prow, a little whirlpool spun. Water was swirling into the boat!

Terror. Heart-stabbing, muscle-tightening, dizzying terror grabbed hold of her body and fuddled her mind. Kneeling in the boat, Jodi stared wide-eyed at the water rising around her. It was icy cold.

A violent shiver contracted her taut muscles and shook her brain into action. In another few minutes the water would engulf the boat. She had to get out before it could suck her under or strike her as it sank.

Clearly, as though Annie were beside her, Jodi heard her sister's years-ago plea. *Learn to swim, Jodi. Please. So you won't drown like Mom and Dad did.*

Thank goodness she had the life jacket, which in her blind haste to get away from the island she'd forgotten to put on. She reached under the seat but couldn't feel the rough canvas fabric.

Sucking in her breath at the chill of the water as it came up almost to her waist, Jodi groped beneath and around the seat.

The life jacket wasn't there. . . .

NOWHERE TO RUN . . . NOWHERE TO HIDE . . . ZEBRA'S SUSPENSE WILL *GET* YOU — AND WILL MAKE YOU BEG FOR MORE!

NOWHERE TO HIDE (4035, $4.50)
by Joan Hall Hovey

After Ellen Morgan's younger sister has been brutally murdered, the highly respected psychologist appears on the evening news and dares the killer to come after her. After a flood of leads that go nowhere, it happens. A note slipped under her windshield states, "YOU'RE IT." Ellen has woken the hunter from its lair . . . and she is his prey!

SHADOW VENGEANCE (4097, $4.50)
by Wendy Haley

Recently widowed Maris learns that she was adopted. Desperate to find her birth parents, she places "personals" in all the Texas newspapers. She receives a horrible response: "You weren't wanted then, and you aren't wanted now." Not to be daunted, her search for her birth mother — and her only chance to save her dangerously ill child — brings her closer and closer to the truth . . . and to death!

RUN FOR YOUR LIFE (4193, $4.50)
by Ann Brahms

Annik Miller is being stalked by Gibson Spencer, a man she once loved. When Annik inherits a wilderness cabin in Maine, she finally feels free from his constant threats. But then, a note under her windshield wiper, and shadowy form, and a horrific nighttime attack tell Annik that she is still the object of this lovesick madman's obsession . . .

EDGE OF TERROR (4224, $4.50)
by Michael Hammonds

Jessie thought that moving to the peaceful Blue Ridge Mountains would help her recover from her bitter divorce. But instead of providing the tranquility she desires, they cast a shadow of terror. There is a madman out there — and he knows where Jessie lives — and what she has seen . . .

NOWHERE TO RUN (4132, $4.50)
by Pat Warren

Socialite Carly Weston leads a charmed life. Then her father, a celebrated prosecutor, is murdered at the hands of a vengeance-seeking killer. Now he is after Carly . . . watching and waiting and planning. And Carly is running for her life from a crazed murderer who's become judge, jury — and executioner!

Available wherever paperbacks are sold, or order direct from the Publisher. Send cover price plus 50¢ per copy for mailing and handling to Zebra Books, Dept. 4405 , 475 Park Avenue South, New York, N.Y. 10016. Residents of New York and Tennessee must include sales tax. DO NOT SEND CASH. For a free Zebra/Pinnacle catalog please write to the above address.

Mary-Ben Louis

SING ME TO SLEEP

ZEBRA BOOKS
KENSINGTON PUBLISHING CORP.

ZEBRA BOOKS are published by

Kensington Publishing Corp.
475 Park Avenue South
New York, NY 10016

First Printing: December, 1993

Printed in the United States of America

For Louis, who gave me love;
For Andy, who gave me music; and
For Bill Jack, who gave me memories.

With thanks to the special friends in North Texas Romance Writers, who give me family.

Prologue

With its strobe light flashing blood-colored circles through the ink-black night, the ambulance had pulled onto the deserted freeway and sped away in the cold rain. A trio of emergency flares cast their faint, eerie red glow on the two remaining vehicles.

Water sluiced down the grim face of the short, stocky traffic officer, his plastic raincoat glistening in the beam of the Austin police car's headlights. He turned toward the waiting witness who had emerged from a passionate pink chrome-laden pickup. A miniature waterfall plunged off the wide brim of the truck driver's white Stetson.

"She's D.O.S.," the policeman said.

"Huh? What's that?"

"Dead on the scene."

"Oh. Figures."

"You saw what happened?" the uniformed man asked.

"In this here downpour? Hellfire, I ain't never seen it rain like this since spring. Like a cow pissin' on a flat rock."

"Yes, sir." He almost smiled at the homegrown Texas simile, until he remembered the young woman's body he had watched being shoved into the rear of the ambulance. "But you must have seen something or you wouldn't have waited after calling the accident in on your CB."

"Yeah? Well . . ."

"Let's go sit in the patrol car so I can write up my report."

He led the way as they sloshed through puddles beside the road and climbed quickly into the black and white. After he closed his door and switched on the dome light, he picked up a clipboard and pen.

"I'm Officer Jamison," he informed the tall, lanky man, who had stretched jean-clad legs under the instrument panel until his cowboy boots disappeared in the gloom. "And your name?"

"Joe Bob Perkins."

"May I see your driver's license?"

The cowboy took out his wallet and handed over the laminated card.

Windshield wipers clicked as Jamison wrote the man's address and other pertinent information on the accident form. "Your phone number?" He added the supplied digits in the proper blank space. "Thank you, Mr. Perkins. Now. What hap—?"

"Call me Joe Bob. Ever'body else does."

"Oh . . . uh . . . all right, Joe Bob. Tell me what happened."

"I was pretty far behind 'em." His tone carried the reluctance of someone not wanting to become involved.

"Them?" Jamison stared down the embankment at the fire-blackened skeleton of a compact car. The sour taste of horror filled his mouth. "There was someone else in the vehicle?"

"Hey, you got it all wrong. There was more than one *car.*"

No second victim. Jamison licked his lips and uttered a sigh of relief.

"Please, no smoking in my cruiser," he murmured as the other man fingered a cigarillo from his western shirt pocket.

"Oh. Okay. It's soaked anyhow." Joe Bob dropped the thin, soggy brown cylinder into the litter bag hanging from the dashboard.

Suddenly the witness's earlier words echoed in Jamison's head. *More than one car.* He laid the clipboard across the steering wheel and faced Joe Bob. "You didn't mention a second car when you called in the accident. Are you trying to tell me that this was more than the case of a driver losing control on the wet, slick pavement?"

"You bet. 'Cept I can't say for sure which one did it."

Thoroughly confused, Jamison reached back into his police academy classes for the patience he needed.

"Joe Bob, if you don't mind, start at the beginning and tell me what happened." When the man beside him fidgeted and appeared about to protest, Jamison amended, "Or what you think happened."

"Okay. Sure. Well, I was ridin' along at a pretty good clip—uh . . . under the speed limit, though—and there was this light-colored compact aways ahead but goin' slower than me. Some low-slung red sportscar whizzed past me and then caught up and banged into the side of the little car. At least three times."

"You mean deliberately sideswiped it?"

"No doubt about it. Even in the rain I could see they hit—from the taillights, y' know? And the little car kept swerving out on the shoulder like it was tryin' to get away. And then another red sports job passed me."

After a few moments of silence, the patrolman prompted, "And?"

"And then my windshield wipers quit."

"They— Why?"

"Hell, I don't know. They been doin' it off and on for months, and I jus' never got 'em fixed."

Jamison inhaled deeply and silently prayed for forbearance. "That's not very smart, you know."

"I guess." Joe Bob's lips spread in a proud-of-himself grin. "But they always start up again—like tonight. After I stopped May Belle—that's my truck—and bent down and jiggled the lever a coupla times and said a few cuss words." He frowned. "But I couldn't see a damn thing when they wasn't workin', it was rainin' so hard."

"Right. But after the wipers started up again, what did you see?"

"Well, I drove on along to the place where the car had caught fire—guess the gas tank blew—and I pulled to a stop on the gravel. Behind one of the red cars. The other one had went—and, no sirree, I don't know which car was which. One hit her and knocked her off the road—on purpose. One stopped—or it coulda been the car what hit her that stopped, y' know?"

"I know." It was all Jamison could think of to say.

"Anyhow, jus' after I parked, this tall man come up to my window. He was drenched, and his shirt sleeve was all tore and black. Looked like it maybe was covered with oil."

"Did he say anything to you?"

"Sure did. He said the woman was dead and for me to use my CB—guess he saw the antenna—to send for you cops—uh . . . police—and a fire engine and a ambulance. Then he yelled, 'I gotta go,' and run to his car and drove off. I called in the accident and waited in May Belle 'til the medics loaded her up—the dead lady, not May Belle—and left."

"You said the man yelled."

"Had to. I never rolled my window down, the wind was blowin' and it was rainin' against it so hard. So I couldn't say what he looked like," Joe Bob grumbled defensively.

"What about the make or model of his car?"

"Couldn't tell. Not in this gully washer. Red, fast, and cost too damn much. That's all I know for sure."

"I don't suppose you got the license number of his red, fast, cost-too-much car." He regretted the sarcasm immediately, but the whole incident had turned into such a muddle that Jamison felt helpless and useless.

"Jesus! I never thought."

"It happens." Jamison shrugged his disappointment.

"Yeah, I'm real sorry. But it was rainin' bullfrogs and baby fishes, and pitch dark 'cept for the taillights, and the fire was mostly already out. I musta got kinda excited, y' know?"

"I know." For the second time during the interview, those words seemed to be the only appropriate response. "Thanks for your help, Joe Bob. And have those wipers repaired."

After the unsatisfactory witness scrambled from the police car and closed the door, Jamison took a deep, cleansing breath and glanced at his watch: 12:03 A.M. "Happy New Year, Officer Jamison," he wished himself with a sigh and picked up the radio mike. When the dispatcher answered his call letters, he said, "I've got a hit-and-run murder. The ambulance left with the victim before I found out. Better send a traffic homicide team."

"Your location?"

"Just inside the city limits. About six miles north of the Northside Medical Center."

The dispatcher signed off, and Jamison hunched down in his seat to wait for the investigators. Fatal auto accidents always made him feel bad, but the hit-and-run kind stirred his blood to boiling.

"Filthy coward!" he growled. And, damnit, that was *all* he knew about the perpetrator.

One

Sliding her attaché case across the matte finish of the black sculptured metal desk, Jodi Turner dropped into the gray leather executive chair. She reached toward the daily calendar in front of her, then pulled her hand back empty. With fingers clenched into a fist to still their trembling, she stared at the previous day's date, unwilling to tear it off.

As long as it remained yesterday, it wasn't March 10, Annie's twenty-fourth birthday. Or what would be her twenty-fourth if she were alive.

Jodi's sigh disturbed the neatly stacked phone messages awaiting her attention.

The date had to be faced. How she'd been dreading it, counting off the days in her head. Five more days . . . three more days . . . one more day . . . until here it was, irrevocable and agonizing.

This was the second Annie's birthday without her, and contrary to what the how-to-cope-with-the-loss-of-a-loved-one books pontificated, it promised to be worse than the first. Jodi hadn't slept her full six hours a night in over two weeks, and she'd eaten nothing since yesterday's breakfast, running instead on the caffeine recharges of countless cups of Coffee-mated coffee.

At that moment her efficient young secretary, holding notebook and pen, stepped into the private office.

"Not now, Mavis," Jodi said in an unusually sharp tone. Nervously, she ran a palm over the shining cascade of sable-brown hair that fell thick and straight well past her shoulders, where it flared into a row of soft curls. "And close the door when you go out. Please."

Hardly noticing the other woman's surprised and puzzled look as she left the room, Jodi sighed again. Then she pulled the March 9 sheet from the calendar, wadded it up, and tossed it into the nearby wastebasket.

Sorrow. Guilt. Frustration. She felt them all, in that order, as she picked up the phone and punched the numbers.

"Austin Police Department."

"Detective Hanley, please."

"May I say who's calling?"

"Jodi Turner. Of Sunbelt Images." Mention of the prestigious advertising/public relations firm oftentimes carried its own clout.

"Yes, ma'am. One moment, ma'am."

The one moment stretched to two or three patience-testing minutes before Jodi heard the slow drawl, "Good mornin', Ms. Turner. What can I do for you today?"

Jodi didn't miss his emphasis of the last word. She simply chose to ignore it. In her friendliest business manner, she said, "You remember me."

"Of course. The Klerkton hit-and-run."

"The death of my only sister," she amended, bristling at his clinical description. "I take that very personally."

"So did I, Ms. Turner."

"Did? Am I to assume the case is closed?"

"No homicide case is closed until it's solved. I explained that when you called a couple of months ago. And the time before that."

"But you haven't done anything more to solve it." Exasperation raised the timbre of her voice a few decibels.

"Please, Ms. Turner. I understand your concern." Detective Hanley spoke more softly than before, causing her accusation, by comparison, to echo loudly in her head. "We've

14

investigated everything and everyone, but we couldn't come up with a suspect."

"Surely there's something else—" She stopped, hearing the unwanted tears welling up around the fringes of her words.

"I don't mean to sound unfeeling, but unless and until we get some new evidence regarding the Klerkton—uh . . . your sister's case—I have to concentrate on the robberies and assaults, the rapes and murders, I *can* solve."

Jodi swallowed hard. She'd probably never know who killed Annie or why. All this time she'd purposely kept at bay the monsters of loss, grief, and loneliness, working herself into a day-by-day physical stupor. At last she knew she had to quell her emotional cowardice, to confront her stalking demons and somehow to vanquish them.

"Ms. Turner? Are you all right?"

How long had she been silent? Too long, apparently. She inhaled deeply. "Yes, Detective, I'm all right. And I'm sorry to have bothered you." She laid the phone in its cradle before a break in her voice could negate her feigned composure.

With her forehead resting on her folded arms on the desk, Jodi finally wept. Except for a few quiet tears at Annie's funeral, she had not once allowed herself to cry. She hadn't dared to start lest she be unable to stop. Now the noisy, gulping sobs filled the room. After a long while they changed to body-quaking hiccups. With Kleenex tissues from her purse, she swabbed her wet face, dabbed the moisture from her lapis-blue eyes, and blew her nose.

Her teardrops had washed away her makeup and her rigid self-control, and had left her engulfed in waves of unfamiliar feelings.

For over a year the most vulnerable, inner core of her heart had denied that Annie was gone forever. To keep up the lie, Jodi had buried herself in her job and closed herself off from all of their mutual friends. Except Irish, who very likely had been responsible for keeping her sane. She had refused to sort through Annie's most cherished and personal belongings. As long as she held herself apart from the awful reminders, as long as she stayed totally involved in exhausting busy-ness, she could almost pretend it had never happened.

But today, on her sister's birthday, Jodi's aching heart finally admitted that Annie would never again laugh or hug or play her beautiful country tunes on her guitar. And Jodi's head admitted that she must relinquish the past and find a way to live—really live—in the future.

Loud voices from the outer office broke into her reverie. The door burst open, and a tall black-haired man in his mid-thirties, wearing skintight jet leather, pushed past a wildly gesturing Mavis.

"I'm sorry, Jodi," the secretary said. "I tried to stop him. He says he's—"

"I know who he is," Jodi interrupted. She thought she might scream, and for self-distraction she gripped the thin edge of the desk until her hands hurt more than did the sight of the intruder.

"Shall I call Security?" Mavis offered.

"No, thank you. But do, please, leave the door open when you go out."

After Mavis departed, the man said, "So you still don't trust me."

Once upon a time that mischievous little-boy grin had blinded her to the real person behind it, but that was before his furious, openhanded blows made her see the dark, secret side of the man she had married.

"What do you want, Quentin?" Jodi stood, careful to keep the desk between them.

She desperately hoped her anger—her alarm, her fright—didn't show on her face. Quentin Turner had always delighted in turning her stormy emotions to his own advantage. Only after she'd learned to remain impassive and mettlesome had she defeated him. He'd never forgiven her for that. But for three years he had stayed away . . . until today.

16

She asked him again, "What do you want? Why are you here?"

Now his smile closely resembled a smirk. "You look awful, sweetie. Puffy eyes, red nose, no lipstick. Been fighting with your boyfriend?"

At the shock of seeing Quentin, Jodi had forgotten about her recent tearfulness. No way would she allow him to dig into her grief and unearth its reasons. To this bully she must appear strong, independent, capable of handling anything he hurled in her direction.

"Tell me why you're here, or I *will* call Security."

"Sit down, sweetie, and relax." While she resumed her seat, he eased himself into the armchair opposite her desk. Unhurriedly, he surveyed his surroundings, then said, "Well, well. I'm impressed. You're only twenty-eight, and already you've made it to the inner sanctum. Jodi Turner, account rep extraordinaire and now second V.P. V . . . e . . . r . . . y nice."

"Quentin . . ." she warned sternly, her eyes darkening to almost black.

"Okay, okay." He reached out to pat her hand. She moved it away barely in time to avoid the contact. He shrugged. "You're the best damn publicist in this town. Probably in all of Texas. Maybe even in the whole Southwest."

Although Jodi was proud of her reputation after ten years of hard work for Sunbelt Images, his compliments meant absolutely nil.

"Cut to the chase, Quentin."

"I need your contacts. Your savvy. My popularity rating's going down the drain."

"Washed down by booze, no doubt, to say nothing of cocaine and those cutie-pies who throw their bras on the stage and go to bed with you afterward so they can read about themselves in the tabloids."

"You read the tabloids now?" He gave her another of those supposed-to-charm smiles. "A straitlaced do-gooder like you?"

"Don't bait me. And don't expect any help from me. Ever!"

Careful, she warned herself. *Don't let him guess how close you are to losing it.*

Slowly, she rose to her full five feet seven and mentally stiffened her spine. "You'd better go. We have nothing further to discuss."

"The hell we don't!" Quentin fairly shouted as he, too, stood and grabbed her arm. "You *have* to take me on as a client again."

Jodi paled as his grip tightened painfully. She jerked loose. The old fear had risen like bile in her throat, but she managed to maintain a visible cool. "The only thing I *have* to do is order you thrown out of this building if you're not out of my office by the time I count to five." After a brief pause, she began. "One."

"You can't do this!" His dark eyes blazed with fury.

"Two."

"You bitch." A feral smile bared his teeth.

"Three."

"I'll get even! I'll pay you back—"

"Four."

"—if it's the last thing I ever do."

"Fi—"

"I'm gone." He wheeled and crossed the room, but at the open door he turned and pointed a defiant, menacing finger. "You'll be sorry, sweetie. And that's a friggin' promise."

As soon as he was out of sight, Jodi, ghost-white and shaking all over, collapsed into her chair with a low moan.

Mavis rushed into the inner office, took one look at Jodi and, reaching for the phone, announced, "I'm calling Security to stop him before he leaves the building."

"No! Don't do that." Jodi hated knowing that her ex-husband's violence could still frighten her. But, even worse, she hated letting Quentin know that. And if she took any action against him, he'd know. And use her fear to make her life a hell. Like so many times before.

Mavis's hand released the phone. "But I heard him threaten you. I mean . . . I shouldn't have been listening, but he was so loud, so angry."

Embarrassed by Mavis's having witnessed the ugly scene, Jodi downplayed her own reaction to it. "Yes, but he's all bluff and bluster. Really. Forget it. I have." *The biggest lie I ever told.* She managed a wan smile and changed the subject. "What's on my schedule today?"

Mavis looked at the blank calendar page. How odd, she thought. Jodi, the most organized and methodical person she knew, always wrote down her daily appointments. Although momentarily taken aback by the unusual query, Mavis, tactful secretary that she was, refrained from comment, consulted the notebook in her hand, and said, "Ten o'clock interview with James Thorne." To schedule an exhibit for the sculptor, Jodi added to herself. "Lunch at twelve with the other Safe Harbor sponsors." To discuss the purchase and renovation of an old mansion as another haven for battered women and their children. "Three o'clock staff meeting." To plan the runoff election campaign for Senator Tannahill. "Cocktails at the mayor's house at six-thirty." To meet the dignitary's nephew from Wyoming, a recently turned-professional rodeo rider who was seeking an agent. "Dinner with Jaime Chavez at eight." To arrange for Chavez, the city's foremost photographer, to create a portfolio for last year's Miss New Mexico to take with her when model job hunting in New York. "And Dr. O'Meara called while you were with your—with that man."

"Irish called? Did he say what he wanted?" Jodi heard her voice, hollow and far away.

"Just that he hasn't spoken with you in over a week."

"I hope you explained that I've been busy." She hadn't intended for her words to come out in a ragged whisper.

Busy. From early morning often until after midnight. Interviews and meetings, luncheons and cocktail parties and dinners, followed by late evenings at the theater or ballet or symphony. Every waking moment job-related. Even her

Sundays were filled with plans and phone contacts to schedule the next week's commitments. There never seemed to be an end to the demands on her time. And she was so tired!

"He said something about today being special," Mavis was saying, "and he wanted to take you to dinner tonight."

He who? Oh, yes. Irish, loving godfather, best friend, and her entire "family." Of course. He'd remembered Annie's birthday, too. And she, Jodi, had been too busy to call the only living person who cared. Busy cramming her days and nights full of appointments and obligations so she would have no time to think about Annie. No time to cry or blame herself.

"No time," Jodi muttered as she rose awkwardly from her chair.

She felt . . . strange. The walls crowded closer, shrinking the room to the size of a prison cell. Her skin tingled, prickled, becoming icy cold as perspiration seeped from every pore. She tried to speak, "No time," but heard only a peculiar, meaningless mumble. Tiny specks of light danced erratically across her vision. Mavis's staring, worried face looked distorted. Everything turned fuzzy . . . and gray. And totally black as Jodi crumpled to the carpet.

Two

The warmth on her face woke her. Jodi opened her eyes, and the sun's rays stabbed them like hot needles. Quickly lowering her eyelids, she wondered where she was. The bed in her own apartment stood in a corner, away from a window and the sunlight.

Then she remembered.

She had fainted in her office.

Damn!

If she hadn't keeled over at work, Mavis wouldn't have summoned Irish, who wouldn't have felt it necessary to hospitalize her for three days of prodding, poking, and pricking, which wouldn't have resulted in her waking up this morning in Irish's cabin seventy-odd miles northwest of everything and everyone familiar.

Whew! Even listing the unplanned changes in her routine left her exhausted. So maybe she was, as the consulting physicians had diagnosed, completely stressed out and in need of R and R.

Lying on her back, Jodi stretched her long legs until her bare toes met the tight foot tuck of the lemon-fragrant sheet. She reached above and beyond her head, grabbed the brass rail, and pulled her arm and shoulder muscles taut, then released them with a lazy sigh. There was something to be said for not having to hurry out of bed and into one of her classic tailored suits to fight the traffic for thirty minutes on her way to work.

But she had fiercely resisted Irish's insistence that she come here.

"If you don't do this, Jodi," he'd sternly promised as she was packing to leave the private hospital room, "I'll personally see to it that Mr. Sunbelt Images himself places you on a compulsory medical leave."

"You wouldn't!"

"I would. And based on the results of your tests, no employer would refuse. Do you want that on your personnel record?"

"Wimpy Jodi Turner, who can't take the pressure? You know I don't. My colleagues, even clients if they found out, might never feel the same about my capabilities."

Irish nodded in agreement. "You haven't had a vacation in over three years, so you're entitled to six weeks off. Arrange it, Jodi, starting tomorrow."

"But tomorrow's my first day back. I can't—"

"Yes, you can. Qualified coworkers, mostly ones you've trained yourself, have been filling in for you the past few days. They can continue for the duration."

"Yes, but—"

"No buts. Either you leave for the lake the day after tomorrow, or I make an appointment with your boss."

"Damn you, Irish O'Meara!"

"Better damn me than bury you."

Jodi threw him a sharp glance. He wasn't teasing. A twinge of self-concern niggled at her stubbornness. "I'm not that sick," she said, but not as convincingly as she might have ten minutes ago.

"Insomnia, vertigo, severe headaches, stomach pain, nausea, weight loss, periods of depression." He grinned, finally, at her look of amazement. "That last little symptom you neglected to mention."

She felt compelled to justify her recent bouts of despondency. "I've had Annie on my mind a lot lately."

22

"Her birthday." His own sorrow was audible, but his following pronouncement hinted more of irritation. "And that confounded, *unfounded* guilt you carry around."

"She begged me to go with her, and I should have!" Jodi wailed.

"Then you'd probably both be dead."

"No. That creep wouldn't have picked on a car with two women in it."

"What if in his demented mind he wanted to destroy both of you?"

Too caught up in her own emotions, Jodi ignored his reasoning. "I knew it would be late when the concert was over. I knew the weather was bad. I should have been at the wheel. Driving at night always made Annie nervous. I knew that. We all did. But no! I decided instead to stay here and have dinner with some new client I can't even remember the name of." Her heart ached with self-condemnation, and her sight blurred with unshed tears.

"So, to prove to yourself that your decision was the right one, you've been working sixteen hours a day seven days a week ever since." Irish reached out to pat her shoulder. "Honey, for quite a while now, you've been wired for an explosion. Quentin's showing up just lit the fuse."

"How did you know he—?" She stopped, then blinked the moisture from her eyes as she locked her suitcase with a click. "Mavis told you."

"Did you think I wouldn't find out?" Irish scolded her.

"He didn't hurt me." The reassurance was as much for herself as for the caring man standing beside her.

"Not physically. Not this time." He swallowed the old fury that rasped his words. "But your reaction to him was an example of what your job stress can cause. A blackout while driving your car, or a mental breakdown, even a fatal heart attack." He raised a hand to prevent the argument he guessed was forthcoming. "That's what I meant by—by burying you." His voice cracked, and a definite dampness pooled in his brown eyes.

A lengthy hush filled the small antiseptic room until Jodi, capitulating with a smile and a kiss on his cheek, clutched the handle of her overnighter and asked, "Do you keep the key to your cabin handy?"

Wearing brand-new designer jeans and an ivory silk camp shirt, Jodi leaned against the redwood railing and listened to the silence. No traffic noise, no sirens, no *boom boom* of the stereo bass in the apartment above hers. Gradually, her city-conscious ears picked out the quieter country sounds. The distant bark of a dog, the closer singing of birds, the nearby hum of a honey bee attracted by the Chloe perfume she always wore.

She moved her head to discourage the insect, then gazed across the fifty-yard stretch of open meadow that sloped from the cabin's rear steps to the Lake Buchanan shoreline. Scrambles of spindly bushes, scattered humps of gray granite, and sprinkles of pink buttercups competed with weeds and grass for footholds in the sandy soil. On the left a dense woodland grew all the way down to the water's edge. The deciduous trees, their leaves an early spring green, stood out glossy and new among the evergreens. Brushed by the bright sun and soft breeze, the lake's surface resembled an expansive sheet of crinkled aluminum foil. Its reflected brilliance hurt Jodi's eyes, so for the second time that morning she closed them to shut out the discomfort.

The dark behind her eyelids suddenly propelled her memory back to last night. Accustomed to traveling only on illuminated urban streets or on highways with wide, empty spaces on either side, she had found the hilly, curving farm-to-market road between the highway and Irish's cabin to be strange, often disorienting. The rural darkness pulsed with a totality she'd never before experienced. Like some hungry, invisible beast, it gobbled up the narrow swath cut by her car's headlights. Mesquite trees and underbrush hovered at the very edges of the pavement, assuming myriad ghostly shapes in the passing cone of brightness.

Even though logic told her it couldn't be true, she thought she was smothering. Braking the car, she rolled down the window and sucked in the pure air of the cool March evening. She felt like a fool, parked in the absolute middle of a perfectly safe road and nightdreaming about monsters. She told herself there was nothing to be afraid of.

But she *had* been afraid.

Squeezing the wooden railing so hard that an errant splinter jabbed her palm, Jodi shivered in spite of the morning's unshadowed sunshine that warmed her shoulders.

Was last night's uneasiness due to her inhibitions about coping with a few weeks of arbitrary exile?

Or was it the illusory forerunner of very real problems she would encounter before she returned to work?

Jodi resolutely filed away the answerless questions, crossed the wide deck, and opened the screen door.

As soon as she entered the cabin's kitchen area, she spied the note. It was attached to the front of the refrigerator with a grinning purple frog magnet. Grinning back, Jodi pulled the paper loose and read the neatly hand-printed message:

> "Welcome! Dr. O'Meara phoned me not to be alarmed if I saw lights in his cabin, that a friend would be using it for a spell. In case you didn't bring any perishables, I put a few breakfast things in the fridge. If and when you feel like saying hello, I'm in the white stucco just west of you. Becky Prentiss."

Stooping to peer inside the refrigerator, Jodi discovered milk, eggs, bacon, margarine, strawberry preserves, and a can of biscuits.

A few breakfast things, indeed. And how thoughtful of her neighbor. Irish had mentioned that a Ms. Prentiss lived next door, someone he didn't know very well who was a permanent community resident.

He'd said, "We met over the fence, so to speak, and she invited me over for potluck supper a few times. She's friendly enough but a very private person. Such sad eyes." He paused, his instinctual compassion apparent, then said, "I left an extra key with her, in case you or Annie ever wanted to use the cabin and I wasn't available."

"Annie had a key. She and Troy spent several weekends up there."

"That's right, they did. But you, now, have always been too much of a city girl," he teased. "Anyway, if you'll feel uncomfortable about Ms. Prentiss having a key . . ."

"Not at all," Jodi broke in. "If you trust her, I'm sure I will, too."

But she and I have different concepts of a proper breakfast, Jodi mused as she walked out to her dark blue Saturn in the graveled driveway. She unlocked the trunk and carried inside a couple of canvas "Save the Earth" bags full of grocery items she'd brought from her apartment.

"Now, *this* is breakfast," she said aloud as she picked up a box of high-fiber cereal and poured a generous serving into the Corning Ware bowl she'd found in a wall cabinet. Removing the lid from the sugar bowl, also taken from the cabinet, she sprinkled three heaping teaspoons of the sweetener over the bran flakes before she added the milk.

Smiling, she recalled Irish's amusement when he'd watched her drop the cereal box into one of the totes.

"Don't forget to take a five-pound sack of sugar," he'd reminded her with a chuckle.

"Cereal is what I like for breakfast, and I like it sweet," she'd retorted. Everyone who knew her well was aware of her breakfast habit, and she'd long ago ceased to excuse it by stating that she seldom ate desserts. "Am I not allowed *one* vice?"

"Sure, honey . . . uh . . . sure, sugar."

At that point they'd howled with laughter, until they grew weak and held each other up by hugging.

* * *

26

When she'd arrived at the cabin last night, feeling tired and nervous, Jodi had only brought her overnighter in. After breakfast, which she ate hurriedly at the serving bar, she unloaded everything else she wanted from the car trunk—cosmetic case, Pullman, garment bag, shoe caddy, and a cardboard carton containing her favorite country-and-western tapes and a dozen paperback romance novels she'd purchased but never had the time to read.

She spent an hour painstakingly storing each item of clothing in the dresser or closet in the bedroom alcove of the huge single-room cabin.

Where to put the novels and tapes? To leave them jumbled together in a box sitting on the floor violated her sense of orderliness.

Just outside the track of the disappearing panel door that provided bedroom privacy stood a walnut state-of-the-art entertainment center. Beside the rack that held Irish's collection of big-band era LPs she found space to stack her tapes. The books she put in an empty drawer of the adjacent desk, on top of which sat the phone, a brown leather file box of stationery and pens, a clock, and a heavy, clear glass paperweight with a photograph glued to its base. Staring back at Jodi was a snapshot of a fourteen-year-old Annie with blond pigtails and herself at eighteen, all dressed up for her first day of work at Sunbelt Images.

Slowly, nostalgically, Jodi ran her fingertips over the smooth glass surface. She'd forgotten about that picture. During the last fourteen months she'd forgotten—on purpose—so many happier days.

Now, here, standing in this completely new environment, Jodi was surprised to discover that the happy memories no longer hurt so badly, but instead offered a kind of solace, the kind she'd been seeking without realizing it.

"Thank you, Dr. Dennis O'Meara, sir," Jodi murmured, "for making me slow down to let the good times catch up."

Once again, as had often been the case since the death of both her parents in a boating accident twelve years ago, her substitute father, with love and wisdom, had maneuvered her into doing the right thing.

Jodi spent a few minutes checking out her large one-room living quarters, which she'd hardly noticed before falling into bed the night before. She approved of Irish's choice of tan leather sofa and recliner, and the three brown denim-upholstered armchairs grouped in front of the wide fireplace across the length of the floor from the sleeping/dressing corner. Brown denim cushions covered the bentwood bar stools on either side of the chest-high divider between sitting and dining areas. Beyond the kitchen appliances and near the west window stood the glass-topped dinette table and four bentwood armchairs.

With her second cup of coffee in hand, Jodi sat at the table and gazed at the array of dazzling colors outside the window. In one flower bed, vivid yellow jonquils were interspersed indiscriminately with purple tulips so dark they were almost black. Another brick-bordered spot boasted pink, coral, and magenta tulips. Familiar flowering shrubs added their rainbow hues: salmon-pink japonica, lacy white bridal wreath, and lemon-yellow forsythia. Before she'd become so obsessed with her job, Jodi used to spend hours in the Austin parks, jogging and enjoying brown-bag lunches, sometimes talking with the workers who taught her the names of the plants they tended.

After rinsing her cup and placing it in the dishwasher, Jodi put on her makeup, donned her navy-blue blazer, and went out the front door. Irish had called her a city girl, which she definitely was, but if she had to stay in the country for several weeks, she might as well get reacquainted with the outdoors.

Although the sun had burned away the daybreak chill, a light dew still sparkled the grass. Sidewalks must be city things, too, Jodi concluded with good humor as she chose to walk in the rutted dirt road to keep her new Reeboks dry.

She'd only taken a dozen or so steps when she sensed that someone was watching her. At first she ignored it, but then she became nervous and apprehensive when the watched feeling persisted. Standing still, she peered in all directions. She even turned to look behind her.

She saw no one.

She resumed her stroll past Ms. Prentiss's garden plot, but the jittery sensation of being watched grew stronger. Instead of stopping again, however, she quickened her pace.

By the time she reached the white Spanish hacienda-style house with its red clay-tile roof, her discomfort had eased.

Jodi sauntered along the curving concrete driveway until she spied a gray-haired woman on her knees violently tugging weeds from a ring of hyacinths that encircled the base of an enormous live oak tree. Even from that distance Jodi could detect the sweet cloying fragrance of the pastel blossoms.

"Good morning," she called out.

"Not today," came the response. "These pesky dandelions are multiplying like rabbits." The speaker glanced back over her shoulder, then straightened, humiliation flushing her cheeks. The woman's lovely young face was strikingly at odds with her frizzed silver-white tresses. If she restyled her hair, wore makeup, and lost twenty pounds, she would be quite beautiful.

"I'm sorry," she said. "I thought you were a neighbor."

"I am. I'm Jodi Turner, Dr. O'Meara's friend. Are you Becky Prentiss?"

The woman nodded and smiled sheepishly. "Yes, and I should've looked before I opened my big mouth. But folks in this neighborhood often walk by and say hello. I thought you were one of those."

"And you were right," Jodi smiled back.

"It's good to meet you, Ms. Turner."

"Jodi, please."

"All right, if you'll call me Becky." She wiped her hands on a faded brown cobbler's smock that had obviously been used for the same purpose on many other occasions.

"I want to thank you for the welcome note and for stocking my refrigerator. And, I'm sure, for airing out the cabin and putting those lovely-smelling linens on my bed."

"It was the least I could do after what Dennis did for me."

Dennis? Jodi suppressed a grin. *Dennis* hadn't called *her* Becky when he claimed he didn't know her very well.

"I cut my hand with a butcher knife. Very badly. I knew a doctor owned the cabin. We'd never met, but I went running over there. Almost fainted, but he fixed me up. Stopped the bleeding, bandaged the wound, gave me a tetanus shot. He advised me to go in to Emergency to get some stitches, but I preferred to chance the ugly scar he warned me about." She held out her left hand to display the long, white jagged streak that crisscrossed the natural lines of her palm. "Hospitals are not one of my favorite things." She smiled in an attempt to soften the unexpected gruffness of her voice, but Jodi saw that Irish had been candid about one detail. Becky Prentiss's large, long-lashed hazel eyes were sad.

"Then I'm glad Irish was here," Jodi said.

"Irish? You call Dennis Irish?"

"It's left over from his high school days." Amused by Becky's amazement, Jodi went on to elucidate. "I think my Mom was the first one to call him that. They were best buddies. My Dad, too."

"Were?" Becky had alertly picked up on the word.

"Yes. Were. My parents died when I was sixteen, and my younger sister and I went to live with him until we were grown."

"What kindness on the part of him and his wife."

"Irish never married. I've sometimes suspected that he was in love once, unhappily, although he's never spoken about it. But we've shared everything else. He's my dearest friend. And my godfather."

"That explains why you call a learned, distinguished *doctor* like him by such a whimsical nickname. I never could."

"Why ever not? If you really got to know him . . ."

"Doctors are so—so clinical."

There it was again. That aversion to hospitals . . . and also doctors. Why? Jodi wondered, then told herself it was none of her business. She was here for a few weeks, and then she'd return to Austin and never see Becky again. Still, she felt compelled to come to Irish's defense.

"Doctors do sometimes have to hurt patients in order to heal them, but Irish would never be clinical, if by that you mean harsh or insensitive," she declared, more crossly than she'd intended.

"If I implied that, I apologize. I was speaking of doctors in general . . . doctors I've known who weren't as nice as Dennis." She paused, then gestured toward the house. "Won't you come in and have a cup of coffee? Or maybe some iced tea. It's pretty warm for this time of year."

"Hot, you mean. When you're pulling up . . . uh . . . pesky dandelions that behave like Easter bunnies." She laughed, and Becky joined in. When the merriment faded, Jodi said, "But I didn't come over to interfere with your schedule."

"What schedule? I've learned not to plan too far ahead. I take one hour at a time, and I spend that hour making myself and the person I love most in the world comfortable and content."

Why hadn't she used the word *happy?* Jodi asked herself. Before she could speculate further, Becky's face lit up with the happiness she hadn't verbalized, and she said, "And here comes that person now."

Jodi looked where the other woman pointed. Looked . . . and kept on looking. Even from a dozen feet away, Jodi could see that the man's eyes were incredible—clear lime-green, almost alienlike in his darkly tanned face. His hair, the color of caramel, tumbled about his ears and onto his forehead in soft, shaggy curls. He was tall and very fit, except his shoulders rounded slightly forward as though he spent long hours at a sedentary occupation. His khaki shirt hung fully unbuttoned. With each step he took, his body swayed, widening the shirt opening to expose his sweat-glistened, sun-bronzed torso. Dusky trails of perspiration trickled through the whorls of tawny hair that covered his chest and came to a V at the waistline of his tight, well-worn jeans. He walked with a loose swagger that drew her attention to his flat stomach, his narrow hips, his . . . quintessential maleness.

Jodi stared until a warm heaviness nudged her loins. What was happening to her? She felt confused and apprehensive. Not since those early days—and nights—with Quentin . . .

She jerked that painful thought-string to a halt.

The approaching man was sexy, true, but she had no interest in sex. Or in any man-woman relationship. Once caught, once betrayed, was enough to last her a lifetime.

When the stranger ambled up to Becky's side, she did the introductions. "Jodi, this is my brother, Luke. Jodi Turner is the friend Dr. O'Meara called about night before last."

Her brother. And his name was Luke. Luke Prentiss. *Luke Prentiss?*

For one second Jodi's agile mind congealed into a mass of putty. Then the excited realization hummed through her brain cells.

"Luke Prentiss, the piano player with *Only in Texas!* My favorite country-and-western band. But I've never seen you in person. Only in group black-and-white photos inside the cassette cases." Jodi stopped after hearing herself gushing like a stagestruck schoolgirl. Swallowing, she tried for a sophisticated restart. "I'm sorry if I embarrassed you. I've certainly embarrassed myself. But I really am an A-number-one fan of *Only in Texas.* I have every one of the band's tapes. Your solos, too." She smiled, looked straight into those fantastic green eyes, and lifted her chin a notch as if to reconstruct the poise she'd let slip away at the instant of recognition.

"Thanks," the pianist said.

When he didn't return her smile, Jodi suddenly felt, for some inexplicable reason, like an intruder.

"It's been quite a while since your last release," she said

nervously to cover her discomfiture. "When will I be able to buy the next one?"

Luke frowned a wordless reply, then stared at his scuffed, sand-encrusted boots.

Puzzlement clouded Jodi's eyes, and her smile became a starched facsimile. Disturbed by the unnamed emotional undercurrents whirlpooling around her, she said, "I should go and leave both of you to your gardening."

But before she turned away, something about Luke called for one more look.

Several beads of perspiration still dotted his forehead, and one drooping curl stuck to his temple like a wet brown comma. Slowly, he raised his right hand to mop his brow.

Jodi couldn't believe what she saw.

Luke Prentiss's fingers, those magic fingers capable of making a piano sing . . . or laugh . . . or cry . . . those fingers were stiff and bent, and that hand and forearm bore the unsightly patchwork of puckered ridges and slick discolored skin that shaped the legacy of all severe burns.

Three

"Oh, God, Luke, I'm sorry." Jodi spoke barely above a whisper, for the shock had stolen her breath.

Luke's eyes sparked with emerald anger, and fury seared his words. "My hand has healed, Ms. Turner, and I don't need your pity." He wheeled and stalked toward the house.

"Wait!" she called out. "You misunderstood. I meant I'm sorry I was so insensitive as to ask you about your next—I should have been more observant." *I should have been noticing your hands instead of being bedazzled by your fantastic green eyes.*

He hesitated, half turned, and gave her a twisted smile that bordered upon insolent. Then he walked on until the arched arcade enveloped him in its deep shade.

Jodi stared after him, overwhelmed by the reality of his tragedy-altered future. After the release of his first two collections of instrumental solos, his popularity had ballooned, and now the balloon had burst. He had every right to be bitter.

Too upset to hold back the probing personal query, Jodi asked his sister, "How did it happen?"

"A gasoline fire."

"How could he have been so careless?" Jodi demanded, inexplicably furious with Luke and, more reasonably, with destiny's foibles. "His hands were his chance to make thousands of people happy."

34

"And make *his* dreams come true," Becky responded curtly. "You think he destroyed that on purpose?"

"No, of course not." Jodi sighed. "I'm sorry. I'm just so stunned. To think how one minute in time can ruin the rest of a person's life. It's not fair."

"Whoever said life is fair?" Becky's smile didn't touch her eyes, and Jodi's intuition told her the woman wasn't referring solely to her brother. "And that's enough philosophizing for one morning," Becky added on a determined lighter note. "Are you sure you won't come in for some tea?"

"I'm sure, Becky, but thank you, anyway."

Jodi needed to get away, to put into focus the feelings that smote her from the instant she saw Luke's scarred hand.

As she trudged back along the dirt road to her cabin, her analytical mind cataloged those feelings in the same manner she might have pigeonholed the pros and cons of a new client. First had come the outrage that a rare talent like Luke Prentiss's had been wiped out. Next, she'd sensed a soul-piercing regret that what was already recorded would be all of Luke's magical music people would ever hear. And then she'd known a heart-wrenching sorrow for the man himself, for his physical pain, for his personal loss of career. For a moment she'd wanted to embrace him, to murmur words of comfort, to absorb a fraction of his misery as her own so that *his* burden would be less.

What am I doing? Fantasizing about holding a stranger in my arms! Just because he's gorgeous and wounded? Cease and desist, Jodi. No more.

Her function for the past five years entailed making over, counseling, and promoting people who desired her assistance and paid big bucks for it. Nobody expected her to dole out free compassion to a disgruntled, rude ex-pianist who obviously wanted to be left alone. *So,* she chastised herself, *why am I doing it?*

Engrossed in her mercurial musing, Jodi failed to hear the car creeping up behind her until the driver honked the horn. She almost lost her balance as she jumped onto the grassy verge to let the car pass.

But the black Cadillac Eldorado with darkly tinted windows came to a halt when it pulled alongside her.

Jodi admonished herself not to be nervous. Walking alone on a country lane was no different from walking alone on a city sidewalk in a quiet residential neighborhood. When she'd confessed to Irish her worry about staying here, he'd reassured her that the Swallows Bluff unincorporated community—a scattering of thirty-odd houses, cabins, and cottages, about half of which were occupied full time—had never had a serious crime.

The person in the car meant her no harm.

Nonetheless, Jodi continued to walk, judiciously hurrying and lengthening her stride.

The car followed her, inching forward. Jodi's heart rate quickened as she tried to decide whether she would be smarter to run or to stop and glare at the imposing vehicle, which seemed to be taking on a forbidding presence of its own.

Finally the car stopped, the front window on the passenger side, the side nearest Jodi, rolled down. The man behind the steering wheel, his features indistinct in the shadowy interior, leaned across the seat and said, "Jodi? Jodi Turner? Is that you?"

From somewhere out of her past emerged the knowledge that she ought to recognize the voice, but she wasn't able to identify it until the speaker—a tall, thirtyish, rather ordinary-looking blond—stepped out of the car and winked at her.

"Troy!" Jodi exclaimed excitedly.

No wonder he'd sounded familiar. Troy Morrell, Annie's lover during the final year and a half of her life, had been like family. Their last time together had been a Christmas dinner at Irish's home to celebrate the holiday and George Strait's recent recording of one of Annie's ballads. That night

Annie had confided to Jodi that the occasion for their next party might well be to announce her engagement to Troy.

While Troy rushed around his car, Jodi said, "I'm so glad to see you. But what on earth are you doing *here?*"

He yanked her close in a bear hug. Beneath her ear his chuckle rumbled in his chest, then he replied, "I'm glad to see you, too," and, as he released her, "I live up there." He pointed to the large cedar shakes lodge that nestled against the hillside overlooking the cluster of lakeside dwellings of which the O'Meara and Prentiss properties were a part. "I can see half the county—well, almost—from my glass-walled den."

"That's wonderful," she said. "I remember. Annie used to tell me about some house you raved about every time you-all came up here. Is that the one?"

"That's the one. I never dreamed it would be mine, but now I can afford it," he finished proudly. Almost boastfully, Jodi supposed, but he'd earned it, as the TV commercial proclaimed, the hard way.

"Yes, you can." Her dark blue eyes smiled into his light blue ones. "And I'm happy for you. Why didn't you answer my note last fall congratulating you on winning both the Song of the Year and Single of the Year awards at the Country Music Association Award show?"

"I guess because talking to you would have made me relive Annie's death all over again." His smile had vanished. He gave her a strange, long, scrutinizing look, then asked, "Are you okay?"

"Better every day. As a matter of fact, that's why I'm here. Irish made me take a vacation."

"Yeah, he always was a little bossy." They laughed at unspoken, shared memories. Serious once more, Troy spoke softly, tentatively. "Uh . . . I've been wondering, what did you do with the things you took from Annie's apartment the day after she . . . uh . . . after the accident?"

"I gave her two guitars to her friend, Ginger Tillman. I'm sorry. I should have asked you if you wanted one of them."

"That's all right." He reached out and gave her arm an affectionate, forgiving pat. "But I would like to have some mementos of hers to keep. To remember her by. I really miss her." He coughed in a vain effort to cover the roughness of his voice. "Uh . . . what happened to her practice tapes?"

"The tapes she recorded her work-in-progress on?"

"Those, and the ones with songs she never finished. And sometimes she wrote down the lyrics or the harmony arrangements on staff paper. What happened to those?"

"I must still have everything. I just dumped all of her music stuff in a big cardboard box and stored it in my closet. I haven't had the courage to sort through any of it yet. But if and when I do, I'll be happy to let you choose something for yourself. Of course, I'll always keep the rest."

"Uh . . . sure . . . I'd expect you to," Troy agreed hoarsely, "but as you say, if and when . . ."

"I'll let you know, Troy, I promise." Jodi gave him a wistful smile, then tossed her flowing mane of dark brown hair as though ridding her mind of a doleful topic. "Tell me about your house. It looks awfully big for one person. Or, do you have a . . . roommate?"

"If you're asking if there's a special woman in my life, no. But I do host a lot of parties. To maintain my image." He grinned impishly, and his average features turned almost handsome. The wholesome boy next door was how Annie used to describe him. "You understand about images."

"I do, indeed. And you're doing a super job with yours." Today he was dressed for the role, wearing a brown suit with a decidedly western cut and fit, together with tan lizard cowboy boots. "I saw you on the *Tonight Show,* and on one of his Thursdays off, Irish watched you on the *Oprah Winfrey Show* with Alan Jackson and . . . I forget . . . some other award winner."

"Garth Brooks." Raising a rallying fist about his shoulder, Troy supplied the other performer's name.

"You've made the big time for sure. Annie would be thrilled."

38

"Uh . . . why don't you walk up the hill sometime and I'll show you my place? It's fabulous. Even has a heated pool. We can take a dip . . . Oops! I forgot. You never learned to swim."

"But I *can*—"

"I know," he interrupted, slapping his forehead with his palm as though he'd solved a major problem. "You *can* loll around on the patio chaise lounge and sip a margarita. That is, if you still like margaritas."

"Doesn't everyone?" Jodi laughed, relishing the renewal of their friendship.

She'd wait until she visited him to reveal her recently acquired skill, that of swimming the length of a not-too-long pool. Troy would be surprised, because he'd often heard Annie tease her about her no-exceptions preference for shower baths over soaking in the tub. Even as a child Jodi had not liked to play in the water, and after her parents' drowning, her reluctance had grown into a near-phobia.

Last winter, when her ever busier work schedule precluded daylight running, Irish had urged her to join a fitness club. There the recreation director had discovered her inability to swim and dared her to try.

Not only was Jodi never one to run from a challenge, but she also recalled how Annie used to beg her to learn to swim.

"What if you *had* to swim or else drown like Mom and Dad? I couldn't bear it if something like that happened to you."

Something different had happened to Annie, something Jodi would always feel partly responsible for. Maybe her learning to swim, her granting Annie's wish in that regard, could in some strange way offer atonement.

The third time she went to the club, Jodi found herself in a black maillot, suddenly able to float and therefore to hold herself above the daunting terror that, to her, lurked in the gloomy depths below the surface. Gradually, she learned how to move her arms and legs to push herself through the water, but swimming would never be one of her favorite forms of exercise.

"I'd like to chat with you some more," Troy was saying, "but I have a lunch date in Austin."

"We'll see each other soon," Jodi said by way of farewell.

"Soon." Troy reentered his car.

Watching him drive off, Jodi considered how fate sometimes balanced her decrees. Luke's career had ended, but Troy's had begun.

Certainly Troy deserved the opportunity. Born into poverty and degradation, he had been living on the street by the time he was fourteen, eventually "adopted" by the owner of a small music store. Troy had taught himself to play the piano and the guitar, and he had struggled for years to gain a respected name as a songwriter and singer. Then he'd met Annie, already a well-known composer of country music; she had adored him, believed in his dream, and used her contacts to open doors for him.

At last, Troy had stepped triumphantly through those doors . . . but too late for Annie to be there to share and enjoy his success. Even so, Troy was lucky.

Luke, instead, had been granted one brief peek through those dream-fulfilling doors, only to have them slammed shut in his face.

As Jodi reached her cabin's driveway, she caught herself daydreaming about somehow counseling and promoting Luke back into the world of music.

It would never happen, of course, but merely imagining it lifted her spirits.

Four

Jodi heard the phone from outside. The door key snagged on the stitching of her jeans pocket, and while she fumbled with the stubborn unfamiliar lock, the ringing stopped.

"Darn it!" she muttered as she entered the cabin and crossed the floor to the closet. Three times she rearranged her blazer on the hanger until it hung perfectly straight from the padded shoulders. As she pushed the navy bone button through its buttonhole, the phone rang again.

Hurrying to the desk, she lifted the receiver and said, "Yes."

"Yes what?"

She could hear Irish's smile.

"Yes, that was you who called a few minutes ago."

"The lady is not only beautiful, she's psychic."

"Not at all. You're the only one who knows I'm here. Except Mavis. And I threatened her life if she bothered me about business or if she told anyone else where I am."

"The lady is also wise." After a moment's hesitation, Irish added, "Quentin is trying to contact you."

An icy shiver trickled along Jodi's spine. Why didn't that man leave her alone? Gooseflesh rose on her bare arms as she croaked, "How do you know?"

"He called your office yesterday, and after Mavis stonewalled him, he called me. He got nothing from me, either."

41

Jodi verbalized the worst possible scenario. "He'll remember your cabin. Sooner or later, he'll find me."

"I doubt it. After all, he lives more than forty miles away from you by the road. Clear around and across the lake. And it's a big lake."

"What?" Jodi barely managed to drop onto the chair before her knees buckled. "Quentin lives up here?"

"Honey, I thought you knew," he said contritely. "The *American Statesman* did a piece on him several months ago . . . said he's living in some condo near the dam."

"Oh, God." Her utterance might have been a moan of protest . . . or a prayer.

"Don't worry. If he figures out where you are, if he phones or shows up on your doorstep, you'll simply swear out a restraining order against him. He'd never have the guts to violate that, because he's a stinking coward."

"I guess." One hand gripped the phone until her knuckles whitened. To steady the other hand's trembling, she pressed it flat on the desk.

Could she discount Quentin's departing snarling "You'll be sorry"? True, his anger had escalated beyond verbal abuse only two times. Once when he had slapped her cheek for forgetting to pick up his favorite suit at the cleaner's, and again several weeks later when he had hit her on the side of her head with his fist after she demanded to know why he'd stayed out all night. On both occasions he'd been falling-down drunk. Sober, he had never actually hurt her.

Could she believe, as she'd vouched to Mavis in the office last week, that Quentin's promise of retaliation for her refusal to help him sprang from bluff and bluster?

Could she accept Irish's perception of Quentin as a weakling who spouted improbable threats?

She had to. Otherwise, her sharp-toothed dread could grind into dust the hard-won foundations of her dignity and self-worth.

In response to Irish's concerned "Jodi, are you all right with this?" she voiced a half-cheery "Sure I am."

"Good. What I called for . . . are you all settled in?"

"Unloaded, unpacked, and uncertain what to do next," she grumbled, and to underscore her point, Jodi yawned noisily into the phone.

He chuckled softly. "Lie on the deck and look for cloud castles in the unpolluted sky. Take a walk in the woods . . . but don't get lost."

Jodi huffed at him. Even in the city, she had learned how to tell north from south and west from east.

"Eat something fattening," Irish continued. "Read a book. Or meet your next-door neighbor."

"I have already," she informed him, then grinned at the memory. "And Becky told me how *Dennis* fixed up her cut hand. Fast work, Casanova, sir."

"Don't be crude," he growled. "She insisted on my calling her Becky, so Dr. O'Meara seemed too . . . uh . . . unneighborly."

"If you say so. You're the doctor."

He groaned at her pun.

"Seriously, Irish, do you know who she is?"

"I have my suspicions, but she didn't mention it, so of course I didn't question her."

"Your suspicions? I don't understand. She told *me*. But then, how could she not, when he walked right up to us as pretty—and I do mean pretty—as you please?"

"I don't think we're talking about the same thing." Irish sounded constrained.

"I'm talking about who Becky is," she said, slightly annoyed by his denseness. "She's Luke Prentiss's sister."

"Who's Luke Prentiss?"

"You know. The piano player with *Only in Texas.*"

"Oh. That country-and-western band you like so much. And Becky's brother is the talented fellow you're always raving about?"

"He's the one, and I met him this morning!" Thrill . . . awe . . . sparkled in her announcement.

"Honey, you meet celebrities every day." Irish was amused,

delighted that she had lost her long-standing underlying indifference.

"I know, but Luke is special." Jodi stopped, embarrassed by the self-surprising admission. "What I mean is, he's *my* favorite country music artist, not a have-to-like client."

"Of course he is." Irish laughed into his phone. "And pretty, I believe you said."

"Damn straight!" Jodi joined in her godfather's merriment. She adored having him tease her. Her own father had been so taciturn, like some uninvolved stranger.

"I'd like to meet this special . . . uh . . . pretty, non-client wizard of the keyboard sometime."

"You can. When you come up to visit. Luke is staying at Becky's. He's sort of at loose ends right now."

"What do you mean by loose ends?" A background voice brought him to pause. "I have to go, Jodi. My next patient is waiting. I'll see you Sunday, or I'll call."

"Okay. 'Bye."

Jodi cradled the phone but remained seated as her unwanted, vagrant thoughts traveled back to Quentin. If she were granted only one wish, it would be never to see her ex-husband again.

She'd certainly felt differently the first time she saw him. With his deep-set black eyes, his engaging little-boy smile, and his sultry drawl, he was unlike any man she'd ever known. But then, although twenty-three, she hadn't known very many men, and none in the Biblical sense.

Quentin Turner had been her first client, her initial assignment as Sunbelt Image's youngest publicist. After working for five years as an artist in the firm's advertising department, which she preferred, she had asked for the available job opening in public relations because the greater salary would make it possible for nineteen-year-old Annie to attend college.

Jodi's artist's eyes had cringed at the young man's attire: a cheap, poorly fitting tan jacket over a pale blue shirt, no tie, too-short reddish brown pants that exposed white socks and black loafers.

"Howdy, ma'am," he said, using the smile and the drawl to full advantage. "I want you to make me famous. I'm a good singer. You don't have to worry 'bout that part." Literally, he had chewed his words.

Jodi Klerkton, determined and suddenly ambitious, welcomed the challenge. In one year, thanks to the respective make-over specialists and to Jodi's tactful urging, Quentin mastered the rules and techniques of how to dress, how to speak, and how to project his average rock 'n' roll baritone and his ubiquitous charm from the stage to vast, loyal audiences.

Quentin used that same twelve months to charm Jodi, too. Never before had she been wined and dined and made aware of her sexual self. The new, all-consuming experience of falling in love dropped blinders over her reason. She made excuses for Quentin's selfishness, his drinking habit, his defiance when criticized or denied something he wanted. From a hayseed she had cultivated a polished, well-groomed star, and she was justly proud of the harvest. Quentin had listened, worked hard, grown into a celebrity and, Jodi had acceded at the time, earned the right to a few excesses. Passion ruled her head, and when her male Galatea swore he would cherish her forever, she joyously became his virgin wife.

During the space of the next year, Jodi found herself humiliated, abused and, finally, betrayed in the most devastating way a man could betray a woman. Naive and gullible, she had fallen for the man she created, only to discover he didn't exist. The real Quentin possessed no conscience, no heart, and no morals. Admittedly, she had been a fool to rely on her emotions, to allow desire to control her decisions; and after an ugly, public divorce, Jodi, drained and miserable, promised herself never to become ensnared in a woman-man relationship again.

For three years she had kept that promise. A handful of

interested men had been privileged to be considered her friends, but when they expected more, Jodi without any regret walked out of their lives.

Then how was it that, with no conscious thought, she had labeled Luke Prentiss "special" . . . and meant it?

Still sitting in the chair in front of the desk, Jodi remembered the misery that clouded Luke's crystal green eyes, the anger that tightened his full sexy lips, the proud departing swagger that refuted her pity.

Somehow Jodi sensed that Luke needed help. But what could she do for him? And why on earth did she feel compelled to try?

Powerful, prestigious men and women in Southwest business, sports, politics, fine arts, and entertainment sought her out and competed for her time, which was always at a premium. They *wanted* her assistance.

Luke Prentiss, on the other hand, obviously did not.

But this is personal.

The reflexes of Jodi's mind had formed the message before her self-protective instincts had the chance to recognize it and close it off.

Her breath caught in her throat. Her heartbeat accelerated.

No! the logical side of her brain cried out in counterpoint. *There is nothing "personal" between me and Luke. And that's final!*

Having solved that problem, Jodi went into the kitchen and solved another. For lunch she'd prepare an omelet with a couple of the eggs Becky had so kindly supplied, and she'd liven it up with some of the dried sweet bell pepper and onion flakes brought from her apartment. Maybe a dash of chili powder as well. Jodi loved spicy foods, even if they had recently caused her heartburn.

Better to have heartburn from eating a tasty meal than from fretting about the surly man next door.

Five

By late afternoon Jodi felt restless, cooped up. She'd had all she wanted of reading for a while. For the past hour, the intermittent gusts of wind outside the cabin had bellowed her attention from the pages of one of the novels she'd brought with her. Maybe a walk in the breeze would blow the boredom out of her existence.

Stepping out onto the rear deck, Jodi was surprised by the increased chill in the air. Towers of white-to-gray cumulus clouds, their fringes stained tangerine, rose, and mauve by the lowering sun behind them, spread across the western horizon. She went inside, donned a thick, cowl-necked navy-blue sweater, and descended the twelve riserless steps.

As she reached the ground, she looked up and saw that the deck floor served as the roof of a storage shed, and the cover for a neat stack of firewood and a patio that sported a redwood benched picnic table and a portable barbecue grill. From there the meadow sloped sharply at first, then gradually to the lake.

As Jodi moved down the steepest part, she maneuvered with care among the erosion-smoothed granite boulders, remindful of half-buried turtles, that lay in her path. Unseen from the deck's height, dainty yellow, lavender, white, and pink blossoms, most no larger than a pencil eraser, clung to the vivid green blades of grass and stems of weeds . . . a

47

multihued carpet of tiny Texas wildflowers. A small white, cream-colored, or yellow butterfly would briefly touch a little pastel bloom, then flutter to another.

With a steady rhythm the wind-whipped, white-capped waves gurgled back and forth over the shoreline pebbles. The air smelled of wet and mold and, faintly, of fish. Breathing slowly and deeply, Jodi found the odors rather pleasant. At the water's edge she turned right and ambled along the narrow beach of gravel and reddish sand.

Several yards ahead, a weathered gray boathouse jutted out into the lake, joined to the land by a short pier that spanned the shallows. Rocking gently on the breeze-stirred surface, a wooden room-sized platform floated next to the building. Jodi spied Luke standing at the wharf's railing. He was working the reel on a fishing rod that leaned across the two-by-four banister, but he was watching her.

Luke studied the approaching woman Becky had called Jodi Turner. She was taller than average and slender, and she moved with a practiced fluid grace. Her long, dark hair, fanning across her shoulders, was a backdrop against her slender neck. Stray sable tendrils blew across her temples and around her ears. New jeans sculpted her going-on-forever legs, and although the bulky sweater concealed the rest of her shape, it emphasized the color of her eyes. Lapis lazuli, almost iridescent, like the feathers of a barn swallow's wings.

Jodi Turner was dazzling. But, more than that, she carried herself with a poise that fairly shouted her confidence in who she was.

He envied her that.

"Hello," she said with a friendly smile as she stepped onto the wharf.

For a few seconds Luke thought she appeared extremely ill at ease, probably taken aback by the unfamiliar unsteady motion beneath her feet. Then he saw her relax as if on cue, a deliberate act of self-control. It angered him somehow, and he frowned.

Jodi noted his scowl, and her smile disappeared. "If I'm

48

intruding, I'll leave." The offer would have been gracious had it not been for the defensive irritation tingeing her words. Was Luke this rude to all strangers, or was there something about her that he disliked?

"You're here. You might as well stay," he grumbled, keeping his gaze fixed on the rod and reel in his hands.

"Thanks a lot!" Jodi wheeled around and stomped to the pier. She departed the floating platform with such force that it pitched violently, slapping the waves with cracking noises. On solid ground she stopped and looked back, prepared to apologize for her overreaction to Luke's acerbic attitude.

Luke had been thrown off balance. He staggered, and to avoid a fall he grabbed the rail, his scarred hand and fingers tightening around it. The fishing rod slid over the banister and into the water with a whispery hiss.

"Damn! Damn! Damn!"

Initially, Jodi surmised Luke was cursing because of the lost, submerged tackle, but then, as the wharf's swaying eased, he lifted his hand from the plank and stared at it. Disbelief and pain warred on his ashen face.

What had happened to his hand now? Jodi wondered. Without hesitation, she stepped onto the wharf again, carefully, and walked the few feet to where Luke stood, still muttering miscellaneous invectives under his breath.

The gentleness of her touch as her hand enclosed his surprised Luke. For the first time since she'd said "Hello," he met her gaze. He saw concern . . . even warmth . . . and he felt a flash of regret for his unsociable behavior.

"Here. Let me see," she said. After placing her left hand underneath his to steady it, she used her right thumb and forefinger to capture and straighten his clenched fingers, one at a time. Jodi gasped. A jagged wooden splinter, larger than a toothpick, protruded from the scar-slick flesh of his palm. No wonder he had cursed. It must be burning like the upper reaches of hell.

And then the realization hit her. Luke had *feeling* in that hand! And she'd seen him instinctively flex wide his fingers when he'd reached for the rail as the wharf had rocked. Moreover, she'd met hardly any resistance when she uncurled his fingers in order to check his palm.

"Oh, Luke, you can feel!" she burst forth without restraint.

"Of course I can!" he shouted. "And it feels like the devil!"

The man, however hurting, still managed to exasperate her. She wasn't about to explain to him her joy upon discovering the movement and sensation in his injured hand. Especially not when she couldn't explain it to herself. Instead, she firmly grasped the offending wood sliver between thumb and forefinger and yanked it out.

"Bloody hell!" Luke screeched.

And blood there was. Spurting from the wound, trickling across his palm, between his splayed fingers and onto Jodi's hand that supported his now-shaking one. Embarrassed by his trembling and by the sight of his blood dripping all over a strange woman's hand, Luke started to pull free. Jodi held tight, then shifted her fingers to push on a pressure point at his wrist.

"Good," she declared after a couple of minutes passed and the blood flow lessened markedly.

"You can let go now. And thanks." He spoke with the same abruptness as before, but his mouth twitched into what Jodi assumed to be a reluctant smile.

"You're welcome." She released his hand.

Luke tugged a handkerchief from his hip pocket and awkwardly wrapped it around his throbbing palm. Jodi walked to the edge of the wharf, knelt down, and swished her hands back and forth in the lake until they were clean. Luke watched, fascinated by her graceful moves and by the way her derriere filled her jeans when she stooped and bent low to reach the water.

Not so fast, Luke reprimanded himself. *She's the doctor's . . . special friend . . . if that's what it's called in medical circles these days. And you're no poacher.*

Jodi stood and faced him, shaking the moisture from her hands. The sun flared from between the cloud pillars, and its brilliance haloed her head, brushing her dark, windblown hair with gold highlights. Even her flawless skin, naturally peaches and cream, took on a golden glow. Her wide apart, black-lashed eyes, set wide apart, reflected the blue of her sweater, and her incredibly kissable mouth shaped an I-hope-you-like-me-better-now smile.

Luke felt the heat flicker in his groin, and he hastily drew enough caution from the bitter well of his past to douse the embers. Jodi Turner was so enticing that it infuriated him. Deep down, he knew the fault was his, not hers, but for his own sake he needed to blame her, so he did.

"Are you a model?" he blurted out.

Jodi asked herself why he always spoke in that abrupt, accusatory manner. And why did it instill in her the impulse to strike back?

"No, I'm not!"

"Well, you ought to be. You're tall and you're beautiful, with fabulous cheekbones, and you move like a model. And you're skinny."

Openmouthed, Jodi stared at him. She was at a total loss whether to be flattered by a few grudgingly bestowed compliments or affronted by the one blatant criticism. After a brief strained silence, she defiantly chose to address the latter.

"I am *not* skinny!" She stopped when she heard her almost-beyond-control denial. Forcing herself to take calming breaths, she started over, placatingly. "If . . . uh . . . if I am . . . uh . . . too thin, it's because I've been ill. Dr. O'Meara sent me here to . . . uh . . . to recuperate." Those mesmerizing eyes made her unbearably nervous!

"I see." He didn't sound at all sympathetic regarding her health. "Then you must be the doctor's favorite . . . patient." He spat out the last word, scorn roughening his voice.

Suddenly, Jodi understood. For some insane reason, Luke

believed her to be Irish's—why hadn't he just spoken the word?—*whore!*

Never in all her twenty-eight years had she been so insulted or so furious. In the blink of those green eyes of his, she crossed the space that separated them and she slapped him . . . hard. Gratified by the amazement registered on his palm-imprinted face, she marched off the wharf. Deliberately, she kicked behind her, hitting the rim of the floating floor with all her strength so that it once more lurched wildly.

This time she didn't stop or look back.

As Jodi angled across the open stretch of meadow behind her cabin, her heart thundered in her chest. Adrenaline still pumped through her veins, and her cheeks reddened with humiliation at the memory of Luke's uncalled-for assumption. Why had he judged her so harshly? He knew absolutely nothing about her.

Jodi halted, but her mind raced like her pulse beat. She'd been terribly upset by Luke's perception of her. Angry and offended, yes, but sad, too, to hear his low opinion of her.

Why, she asked herself, should she care what Luke Prentiss thought about her? He was a stranger. She'd never see him again after her exile ended and she returned to Austin. Whether or not someone approved of her life-style had never before posed a problem. She wanted Irish to be proud of her. Besides him, she felt no obligation to please any man, and she was determined to keep it that way.

If Luke despised her, she could live with that.

But she wouldn't like it.

Smiling wryly at her confused and confusing logic, Jodi hurried on toward the cabin.

A new awareness assailed her, something entirely unrelated to Luke. Or was it?

Somebody was watching her. Again. Like this morning when she had walked to Becky's house. Had it been Luke who had watched her earlier? Maybe. Because both then and now, a vague sensation of acute dislike partnered the feeling of being covertly observed. And Luke had not attempted to disguise his belligerence toward her. But for him to spy on her . . .

The possibility raised the same disturbing ambivalence as had his unfair assessment of her bedroom habits: indignation, along with a nameless ache deep in her soul.

Jodi recounted to herself the other times when she'd felt insecure and unsure. When her parents died and she had to become an immediate sixteen-year-old adult to take care of Annie. When Quentin destroyed their marriage and she had to cope with the idea of failing at something important. When Annie was killed and she had to find something satisfying to fill the void in her life.

And now she was being strangely and irrevocably drawn to an implacable man who had no interest in or respect for her.

The truth—the challenging truth—hurt today, just as it had on those other occasions in the past.

You took charge then, and you *handled everything just fine,* Jodi consoled herself. *You can do it once again.*

Sure she could.

But how?

When Luke stepped up onto the dark cabin porch, he heard the music—Patsy Cline singing *Crazy,* Willie Nelson's ageless love ballad. Luke smirked. He'd sworn he would never again be so foolish as to be that kind of "crazy." If Corinne, his former manager and booking agent, had accomplished nothing else for him, she had taught him that. In the process of learning the grim lesson, Luke had also discovered how a woman could be warm velvet in the boudoir and cold steel in the office. And when push came to shove, the hard metal had survived, and the shining softness had ended up as the tangled threads of his frayed dreams.

" *. . . crazy for lovin' you.*"

Luke knocked on the front door, and a few seconds later

the outside light came on. Purposely, he stood where the woman inside could identify him through the peephole. He thought she might not acknowledge his presence. After all, three hours ago she'd slapped him so fiercely that his jaw had stung for several minutes. Remembering, he reached up to touch his cheek, just as the door swung open.

"I hope it still hurts," Jodi said tersely.

He hadn't expected her to put out the welcome mat, but her frontal attack shocked him into speechlessness.

"If you care to come in, I believe there's some pain-killing ointment in the medicine cabinet." She stepped back in order for him to enter the cabin.

He did, barely. "How about feeding me some crow instead?"

He smiled . . .

. . . and had no inkling of the butterflies her stomach acquired.

Her expression remained unreadable. Shifting self-consciously from one foot to the other, Luke dispensed with the smile . . .

. . . and she thought the room surely had grown dimmer.

"I came to apologize." He spoke softly, tentatively.

She forced herself to look away from the distress in his eyes. "Then do it, and I can get back to enjoying myself." She felt shamed by her intractableness. But *he* was the one who earlier today had drawn the battle lines. She would not retreat.

"Are you always this unfriendly?" Luke wondered aloud.

"Hah!" she scoffed.

"Okay, okay. I deserved that." He paused. "I deserved the slap, too." Together with the admission, he gave her another smile, this one accompanied by wariness.

"Yes, you did." But she sounded less testy.

"We've actually agreed on something." Solemnly, Luke moved a step closer. "Truce?" He thrust out his hand.

Jodi took it but, noting the bandage encircling it, was careful not to squeeze.

"It's not very sore," Luke said. "Becky's great at first aid. She used to be a school nurse before—" He paused momentarily. "She's had a lot of experience with minor cuts and bruises."

"And humongous splinters." Jodi chuckled, hoping to dispel the last vestiges of tension between them.

More than willing to extend the cessation of hostilities, Luke laughed with her. He told himself he simply didn't want to fight with a neighbor whom his sister apparently liked. When Becky had heard his slightly biased story of the encounter on the wharf, she had given him what-for while she cleansed, medicated, and bandaged his palm.

"May I sit down?" Luke asked.

"Of course. Pardon my bad manners."

He removed his jacket, laid it across the arm of the leather sofa, and sat down beside it. She chose the recliner but perched on the edge of the seat cushion. Her body language indicated to Luke that she anticipated more than the disgruntled apology.

"Ms. Turner, I want to explain—"

"Jodi, please. Call me Jodi."

He nodded.

She was beginning to understand that Luke Prentiss was a man of few unnecessary words. Perhaps that supplied the reason for some, if not all, of his brusqueness.

"Jodi." He crossed and recrossed his work boots at the ankles, first one and then the other. Clearing his throat, he began again. "Jodi, I want to explain about this afternoon. When I assumed . . . whatever . . . about your relationship with Dr. O'Meara." He swallowed audibly but bravely met her girding-for-battle gaze. "I was wrong. You see, Becky had told me the doctor was lending his cabin to a *special* friend. And when I saw his friend was a woman—a very lovely and much younger woman—well, I mistakenly connoted the word *special* with—with—" He sighed heavily and squirmed in his seat. "I'm sorry."

Suddenly, Jodi felt the astonishing urge to stand, walk

over, and put her arm around him. He looked utterly miserable. Intuitively, she guessed that Luke didn't apologize often. She suspected he usually did his own thing and without repentance let the chips fall where they might. Certainly, he was different from any man she'd ever met. In the instant of that discovery, Jodi didn't know whether she applauded or deplored his individualism. She did know she wanted to find out.

Six

"Apology accepted." Not ready to declare a full surrender, Jodi managed to maintain a facade of annoyance.

In reality, once the smoke from their battles thinned, she'd begun to figure out the reason for Luke's animosity. His leap to such an unwarranted conclusion about her undoubtedly reflected his distrust of all women. Some woman must have hurt him deeply, and to protect his heart from another wound of that sort he wore his defensive ire like a bulletproof vest. Jodi understood how a strong, stubborn man might handle his emotional reclusiveness the way Luke did. After all, she herself used a careful indifference to forge her own shield against further heartbreak.

"Friends?" Luke gave her another one of his butterfly-creating smiles.

Jodi's shield promptly melted under the green fire of his eyes.

Indifference, she admitted, was no longer possible. But she hung on to the carefulness like a dislodged mountain climber clinging to her safety rope.

"I guess." She slid back and settled on the recliner.

"So you're not a model," Luke said.

Here we go again, Jodi moaned inwardly.

"What *do* you do?" His tone held no rancor, only curiosity.

"I'm a public relations rep. With Sunbelt Images."

"A good firm."

"Yes, it is. So why aren't we your agency?"

She'd intended the question to tease, but he reacted by throwing his shoulders back, stiffening his spine, and moving forward from the back support of the sofa.

Then she remembered. Luke no longer needed an agent. How thoughtless could she be?

"Now I'm the one to apologize." Nervously, she ran her palm over her head and down the dark fall of her hair. "I forgot about your . . . injury."

His expression brightened. "That's a compliment!" Noting her astonishment, he went on, "You forgot I'm 'that poor cripple.' "

"You are not!" *I may as well explain to him my denial while I explain it—with care—to myself.* "You're my neighbor, and you're Becky's brother." *There! That should set us both straight about any hormonal urges.*

"Your *friendly* neighbor and Becky's *friendly* brother," he corrected with a grin.

"I'll buy that." A short, surprisingly comfortable silence ensued. Then, "Earlier, you said Becky was a nurse 'before.' Before what?" An oddly closed look crossed Luke's face. "I mean, does she work at another job now? Or, am I being too nosy?"

"She doesn't talk about herself much." He paused, then added, "But I don't think she'd mind our *friendly* neighbor knowing."

"I don't want to pry."

Jodi respected a person's sometime need for privacy. That belief was the fulcrum for the seesawing balance she strived to achieve for her clients: their empowered publicity versus their right to keep personal matters personal.

"Becky writes books," Luke said.

"That's great. Is she published?"

"She is."

Hearing the brotherly pride in those two words, Jodi waited expectantly. When Luke volunteered no additional information—the exasperating and intriguing man of few words!—she loosened the reins on her curiosity. "What are the titles of her books? Who's her publisher? Does she use a pseudonym? I have writer clients, and I try to stay current with publishers' lists, but her name doesn't ring a bell."

"Becky Shannon. Her two given names. She writes children's books. About a squirrel she calls Feisty. Three published so far."

"Excellent. How are her sales?"

"I never asked her." Luke bristled, but Jodi, the inherent publicist, failed to recognize the warning.

"Whatever her profits are at present, Sunbelt Images can probably increase them by at least ten percent."

"She doesn't need your help." His face flushed. His eyes flashed danger signals.

"You're angry again," she said, dumbfounded by his turned-around attitude. How could they be friends when he was so touchy?

"You bet I am! If Becky wanted an agent, she'd have one."

His antipathy hurt her feelings, and she didn't understand why. Usually, she was impersonal and businesslike when her expertise was rejected. This time she felt compelled to persist. "But—"

"She keeps a low profile. Her choice. Leave her alone," Luke snarled.

"All right!" she snapped. "I'm sorry!" Luke's agitation puzzled her. She'd offered her professional assistance, and he behaved as though she'd jeopardized Becky's well-being.

Sensing Jodi's perplexity and not wishing to pursue the subject any further, Luke took a deep breath and exhaled it in a prolonged susurrus. "We always seem to be saying 'I'm sorry.' " Picking up his jacket from the sofa's arm, he rose to his feet.

"Yes, we do, don't we?"

To Luke she sounded wistful, like a little girl whose playmate was leaving the party mad.

Playmate? Where had that come from? For him to "play" with this exquisite career woman would result in losing the game even before the party began. She spelled danger, a threat to his safe, uninvolved existence that strove for neither win nor loss.

Jodi watched him scowl and shrug his shoulders. She stood and started slowly toward the front door while he slipped his arms into the jacket sleeves.

Moving ahead of her, Luke reached the door and opened it. He stepped outside, turned and, his voice gruff, said, "But we're still friends," then hurried off the porch.

Nonplussed, Jodi stared into the darkness that enveloped him. The man was unbelievable! Mercurial. Fascinating. Dangerous. Did she dare to risk the danger? Reflecting on the imagined rewards should she take the risk and survive, Jodi lingered in the open doorway until the blustery north wind chilled her to the bone. Only her heart felt warm, glowing with its new freedom from its erstwhile bonds.

Outside, the gusting wind buffeted the cabin, whistling and keening around the corners to keep Jodi awake. A limb of the huge pecan tree, planted to shade the driveway, rubbed against the window glass, squeaking like a fingernail scraping a blackboard. Somewhere a garbage can lid banged and clattered as it blew away. Although Jodi snuggled under the extra blanket she'd found in the closet, she still felt the bitter cold that seeped in around the windowsills and under the doors. The built-in electric heater in the bathroom cast an orange-red glow across the bedroom floor, but its heat provided no contest for the chill that pervaded the cabin.

Jodi's muscles tensed, and the tenseness made her colder, which caused more tension. Her rising anger exacerbated her inability to relax. If she could get her hands around Irish O'Meara's throat . . . But he was sleeping miles away, comfortable and unaware, in his central-heated house. She was here, and she had to do *something*.

Build a fire in the fireplace? Even if she'd never built one, she assumed anyone could accomplish such a simple task. But what if she accidentally set fire to the cabin? Besides, all the wood was stacked under the deck, and she was loath to venture out into the dark and the weather. She sought another alternative.

Her sweats. Why hadn't she thought of them earlier instead of lying here shivering and muscle-tight and unable to doze off? Shrieking when her bare feet met the frigid hardwood floor, Jodi ran to the armoire for her sweatsuit and yanked the pants on, heedless of her nightgown bunching at her waist. Her teeth chattered. Until now she'd always believed that only happened in books. Quickly, while in the process of rushing back to the bed, she pulled the top of her sweats over her head.

"Mmmm," she sighed when under the covers she felt warm for the first time in hours. Sleep enfolded her before she completely relaxed.

At daybreak, Jodi reluctantly crawled out of her cozy nest. Scrambling around for her satin scuffs and wishing they were furry booties, she streaked across the room, grabbed the phone, and punched the familiar numbers.

Following the third ring, a crisp male voice said, "Hello. You have reached the residence of Dr. O'Meara. After the tone, please leave your message, and I'll return your call soon."

Beep!

"Damnit, Irish!" Jodi yelled at the answering machine, her words spurting little puffs of vapor into the air. "This house was built—"

"Good morning, Jodi." It was the same voice, unrecorded and fuzzy with sleep.

"—for *summer* living! A norther blew in up here last night, and it's freezing my buns off!"

"Oh, Lord! I forgot to—"

"I'm leaving this dump as soon as I can pack! I'd rather

die of job stress than pneumonia!" With every declaration, she grew angrier and louder.

"It is not a dump," Irish stated, quietly but adamantly. "It has a state-of-the-art entertainment center and expensive furniture and the best appliances money can buy."

"The garbage disposal doesn't work," Jodi informed him, jubilant over the puny triumph.

"Oh? Well, call a repairman and have it fixed."

"I won't be here that long."

"Yes, you *will.*"

"I'm not spending another night in this—this walk-in freezer." She thought her nose and ears must surely be turning blue.

"Not necessary."

"You're going to call forth a heat wave," Jodi snapped, exasperated by his calm when she was so upset.

"No, but if you'll cool off—"

"Hah!"

"—and listen, I'll tell you how to get warm. In the storage shed below the deck are two large electric heaters with circulating fans. The key hangs on the brass hook near the back door. Plug one of the heaters in in the kitchen and the other into the socket behind the desk, and the whole place will be comfortable in a few minutes. I forgot to tell you about the heaters. I'm sorry."

"Oh. Okay. And thanks." She placed the phone in the cradle as the thought surfaced. *Now I can stay.*

Jodi grimaced. What was happening to her? Since her arrival the night before last, she'd changed into a woman without control over her motives . . . or over her emotions. It was a new and baffling . . . and wholly alarming . . . experience.

Annie, often chided by Jodi for her impulsiveness, had once said to her, "You just wait, big sister. Someday you're going to discover a different you underneath all that structured composure and regimented planning. It'll scare the hell out of you at first. But, I promise you, the other Jodi will be happier."

A half-sad, half-amused smile curved Jodi's cold-stiffened lips. If Annie were alive to witness her sibling's current indecisiveness, she'd tease Jodi unmercifully.

"It's scary all right, kiddo," Jodi murmured to the one who couldn't hear her. Or maybe she could. Did angels giggle? Jodi speculated . . . because she envisioned Annie doing just that.

After marveling that she had reached the point where she could find anything humorous about Annie's being in Heaven, Jodi pragmatically switched her mind sights to the more mundane matter of electric heaters. Rebelling at the idea of encountering the frigid outdoors, she put on her Reeboks and a heavy sweater and walked toward the rear door. What needed to be done, she would do. Hadn't that always been her internalized creed?

Minutes later and halfway up the steps, Jodi almost dropped the second of the heaters when she heard Luke's voice ask, "Need help?" Without looking behind her—from his voice she guessed he stood at the bottom of the stairs—she said, "I don't like people sneaking up on me."

"I wasn't sneaking. I run past here nearly every morning." Now he sounded closer, directly below her. "I'll carry that the rest of the way."

When he reached around her to relieve her of part of the heater's weight, Jodi's center of gravity shifted. Her head swam as she peered through the eye-level open space where there was no riser. Momentarily disoriented, she rocked backward. Luke quickly steadied her with his free hand.

"You okay?" he asked worriedly.

She was *very* okay, she realized. His hand, even through her clothes, felt warm and strong and . . . *there*. An unexpected rush of desire struck her, and without answering him, Jodi sucked in a long, trembly breath.

"Stand still," he commanded crisply. Carefully, he squeezed by her on the steps, then hoisted the heater onto his shoulder, carried it up, and set it on the floor beside the first one.

Having regained control of her equilibrium and of her runaway libido, Jodi moved up to the deck, and when Luke wheeled around, he bumped solidly into her.

To prevent her falling, he grabbed her upper arms with both his hands and tugged her safely toward him, growling, "I told you to stay put."

For the briefest of instants she traitorously allowed herself to delight in the feel of his body touching hers from breasts to thighs, before she put her palms against his chest and pushed him away. "I don't take orders from you," she said, actually more disturbed by her reaction to his embrace than by his bossy manner.

"Or from anyone else, I suspect," he murmured, taking the sting out of the remark by bestowing on her his heart-stopping smile. "If I asked, very nicely, would you please make me a cup of coffee?" He opened the door and moved back for her to precede him. "It's cold out in this wind and"—he followed her inside—"it's colder in here! Jesus, Jodi! You spent the night in this . . . wooden igloo?"

Gazing at her under the kitchen overhead light, he considered her not only unfathomable but also probably the most beautiful woman he'd ever seen. Even without makeup and with her dark hair tousled about her face and with her figure hidden beneath the bulky clothing, she stole the last air from his lungs.

Hearing his ragged gasp, Jodi refused to meet his penetrating crystal green eyes. She must look awful! Her face as bare as a newborn's bottom, her hair tangled after a night of tossing on her pillow, and wearing the same sweats she'd finally fallen asleep in. Remembering the nightgown still bunched at her waistline, she blushed.

Watching the flush deepen on her cheeks, Luke anticipated an outraged response to his question, and to offset it, he said, "It's a fine wooden igloo. But it needs heat." With that, he hurried outside for the wherewithal to fill the need.

Jodi dashed into the bedroom and ran a comb through her hair. It crackled with static electricity. She picked up her lipstick, then dropped it unused into the plastic tray. If she put color on her lips, Luke would notice . . . and guess how embarrassed she was about her appearance. She'd be damned if she'd concede him that victory.

By the time the installed heaters had made a dent in the chill, the coffee was ready. Luke took a few sips from the mug Jodi handed him, then spun on his bar stool to give her a mischievous little-boy grin. "If I ask you something, will you promise not to get mad?" The gleam in his eyes was not that of a little boy.

"I can only promise to try." *As long as you look at me like that, I'll promise anything.*

"Last night, why didn't you build a fire in the fireplace?"

"If I tell you why, will you promise not to laugh?"

"I can only promise to try."

Jodi was the one who laughed. Luke was fun . . . when he forgot to thrust her into that females-are-not-to-be-trusted pigeonhole.

"All right, I confess," she said. "I don't know how to build a fire. It sounds ridiculous, I suppose, but I was afraid I might do something wrong and set the cabin on fire."

Solemnly, Luke reassured her. "You wouldn't have. This cabin's not going to burn down. Not because of a quote-wrong-unquote fire in the fireplace." He paused. "How about a former Boy Scout giving you a few pointers?"

He was dead serious. He cared that she worried about a flaw in her how-to knowledge. His solicitude started her heart double-timing against her rib cage. *Get real, woman,* Jodi reprimanded herself. *He's merely acting out the role of "friendly" neighbor.* Aloud, she said, "I'd appreciate that."

"Lesson number one coming up." He started toward the back door, hesitated, then added with a chuckle, "First, you need logs."

"Smart ass," Jodi retorted as she wadded her paper napkin and threw it at him, hitting the noisily closed door instead.

Later, Jodi stood at the side of the fireplace, listening to Luke's clipped instructional commentary and watching his every move. Laying the kindling and logs on the grate proved as simple as she'd expected. What surprised and impressed her was the dexterity with which Luke handled the small assorted bits of fire-starter wood. Sometimes his fingers dropped a piece, but each time he awkwardly managed to pick it up again and place it, if a bit clumsily, on top of the other chips.

Clearly, Luke's injured hand was not as constricted as she'd earlier surmised. And she recalled his reflexes yesterday when he'd almost fallen on the lurching wharf. He'd never be able to play like he had before, of course, but maybe if he wanted to play the piano again . . .

Therein lay the dilemma. Jodi had no inkling of what Luke wanted, and her intuition cautioned her this was not the time to ask.

Glad the phone rang to divert her attention, she hastened to the desk.

After lighting the fire with a long match held at arm's length, Luke straightened and watched her cross the room. She might not be a model, but she definitely moved with a model's grace and confidence and with just the right amount of hip sway to tantalize. When she spoke into the phone, he couldn't avoid overhearing.

"Hello . . . I knew it was you. I have heat now, so . . . *What?* . . . Oh, my God! When? . . . Tell the police I'll be there in . . . two hours, maybe less . . . Yes, I'll drive carefully."

At the word *police,* Luke had moved quickly to Jodi's side. The moment she put the phone down, he spoke. "What's wrong?"

When she turned toward him, he saw the disbelief and disquiet in her eyes. Her hand still fiercely gripped the phone as though its cool smoothness represented her one hold on reality.

In a voice amazingly natural, considering the tension on her face, she answered his question. "Sometime yesterday someone broke into my apartment . . . and trashed it."

Seven

"Damn," Luke muttered. How could Jodi just stand there? If his place had been burglarized, he'd be cursing like a fiend and pounding his fist on the desk.

I have to handle this. I have to handle this, Jodi repeated over and over to herself . . . until she gained the control she sought. Even as she congratulated herself for not having lost her composure, she realized Luke wasn't going to be satisfied with her simplistic statement of the facts.

"You told the person on the phone to tell the police you'd be there," he said. "Who discovered the break-in?"

"Mrs. Carson, the apartment manager."

"Why did she call you before she notified the police?"

"She didn't," Jodi explained impatiently. "She doesn't know where I am. She called Dr. O'Meara and he called me."

"I see." But he didn't, really. Apparently, only the doctor was aware of Jodi's whereabouts. Such secrecy seemed strange, especially since she constantly required media contacts and exposure to do her job. Whatever . . . or whoever . . . Jodi was hiding from, Luke discounted any further questioning. It certainly didn't involve him, and once her vacation ended, their paths would likely never cross again.

Jodi interrupted his musing. "I don't want to be rude, but I have to get ready now."

"Oh. Sure."

When he opened the front door and paused to look back over his shoulder, she was already moving toward the bedroom alcove. "Let us know how it goes."

Now, why had he said that? he wondered. It was no business of his what Jodi found at her Austin apartment. On the other hand, he rationalized, any good neighbor would be expected to express concern over another's misfortune.

"I will, and thanks," he heard her answer as he shut the door behind him.

Thirty minutes later, Jodi drove along the narrow winding road that two nights ago had made her so uneasy. In the daylight, the trees crowding the shoulders formed a glorious sweep of every shade of green from lettuce-light to near-black. Shards of frost sparkled like sunstruck crystal on the grass and weeds edging the ribbon of asphalt. Sprinkled among the glitter, a few pink primroses, having dared to challenge the calendar by blooming early, drooped limply on their stems. Jodi saw none of the passing beauty. Other than frequently reminding herself not to drive too fast on the unfamiliar road, her thoughts centered on wondering and worrying about what the thief had stolen from her.

Replaceable were the computer, television, radio/tape player, and portable kitchen appliances, but not so the costume jewelry pieces Irish had given her on birthdays and Christmases, nor the Meissen teapot her great-grandmother had brought with her from Germany, nor the paintings.

"Please," Jodi pleaded aloud. "He didn't take my paintings."

As a teenager, Jodi had dreamed of someday becoming an artist, and her teachers had encouraged her, claiming she showed promise. She planned to graduate, get a job, and save her money to pay for art lessons; but when her parents died, her priorities changed. Although Irish gave the sisters love and a home, Jodi felt responsible for Annie's education, so after graduating from high school, she secured a job in the commercial art department of Sunbelt Images and opened a savings account to send Annie to college.

The day before her twenty-first birthday, Jodi had strolled past the small art gallery near the office building where she worked. Although she often lingered on the sidewalk to admire the paintings displayed in the window, she had never gone inside. On that particular afternoon, a remarkably unusual painting caught her eye. The ocean scene depicted a rough, empty sea with an approaching storm filling the upper third of the canvas. The artist's technique was truly unique. Watercolor blues and greens overlapped and blended mistily to shape the rolling waves, while the threatening storm clouds stood out in three-dimensional oils, many streaks and shades of gray layered on with a palette knife.

Entering the shop, Jodi inquired about the painting. The saleslady, who introduced herself as Norma Sanders, the proprietor, informed Jodi that the artist was a Texas woman who a few years earlier, in her mid-thirties, had died of cancer.

"Elaine Joseph was very gifted," the owner continued. "There aren't too many examples of her work around. In the future, the one in the window may be worth ten or twenty times what it costs today." She quoted the price—probably reasonable, but expensive for someone earning Jodi's salary.

"I'm not buying it for speculation," Jodi said. She could hardly believe she'd already made up her mind to spend the equivalent of three months' savings on a framed, eight-by-ten-inch rectangle of water and sky! To assuage her guilt for the expense and impulsiveness, she'd call it her very first birthday present to herself. "I suppose it sounds foolish," she tucked in her chin in embarrassment, "but it speaks to me."

"It says, 'Hang me on your wall'?" The other woman smiled understandingly as Jodi gave her a startled look and nodded in affirmation. "That's why painters paint. To earn the ultimate praise, which is to give pleasure to people like you."

For a brief moment, as Jodi drove along the country road, she enjoyed the pleasant memory . . . until she remembered she also possessed an original Winslow Homer, considerably more valuable than the Elaine Joseph.

Jodi and Norma Sanders had become friends of sorts, chatting about art and artists whenever Jodi visited the gallery. With her first bonus check as the company's second vice president, she'd bought the Winslow Homer, another ocean scene. She treasured the two paintings, not only for their beauty, but also because they betokened the plateaus of her career success.

Why had the robber picked *her* apartment to break into? Anger, blazing and hurtful, rose through the worry to the surface of her emotions. *If that son of a bitch has taken my paintings and if he's caught, I will personally . . . spit in his face!*

Without conscious intent, Jodi grinned and eased her tight grip on the steering wheel. How many times in their childhood had Annie, when upset with someone who'd done her wrong, threatened to spit in that person's face? Later, the Klerkton girls had utilized the phrase between them as a war cry for their aggressive independence, and this morning Jodi found in its use a much needed solace. She guessed she was at last beginning to discover the silver lining in the cloud of her loss of Annie.

Having reached the divided four-lane highway, Jodi sped toward whatever awaited her. Several times the speedometer registered seventy-five and she forced herself to slow down, only to have her foot press heavily on the accelerator again. Once she arrived at the city's outskirts, handling the heavier traffic claimed her full attention until she parked in her assigned spot behind the apartment complex.

A police patrol car was pulling away from the curb. Wondering why the officers left before her arrival, she dashed inside the building, down the corridor, and flung open the door to her apartment.

Jodi stood stock-still. Her heart thundered in her chest, and a whispery, "No! Oh, please, no!" sputtered from her mouth.

Papers were strewn everywhere. The drawers of her desk had been yanked out and, along with their dumped contents, thrown to the floor. Receipts, letters, bank statements, personal papers, and notes regarding future work ideas were scattered across the carpet . . . among her books. Every volume had been pulled from the wall of shelves. Some had landed closed, some open, but each one's position suggested violence on the part of the burglar.

Someone tapped Jodi on the shoulder. Startled, she gave a shriek.

"It's all right, Ms. Turner," a soft-spoken, drawling male voice said.

Jodi looked up at the person who had touched her. He was short and stocky, in his late fifties, with receding mousy brown hair and coffee-brown eyes that held the same sympathy and concern as when he'd interviewed her here the day after Annie's murder.

"Detective Hanley," Jodi said.

"Too bad we meet again like this." His beefy hand made a sweeping motion in front of his barrel-shaped chest.

Sudden alarm blanched the color from Jodi's cheeks. He was a *homicide* detective!

"The robber killed someone?" she gasped. The apartment manager was alive; she'd informed Irish of the break-in. "Oh, God! Nita! The maid! I told her not to come until I contacted her."

"No, no, Ms. Turner, no one has been killed," the detective hastened to reassure her.

A long, hissing sigh of relief escaped Jodi's lips before she asked, "Then why?"

"Why am I here?" At Jodi's still-half-stunned nod, he explained. "I happened to be in the squad room when the patrolmen on the scene called for an investigator. I recognized the address and apartment number as yours, and thought you might like to see a familiar face when you got here."

"I . . . Thank you."

Another plainclothes officer, a flash camera in his hand, walked out of the bedroom and approached them.

"Ms. Turner, this is Detective English. He's in charge here." The homicide detective stepped away, acknowledging the younger man's authority.

"Ms. Turner, I'm sorry about this," said the tall, rangy redhead with a boyish, freckled face. "Quite a mess, isn't it?"

"To put it mildly," Jodi groaned. It was a neatnik's nightmare.

"I've already taken photos and fingerprints, although he probably wore gloves. After I get your prints"—he removed a kit from the briefcase propped against the wall—"I can eliminate those."

Jodi cooperated silently during the procedure, thinking she was somehow helping to apprehend the crook. After cleaning the ink from her fingertips with the offered Handi-wipes, she felt ready to deal with any further vandalism.

That was when she remembered the paintings. She hurried through the paper clutter, which crackled and rustled under her feet.

Inside the bedroom, she wheeled with apprehension and looked toward the walls flanking the doorway. They were still there! *Bless you, Mr. Break-in, for not knowing the worth of my paintings!*

Every bone in Jodi's body seemed to turn to mush as she faltered across the room and dropped onto the bed. Her hands shook. Her mouth went Sahara-dry. Her eyes burned and her throat ached with unshed tears. Whether from relief about the seascapes or from delayed reaction to the fact that an intruder had violated her home, she didn't know. Maybe both.

"Ms. Turner? Are you all right?" Detective Hanley stood in the opening between the rooms, an anxious expression on his florid face.

"Yes," Jodi breathed. "No. I don't know." She smiled sheepishly. "I think my knees betrayed me."

73

"It happens." He smiled back, then waited patiently for her to pull herself together. From his encounters with her following her sister's death, he knew Jodi Klerkton Turner to be a woman of more-than-average courage and inner strength. Therefore, her next caustic, vengeful declaration was not surprising to him.

"Maybe it'll help catch the bastard if I tell you he's no art connoisseur."

Detective Hanley directed his gaze to where she pointed with a slightly trembling hand. "Valuable, are they?"

"Very valuable. And I'm so thankful he didn't know that."

The other detective had entered the bedroom in time to hear their last comments. He said, "I'd like to know what *is* missing, if you don't mind checking."

"Of course." Jodi rose from the bed and turned.

With a gasp, she noticed the contents of her dresser drawers lying on the floor in untidy heaps of pastel satin and lace. A terrible fury assailed her. Someone mean and ugly had invaded her privacy and touched her most intimate apparel.

"How dare he!" she muttered gratingly as she neared the dresser. Strangely, the perfume and lotion bottles remained undisturbed. Uneasily, Jodi raised the lid of her carved teakwood jewelry case. After a few seconds careful perusal of the hinged trays, Jodi found everything exactly as she had left it, neat and in perfect order. Uttering a grateful sigh, she said, "He didn't take my jewelry."

The closet, however, she discovered with renewed anger, exposed another spurt of viciousness. Stepping gingerly among the jumble of hats, shoes, blankets, sweaters, T-shirts, and photo albums, she kicked aside their sundry containers. Her dresses had been shoved to one side or the other and clung precariously to tilted hangers. But, as far as she could determine, nothing was missing.

"I don't understand," Jodi murmured with a perplexed frown.

"Understand what?" This from Detective English, who had come up beside her.

"He didn't steal anything. He just made a horrendous mess."

"Let's check out the rest of the apartment," the officer in charge suggested.

The trio moved back into the living room, where an amazed Jodi indicated that the computer, as well as all the other portable items a robber would be expected to carry away, was still there. The Meissen teapot perched on its corner shelf. In the small kitchen/dining area, the only sign of the burglar's presence was the minor shifting of dinnerware, cooking utensils, and canisters from their usual locations inside the cabinets.

"This is crazy," Jodi said, shaking her head in bewilderment as, at the stainless steel sink, she washed the remainder of fingerprinting ink off her hands. "If he didn't want any of my belongings, why did he break in?"

"Maybe he was looking for something specific," the homicide detective suggested, his demeanor pensive and grave.

"Yeah," Detective English said. "Money. For dope. He sure checked all the likely hiding places."

"But he could have taken so many things and sold them," Jodi said wonderingly.

"Maybe he heard a noise in the hall while he was searching for cash and ran before he had a chance to pick up what else he'd planned to take with him. Probably some half-stoned kid. Not a professional thief, certainly, because he left the hall door open. That's what attracted the manager's attention."

The younger man's deductions made a weird kind of sense. Jodi knew criminals on drugs often behaved in a bizarre fashion. Breathing a sigh, she willingly accepted the police officer's explanation of what had happened.

"It's lucky Mrs. Carson didn't come in while he was still here," Jodi said. "She could have been hurt or even killed."

Shudders, visible to the two men, smote her. Her face paled and her eyes, wide with the horrible possibility, darkened to near black. Thank heaven it hadn't occurred.

"But she wasn't. She's okay." Detective Hanley reinforced her relief.

"That's right," Detective English seconded. "The patrolmen took her statement before they had to leave on another call, while I was taking pictures in here." He paused. "I'm through, unless you have a question." Jodi shook her head. "If need be, where can I reach you?"

"For a few weeks I'll be staying at Dr. O'Meara's cabin on Lake Buchanan. The phone number is 555-3497."

Detective English jotted the information down in his pocket-size black notebook. "Unless the perpetrator left fingerprints and we have them on file, I doubt if we will ever learn his identity. Sorry."

"You'll let me know?" Jodi requested.

"Yes, ma'am." He picked up his briefcase and camera and left.

At the hall door, Detective Hanley hesitated. "You better have this jimmied lock replaced with a dead bolt," he advised. "It's safer." Then he, too, departed.

Jodi promptly phoned the maintenance man, who lived in a room in the basement. When he heard her name, he inquired about the extent of the theft.

"That's good," he said after Jodi explained. "But he might be back."

Startled, Jodi bit back a denial. That aspect of the crime hadn't occurred to her. Surely one of the policemen would have warned her if he thought it possible. Of course, Detective Hanley *had* insisted she use a stronger lock.

"Maybe," Jodi replied after the moment's silent concern. "So could you please install a dead bolt lock on my door today?"

"Be right there. Soon as I fix a leaky faucet in 2B. I already went out and got the lock first thing this morning, right after Mrs. Carson told me about the break-in."

"Thank you, Mr. Williamson."

Hanging up the phone, Jodi felt more positive about her situation . . . until she turned and looked around her at the sea of higgledy-piggledy papers and books. With utter dismay, she waded through them to the bedroom, where waves of defilement washed over her. For a few moments she almost drowned in anger and in a savage need to strike back at the person who had done this to her. Only her ingrained self-discipline provided a life jacket of calming control.

As she stooped to retrieve a wisp of orchid and ecru lace and started to lay it on the bed, she groaned in disgust. That man had put his vile hands on her panties, her bras, her slips, her nightgowns. Every garment was dirty, degraded. Jodi grabbed up the rest of her lingerie and, half stumbling to the bathroom, shoved the befouled load deep into the clothes hamper. None of it would touch her bare body until it had been laundered . . . twice! Swallowing the nausea rising in her throat, she understood why a raped woman's first instinct after the crime was to take a long, cleansing shower.

Jodi sighed raggedly and with a determined energy tackled the closet's strewn contents. Just as she was returning the last refilled cardboard box to its place on the shelf, someone knocked on the door.

Remembering the broken lock, Jodi stood statue-still. What if that were the burglar, returning to steal what he'd left behind? Anyone who created such havoc had to have been motivated by extreme urgency. What if desperation had driven him back?

Then she thought of the expected maintenance man, and Jodi started to breathe again. Besides, anyone planning to harm her wouldn't announce his presence. He'd simply sneak in through the unlocked door.

"I'm coming!" she called out as she scampered across the paper-cluttered carpet.

Pushing the door open, she beheld the one person capable of brightening her depressing day. Tall, trimly fit for forty-eight, with thick salt-and-pepper hair and the kindest blue eyes in the world, he'd never looked finer.

"Irish! I'm so happy you're here." She reached out and by one arm tugged him into the room.

He took a couple of steps, saw the papers scattered all over, and grunted. "What an awful sight for you to walk into."

"This was the *best* part," she told him, making an effort to chuckle.

Irish set the plastic bag he was carrying on the floor beside him, then gave her a hug. "I'm glad you, and your sense of humor, are okay." His voice cracked the slightest bit before he managed to clear his throat. "You *are* okay?"

"Yes, besides still being mad as hell. Oh, I groped my way through fear and vindictiveness, but straightening up the bedroom gave me something tangible to concentrate on." She gestured toward the plastic bag, at the same time reading aloud the words printed on it. "Angelina's Deli. Dare I hope that's lunch?"

"Late lunch or early dinner, whichever. It's after three. I figured you wouldn't stop to eat until you had every tiny little thing back in its proper place." He gave her a teasing smile.

"Yeah?" Picking up the food, she headed for the kitchen. "Well, I'm stopping now, doctor, sir, because I'm famished."

"I brought beef minestrone and garlic bread and some of those hot pickled peppers you like." Irish followed in her wake through the sea of papers.

"Yum," Jodi responded, licking her lips as she took a pan from a cabinet and poured the soup into it. While it heated, she set out the plates, bowls, and silverware on the breakfast table.

Watching her work, her movements not as smooth or natural as she would have liked them to be, Irish asked, "Feel like telling me what the burglar stole? I hate to ask, but . . . the paintings?"

"They're safe." Pouring the steaming soup into the bowls,

she motioned for him to sit down, then sat across from him. "Luckily, he didn't steal a thing. He just turned everything topsy-turvy."

Irish gave her a quick, anxious glance, then commented, "Strange. He must have been looking for something in particular."

Jodi halted a spoonful of spicy minestrone halfway to her mouth, then returned it uneaten to the bowl. She'd remembered. "That's what Detective Hanley said."

"Why was *he* here?" Like Jodi, Irish had lost faith in the police department's solving of Annie's case, although the professional in him was compelled to admit and accept Hanley's lack of evidence.

Briefly, Jodi explained the homicide detective's presence, but uppermost in her mind loomed the sudden realization that both the experienced law officer and physician had hinted at the same disturbing possibility.

"You think the man who broke in here might have targeted *my* apartment? On purpose?" She didn't care at all for the path this conversation was taking.

"Eat your lunch, Jodi."

"But—"

"This subject's not good for your digestion. We can talk about it later. Eat." Following his own advice, he sipped his soup and gnawed on the crusty bread.

Silently, Jodi obeyed him, feeling like a chastised youngster who focused on the familiar in order to avoid confronting something unpleasant that awaited her.

"That was delicious," she said after she swallowed the last bite of her meal. Her mouth set in a stubborn line. "Now. It's later. So . . . what did you mean about the robber hunting for something specific . . . here?"

Irish dodged the question by asking one of his own. "What else did Hanley have to say?"

"Nothing. But the inspector in charge—his name's English—believes the robber was some kid looking for money

79

to buy drugs, and got scared and ran away when he heard noises outside in the hall."

"Makes sense to me." Irish's eyes avoided contact with hers.

Jodi noticed, and she pressed the matter. "I can't imagine what the man would think I'm hiding here, can you?"

"No, I can't." This time he met her gaze squarely and smiled. "I'm sure the investigator's theory is right."

He sauntered into the living room and, while Jodi rinsed the dishes and stacked them in the dishwasher, began to pick up the books and return them to the shelves. Jodi could postpone organizing them; he'd insist upon it.

"What about a new lock on your door?" he called out.

"That's taken care of, or will be." She walked up behind him. "The maintenance man promised to do the job this afternoon."

"Good. I have to be at the hospital for a five o'clock consultation"—he glanced at his wristwatch—"and I don't like your being here alone when anybody could just open the door and walk in." Kicking at a nearby pile of papers, he asked, "What about these?"

"I'm too tired to sort through everything today," she admitted with an uncharacteristic listlessness. "For now, I'll gather them up and stuff them in the desk drawers, out of the way."

"Smart idea," Irish approved, pleased that Jodi was less fixated on a place for everything and everything in its place. He bent down and picked up a long, fat envelope.

"You don't need to help." She took the bank statement from him. "It's almost time for your appointment, and I'll be okay. I'm just glad you had a chance to come by. And thanks for lunch." She leaned over and planted a kiss on his stubble-shadowed jaw.

After Irish left, Jodi busied herself with the room's remaining disorder. During that half-hour, Mr. Williamson arrived and, after a brief flurry of drilling and pounding, showed her how the lock worked, then handed her the keys.

Then he scurried away, grumbling about the sticking cabinet doors in 3C.

The sudden, lonely silence gave Jodi the jitters. Moreover, a faint aura of menace hung in the room, much like the way the scent of a woman's perfume lingers when she's no longer there. The eerie sensation probably stemmed from her frazzled nerves, but it was genuine, palpable, and Jodi couldn't ignore it.

"I'm out of here!" she declared, welcoming the sound of her own voice in the oppressive quiet.

Hastily, Jodi penned a note to Mrs. Carson saying that she was going away again, then deposited the message in the manager's mailbox and hurried out of the building.

Later, as she traveled the narrow winding road to the lake, Jodi experienced a newfound comfort in the closeness of the trees, barriers perhaps against the disconcerting malice she'd left behind. Contrary to the morning trip, her artist's eyes savored the passing montage of the many interwoven shades of green, gold-brushed by the fingers of late afternoon sunlight that pointed through the gaps between the rolling western hills.

Happy to be on her way to the cabin, and totally surprised by the realization, with a weary smile she negotiated the sharp turn into the rutted dirt lane.

Eight

Jodi had anticipated lying awake all night with her flash-backed emotions flipping like Rolodex cards, from anger to revenge to relief to fright and back to anger. But while she showered, not only the soapy water drained away, but also the adrenaline that had pumped through her veins for hours. Seconds after she slipped beneath the covers, she collapsed into dreamless sleep.

The next morning, still slumber-groggy and waiting impatiently for the coffee to drip through, she jerked to alertness when someone pounded once, twice, on the back door.

Memories of yesterday flew to the forefront of her mind. Had she double-checked that lock before falling asleep?

"Who's there?" she called out, a quaver in her voice.

"Who the hell are you expecting?" came the vociferous response.

Luke.

Jodi labeled herself an idiot for the momentary fear . . . and only then remembered her promise to call from Austin to let the Prentisses know about the break-in. Maybe a mild annoyance on Luke's part was justified . . . but anger? He seemed to go around *hunting* for something to be angry about . . . and the habit backfired. It made everyone . . . or Jodi, at least . . . angry with *him*.

"You're too early!" She remained seated on the bar stool, one slippered foot hooked behind a rung.

"You're not asleep!" Luke yelled.

"Not after all the racket you're making!"

"I saw your light!" He paused and lowered the decibels of his voice, even adding a slightly cajoling note. "Open the door, Jodi. I'm getting a raw throat shouting out in this cold air."

Jodi rose and sauntered to the door, unlocked it, and quickly stepped backward because she had a hunch what was coming. She was right. Luke yanked the door open and plowed inside, barely halting before his sweats-covered body bumped into her navy-robed one.

Jodi looked up into a pair of pale green, accusing eyes and reacted in kind. "It's not that cold this morning."

"You didn't call us," he growled.

"I forgot." Her admission contained no hint of regret.

He stood so close Jodi could feel the heat emanating from him. Hastily, she walked away and busied herself with the coffeemaker. Her hand trembled when she took a mug from the cabinet. *Because I'm furious with him for scaring me,* she told herself. Her shaking had nothing to do with the strange warmth in the pit of her stomach. Of course it didn't.

Luke watched the way her silken robe, which exactly matched the color of her beautiful eyes, clung to her feminine curves and shifted and clung again as she moved under the kitchen ceiling light. When she raised her arm to remove a mug from the shelf, the smooth satin caressed her breasts. He wondered how that handful of soft, warm flesh would feel . . .

Stop thinking crazy, Prentiss! She's an ambitious, career-priority female on a sabbatical. In real time, she's another Corinne. So cool it.

He loudly vented his self-annoyance. "Well?"

"Well what?" Pouring her coffee and adding the non-dairy creamer, she deliberately took her time.

Luke wanted to wring her lovely, slender neck. "Well, what happened at your apartment?"

Jodi ducked her head. Still coping with the effect his nearness had had on her breathing, she blew a sighing word out through her pursed lips. "Oh."

Luke heard the exhalation and waited, searching her face, half hidden by the fall of her dark hair, for more signs of distress. The wish, the need, to erase her worry dumbfounded him.

Finally, Jodi looked up into his eyes, which registered curiosity . . . and some other emotion for which she had no name. With a tremulous smile, she said, "The robber left the place in a shambles, but he was scared away before he had a chance to steal anything."

"Good," Luke grunted. Then, without volunteering a smile of his own, he turned away.

Jodi reached into the cabinet for a second mug. "How about some cof—? Darn!"

At the sudden, sharp sound of the door slamming shut behind him, she'd dropped the cup. It glanced off the edge of the counter, fell to the floor, and broke, providing another startling noise. Bending over to pick up the pottery shards, Jodi reprimanded herself for being so jumpy. She'd never been a nervous person, and simply because some half-stoned juvenile had made her a crime victim was no reason to be skittish now. That would afford the creep a victory, and her forte was winning, not losing.

Speaking of winning, Jodi mused with a wry grimace, *who won this morning's round, Luke or I?* His bewildering, mercurial changes of mood and behavior intrigued her. As did his incredible green eyes. And his sexy mouth.

Where had *that* come from? "Sexy" held no attraction for her, nor did the grumpy man next door. With that conclusion firmly fixed in her thoughts, Jodi dumped the mug fragments in the garbage can and piled three spoons of sugar on her cereal.

As she drank the last of her second cup of coffee, the phone rang. It was Becky.

"I hope I'm not calling too early," she began, "but I've been wondering how yesterday went."

84

"Not nearly as bad as it might have been. Didn't Luke tell you?"

"No. Did he stop by on his run?"

"He only stayed a few minutes." *Just long enough to infuriate me.*

"We didn't talk after he came back. He was in a hurry to shower and get to work."

"He has a job?" Why did that surprise her? Piano playing wasn't the only way to earn a living. She just hadn't pictured Luke doing anything else.

"He works part-time for the Millers," Becky said. "They own a mom-and-pop grocery store about a mile on down the road past the turnoff to our house."

"I see."

"Jodi, would you mind coming over here for a chat?"

"No. Why?"

"I'd come there, but I'm expecting an important call from my editor. Luke said he told you I write children's books."

"He did, and I think it's great."

"Thanks. But I don't want to talk about me. I want to hear what happened at your apartment."

"All right. In about an hour."

"Fine."

In keeping with the Spanish hacienda-style house and the bright, multicolored terrazzo floor and wainscoting of the entrance hall, Jodi thought the room that she entered ahead of Becky would contain dark, massive, ornately-carved antiques. Instead, the furniture was modern and white, wicker or painted wood, upholstered with a soft peach or a mist green or a dainty floral polished fabric combining the two colors. On stark white walls hung small unframed Monet and Cézanne reproductions in asymmetrical groups of three or four. Jodi's footsteps sank into the green carpet as though she trod on thick, lush grass after a soaking spring rain. In fact, she had the improbable impression of standing in a cool, airy garden . . . under a roof.

"This is lovely," she applauded. "Probably the pinnacle of your interior decorator's success."

Becky chuckled. "That's probably the nicest compliment I ever received."

She took Jodi's sweater, laid it over a chair arm, and with a gesture invited her guest to sit. Jodi chose the sofa, Becky settling beside her.

"I hate gloomy, depressing rooms," Becky said. She lifted her shoulders to hide their barely perceptible shuddering. "So I had all the walls repainted before I moved in. Then I bought light, cheery furnishings."

"You refinished the piano yourself?" Jodi guessed that under the upright's white enameled finish lay the genuine mahogany or walnut patina of a rare vintage instrument from another era.

"Yes. It belonged to Great-grandmother Prentiss, who studied to be a concert pianist but gave it up to be a wife and the mother of four sons. Luke is the only one in the family who inherited her talent." A shadow crossed her features, and her hazel eyes darkened with the sadness that never quite left them.

"Does he play at all now?" Jodi asked.

"Oh, no!" Becky gasped. "Never!"

"But he can use the fingers of his right hand," she insisted.

"For some things, yes." Moisture shone in Becky's eyes as she looked disbelievingly at Jodi. "You remember how he played. His fingers rippled over the keyboard like musical lightning. Can you imagine how he'd feel, making those clumsy, pounding sounds a little boy makes when practicing his scales? It would kill him." Her voice cracked, and one teardrop slid down her cheek.

Jodi pretended not to notice Becky furtively brushing the tear away, having learned firsthand that setbacks and compromise didn't kill. But sympathetic toward her hostess's mood, she refrained from saying so.

"Luke has accepted the fact that he can't play anymore," Becky continued in a stronger voice. "He likes his job."

"At a grocery store, you said."

"They also sell fishing tackle and hardware, and it's a feed store, too. Herbert and Maggie are in their late sixties. They depend on Luke to drive into town for their supplies, to move or lift heavy cartons, and to stock the high shelves. He clerks on holiday weekends if he's needed, and whenever the Millers go to visit their daughter in Waxahachie. They like being able to summon Luke at a moment's notice, and I think he likes not having a predetermined work schedule."

"A mutually satisfactory arrangement," Jodi commented, although she found it impossible to think of Luke as a happy, permanent grocery clerk.

"Exactly."

Did Becky sound unduly defensive? Perhaps she, too, in spite of everything, still thought of her brother as a pianist.

"Well," Jodi said, "I'm glad I can buy milk and bread without having to drive those nineteen crooked miles to Burnet. I don't suppose the Millers run a washateria, too?"

"Washateria?" Becky frowned in puzzlement.

"Irish says I have to stay here six weeks, and there's no washer or dryer in the cabin."

"Use mine," Becky offered. "Any time."

"Thank you, but I wasn't hinting—"

"I know that, Jodi. Neighbors help out neighbors." She paused. "I hope I'm not prying, but . . . if Dennis sent you here . . . I mean, have you been ill?"

"Just job stress," Jodi answered glumly. She hated admitting her inability to handle the problem without Irish's intervention.

" 'Just'?" Becky placed a hand over Jodi's, then gently squeezed it. "Stress, on the job or off, can be serious, and it's certainly nothing to blame yourself for or be ashamed of. I know." She avoided Jodi's curious glance.

Jodi sensed that Becky's last two words implied more than encouragement, but before she could come up with a tactful response, the phone rang.

"That's probably my editor," Becky said and, looking relieved, hurried to take the call.

Jodi moved to the far end of the long room. Nevertheless, she couldn't help overhearing Becky speak with disgust to someone about an artist who didn't "know beans about squirrels."

"Hers look like chipmunks," Becky scoffed. "Have her do the sketches over. . . . No. I mean all of them. . . . I don't agree, and let me remind you, my new contract gives me full illustrations approval. . . . Just tell her. If she wants the job, that's how it is." Becky muttered a sailor-made curse as, with exaggerated care, indicative of restrained violence, she placed the phone down.

Turning around to face Jodi, she said, "Sorry about that."

"It sounded to me as though you're entitled."

"Maybe. The woman who illustrated my other books had triplets two months ago, so her art career is on hold. The new prima donna artist wants to create an entirely different squirrel, which my young readers—and I—absolutely will not accept."

"It's a good thing your contract lets you have the final say."

"That's why I insisted that clause be included," Becky explained as they resumed their seats. "Janette had confided to me that she was expecting two babies more than the one she and her husband had been hoping for for eight years. I took it for granted that I'd soon be working with an untried illustrator."

"May I read your manuscript sometime while I'm here at the lake?"

Becky stared at her in amazement. Then she gave a nervous little laugh. "You want to read a story about a squirrel named Feisty, written for children between the ages of seven and nine?"

"Yes, I do. Didn't Luke tell you I work for Sunbelt Images?"

"No." Becky's expression changed to solemn, almost grim. "But I don't need—"

"An agent. I know. Luke made that point abundantly clear."

Did he ever! Her professional ego still bore the bruises of Luke's wrath, and judging from Becky's contrite glance, her tone of voice had exposed a few of those leftover black-and-blue marks.

"I'm sorry if he was rude," Becky said. "He's very protective of me."

"I understand." But she didn't.

Becky Prentiss needed no "protector." The woman who a few moments ago had delivered the ultimatum regarding her book's illustrations had demonstrated a laudable capability and willingness to take care of herself.

"I'm just curious, I guess." Jodi went on to explain the reason for her request. "Like anyone who doesn't—can't—write a book. During the past five years I've handled the publicity for two—no, three—writers, but I've never seen or been involved with a work still in progress."

"That's why you want to read mine?" A lingering skepticism tinged Becky's query.

"That's why. As a friend. A curious friend."

"Well . . ." Becky rose and left the room. In a couple of minutes she returned and laid several computer printout pages in Jodi's outstretched hand. "That's a rough draft of *Feisty's New Friend*. The same one the illustrator's working with. You'll find handwritten changes in the margins and between the lines, but I'm sure you can figure it out. And please, feel free to write on it yourself if you have any comments."

"Thank you. I'm honored."

"Now," Becky's tone dismissed all further talk about her work, "tell me about the burglarizing of your apartment. How he got in. What he stole. What sort of damage he did.

What the police say." She stopped for a breath and grinned. "I'm babbling like a—a curious friend."

Pleased at the rapport developing between them, Jodi smiled at Becky's use of her own earlier phrase. She looked across the sofa at her neighbor. For an instant she was mesmerized by the remarkable contradiction between Becky's pretty, mid-thirties face and her silver-white hair . . . and wished she were a portrait painter.

Becky was watching her expectantly, waiting to hear about the break-in.

While downplaying the range of emotions she'd been prey to, Jodi related the bare details Becky had asked for.

"Strange." Becky frowned. "In your job, do you discover things about clients, secrets the tabloids would love to get hold of?"

"Sometimes." What brought that up? Jodi wondered.

"Have you ever kept that information in files in your apartment?"

"Heavens, no!" The idea disgusted her and the supposition affronted her. "I never put that kind of garbage in *any* file! My goal is building images, not tearing them down!"

"Okay, okay. Sorry I asked. I guess my writer's imagination went into overdrive. It occurred to me that if you did have information like that somewhere, the burglar could steal it and get rich blackmailing your clients. Or you."

Jodi laughed heartily, easing the brief tension between them. "You should be writing mystery novels instead of books for children." She grew sober. "Like the detective said, the burglar was someone who needed cash for a fix. And while he hunted for it, he made one god-awful mess. He just happened to pick my apartment at random."

Jodi believed that. She wanted to believe it. She *had* to believe it. Otherwise, the crime raised too many unknown, unanswerable questions. Frightening questions.

Nine

Those questions, still unspoken, hovered like distant storm clouds on the outskirts of Jodi's mind while she chatted with Becky about nothing important. When she said goodbye and walked along the rutted road toward the cabin, the questions suddenly encompassed a bizarre logic that hit Jodi with the force of a Texas tornado.

What if someone *had* deliberately broken into *her* apartment? Could his purpose have been not to steal, but to leave a disconcerting path of destruction through all of her neatly organized belongings? To manhandle her personal apparel and possessions? He'd created exactly the kind of chaos that was sure to disturb her the most. Who would know that . . . and use the knowledge to assault her peace of mind?

Quentin, of course.

Why hadn't she thought of him sooner? Characteristically, one way or another, he'd always paid her back for making him angry, for crossing him. It had usually been with vituperative curses or loveless sex. Then he'd hit her that first time, slapped her face brutally hard, simply because she failed to run an errand for him. Later . . .

Jodi shut off the ugly memories. With Annie's and Irish's encouragement and support and with the aid of a tough-minded lawyer, she'd broken free of Quentin's violence. That brief, demeaning phase of her life was over.

But was it, really? Might the devastation in her apartment have been a reprisal against her refusing to take him on again as a client?

Should she report her suspicions to Detective English? No. There was no proof, and if the police questioned Quentin, guilty or not he would retaliate in some other, far worse manner. He'd promised to get even. She just hoped trashing her home had satisfied his vindictive urges. If not, what else did he have planned for her?

Jodi shivered despite the warm sunshine on her shoulders and back. She felt exposed . . . vulnerable. To what, she didn't know. For a few seconds she even had that earlier, unexplainable sensation of being watched.

Although feeling somewhat overreactive, she nevertheless hurried her footsteps until she reached the cabin. She unlocked the door and rushed inside, then halted just past the threshold to catch her breath and to savor the secure embrace of the one place where Quentin had never been.

He'd known Irish owned property somewhere on Lake Buchanan's shoreline, but he'd always refused to come here when Jodi or Irish suggested it. Bright lights, earsplitting rock and roll music, and adoring groupies had been as necessary to Quentin off stage as on. And Jodi, unwilling during those days to admit or confront the problems in her new marriage, had declined Irish's invitations to his vacation cabin, claiming a desire to be near her husband. Instead, she'd remained in the city, alone, working long hours even then to hide the emptiness in her life.

A couple of days ago Irish had told her Quentin lived in a condo across the lake. Had Quentin sought out the cabin's location? Had he discovered she was staying here? Was he watching her, stalking her, with some nefarious purpose in mind?

Jodi whirled and slammed the door closed with a loud, protecting thud.

Immediately she felt better . . . calmer.

For a few moments she'd relinquished her closely guarded

self-control to yesterday's fears. Aware that the short-lived paranoia had sprung from the resurfacing of upsetting memories, Jodi vowed not to let it happen again. She'd learned through experience that the best and surest way to bypass unwanted thoughts was to reroute her thinking, to patch new, pleasant data into her emotional arteries. And this time she knew she held the corrective mind surgery in her hands.

Jodi set the manila file folder containing Becky's manuscript on the desk, then took off her sweater and laid it across a chair back. It slid to the waxed hardwood floor in a clump of turquoise cashmere. Jodi gave it an irritated look and, mentally snubbing her nose at her neatnik fetish, left the sweater lying there. Retrieving the file folder, she settled in the recliner and began to read.

Feisty's new friend turned out to be a Persian kitten named Puff. Although cats and squirrels are enemies by nature, neither animal in Becky's tale knew that, so they would share wonderful adventures, some daring, some just plain fun.

As Jodi read the first printout page, pencil in hand because she habitually read nothing without one, she unconsciously drew in the left-hand margin a tiny spare but realistic sketch of Feisty and Puff at play. Realizing what she'd done, she made a moue and turned the pencil over to erase her doodling. Before she did, however, she stopped.

Becky said I could write on her rough draft. Maybe she didn't mean draw—Jodi smiled as if she were getting away with some mischief—*but I'm enjoying this. So why not?*

She continued to read, penciling in additional scenes. Episode after episode, she was impressed by Becky's talent. Not only did Becky understand how to entertain children, but in the process she also subtly managed to teach a valuable lesson: Animals—or people—who were totally different from one another could still be friends, even though outsiders sometimes expected them not to be.

Judiciously, Jodi glanced back over her hastily drawn handiwork. It was *good!*

She gasped as, like an electric shock, a painful self-analysis stunned her.

Once upon a time, as a naive adolescent who fantasized about someday becoming a famous artist, she'd filled every blank space on her schoolwork and tablets with all kinds of scribblings and drawings. The habit lingered, grew, and earned for her stepping-stone salary increases after she went to work for Sunbelt Images. But when she forsook the commercial art department for a better-paying position as a public relations representative, she had stifled the urge to draw anything. Like jamming the glass stopper in a bottle of too-heady perfume. If she couldn't be an artist, she'd refuse to insult her dream by placing even so much as a miscellaneous doodle on a scratch pad.

The words on Becky's computer printout pages blurred and ran together as the bitter tears filled and overflowed Jodi's eyes. Quietly, the years of self-castigation drained down her cheeks and out of her soul.

She knew that if she had it to do over, she'd still choose the job change in order to finance Annie's college education, but she wouldn't seal off her own needs. In those days, to prevent the weakening of her resolve to do all and be all for her orphaned sister, she'd gone to the other extreme by being too hard on herself.

And obviously that same punishing of self had contributed to her burying herself in her work following Annie's death.

Oh, Annie, who killed you? And why? You never hurt anybody in your entire twenty-two years.

Someone had taken Annie's life when she had the most to live for. She was planning to marry the man she loved and was selling her country songs almost as fast as she composed them.

It wasn't fair!

Some damn ghoul out there was walking around with a ghastly dark secret: He'd used her car to commit cold-blooded murder . . . and gotten away with it.

So far.

Maybe for always. Because Detective Hanley's investigative skills had failed to uncover a single clue to break the heart-wrenching deadlock.

If only . . .

No, Jodi told herself as she wiped the tears from her face with her knuckles. *I have to stop hoping . . . just like I have to stop blaming myself for not going with Annie that New Year's Eve to the Clint Black concert in Dallas. My being in the car wouldn't have saved her.*

Irish was right. She had to let it all go—the guilt, the grief, the frustration—so her wounded spirit could heal and her pressure-ridden body could find peace.

Exhausted by the tangled emotions of the past few minutes, Jodi laid her head back against the padded leather headrest, uttered a sighing moan, and lowered her tear-swollen eyelids.

When she awoke, she glanced at her wristwatch and was amazed to discover she'd slept almost three hours. Initially, she felt foolish, even at fault for being lazy, but then she remembered why Irish had persuaded her to come here. To forget clocks and calendars, and to do whatever she wanted without feeling obligated to do something else.

However, for someone who for many years had pre-planned every waking hour, the inactivity created a stress of its own.

You didn't think of that, did you, Irish? she railed at her godfather.

But he had. As on so many other occasions, he'd given her the answer before she asked the question. He'd already suggested an alternate agenda.

Read a book.

She'd done that.

Take a walk.

She'd rather sit here on her duff.

Play your tapes.

A pleasant way to occupy her time . . . and her thoughts . . .

without burning up the meager storehouse of her current energy.

Jodi moved Becky's manuscript from her lap to the end table. Standing, she stretched her arms high above her shoulders and shifted her weight from one foot to the other, jump-starting her stiff muscles. She walked over to the entertainment center and looked through the stack of small plastic boxes she'd brought with her, until she found the tape she sought. On it were Luke's early solos, the ones prior to the release of his two all-instrumental singles. Each *Only in Texas* record featured one ragtime solo number, and Jodi had dubbed all of those onto a special tape, which she now slid into the deck. She pushed the PLAY button.

On her way back to the recliner, during the first notes of the rollicking rhythm of "The Entertainer," she paused to open the front door. The Quentinized ghosts had been disposed of, and she wanted to breathe the clean, bracing air and hoard the reflected warmth of the spring sunlight that tracked across the floor. Glad she wasn't in her office trying not to be late for her next appointment or trying not to react with a shiver to the ululation of a siren on the street two stories below, Jodi sat down and propped the heels of her Reeboks on the footstool.

The second of Luke's solos was "Under the Double Eagle," its martial fervor, remindful of Sousa's marches, never failing to accelerate Jodi's patriotic heartbeat.

In contrast, the syncopated, stumbling melody of "Kitten on the Keys" made her smile. As always, it brought back happy memories of Patches, her childhood pet who had created his own feline composition as he trod up and down the ivories of her parents' piano.

Next came "Maple Leaf Rag," which also yielded the trademark of every solo Luke performed. Somewhere in the rendition, he hit one grating, discordant chord. Those not acquainted with Luke's deliberate tongue-in-cheek clunker silently asked themselves, "Did I really hear that?" then went on to enjoy the remainder of his harmonic perfection.

Luke's knowledgeable fans, like Jodi, eagerly waited for that lone blink-of-the-eye "mistake" the first time they heard Luke play any song, then delightedly thought, "There it is!" and considered themselves privy to an inside joke.

The lilting soprano strains of "Nola," the last song on the tape's A side, had barely begun when Jodi heard heavy footsteps running up the front steps and across the porch.

Before she could gain her feet, Luke stormed through the open doorway, shouting, "Stop it, damn you, stop it!"

Startled by his noisy intrusion, Jodi rose quickly and, as she whirled toward him, yelled back, *"You* stop barging into my house like a rampaging bull moose!"

Then she saw him. Body rigid, his forehead sheened with sweat, eyes narrowed to unreadable slits, lips stretched wide in a frightening, feral grimace.

Speechless with astonishment, Jodi could only stare. Why on earth was he so furious with her?

"Turn . . . off . . . the . . . tape," he rasped, his jaw muscles quivering as he clenched and unclenched his teeth.

Suddenly, she understood. Horrified by what she had done, she sprinted to the entertainment center. Luke wasn't angry. He was in agony—because she'd played his music, and he'd heard it and been reminded of everything he'd lost.

Jodi pushed the STOP button and, before she faced him again, scrambled through her regret-befuddled brain for a proper apology. Inadequate though it was, the only thing she could come up with, however often it had already been used between them, was a breathy "I'm sor—"

In mid-sentence she turned . . . and clamped her mouth shut. She was alone.

"Luke! Wait!" She couldn't let him go without an explanation!

When she'd selected his tape, she hadn't said to herself, "I can play this now because Luke's at work." But Jodi *knew* she would never ever have played it if she'd had any idea he might be within earshot. Not even if he were completely adjusted and reconciled to the tragic ending of his burgeoning musical career—as Becky had inferred he was—and as she, Jodi, had just inadvertently, cruelly proved he wasn't.

She rushed through the open door and out onto the porch, calling his name again. He kept on walking, slowly, his shoulders slumped, his shuffling steps dragging in the dirt like those of an old, sick man.

At that moment, Jodi hated herself.

The next moment, her phone rang.

Damn! Talking to Luke would have to wait. Maybe she could ignore a clock or a calendar but not a ringing phone. What if it were the Austin police calling to tell her they'd caught the robber? Or, better yet, that they had finally by some miracle learned the identity of Annie's murderer?

Ten

"Hello?" Only in her office did she answer the phone with "Jodi Turner." There were too many crazies out there for her to indiscriminately volunteer her identity.

"Jodi, are you enjoying your vacation?" a man asked without preamble.

Who was he? Who had found out she was here?

Jodi's heart skittered in her chest as the wheels of memory spun in her head. She knew she ought to recognize the voice, and because she didn't, it had to have been a long time since she'd spoken to him over the phone. She prided herself on remembering phone voices, a talent that pleased and flattered her clients. But she was unable to assign either a name or a face to the speaker on the other end of the line, and the inability unnerved her.

Lately, it seemed, a great many things unnerved her. Jodi laid the blame squarely on Quentin's unexpected reentry into her life. And on the break-in.

"Jodi? Are you still there? It's Troy."

Troy! Of course, she thought with relief.

"Hi, Troy. Sorry I didn't answer right away, but you caught me downing the last of my coffee." A viable excuse, she thought, preferring the fib to an admission that she'd forgotten he lived nearby.

"Are you enjoying your vacation?" Troy repeated.

"I like sleeping late."

He laughed. "I think that's called damning with faint praise. You miss the Tex-Mex food."

He knew her better than she realized. She, Annie, and Troy had spent a fair amount of time together that last year and a half Annie was alive.

"Especially the *fajitas*," Jodi admitted, striving for a light-heartedness to match his because he needed to forget Annie and get on with his life.

Troy continued his teasing. "I bet you've already been back to the city."

"Well . . . yes, but it was necessary."

"Necessary?"

"A problem at my . . . ah . . . office." She didn't want to tell Troy about the ransacking of her apartment. Out of allegiance to her sister, he might wax overly protective. Irish's "protecting" had left a big enough dent in the walls of her fortress of independence.

"No more problems?" Troy sounded ready and willing to assist her. His solicitous attitude solidified Jodi's decision not to disclose why she'd gone to Austin yesterday.

"Everything's okay," she assured him.

Not really. She was haunted by the look on Luke's face when he'd shouted at her to turn off the tape. Without meaning to, she had figuratively rubbed his nose in his undeserved failure.

"Troy, I'm sorry, but I have to hang up. There's something important I need to take care of."

"In Austin?"

"No. Here."

"Oh. Well, don't forget you're coming up the hill to see my new house and have a margarita."

"I'll let you know," Jodi said, impatience brittling her half-promise as she cradled the phone.

Grabbing the sweater off the floor and the cabin key off the desktop, she headed for the door. Luke's pained expression, his handful of anguish-hoarsened words, the defeat so apparent in his departing steps, tore at her conscience. Somehow she had to ease the hurt her blunder had caused.

The phone rang again.

"Shit!"

Hurrying to the desk, she lifted the receiver, her "Hello!" unmistakably irritated.

"Ms. Turner? Detective English of the Austin P.D. Am I calling at a bad time?"

Jodi inhaled deeply, then released her frustration in a noiseless sigh. Dredging up her stay-calm-no-matter-what public relations persona, she responded, "Not at all. Do you have some news for me?"

Idiot! Of course he did, or he wouldn't be contacting her.

"Yes, ma'am. We ran the fingerprints through the computer, and one set's on file."

"Good." They'd find the crook, and her embattled nerves could normalize.

"Juanita Sancho."

"That's my maid!"

"Yes, ma'am. We brought her in for questioning this morning. She claims she's innocent."

"She *is!*" Mortified, Jodi dropped onto the nearest chair. "This is my fault. I should have told you about her, but I was so rattled."

"You're aware she spent a year in prison for assault with a deadly weapon?"

Fury crackled in Jodi's reply. "For using her son's baseball bat to defend herself and her son against a drunk, abusive husband." She paused. Taking her anger out on the detective was unfair. "I met her right after she got out on parole, when I spoke to the women at Safe Harbor about my own experience."

"You were a battered woman?" Disbelief colored his query.

"Not in the true psychological textbook sense. I was lucky, able to realize what was happening and walk away with only a few bruises." And a determination never to fall

101

in love again. "Nita's case was different. She wound up with low self-esteem, no job experience, not even a high school education. She needed an income to take care of herself and her son, so I hired her and recommended her to a few colleagues. None of us has known one second of regret. She's completely trustworthy. Nita has a key to my old lock. There would have been no reason for her to break in. I just wish I'd explained this to you yesterday."

"I just wish the fingerprints had turned up the real perpetrator. No, that's not right. I don't mean I wish your friend was the guilty one."

His *gaffe* earned a soft chuckle from her. "I understand."

"I'll inform you if anything else develops, but I'm not optimistic."

"Thank you anyway."

"That's my job, ma'am. Goodbye."

"Goodbye, Detective English."

Glowering at the replaced phone and daring it to stop her again, Jodi scurried across the floor. On the porch, with the key dangling in her hand, she stopped herself.

By now, she conjectured, Luke would have buried his dejection in his unreal reality. His stubborn pride would have delegated the incident with the tape to the only place where he could exist with it: the Land of It-Never-Happened. If she went bounding over there with an apology and an explanation and compassion, he'd probably growl at her and do another disappearing act.

But if she had a second reason, a valid one, to go . . .

Feisty's New Friend.

Minutes later, carrying the manuscript folder in the crook of her arm, Jodi was halfway to the Prentiss house before it occurred to her that in her haste she might not have locked the cabin door behind her. She hesitated briefly, then shrugged her shoulders. According to Irish, crime was nonexistent in the Swallows Bluff community. So she moved briskly ahead, focusing her energy and attention on her upcoming talk with Luke.

Not until after the fourth insistent peal of the doorbell did Luke answer its summons. Through the screen of the storm door, he grumbled, "Becky's not here."

"Oh? I wanted to return her manuscript." Jodi held out the folder.

Luke couldn't have looked more stunned if she'd just told him she was there to confess to being a humanoid straight off the Starship Enterprise.

"She let you read it?" He very nearly squeaked.

"Yes, she did. And I liked it."

"She never lets *anybody* read her work in progress!"

Jodi detected the jealousy hidden within his surprise. Darn! To begin their conversation she'd picked what she thought would be a safe subject. Instead, she'd managed to relight the fuse of his hostility.

"Both her editor and illustrator have seen it," she offered him with a cool-down logic. "And I was interested. Maybe that's why she let me—"

"I told you," he snarled. "Becky doesn't want an agent. She sells plenty of books without all that hype."

In spite of promising herself that this time she absolutely would not react to his absurd animosity, Jodi nevertheless felt the heat from the flare of her own fuse. It burned in her voice. "If you'll . . . *please* . . . open the damn door and take the manuscript, I'll go home. And then you can be obnoxious by yourself."

She'd had it with trying to be civil to Luke. Even if she was sorry he was no longer a pianist. Even if he was the handsomest, sexiest man she'd ever known.

Jodi gulped. *I have to get away from here.* Self-preservation shifted into high gear as she shoved the folder under her arm, spun on one heel, and almost tripped over a huge urn of ferns at the base of one of the arched columns. Concentrating on keeping her balance, both physical and emotional, Jodi failed to hear Luke call her name. Only when he touched her shoulder . . . and she dropped the folder in a startled reflex . . . did she realize he'd followed her out onto the shaded arcade.

Without a word he stooped and, with his scarred hand, began to pick up the spilled manuscript pages. Although he fumbled with a few, he gathered all of them while Jodi watched and speculated again, with a spark of hope, on the degree of constriction in his fingers. The fact that he used his crippled hand for tasks he could have done easier and better with his left one indicated to her a subconscious reluctance to admit total defeat.

If only he weren't so withdrawn into his pain . . .

Returning the pages to her, Luke said, "Bring those inside, and I'll give you a Coke for your trouble." He was smiling!

Jodi stared at him in amazement and wondered when she'd learn not to react in kind to his volatile flashes of temper. If she'd only stay calm and be patient for a little while, he'd revert back to the congenial neighbor who was looking at her with a twinkle in his fabulous green eyes and an I-dare-you-to-accept-my-invitation grin on his sexy mouth.

Jodi's annoyance evaporated as suddenly as it had blazed. She smiled back at him and stuffed the manuscript pages in the folder. "How did you know I can never turn down Coke?"

"I hoped." He held the door open for her to precede him into the gardenlike living room. "Find a comfortable chair while I go get the liquid bribe." He tossed another endearing, crooked grin over his shoulder as he left the room.

Why couldn't he always be this nice, this friendly, this much fun? Jodi asked herself.

She knew why.

Deep down, Luke Prentiss was a fiercely angry man. And justifiably so, because of destiny's low blow. One day his fingers had made magical music and his two solo releases had both made the charts. The next day his right hand had been damaged and his dream career had burned up like tissue paper in the flame of a match.

But if he were ever to be happy, or even content, Luke had to work his way through denial and bitterness to some form of lasting acceptance. She'd lost Annie; Luke had lost his ability to play the piano professionally. She was finally regaining her old self—no, a new and different self—without Annie. Maybe she could help Luke get in touch with a new, different Luke, without his flexible dexterous fingers.

Jodi dropped the file folder on the coffee table and took a seat in front of the television. An old Jimmy Stewart movie was on—*The Stratton Story.* She watched it for a moment . . . until nostalgia swept her backward into a time warp. She saw herself, a sentimental adolescent sobbing over the movie's bittersweet story . . . or over her father's unhappy life, she wasn't sure which.

"Why the sad face?" Luke asked. He stood beside her holding two glasses of Coke.

Glancing up, she couldn't avoid noticing the stark difference between his hands—one naturally tanned and blue-veined with wiry dark hairs growing between the knuckles, the other slick and hairless, dull red in color and scar-puckered.

"You looked so glum, so far away when I walked in." Luke handed her her drink.

After a sip of the cold, sweet, biting beverage, Jodi gestured toward the TV screen. "Reminiscing, I suppose. When I was a young girl, that was one of my favorite movies on the late late show."

"You're a baseball fan?"

"No."

"Isn't the movie about baseball?" Apparently, he'd simply turned on the set for noise to fill the empty house.

"No. It's about a big league baseball *pitcher* whose leg was amputated and who overcame unbelievable odds in order to pitch one more time."

Jodi watched the fury smolder in his eyes. Stubbornness

105

tightened and thinned his lips. "Is this your none-too-subtle way of lecturing me?"

And make you run away again?

She answered quickly. "No."

As she stared unseeingly at Jimmy Stewart and June Allyson in a loving embrace, Jodi marveled that coincidence *did* happen in real life as well as in romance novels. If she'd searched for weeks, she'd not have come up with a better device than this old comeback movie to make her point. She realized she would have to share a part of herself, but for Luke she was strangely willing. She didn't hesitate to label the seed from which her staunch independence had sprouted.

Her beginning came out soft and sorrowful. "I was thinking about my father."

"Your father?" Visibly relaxing now that he knew she didn't intend to preach to him, Luke sat nearby and drank from his moisture-beaded glass.

Jodi took several sips from her own while she collected her thoughts. Paramount was her goal not to cause Luke any added distress.

"My father, my mother, and Dr. O'Meara—we've always called him Irish—grew up together. As far back as the boys could remember, they planned to be partners, Irish the physician and Dad the pharmacist, and build their own clinic. During their senior year in high school, my parents fell in love and . . . I began to be. They married the week after graduation, and through the years Dad held a multitude of menial or blue-collar jobs to support his wife and children. I—I had a younger sister."

Luke responded to the break in her voice and the deeper grief that darkened her eyes. "Had?"

"She died." Jodi exhaled, licked her lips, then continued. "Dad blamed Mom . . . and me . . . and Annie . . . his responsibilities . . . for keeping him from being a pharmacist. To make it worse, Irish of course did go on to college and med school."

"Your father felt like a failure."

Is that how you feel? Hearing the empathy in Luke's announcement, Jodi almost spoke the words aloud.

Instead, she said, "Yes, but the saddest thing is that he didn't have to be. Many, many times Mom offered to help out, to get a job. Dad could have gone to night school for his college diploma. There were scholarships and student loans available. At least he should have *tried!* But no, he was too proud to admit he was poor and too stubborn to ask for help. After Irish went into practice, he offered to lend Dad the money. I think that was when Dad hit bottom. He started to drink more often, couldn't keep a job, turned into a constant whiner wallowing in self-pity. Our whole family suffered, and I swore right then I'd never give up on myself or be a quitter like him."

"Where are they now? Your parents?" Luke set his glass on the end table, then reached for Jodi's and placed it beside his.

"They died twelve years ago. They were fishing in a small rented bass boat when a thunderstorm blew up. I'm sure Dad was drunk—he took two six-packs with him—and Mom never learned to swim. When they didn't come home by midnight, I called the police. After daybreak they discovered the capsized boat on the lake, and then the divers found their—their bodies."

"Tough." A single gruff word, but it echoed the sympathy in Luke's expression. "Your little sister was with them?"

"Oh, no. After that, she and I lived with Irish until we were grown. Annie was ki—she died in a car accident a little over a year ago."

"Jesus H. Christ!" He gently, compassionately laid his left hand over hers.

Ever so briefly, his fingers squeezed hers, and even in the moment of unhappy remembering Jodi felt the warmth spread from her hand to somewhere below the pit of her stomach. Drawing in a ragged breath, she was suddenly aware that although Luke used his scarred hand for practically everything, he'd touched her with his unflawed one.

107

Luke had deliberately touched Jodi with his unflawed hand. In his memory lingered the shock, sharp and cutting, of Corinne's horrified gasp and hasty pulling away the first—and only—time he'd reached for *her* hand with his still raw, wounded one. Luke flinched inwardly at the prospect of a similar reaction from Jodi.

"Your whole family wiped out by tragedy," he murmured, consolingly patting her hand. "By two tragedies."

Luke began to see that to her the surrender to those debilitating personal losses had been unthinkable, so she'd fought back by making herself into a strong and independent woman, one who turned toughly combative if she sensed herself weakening. He was beginning to suspect Jodi wasn't the cold, heartless career woman he'd originally pigeonholed her to be. He didn't know yet exactly who she *was,* but suddenly, inexplicably, he knew he wanted to find out.

"I'm so sorry." When he saw the bleak, stricken look beclouding her lovely midnight-blue eyes, he removed the comfort of his touch and gave her what he believed she needed . . . and wanted. "And you definitely are *not* a quitter."

Jodi rewarded him with a brave, determined smile. "Which is really why I'm here."

Luke frowned in puzzlement and brushed a caramel-colored curl up off his forehead. It fell right back, creating in Jodi a sensuous urge to try her luck at taming it.

She directed her gaze away from that tempting curl. "I followed you to finish the conversation you ducked out on and to tell you I wouldn't have played your tape if—"

"Say no more," Luke interrupted, waving his right hand, ridged palm out, back and forth in front of his smiling face. "I overreacted. You thought I was at work, and I just happened to be walking home, and your door was open."

"You walked all the way home from work?" She was glad to change the subject.

Luke laughed, a hearty, full-throated guffaw that sparkled his eyes and made him look five years younger.

He should laugh more often, Jodi thought, intuitively guessing that his joyful moments occurred far too seldom.

"I bet you take a taxi in Austin, even for a few blocks," Luke said, leftover mirth removing the sting from his accusation.

"I do not!" Jodi grinned at him. "I drive my car."

"Well, I don't own a car anymore." Sometimes he still missed the little sportster he had sold to pay his hospital, surgery, and therapy expenses. "Becky needed hers today. Besides, my job's not quite a mile and a half from here."

"At the Millers' grocery store. Becky told me."

Luke sobered instantly, and his demeanor acquired the closed look Jodi had come to expect. "She told you a hell of a lot."

"Is your job a secret?" Jodi demurely asked.

"No," he snapped, "but maybe some other things are."

"Then I'm sure Becky won't reveal those," she countered sweetly. Refusing to be baited into another argument, Jodi decided not to pursue the matter. She rose and, followed by Luke, moved across the room. "Thanks for the Coke."

Typically, when he held the door open for her to step outside, his "You're welcome" sounded exceedingly like a drawn-out grunt.

When Jodi twisted the cabin doorknob and shoved, nothing happened. Good. So she *had* locked up after all. Turning the key in the slot, she opened the door and stepped inside.

An eerie feeling assailed her, not unlike the earlier sensations of being watched. But she was *inside* . . . where this morning she'd felt safe *after* she'd closed the door. Now she felt as if she'd shut herself up *with* the watcher.

Her trembling hand flipped the overhead light switch. Sundown was yet an hour away, but she demanded illumination in the room's dim corners and around the bulky furniture. Walking carefully and quietly, she lit every table lamp as she went through the cabin. Her fast breathing sounded too loud. She nervously peered into the bedroom alcove and the shower stall. Entering the kitchen area, she checked behind the serving bar. Lastly, she made certain the door leading out onto the deck remained locked.

Only then, after verifying that she was alone in the cabin, did she throw off the tension and berate herself for yet another attack of groundless paranoia.

"Damn you, Quentin," she muttered. Because of her ex-husband's threats, she'd allowed herself to become the victim of foolish imaginings. She had to stop. Now. This minute.

From the foolish to the sensible, Jodi decreed as she removed a small steak from the freezer to defrost. After a quick shower and a dinner of broiled rib eye and tossed salad, she planned to sit in her panties and robe and read till bedtime. At the armoire, she pulled out the underwear drawer.

Jodi opened her mouth to scream, but the shock of what she saw had sucked the air from her lungs. Prickles of fright and frissons of revulsion crept down her rigid backbone. Intermittently, she felt icy cold, fiery hot, then cold again. When, desperate for oxygen, she finally took several noisy, jerky breaths, a slight odor of musk affronted her nostrils.

Not the usual, expected fragrance of her Chloe sachet.

But then, nothing was the same as when she'd closed that drawer. Her lingerie had been tumbled and stirred about as though by a portable water-free washing machine.

She *always* folded and arranged her bras on the left and her panties on the right, even in a drawer in an out-of-town hotel when she stayed overnight. No exceptions. None. *Ever.*

Someone had been inside the cabin while she was gone!

"Who? How? Oh, God, *why?*" Jodi whispered in an unrecognizable voice. She collapsed on the side of the bed, her shaking hands grasping and bunching the bedspread so tightly the wrinkles might never come out. A faint, uneven thumping scared her anew until she identified it—her shoe heels striking the bare floor. The uncontrollable tapping set her teeth on edge.

110

To stop the racket, she stood quickly. Her head spun. Waiting until she felt steady enough, she then moved gingerly toward the phone to call the Austin police. No, the Burnet County sheriff's office . . . because she was in Swallows Bluff. The community with no crime.

"Hah!" she snorted.

The undiluted spurt of disgust and fury somehow rejuvenated her stunned, saner brain cells.

Jodi halted her trek across the floor as an interview with the sheriff's deputy played in her head.

You say the door was locked when you came home?

That's right.

There's no sign of forced entry.

I know.

But you immediately suspected something wrong. Why was that?

I had a feeling.

I see. A feeling. Uh . . . is anything missing?

No. But my lingerie drawer has been messed up.

At that point the officer, rather than question her further, would be disposed to cart her off to the loony bin.

"Damn!" Jodi thundered the curse into the uneasy silence.

The officer would think her a fool. If the truth be known, at the moment she *felt* a little foolish.

Because of recent worrisome circumstances, she admitted to being less in control of her emotions. Had she overreacted to finding a drawer of underwear in disarray? Could she herself have closed the drawer with such force that its neatly stacked contents had toppled over?

It *could* have happened that way.

But Jodi didn't really believe it had.

Eleven

Not since Jodi began kindergarten had she slept all night with a light on. And last night hadn't really changed that because although the low-wattage lamp on the dressing table burned from dusk to dawn, Jodi spent every hour awake and restless. She wasn't afraid the intruder would return; she simply needed the pool of dim light to drown the dark, offensive aura his presence had left behind.

At first she wondered if this had any connection with her apartment break-in. Until proven otherwise, she would continue to believe Quentin responsible for that, but this recent event lacked the earmark of her ex-husband's style, which was retaliatory violence. He would have torn the place apart. Also, although the apartment door lock had been jimmied, whoever entered the cabin had discovered she'd failed to lock up . . . and flipped the night latch when he departed . . . or had, like the private investigators on TV, used a lock pick.

There was another difference between the two episodes. An alarming difference. The incident this afternoon insinuated more daring and more stealth on the part of the interloper . . . and therefore more danger to her. Not only had he invaded her space, but he'd done it with an arrogance that was maddening. He defied her to *prove* to anyone else that it had happened, as if he were playing some fiendish

112

game, taunting her to join in and already certain he would win . . . because she didn't know the rules.

Conversely, Jodi spent some of her sleepless minutes trying to convince herself that if the deed had been done at all, it wasn't such a big deal. Inconsequential misdemeanors were committed hundreds of times a day . . . everywhere. Even in rural communities. So why couldn't she think of this event as an unexplainable nuisance and factor it into her usual I-can-handle-this mode? Because her intuition insisted the game was yet to be played out and because, whoever he was, *he* was in control. All *she* could do was devoutly hope her instincts were wrong, that she herself had accidentally shuffled her bras and panties . . . and be wary.

Daylight finally chased the seen and unseen shadows from the big room and from her mind. Jodi donned her sweats—and the same lingerie she'd worn yesterday—then ate her cereal and drank three cups of coffee while she waited for nine o'clock. Leaving the dirty dishes on the breakfast table, she searched for and found Becky's name in the thin Burnet phone directory.

Becky picked up on the second ring. "Hello?" Evidently, she too was careful not to announce her name to strangers.

"Becky, this is Jodi. I hope I'm not calling too early."

"Goodness, no. Is something wrong?"

"Wrong?"

"Luke saw your light when he woke up around three this morning. Said he almost called to check on you; figured reliving all that stuff about your parents and your sister was keeping you awake."

Two ideas struck Jodi simultaneously. First, that Luke and Becky shared everything, including their new neighbor's history, just as she and Annie might have done. That made Jodi wistful. But learning Luke had worried about her rapidly overlapped and surmounted her sorrowful thoughts.

Jodi hastened to reassure the woman waiting on the other end of the line. "I was wakeful, and then I fell asleep with

113

the light on." A half truth. "I'm sorry Luke was worried." A complete lie.

She heard Luke's voice in the background, but not his words, and then Becky's "She's okay."

"What I called for," Jodi added, her pulse quickened by the idea of Luke's lingering concern, "is to ask if I can use your washer and dryer this morning."

"Any time. I'll be here all day."

Luke, too? Jodi wondered; then hastily shoved her curiosity beneath her habitual noninvolvement. Whether he would be home or not was none of her business, and besides, she didn't care either way. No; strike that. She did care, but she gave herself a scolding and a command to quash all feelings except those of a casual, soon-to-live-elsewhere neighbor.

Jodi hurriedly gathered her dirty clothes, plus every piece of lingerie she'd brought with her from Austin, and carried them to Becky's in a clean pillowcase. If the older woman noticed the preponderance of underwear as Jodi loaded the washing machine, she refrained from comment.

Instead, she remarked on Jodi's visit the day before. "Luke said you liked *Feisty's New Friend.*"

"Very much. You're a talented writer." Jodi started the washer.

Becky voiced her thanks and preceded her guest into the Early American kitchen, where braided earth-tone area rugs brightened the hardwood floor. Herbs in tiny clay pots rested on the windowsill and spiced the air.

After motioning Jodi to one of the pine cane-bottom chairs, Becky poured coffee into a couple of brown crockery mugs. "Black? Or cream and sugar?"

"Just cream, please."

Becky removed a small pitcher from the refrigerator and handed it to Jodi, who added a dollop of its thick butter-yellow contents to her mug before setting it on the waxed pine tabletop beside the Blue Willow bowl of jade plant.

When Becky sat down, Jodi broached the subject that had bothered her since her arrival, an issue she guessed her hostess might be reluctant to raise. "I hope you didn't mind my doodling in the margins of your manuscript."

"You did? I haven't looked at the copy you had. But I said you could write on it." She renewed her permission with a bright smile. "I can print out a clean copy if I need another one."

"I feel honored that you let me read it." Jodi paused. "I suppose Luke told you it made him angry."

"No, he didn't." Bewilderment mingled with her surprise.

"He assumed I want to maneuver you into hiring me as an agent," Jodi said. "And that wasn't the first time he's accused me."

"Oh." Becky stared at her mug, which she turned in uneven circles on the smooth wooden surface.

"I'm not doing that," Jodi said tersely. "And I wish Luke weren't so distrustful. I want to be your friend, not your agent."

Becky's lifted gaze shimmered with moisture.

"Please," Jodi hastily added, "I didn't mean for what I said about Luke to upset you."

"It's not that," Becky murmured. "It's been so—so long since I—I had a friend." She wiped her eyes and forced a shaky smile.

"I can't believe that," Jodi protested. She'd liked Becky from the moment they met. Becky was thoughtful, kind, amiable. Anyone would enjoy being her friend.

"It's true." Becky uttered a nervous laugh, then took a long, ragged breath. "Have you ever heard of Rebecca Avery?"

"The name Avery rings a bell, but I can't place it offhand."

"Senator Aaron Avery," Becky prompted, barely above a whisper.

"*That* Avery!" Disgust sharpened her voice. "The one who was killed in a private plane crash several years ago."

"Three years," Becky mumbled.

Jodi wasn't listening; she was remembering aloud.

"I remember, the local media turned the affair into a circus. And I do mean affair. The senator had been playing around with his secretary for months. She also died in the accident. They were returning from a weekend in Vail when the senator's plane plowed into the side of a mountain." She frowned as she recalled more details. "His wife was pregnant. I saw her once, coming out of her house, and a TV news reporter was skulking on her front steps, determined to squeeze out the last drop of her grief and humiliation for the ten o'clock news. And later, Hollywood made what television likes to call a docudrama based on the sensationally slanted news stories." Jodi's sneer bespoke her opinion of such movies. Her vociferous tone softened to one of sympathy. "I've often wondered what happens to the *real* people after the blood-sucking frenzy dies down."

"I can tell you about one of them." Becky fixed her gaze on a spot beyond Jodi's head. "Aaron Avery's . . . widow . . . lost her baby. Then she . . . suffered a complete breakdown. After fifteen months in a . . . mental hospital, during which her hair turned white, she . . . took back her maiden name and . . . vanished off the face of the news media's earth."

"You?" In shock, Jodi stared at the woman who had just related the most personal degradation and horror imaginable.

The Rebecca Avery whom Jodi had seen briefly on the TV screen wore an expensive canary-yellow Mother's Work maternity suit. She'd been thin to the point of frailty, with pale sunken cheeks, close-cropped black hair . . . and heartbreakingly sad, downcast eyes.

It took a few quiet seconds for Jodi to reconcile that image with the overweight, frumpy woman who sat beside her. Then a jumble of emotions grabbed her—sorrow, sympathy, respect, and admiration for the victim who'd fought her demons and won. Those feelings still rocked her as she laid her hand over Becky's and gave it a gentle pat.

"You," she repeated, this time with a whispering roughness. Jodi swallowed to displace the lump in her throat. "I'm so sorry. I should have recognized you."

"No, you shouldn't have." Becky managed a crooked, feeble smile. "I know I've changed. I wanted it that way. No more Rebecca Avery. I can't bear to live with her . . . and her past." Tears misted her eyes but she blinked them away.

Jodi understood a lot of things now. Luke's near obsession to protect his sister from further publicity even as a writer. Becky's evolvement into the plump person who wore drab, ill-fitting clothes to erase all resemblance to the Rebecca Avery who'd been hurt beyond comprehension, then forced to watch her anguish and betrayal spread across the country in newspapers and on radio and television.

"How ghastly that time must have been for you," Jodi said. "But you survived. You didn't give up." Her laudatory tone turned brittle when she continued. "My ex was unfaithful, too. Men can be such assholes."

"Present company excluded, I hope." Luke, his expression solemn and inscrutable, leaned one hip against the doorframe, his booted feet crossed at the ankles. He looked as if he'd been standing there quite a while. He looked totally, annoyingly, excitingly male.

The spurt of Jodi's heartbeat, the flutter in her stomach, the color she felt warming her cheeks—all were so unexpected and upsetting that she muttered something about checking the washer and fled to the utility room. But as she transferred her clothes to the dryer, she couldn't escape the voices in the adjoining room.

Becky's accusing: "You embarrassed Jodi."

"How, for God's sake?" Miffed.

"Probably because you overheard her talking about a very private matter. Her husband's infidelity." Exasperated.

"Am I supposed to knock before I walk into my own kitchen?" Defensive.

"Of course not. Forget it." Capitulating.

"Why did you tell her about that sonofabitch you married?" Obviously angry.

"How long *were* you eavesdropping?" Becky wanted to know.

"Long enough. Why did you tell her? She's a stranger! She can blab your whereabouts all over—"

"You *are* an asshole!" Jodi interjected as she trounced into the kitchen and threw Luke a black scowl that would have daunted 007. "I may not have known Becky a week, but I'm her *friend.* And to me that means loyalty and caring and— Damn you, Luke Prentiss!"

Sudden unwanted tears welled up in her eyes and overflowed onto her flushed face. The last few hours of fear, doubt, and confusion had finally rolled up like a runway carpet and tautened into a battering ram that smote and wrecked the self-control she was so proud of. And her sudden unwanted reaction to Luke's unannounced appearance and disturbing sexuality formed the steel-hard point of the emotion-spawned weapon.

A weeping Jodi stunned Luke into incredulity. In every one of their verbal skirmishes she'd come off scrappy and strong, sometimes spitting and snarling like an alley-wise cat. Nothing in their brief acquaintance had prepared Luke for the forlorn little kitten image who slumped against Becky's refrigerator. He felt as if he'd taken a sucker punch to the gut.

"Now see what you've done!" Becky fumed at her brother.

What I've done, he thought, *is behave like a judgmental jackass.* His insides squirmed and knotted with guilt.

Slowly, silently cursing himself with every stride, Luke moved toward Jodi. Once there, he murmured "I'm sorry" and, with his right index finger, captured one of the pearly spheres on her wet, ashen cheek.

"Don't!" Jodi shrieked, and abruptly turned her head away from his reach.

She couldn't bear the shame of having cried. She couldn't bear the shaft of burning desire, the longing to feel his arms around her, that his tender touch ignited.

118

She saw Luke, his hand still suspended in midair, stare at her with glittering green eyes, an unfathomable expression on his face.

For an instant after Jodi jerked her head aside, Luke felt nothing, his benumbed brain unable to comprehend what had happened. Then, as though a second fist slammed into his stomach—or into his heart—he understood. He'd been so intent on offering solace to Jodi that he'd forgotten . . . and had repulsed her instead by touching her with his ugly, scarred finger.

"Oh, God," Luke moaned softly.

He couldn't bear the shame of her rejection. He couldn't bear the onslaught of desire, the longing to hold her close and not be punished by her sickening withdrawal.

He let his hand, now trembling, fall to his side and, careful not to brush against her, squeezed through the door into the utility room. Then, with his palm he struck the outside screen door so hard that it hit against the wall of the house before it banged shut behind him.

Jodi broke the reverberating silence with a sputtering sigh. Luke had run away again. He was a master at coaxing her long-dormant feelings out of their safe hidey-holes and then fleeing the consequences he'd wrought.

With misgivings, Becky had watched the exchange between Jodi and Luke. The hurt in Jodi's eyes prompted her to say, "I don't usually apologize for Luke's bad manners, but—"

"Why bother?" Jodi interrupted, sarcasm evident as she stiffened her spine and stepped away from the side of the refrigerator.

"Because this time he had a good reason." Becky ignored Jodi's huff of disagreement. "He's going to hate me for telling you this," she added under her breath, seeming almost to be talking to herself.

"Then why do it?"

"Heck if I know." Becky's chuckle astonished them both. She motioned Jodi to the chair she had previously occupied, warmed the coffee in the mugs, then reseated herself. "Maybe," she said, "because I want you to like my brother."

Like? Bemused, Jodi quizzed herself. *Infuriated by?* Often. *Attracted to?* That also. But *like?* She preferred to stick with *infuriated by.*

Becky expected a response, and Jodi owed her a courteous one. "He's still dealing with the loss of his career."

"Yes, but that's not why he ran out of here like he was being chased by a swarm of killer bees." Becky sipped from her mug.

Should she go on? Did she have the right to shine the spotlight of her friendship with Jodi on Luke's soul-deep wretchedness? Becky sensed in Jodi's waiting attitude some of the same compassion she'd encountered from Jodi when she'd revealed her own secreted past. A precognition of Jodi's ability to help Luke in a way she herself never could led Becky to throw the mental switch and illuminate her brother's worst nightmare.

"It was the way you acted when he touched you." She spoke softly, praying even as the words left her mouth that she'd made the right decision.

Jodi recalled her immediate sensation of comfort, then the awakening of a need she'd not experienced for more than three years . . . followed by the necessity for her quick denial. Had Luke been embarrassed by her Eve-to-Adam response? Was she that transparent? Lord, she hoped not.

"I don't understand," she said, nervously licking her lips.

"Luke barely brushed your cheek, but you cringed and shouted 'Don't!'."

Why did Becky sound angry? Still puzzled, Jodi dared not disclose the real reason for pulling back from Luke's passion-stirring caress. "He—he surprised me," was all she could think of to say.

"Because he touched you with his *crippled* hand!"

The accusation—the revelation—hung in the air like a balloon of dialogue in a comic strip.

"No!" Jodi contradicted. "I didn't even notice which hand he used! It wouldn't have made any difference, anyway."

"It made a difference to his fiancée." Becky grimaced at the memory. "She couldn't stand the sight, or the touch, of his burned hand. She broke off the engagement while Luke was still in the hospital."

"How awful! How could she?"

Yesterday she'd wondered why Luke patted her hand with his left one when he used his right one for everything else. Now she understood.

"He thought I was reacting the same way she did," Jodi gasped. Appalled at her unintentional blow to Luke's pride, she had to swallow the tightness in her throat before she could speak. "Oh, Becky, I have to tell him—"

Becky caught Jodi's wrist as she pushed her chair back from the table. "Not now," Becky pleaded. "He'd know I told you, and he'd never forgive either one of us."

"But—"

"Give him a chance to put it in perspective. I think he'll realize he misinterpreted your action. Just as I did. And I'm truly sorry about that."

"It's all right. Like I said, he surprised me." Without volition, she turned her explanation inward. "I've never known tenderness like that from a man." Hearing the plaintiveness in her statement and catching Becky's questioning glance, Jodi blessed the timely intrusion of the clothes dryer buzzer. She scrambled to her feet. "I'll fold my things and take off so you can get some work done." Heading for the utility room, she said, "And thanks."

"Use my washer and dryer any time. I already told you that."

"No. I mean thank you for the girl talk. For the sharing."

Later, as Jodi sauntered along the grassy verge of the rutted road, the pillow slip slung over her shoulder, she considered that first evening in her cabin when Luke had apologized for having misjudged her relationship with Irish. He'd offered his hand and she'd shaken it, both gestures automatic and normal, practically thought-free.

But this morning Luke's insensitivity had caused her to cry, and a sincere regret—an *emotion*—had figured in his fingering away her teardrop. Impulsively, he'd exposed his feelings. And, as in the case of his fiancée, she, Jodi, had scorned his tender caring. Or so he believed.

No wonder Luke had run away.

Now Jodi was glad Becky had prevented her from racing after him. Whatever she might have said to him would have been wrong. No spoken words could repair the scar tissue over the wound to his spirit she had so unwittingly reopened. He wouldn't believe her words. Or trust them.

Only her actions and time would prove to Luke she wasn't like the intolerant and cruel woman who had destroyed his sense of self-worth.

Whoever that woman was, Jodi hated her. And envied her. Because once Luke had loved her. Maybe he still did.

As Jodi ascended the cabin steps and unlocked the front door, she refused to analyze or even admit to the momentary thrust of pain in the region of her heart.

Twelve

For nearly seventy-two hours, Jodi avoided the Prentisses. Or rather, since neither Becky nor Luke contacted her, she willingly distanced herself from them. She wanted space and time to assimilate the incomprehensible, deplorable facts Becky had told her: Aaron Avery, the senator who'd been unfaithful to his pregnant wife, was her late husband, and Luke's fiancée had dumped him because she couldn't stand the sight or the touch of his burned hand.

Once again Jodi was reminded how unfair life could be. That train of thought sent her straight back down yesterday's track of wrong turns and dead ends. It naturally followed that she'd reminisce about Annie. Sometimes Jodi wept, sometimes she smiled, but always she felt lonely and bereft. She refrained from calling Irish because she was in no mood for a cheer-up lecture. Instead, she longed for someone's shoulder to cry on.

Troy. He would understand. He, too, still missed Annie. Hadn't he said so during their recent happenstance meeting out on the road?

Jodi looked up his phone number. A female voice answered. "Troy Morrell's residence."

Jodi started to hang up, then chided herself for the poignant stab of betrayal. Troy no longer owed his loyalty to her sister. He'd been wonderful to Annie, and Jodi shouldn't be rude just because she'd expected him to be available to grieve with her.

"Hello?" The fretful voice demanded acknowledgment.

"Hello. I'm Jodi Turner. May I please speak with Troy?"

"I'm sorry, Ms. Turner, but Mr. Morrell's not here. I do his cleaning. He went to Nashville for a few days."

"Will you please leave him a note that I called? And thank you."

Unable to commiserate with Troy, Jodi decided to point her restiveness in another direction, one that would produce tangible benefits.

She drove to Austin and passed several boring hours restoring order to the jumbled personal papers she'd picked up off the floor and stuffed into desk drawers the day of the break-in. To relieve the tedium of reading and sorting, she declared time-out for a couple of phone calls.

First, she tried to reach Irish, but his office nurse informed her he would be in surgery the entire afternoon. A longtime patient and friend had insisted Irish be present in the operating room during his liver transplant. Jodi knew it had not for a moment occurred to Irish to be anywhere else.

"Evelyn, will you check his calendar?" Jodi requested. "See if he's jotted down anything for the weekend?"

After an audible rustling of paper, Jodi heard the smile in the nurse's reply. "On Sunday, it says, 'Check on Jodi. Take steaks.' Is that what you wanted to find out?"

Jodi laughed. "Absolutely." Then, almost as though she hadn't been considering the matter all day, she added, "And please, tell Irish to bring two extra rib eyes. And a quart of that hot German potato salad from Angelina's Deli."

"Ah!" Evelyn said. "You're planning a party."

Jodi had come to the conclusion that a four-on-four conversation would amiably reconnect her with Luke without her having to refer to the emotional scene that had parted them.

"You catch on fast," she told the woman who'd known her most of her life. "See you, Evelyn. 'Bye."

Jodi filed for a while, then phoned Nita Sancho.

"Hi," chirped a young boy. "I'm Hector. Who're you?"

"I'm Ms. Turner. Remember? Your Mom works for me."

"Does she have to *today?*" he squeaked. "You're sup-posed to be gone away."

Jodi chuckled. Evidently, the bright little fellow had other plans for his mother's special work-free Friday. "I am. Gone away. But I need to speak to your Mom."

"Aw, gee. Mom! Phone!" His shout blasted Jodi's ear-drums.

The next voice she heard was plainly that of a compliant, subservient maid. "Juanita Sancho here. May I help you?"

"Nita, it's Jodi."

"Oh, hello!" Friendliness rang in Nita's greeting. "Do you need me this afternoon?"

Jodi could almost see the eager child fighting back the tears of disappointment. "Don't you and Hector have some-thing planned?"

"We were going to the park to watch the older boys play soccer, and then have a hamburger and fries at McDonald's." She paused and, from the sound, had turned her head away from the mouthpiece. "Hector, what did you say to Ms. Turner?" Then, back to Jodi, "Was he rude to you?"

"Not at all. And don't scold him. If anyone deserves a scolding, it's me."

"You?"

"For allowing you to be upset and embarrassed by De-tective English. For failing to explain to him that you're my employee . . . that I'm aware of your history and trust you implicitly."

"Oh, that. Jodi, I *am* on parole, and a crime *was* com-mitted, and my fingerprints *were* there. The police were just doing their job."

"I'm so glad you aren't angry with me."

"Angry? With the person who fixed it"—her words grew thready—"so I could get Hector out of that foster home . . . and back with me . . . after I moved into Safe Harbor?"

"I didn't fix anything. The judge did."

Contradiction strengthened Nita's voice. "After *you* found and paid for a lawyer to plead my case."

As always, Nita's worshipful gratitude made Jodi uncomfortable. "That was in the past," she insisted. "For now, you and Hector go enjoy your outing."

"Will you need me next Friday?"

"No, not for a few weeks. And I'll have to meet you here. I had a new lock put on the door, and you don't have a key yet."

The two friends exchanged farewells, and Jodi attacked the last stack of bills and receipts. After finishing the chore, she stopped at her favorite restaurant for *fajitas* before she tackled the seventy-five-mile twilight drive to the lake.

Barely inside the front door, Irish gave Jodi an awkward hug, then strode to the kitchen and emptied his hands of the package of steaks and plastic carton of potato salad. While Jodi stored the food in the refrigerator, Irish turned and surveyed the big room, pleased to be there for the first time since last summer. He really ought to come more often, he mused as he took in his surroundings.

Suddenly, he slapped his forehead with his palm and declared, "I don't believe it!"

"Believe what?" Jodi came up behind him.

"Dirty dishes here on the bar. Loose sections of the Sunday paper scattered all over the floor. Your robe left on the sofa." He stopped for a breath. "Jodi, honey, are you ill?"

As humiliation and guilt heightened the color in her cheeks, Jodi tucked her chin so that she missed the twinkle in Irish's eyes. "I'm all right. I overslept, and then I read the funnies and business page while I ate breakfast. I wasn't expecting you quite this early. I'm sorry. I'll tidy up in a jiffy."

She took one hurried step before Irish grabbed her arm and pulled her against his chest. His chuckles rumbled in her ear. "Don't you dare." He met Jodi's confused gaze with a broad grin. "I feel like shouting 'Hallelujah!' I love seeing this place messed up! Ever since you and Annie came to live with me, you've been so damn . . . ah . . . tidy, sometimes I wanted to scream. But how could I fuss at you for being so neat when your peers had to be threatened with grounding before they straightened their rooms?"

His grin faded as he spoke, and Jodi, feeling like that orphaned adolescent of long ago, responded before she thought. "I didn't want us to be any bother."

As Jodi's admission echoed in her head, she grew still, almost rigid, in Irish's embrace. The grown-up Jodi, through the capable, empathetic performance of her job duties, had learned to ferret out why clients did what they did and why they'd become who they were. So why had she never guessed the reason behind her own place-for-everything-and-everything-in-its-place obsession?

"Oh." Even muffled against Irish's chest, her one word of astonishment said it all.

"Oh, indeed." Irish released her and stepped back. He looked chagrined, slightly sorrowful. "I should have figured it out. As the saying goes, I must have been too close to the forest to see the trees. I was trying as hard as you were to do things right, to be a satisfactory father figure. How could I possibly berate you for a praiseworthy habit? I knew nothing about rearing two little girls. . . ." When Jodi started to speak, he waved a silencing hand and said, "To me, twelve and sixteen *were* little."

"I wasn't going to argue with that," Jodi told him. "I just wanted to tell you nobody could have been a wiser, more loving parent."

Scrutinizing Jodi's adoring face, Irish cleared his throat—twice—before his response got past the lump of emotion. "I don't know about that."

"I do." Jodi grinned and lightly thumped his nose, a gesture she used to employ after he'd taken her to task for some minor infraction of the O'Meara Rules of Behavior. Then, and now, it was her way of saying, "I hear you, and can we please change the subject?"

They moved through the cabin and plopped down on the sofa, once Jodi, with thumb and forefinger, fastidiously removed her robe from the seat and dropped it on the newspaper clutter.

Laughing heartily, Irish said, "I don't have to ask if you're taking it easy."

"I'm eating regular balanced meals." On her fingers, she counted off his prescribed cures. "I've read a book. I don't watch the clock."

"How about the insomnia?"

"So far I've had two bad nights. One when I nearly froze to death. That was your fault," she pointed out.

"And what caused the second?"

"Just restlessness, I suppose." Determined not to worry Irish with an account of how her tumbled lingerie had made her temporarily crazy, she concluded with, "But I do take naps if I'm tired."

"Are you jogging?"

"Not yet." Jodi frowned. "You told me to relax. I've been relaxing."

"Commendably so." Irish motioned toward the fuzzy blue robe lying at his feet and obtained the result he hoped for: a near giggle from the woman who sat beside him, in soiled, wrinkled sweats and no makeup, bearing little resemblance to the structured, driven business executive who'd fainted in her office. He smiled fondly at her. "Try getting more exercise. You'll sleep better."

They settled into a familiar routine, sharing their news since last they saw or spoke to each other. Jodi related the details of her trip in to the city. Irish was still searching for a new reliable yard man. Also, according to him, Mavis had contacted him to hear how her boss was feeling. Then Jodi told Irish about her unexpected encounter with Troy and about his purchase of the nearby hillside house.

"Good. If you get lonely, you can seek out his company."

"I didn't think you liked Troy."

"He's all right. What I didn't like was the way he blatantly used Annie's contacts to further his career."

"She wanted to help. She loved him."

"Yeah. And he used her love, too," he grunted. At Jodi's quizzical glance, he explained. "Getting her to sleep with him without a marriage license, or at least the promise of one."

"You're an old fuddy-duddy." Jodi reached over to plant a kiss on his cheek.

"Well, I don't have to worry about you being around Troy. He's not your type." Irish paused, and a merry sparkle glinted in his blue eyes. "Speaking of your type, what happened to that 'pretty as you please' piano player I'm supposed to meet?"

He never forgot a thing he could tease her with. Today, she'd pay him back. Her gaze mirroring his merriment, she answered his question with one of her own. "Are you really interested in Luke, *Dennis,* or are you hinting at an excuse to see his sister again?"

Irish refused to take the bait. Solemnly, he replied with, "I realize your appetite is improving, but I doubt if you plan to eat three steaks plus all that hot potato salad, which by the way you know I don't care for."

"You always were able to foretell my mischief." Jodi tried to sound exaggeratedly contrite, but she wound up joining Irish's contagious laughter. "Okay. You got me." She rose from the sofa. "I'd better go extend the invitation."

"You haven't asked them yet?" The query contained genuine disbelief. "This from the woman who subsists on schedules and charts?"

"It was your dictum that I forget calendars and clocks," she saucily reminded him as she approached the desk.

Jodi had purposely delayed inviting the Prentisses. If they had time to mull over their last unfortunate meeting, they might decline. But if they had to give an immediate answer, they might simply react as good neighbors.

She was right. Becky, who answered the phone, graciously accepted and insisted upon bringing dessert.

"That'll be great," Jodi told her. "I hadn't even thought about dessert. I'm just not a sweets eater."

"Except for three heaping spoonfuls of sugar on your cereal," Irish groaned from across the room.

Jodi ignored him, hung up the phone, and rushed to shower and change clothes. While Irish waited, he put a Glenn Miller tape in the stereo. He was singing along with "Little Brown Jug" when Jodi opened the sliding door and came out of the bedroom alcove. She wore new jeans and a blue chamois pullover and had arranged her hair in a single thick braid pulled forward over her shoulder. For one flash-backed instant, she became that youthful girl he'd moved into his home twelve years ago.

"I was wondering," she said, "could we do the steaks outside, do you think?"

"Let's go check."

Of one accord, they walked out onto the deck. The day was sunny and windless, the sky an azure backdrop for a handful of cottonball clouds. The air smelled clean and fresh, spring's fragrance of new beginnings. Spread out beyond the verdant meadow, the lake lay smooth and silver-blue, like polished pewter.

"Definitely shirtsleeve weather," Irish pronounced. "I'll get the barbecue grill ready and clean off the table and benches." He'd already descended a couple of stairs.

"I'll tell Becky where we'll be. They can come over by the back way."

Two hours later the guests arrived. Carrying a large Pyrex dish of what looked like brownies, Becky led the way. When she stopped to deposit the dessert on the plastic-covered table, Luke moved past her and held his hand out to Irish.

"Dr. O'Meara," he said, "I'm Becky's brother, Luke."

Without so much as a blink of surprise or a twitch of hesitation, Irish grasped Luke's scarred hand and gave it a firm shake. "Glad to know you, Luke."

Jodi was proud of and relieved by her godfather's reaction, or lack of reaction, to what must have shocked him as badly as her first sight of Luke's deformity had stunned her. Once he and Luke broke eye contact, Irish did glance at Jodi as if to reprimand, *You could have warned me.* The silent exchange went unnoticed by the siblings, both of whom appeared tense, unsure. With a friendly smile, Irish walked over to Becky. "So, we meet again."

"Good morning, Dennis. I hope you've been well."

Jodi thought Becky's formality rather endearing, but apparently the man for whom it was intended did not.

"I think I'm going to be sick—" he stated grimly.

"Oh, no," Becky gasped.

"—at heart if you don't stop calling me Dennis." His smile returned, and Becky blushed. "My medical colleagues address me as Dennis, but all my friends call me Irish."

"I'd feel strange." A weak-voiced Becky stared at the concrete floor. "You're a doctor."

"I'm not *your* doctor."

"No."

"Am I your friend?"

"I guess. Yes. Of course you are." Finally she met his gaze and discovered it to be honest and warm.

"Then I'm Irish." To give Becky the opportunity to get over her shyness, he directed his attention to her brother. "To you, too, Luke."

"Works for me," the younger man agreed with a nod and a mind-boggling smile.

Jodi delightedly watched the trio until Luke's smile roused her vulnerability to him, at which time she burst forth with, "I'm going to start a fire."

Lady, you already have, Luke thought when he let himself look squarely at Jodi for the first time since his arrival. She was drop-dead gorgeous. The soft lapis-blue top, the exact color of her black-lashed eyes, clung to her breasts, one of them caressed by the loose curling ends of her sable-brown plaited hair. That braid would lie heavy, silky, in his palm if he lifted it from its resting place . . . and if in the process his fingers barely brushed the swell beneath it. . . . He felt the weight in his groin.

Jodi felt the impact of Luke's sensuous stare. Nervously, she picked up the can of lighter fuel that sat on the ground beside the barbecue grill.

"Better let me do that," Irish suggested.

He was subtly reminding her how in the past he or Troy had always performed the task for her. Well, under Luke's watchful gaze, she didn't intend to appear dependent or helpless.

"No," she said sharply. "I'll do it."

Unscrewing the lid, she poured a liberal amount of the fluid over the briquettes. The acrid odor burned her nose. She sniffed as she took a match from her jeans pocket.

"Jodi," Irish began.

She stopped him with a fierce look.

To be sure her headstrong deed didn't fizzle into nothing, she added still more of the odious liquid. Acting quickly, because the fumes made her eyes water, Jodi set the can down and struck the match on the outside of the grill bowl. Just before she dropped the match on the charcoal, Luke's voice bellowed, "No!"

With a loud *whoosh,* a chest-high geyser of orange flames shot in the air . . . a millisecond after Luke grabbed her shoulders and roughly jerked her backward. Blinded by the flash, Jodi felt the searing heat on her face, then the bruising pain of fingers digging into her flesh. Although dimly cognizant of Irish's and Becky's horrified cries, the dominant sound was the seemingly endless hiss of air emptying Luke's lungs.

The full impact of the catastrophe she'd so narrowly escaped smacked Jodi hard. Her knees buckled. She slumped weakly, gratefully, against the solid strength waiting behind her. Luke supported her by quickly reaching around her waist to pull her tight against him. To Jodi, the warmth of his body touching hers from thigh to chest, his forearms pressing the underside of her breasts, was almost as hot, almost as scary, as the fiery blast from the grill had been.

After a shuddering, fortifying breath, she murmured, "You can let me go now."

He did.

Jodi felt strangely cold despite the nearby tongues of flame still dancing above the reddening coals.

By then Irish and Becky had rushed to her side. She was unable to separate and distinguish their simultaneous exclamations of dismay and concern.

Turning around and smiling shakily, she reassured them. "I'm not hurt. I'm all right. Don't worry. Everything's okay."

But everything was not okay.

Thirteen

As Jodi turned away from the grill to speak to Irish and Becky, she saw Luke walk woodenly to the ice chest and, without pausing for a breath, gulp down a beer. When he set the empty down, his hand shook so violently that the can missed the table and fell, clinking on the edge of the patio.

Immediately, she guessed what had happened. In his mind Luke had relived the other fire, the one that had burned away his dream and forever altered his life. Jodi covered the distance between them in four hurried steps.

"Luke?"

Not until she reached out and clasped one of his trembling hands did he acknowledge her presence.

"Leave me alone," he muttered, avoiding her eyes.

"After I thank you for what you did." She waited, tightly holding on to his hand until the trembling eased somewhat. When she realized he wasn't going to say anything, she spoke again. "You saved me from being badly burned . . . the way you were. That was a very brave thing."

"Brave?" His mirthless cackle serrated her nerves like a dull knife blade. Finally his gaze, full of despair, touched hers. A bitter, self-accusing mockery of a smile stretched his lips. "Brave? I was scared to death!"

Luke, his heart slamming against his ribs so noisily he thought Jodi surely must hear it too, loathed as never before his fear of fire. He cursed himself for allowing the fear to surface. Most of all, he hated that Jodi had witnessed his reaction to that fear.

Then why in God's name had he *admitted* his cowardice? Because he wanted to stop Jodi from being nice to him. Because he couldn't trust the grateful, adoring look in her eyes. She was even tenderly holding his hand as though the ugly scars didn't matter. If he wasn't careful, he might begin to think, to hope she cared, really cared . . . and, far more than fire, he was afraid of being used, discarded, and made a fool of by another woman.

Watching the expressions as they played across Luke's face, Jodi finally understood. Paramount to Luke's remembered pain and sense of loss, he felt . . . shame . . . because he'd permitted her to discover he wasn't made of perfect, emotionless stone! The impulse to comfort him with a hug, counteracted by the denying pull-back of her muscles, created an actual ache in her arms. She gritted her teeth. Luke didn't want sympathy, nor did he need it. What he needed was the gift of someone else's confession of weakness.

Jodi released his hand and, as lightly as she could manage, said, "So what? Everybody's afraid of something. Me, I'm absolutely terrified of thunderstorms." She shivered in emphasis. From the tightening of Luke's mouth, she could tell he didn't believe her.

Irish strolled up just in time to overhear Jodi's revelation and, deducing the motive for it, vouchsafed, "That's true. Most kids hide under the covers. Not Jodi. After a thunderstorm passed over, I'd find her crouched in the dark corner of her clothes closet, trembling like a leaf in a high wind and white as a ghost."

Fondly patting her godfather's arm, Jodi added, "And he'd coax me out, and we'd go have a cup of hot chocolate." She laughed. "To this day, hot chocolate reminds me of thunder and lightning."

"So . . . now you don't like hot chocolate," Luke concluded. A halfhearted smile washed away some of the strain on his features, and his body frame relaxed a bit.

Becky, who had remained quiet all through the trialogue she sensed might help her brother, now approached him, stood on tiptoes, and placed a kiss on his cheek. "I'm so proud of you." A sob rising in her throat prohibited her from saying more.

"We all are . . . and thanks." Irish's voice, too, was ragged with suppressed emotion. Then, observing in Luke a renewal of tension, Irish quickly appropriated a good-ole-boy persona. "Hey, people, let's get this show on the road. I'll manhandle the steaks. You-all set the table and bring the rest of the grub downstairs."

During the meal, Jodi and Irish did most of the talking. Because of the past she so scrupulously shunned, Becky had few remember-whens to offer, and the still-haunting fire reinforced Luke's usual taciturnity. Irish entertained them with amusing tales about his pranks in medical school and, to Jodi's consternation, related one of the scrapes she had gotten into.

He said, "One day in her sophomore algebra class, instead of concentrating on what a student was drawing on the blackboard—"

"Oh, no," Jodi interrupted. "Not that awful story."

"Awful but true," Irish tossed back at her.

"Tell us," Becky urged, her hazel eyes alight with glee.

Irish ignored Jodi's graphic threat on his life. "Well, instead of copying the algebra problem, Jodi drew an uncanny likeness of her teacher in her notebook. Except it was a caricature—and the teacher had an enormous bulbous nose."

"Oops," whispered Luke, looking as though he were finally enjoying himself.

" 'Oops' is right," Irish seconded. "Miss Prow—that really was her name, I swear," he maintained when Becky and Luke protested—"Miss Prow happened to stop at Jodi's desk, glance down, and . . . suffice it to say, Jodi was suspended from classes for three days."

"And I received a semester grade of C-minus in algebra, and A's in everything else," Jodi dramatically complained, unsuccessfully struggling to keep a straight face in view of the trio's gusto.

Once the jollity subsided, Becky directed a serious question at her hostess. "Did you study art?"

When Jodi hesitated, Irish answered for her. "I think Miss Prow frightened off any talent Jodi had. That incident happened right after she and her sister came to live with me, and as far as I know, that was the last thing Jodi ever drew."

"But she *does* have talent!" Becky asserted.

She looked away from Irish's bewilderment and into Jodi's perturbed, don't-do-this gaze. Becky understood none of what was occurring beneath the lid of Jodi's emotions, but she did understand she'd opened a can of worms and somehow had to re-cover the wriggling mistake. The truth, she'd learned the hardest way, was the best place to start.

"The sketches you made on my manuscript are incredible," she told Jodi.

"Thanks," Jodi said. "Pass me the brownies, please, Irish."

"You don't eat brownies," he snapped. "And don't change the subject." He turned to Becky. "What sketches? What manuscript?"

Briefly, shyly, Becky explained about her children's books, then once more praised Jodi's clever drawings of the squirrel and kitten in the rough draft's margins.

"Jodi, why didn't you tell me you were interested in art?" demanded an astonished Irish. "Surely you knew I'd have paid for the lessons."

"That's *why*. Annie and I cost you enough. Our clothes, our food, all the *necessary* things. Art lessons would have been a luxury," she ended softly, sorry that she'd exposed her heretofore unstated girlhood credo in front of Luke and Becky.

"My God," Irish breathed.

In those two words, Jodi heard exasperation, regret, and sadness. He shouldn't be feeling any of those emotions. She touched his hand that held the beer can. "It's no big deal. And"—she presented him with what she hoped was a sassy smile—"I *do,* too, want a bite of your brownie."

For quite a while, the conversation was confined to remarks like "Hand me a paper napkin" and "Would you like another beer?" Each of the four was obviously holding his or her own thoughts close and private. When Jodi could no longer bear the strain, she jumped up and said, "Irish, if you'll douse the fire, or do whatever it is you do to make it safe to leave unattended, I'll clear the table."

"I'll help you," Luke volunteered as he rose and began to pick up the plates.

Jodi opened her mouth to protest, then thought better of it. "Great," she agreed. Maybe Luke wanted to avoid assisting Irish with the still-hot coals. "You can throw the scraps on the ground for the birds and animals. The garbage disposal is on the blink."

When Jodi and Luke went up the steps with their initial load, Irish stayed seated. His shoulders slumped forward, his chin resting on his interlocked fingers. Becky got up, walked around the table, and scooted along the bench until she sat near him.

"Dennis—Irish—"

At the second name, he looked up at her, his gaze filled with misery.

"I was going to ask if you're all right, but I can see you're not."

"No, I'm not," he grumbled.

Becky knew he was figuratively kicking himself, and she knew why. But she sensed he needed to say the words. She waited, concerned by the hurt on his face.

"I've loved Jodi since the day she was born. Why didn't I ever know she had that talent? And after she came to live

138

with me, why didn't I realize she wanted to take art lessons but dared not tell me because they weren't . . . *necessary?*"

"You're a fortune-teller?" Becky quizzed, forcing a smile she didn't honestly feel.

In spite of his distress, Irish smiled back at her. She possessed such an aura of quiet composure, calm and calming. He'd noticed that about her before. It was a quality he with his Hibernian temperament admired and oftentimes envied.

"No," he said grudgingly, "I'm not a fortune-teller. But I am a physician, supposedly enlightened about human nature as well as about the number of bones in a human skeleton."

Unnoticed, Jodi and Luke came down for the leftover food and made their way back up to the kitchen.

"I think—no, I know," Becky corrected herself, "you're a wonderful substitute father. Jodi obviously adores you. It's also obvious she grew into a strong, caring young woman, well-adjusted and successful. You don't believe your guidance, your influence, contributed to the kind of person she is?"

"Yes, but what if she'd rather have been an artist?" His plaintive question sprang from self-punishment.

"When Jodi made her choices, for whatever reasons, she wasn't a baby," Becky declared in an impatient, scolding manner. "And you are not to blame. She may yet choose to study art . . . if she really wants to." She paused, then made a conscious and totally unexpected decision to carry the subject further. "You sent Jodi here to recover from stress, partly caused, I suspect, by her sister's death in a car accident."

"I don't see what one thing has to do with the other."

"Sometimes, when a person suffers the loss of a special loved one, *her* life, too, or the way she's lived it, is utterly destroyed. And after she eventually works her way through the tunnel of grief, she may choose to create a new life-style for herself, one she likes much better." Bravely, almost defiantly, she met his kind blue eyes. "That's what I did."

Irish had guessed what she was going to reveal, and his compassionate nature, one of the traits that made him an excellent doctor, wished she wouldn't. He knew what the admission would cost her. Now that she'd capsuled her past in four succinct words, he owed her the same honesty.

"I know," he said, feeling as helpless and inadequate as when he had to inform a patient he or she was terminal.

Becky's eyes widened, and she uttered a faint hitching gasp. "You know? What do you mean, you know?"

"I know who you are . . . were . . . are . . . Damn!" Which verb was the right one?

Unbelievably, Becky *smiled*. It was a feeble, sorrowfilled smile, but it accomplished its purpose. It gave her courage and turned Irish's discomfort into respect.

"Yes, I *was* Rebecca Avery. I'm surprised you recognized me. I've changed a lot."

"Not that much. The night they brought you in to Emergency—when your baby died—I was there to help with a patient of mine. I saw your lovely heart-shaped face. Your eyes awash with tears and heartbreak. The first time I saw you, met you up here, I remembered that face, and your eyes, and that awful night."

"You never said a thing." Becky blinked away the moisture forming in her eyes.

"It was none of my business. And you can be sure I won't tell anyone," he promised.

"Jodi knows." At his look of denial, Becky added, "I told her. We were talking about stress or ex-husbands or some woman thing, and I found myself telling her my story. She's a good listener."

"Jodi's a good everything," Irish stated proudly.

"Which leads us back to where we began, the point being . . . so far, Jodi has chosen well for herself."

"What have I chosen?" Jodi wanted to know as she and Luke joined the two still sitting on the redwood bench.

"Not to eat brownies or drink hot chocolate." Although

Irish's mouth grinned, his eyes cautioned her not to pursue the matter further.

Jodi took the hint. "They're bad for my teeth. The *doctor* knows!" Her guttural, raspy pronouncement parodied the decades-ago radio announcer on *The Shadow.*

Everyone laughed.

Soon after that, the Prentisses departed, slipping through a gap in the brilliant hedge of red-top photinia. Jodi climbed the steps one final time and tidied up the kitchen and living area while Irish took care of storing the barbecue grill.

When he entered the back door, Jodi, her curiosity ready to burst at the seams, accosted him with, "What were you and Becky saying about me?"

"She was reminding me that you're good at what you do and that your life's not ruined because I didn't have enough sensitivity to see your talent and pay for art lessons."

"She's right." Jodi continued to speak as they walked across the cabin and sat side by side on the sofa. "You were both so serious for so long, you didn't even know when Luke and I came and went."

Irish chuckled. "Why don't you come straight out and ask me what else we talked about?"

"Well . . . I didn't want to be too nosy." She pretended a nonchalant disinterest.

"Hah!" Irish jeered. After a beat, he turned solemn. "Becky confirmed what I already knew. That she was . . . is . . . was"—that damn verb again!—"Rebecca Avery."

"I suppose you know she told me?" Irish nodded. "I didn't recognize her. She's so unlike the woman I saw on the TV news. But *you* knew."

Irish explained about the night in Northside Medical Center's Emergency Room.

"Earlier this week, when I asked if you knew who Becky was, you said you had your suspicions," Jodi recalled. "But then you clammed up as soon as you realized I was referring to her being Luke Prentiss's sister."

"I could empathize with her desire for anonymity. And I

141

honored it. I figured she'd tell you if she wanted you to know. She had to trust you first—not to give her away."

"Why couldn't Luke have understood that?"

Irish was struck by the bitterness in Jodi's question. Grave, insightful concern clouded his eyes as he waited for her elucidation.

"When he overheard Becky discussing her past with me, he immediately took it for granted that I'd go out and blab to the whole news world where Becky is and the name she uses and . . ." She broke off because she felt anew the ire and ache of Luke's distrust . . . and Irish was staring at her in a strange way.

"Did it occur to you that he might have been protecting himself as well as his sister?"

"Protecting himself?" The possibility stunned her, befuddled her.

"Luke suffered a severe trauma, maybe more emotional than physical, when his hand was burned. Has he told you how it happened?"

"Becky just said it was a gasoline fire. Luke doesn't talk about it at all."

"I think Luke doesn't talk about a lot of things." Jodi threw him a how-did-you-guess look. "That's what I meant about protecting himself. He's in hiding—every bit as much as Becky is. The difference is, Becky's content, at peace with her new life. Luke is angry, mixed up, miserably unhappy."

"Because he lost his career." Jodi related the incident of her playing Luke's tape and also how he hadn't touched a piano since his injuries.

"He lost more than a career, honey. He lost his music. No. For some reason, he *threw* his music away. So . . . he has literally thrown himself away. He feels useless, worthless, less of a man."

Jodi almost disclosed the information about Luke's broken engagement because her heart, having succumbed to its own wounds, told her the selfish woman's callous, untimely

142

rejection was the blow that had completely crushed any urge Luke may have had to fight back. She'd kept only a few secrets from Irish, but this one belonged to Luke until he was ready to tell it.

Not for the first time did she say to Irish, "Maybe you should have studied psychiatry," but she'd never meant it more than now.

"I did," he grinned in response. "In the University of Real Life."

Jodi further lightened the mood by repeating for the second time that day the gesture she hadn't thought of in years. Playfully, she thumped his nose.

Fourteen

While the day of the barbecue dinner had provided shirt-sleeve weather, the following afternoon mimicked pure summer—above eighty degrees and sultry to the point of being oppressive.

I have a colossal case of spring fever, Jodi decided as she backhanded the perspiration off her forehead. Although drowsy, she knew a nap would only make her more listless after she awoke. This was the moment to swallow Irish's next medicine: jogging, to get her blood circulating and wake up her lazy brain cells.

Too warm for sweats, she elected to run in the T-shirt she was already wearing. She did exchange her shorts for jeans, to protect her legs from brambles and chiggers.

At the foot of the deck steps Jodi turned left, away from the Prentiss property, through the dense woodland that bordered the lake. She located a faint path, probably the one Luke took every day, and loped along it until she became so winded her chest ached. *I'm out of practice,* she complained as she halted for a few cool-down stretches of her tired, tight muscles. The trunk of a fallen tree, a handy place to rest, beckoned her.

Sitting, listening to her breathing slow to normal, she remarked to herself how quiet it was. Then, gradually, she heard the voices of the woods. Birds everywhere, some of their calls identifiable from her walks in the city park: the shrill *chip chip* of a male cardinal setting his territorial boundaries; the shrieks and wing clatter of a flock of grackles taking flight; the squeaky-hinge cry of a blue jay summoning a mate to discovered food. Countless sparrows cheeped and fluttered around her, then settled, unafraid, to peck at the winter-decayed leaves, overturning them in search of insects. Not too far away a dog barked and, as if on cue, another one answered from across the lake. Perched on a low pecan tree limb, a fat squirrel switched his tail and chattered angrily at her for coming too close. Jodi thought of Feisty and longed for a sheet of paper so she could capture the image of the fussy furry animal overhead.

"I'm being silly." At the sound of her voice, the sparrows feeding nearby screeched and took refuge on the branches near the squirrel. "I came out here to jog, not to draw."

With that she rose, brushed the dead leaves and shreds of rotten bark from her jeans, and ran slowly down the path. Before long, she grew so hot she feared she might faint. Sweat rolled down her face, between her breasts, and matted the T-shirt to her back. Stopping, Jodi gasped repeatedly for breath, pulling in meager supplies of choking humidity. Willing her knees to support her despite their unsteadiness, she lifted the fall of her hair to let the air cool her nape.

There was no more air, no more bird sounds, no more sunlight streaking through the gaps between the trees. A flash of lightning suddenly obliterated the shadows, and thunder shook the ground beneath Jodi's feet.

Oh, God! A thunderstorm . . . and no place to hide! No covers to slide under, no closet to flee into. The adult Jodi sought a false courage during the storms by surrounding herself with people, never staying at home alone. Here she was alone, surrounded only by a canopy of towering trees, any one of which could serve as a lightning rod.

Terror held her rigid, perspiring from every pore, gasping for air like an oxygen-starved guppy. Until raindrops the size of half dollars beat at her with the force of catapulted pebbles. Rain and fright blurred Jodi's vision as she began to run. The forest crackled with lightning and reverberated with thunder, nullifying her sense of direction. When her legs and lungs could carry her no farther, she collapsed onto the layered, slick, moldy-smelling leaves. Her continuous tears mixed with the water that sluiced down her pale face and onto the thoroughly soaked T-shirt. A sudden gust of cold wind helped to freshen the muggy air, but it also chilled her to the marrow of her bones.

Shivering, still breathing hard, Jodi blinked away the tears and raindrops and anxiously looked around. There was no path. She was lost!

Nearby loomed a cluster of huge boulders. One, Jodi saw, had a concave base that formed an overhang. Struggling to her feet, staggering all the way, she reached the rocks and lunged under the ledge. A field mouse scampered past her out into the downpour. Jodi barely noticed. No varmint on earth was as frightening as the wrath of the storm. Here at least she felt safe from being struck by lightning.

Jodi slid back against the gritty stone wall and took stock of her "cave." Deeper than expected, it offered ample protection from the blowing rain. The wind whistled through the tiny canyons among the rocks above and behind her, imitating the whimpers of a child. Or was the whimpering coming from her?

The scream, she knew, was hers, as the whole world turned blue-white and a sharp, acrid odor filled her nostrils. A second later, the boom of thunder assailed her eardrums . . . followed by the *crack* as a tree snapped and deposited its thick top limbs across the front of Jodi's shelter.

Running through the woods, Luke determined from the roiling leaden sky and the heavy stillness in the atmosphere that he'd never reach the open meadow behind Jodi's cabin before the storm hit. Loath to be caught beneath lightning-attracting trees, he abandoned the path and made a dash for what the old-timers called Umbrella Rock. But he wasn't fast enough. On the heels of the first lightning and thunder arrived a deluge of enormous stinging raindrops.

He had come within a scant five yards of the eroded notch at the base of the largest granite boulder when he saw the white-hot lightning bolt strike the tree, felt the electricity lift the hair on his head, smelled the nose-burning ozone. Momentarily deafened by the thunder, then realizing how lucky he'd been, Luke raced for shelter. The ancient borer-weakened cottonwood, its trunk blackened and slightly smoking, splintered noisily and, in a gust of wind, toppled over. It missed Luke by inches . . . and blocked his entry into the cave.

The ends of broken branches abraded his hands as he tugged them aside to make space to crawl through. Scrambling around the bulk of the cottonwood's crest, Luke flung himself under the overhang of Umbrella Rock. He landed, not against dry stone but against something soft . . . and sopping wet. Something whose spine-tingling wails mingled eerily with the moaning wind. Luke scuttled to one side, off what he presumed to be some poor drenched creature of the wild.

Through the gloom he stared at Jodi's ash-gray, fear-contorted face. Her dazed eyes, wide and awash with tears, stared back at him. The whining sound from deep in her throat seemed to go on forever, wrenching Luke's heart.

"Jodi?" His croak was lost in the uproar of wind and rain. He tried again, louder. "Jodi, it's me. Luke." He touched her bare, frigid arm.

Startled, she hunched away from him, but her mewling ceased. "Luke?"

He couldn't hear her whisper, but he read his name on her colorless, trembling lips and read the disbelief in her eyes. "Yes, Jodi, it's me."

Like a drowning person grabbing at floating debris in floodwaters, she clutched his front and held on. She was shaking so hard that Luke vibrated with the contact.

Gently, he loosened her grip, twisted out of his waterproof

147

jacket, and draped it across her shoulders. "There. That's better," he said in her ear.

It *was* better. Jodi felt the difference at once. The warmth from Luke's jacket, from Luke's body, seeped through the T-shirt and touched her skin with . . . reality. The hovering thunderstorm ghouls receded a few inches, allowing her a peek at Luke's worried features. He was real. She hadn't hallucinated the whole thing after all.

"Th—thank you." She tucked her chin and huddled deeper into the jacket.

Without a word, Luke turned slowly, pulled her against him, and tightened both arms around her. Gradually, as he shared his body heat with her, her violent shivering gave way to an occasional spasmodic jerk when lightning flashed or thunder rolled.

Jodi began to feel more like Jodi Turner and less like some nameless clump of uncontrollable muscles and nerves. She began to feel the old need for someone to talk to, for someone to talk to her and overcome the lack of courage that thunderstorms always caused.

"Luke?"

He'd hoped she'd relaxed a bit, but the wistful plea as she said his name bespoke her lingering unrest.

"Are you all right?" he asked, not knowing what else to say.

"Y—Yes. Will you talk to me?"

"What about?" He was out of practice at making conversation, and he'd never been adept at comforting damsels in distress.

"About your band."

It's not my band anymore! Didn't she realize what she was asking of him? Probably not, because she was still addled by her stressful reactions to the storm raging only a few feet away.

Luke took a deep breath and lessened his grip on her. Quickly, she squirmed close again, and he knew he couldn't refuse her anything. Not today. Maybe not ever. And that possibility frightened him almost as much as the tempest outside their hideaway frightened Jodi. Luke shifted his weight and hers so they were both more comfortable.

"What about my—my band?" Speaking the phrase out loud hadn't been quite as difficult as he'd imagined it would be.

"Anything. I don't know. Why you call it *Only in Texas.*"

Her soft, indecisive request bore out Luke's conjecture that she was still enmeshed in her phobia. Later, she might not remember what he told her, but he had a strange yearning to tell her anyway. Maybe talking about the past would erase it from his mind—and from his heart—once and for all, so he could give up the dream that never completely went away.

"Once upon a time," he began his personal, private fairy tale, "there were three college guys. At Texas A & M. For fun they started a three-piece band, Phil on guitar, Gus on the bass, and . . . and . . ." He stopped and ran his tongue around and over his dry lips. *I can't do this.*

Jodi helped him. "And you on the piano."

"Right." He laid his hand on the top of her wet head to nestle it under his chin. He didn't want her to look up and see in his eyes the dying of his happiest memories. She'd already witnessed enough death. He sighed, then continued. "Classmates asked us to play at birthday dances, fraternity bashes, end-of-finals celebrations. Sometimes they even paid us a few dollars." Recalling those gigs made him smile a little. "After graduation the *Texas Two-Steppers*—that's what we called ourselves then—added a second guitarist and a drummer and cut a demo record. The local disc jockeys gave us a lot of air time."

"What about *Only in Texas?*" Jodi persisted. For the first time, she failed to cringe at a lightning flash.

Luke was glad his chatter had distracted her. He was also glad—and astonished—that he was distracting himself from his self-identity as a failure. With pride—a feeling long unfamiliar to him—he answered Jodi's question.

"We began to branch out. We played mostly country-western, of course, but we crossed over into popular music, too, and folk tunes, honky-tonk, big-band oldies, even gospel sometimes. So we decided we needed a new name, something that indicated our diversification. But one or the other of us kept vetoing every suggestion 'til one night after rehearsal Gus, totally frustrated, said 'Where on earth would five country-western junkies make trouble for themselves by tackling so many different kinds of music? Where else, I ask you. Only in Texas.' We all looked at each other and started to laugh like crazy—and that's how we became *Only in Texas*." Nostalgia raised a rumbling chuckle in his chest.

Jodi leaned back out of his embrace and smiled up into his incredible light green eyes. "That's a nice story. Thanks for telling me."

Luke cleared his throat and diffidently dropped his gaze. He hadn't talked so much at one time in months. He felt embarrassed—but somehow good—about blabbing those old memories. Jodi had listened as though she really cared.

Luke's body tensed. Hell, listening was what she got paid to do! Listening . . . and molding people into objects she could use to obtain money and prestige for herself. Like Corinne.

Jodi sensed Luke's change of mood when his muscles contracted and hardened. Was he sorry he'd laid bare a fragment of his past? When she asked him about the band, she'd been selfish, nervous, thinking only of her need for the sound of a human voice to drown out the thunder.

Now she listened to the near silence. At some time during Luke's *Only in Texas* chronicle, the lightning, thunder, and torrential rain had ceased, as suddenly as they had begun. Only the wind remained.

"Storm's over," Luke announced gruffly, unnecessarily. He grabbed her shoulders and pushed her none too gently away.

The stone behind Jodi's back was cold, even through Luke's jacket. The look in Luke's eyes was colder. He seemed to be warning her not to perceive their moments of closeness as anything other than survival-of-a-thunderstorm tactics.

The storm was over. So was the closeness.

So be it, Jodi acquiesced as, without audible comment, she scrambled to the front of the overhang. Her I-don't-need-him indignation wavered when she encountered the imprisoning treetop.

"Curses!" she muttered through clenched teeth.

"Let me." Alternately grunting and mumbling unintelligible obscenities, Luke managed to clear a space for her exit. He followed her out into wind gusts bitterly cold and strong enough to make him wobbly on legs stiff from crouching so long in the cave.

In spite of the icy wind, Jodi almost tore Luke's jacket from her shoulders, then thrust it toward him with a terse, "Thanks."

Luke watched the gale rock her, too. She had to clamp her mouth shut to shush the chattering of her teeth. But her eyes remained two dark blue battle flags of unrelenting independence. He glanced down, away from her defiant glare . . . and sucked in a gasp.

The wet, thin cotton fabric of the white T-shirt clung to her pale skin like transparent spandex. Luke's hungry eyes picked out the delicate lacy pattern of her bra and, beneath that, the subtle rosy tint of her pebbled breasts. When his body began to react in a normal, female-deprived fashion, he pulled his gaze away and snapped, "Put the damn jacket back on!"

Jodi, who'd noticed his perusal of her barely concealed nakedness and been devastated by her own feelings, hastily donned the wrap and frantically zipped it closed.

Luke grumbled, "Now you won't freeze." He hoped she'd think concern for her well-being his motive for ordering her to cover herself. He never expected to be pleased to be standing outside, coatless, in an intensely biting north wind, but it worked almost as well as a cold shower.

Miserably, Jodi followed a silent Luke through the soggy underbrush to the path and then toward the cabin. She had no wish to converse with him, and even if she had, the fierce gale would have blustered her words away like the tender leaves that were being wrested from the dripping trees overhead.

At the bottom of the cabin steps Jodi assumed the lead. She unlocked the door and, once inside, shrugged out of the jacket and handed it to Luke. Now he'd leave—he always left abruptly—and she wouldn't have to wonder, as she had all the way from the cave, what to say. The flash of heat in his eyes had taken her by surprise. She had no inkling of how to make small talk with a man—a sexy man—who'd gaped at her bare-looking breasts with raw desire . . . and made her writhe inside with a passion long stifled and almost forgotten.

"Take off your clothes," that sexy, arousing man commanded.

"I beg your pardon?" Jodi blushed. Had Luke read her wanton thoughts?

"Unless you like having pneumonia." From the twinkle in those fabulous eyes, he was enjoying her embarrassment to the fullest.

"Oh." Irish's teasing had taught Jodi to laugh at herself, so smiling at Luke was easy. She shrugged. "I'll just be a minute."

Apparently, Luke, who was rummaging through her kitchen cabinets, had no intention of leaving. "Instant coffee?"

"In the jar beside the coffeemaker," she told him as she headed for the bedroom.

Actually, it took six minutes for her to strip, towel off the dampness and put on dry underwear, jeans, and a cowl-neck sweater. She turbaned a fresh towel around her hair and slid her feet into her slippers.

Just as she pushed open the folding door, the phone rang. Jodi hurried to catch it, vaguely aware of Luke's footsteps behind her.

Bringing her a mug of coffee, Luke followed her to the desk and waited impatiently while she spoke to the caller.

"Hello? . . . Who *is* this? . . . Quentin? . . . Well, I don't want to talk to *you!* . . . I told you before, I'm not going to help you. Get another agent . . . I don't *care* who! Just leave *me* alone! If you don't, I'll swear out a restraining order."

At the words *restraining order,* Luke, concerned and frankly curious, moved closer . . . close enough to hear the other man shouting at Jodi. But he couldn't quite make out what was being said.

"I don't owe you one damn thing!" Jodi yelled into the mouthpiece.

This time Luke clearly overheard the man's loud, threatening response: "I could *kill* you for this!"

Fifteen

The threat echoed in Luke's ears and probably in Jodi's as well, for her hand that held the phone was noticeably trembling. Luke reached over, twisted the instrument out of her tense fingers, and slammed it onto its base. Vociferously, he demanded, "Who in the hell *was* that?"

"Don't shout at me!" Jodi screamed back at him.

"Okay, okay!" Luke loudly agreed, then realizing he wasn't complying, he repeated his question more quietly. "Who was that on the phone?"

"My ex-husband." Limp and worried, Jodi dropped onto the desk chair. Quentin had no right to inject himself into her life again.

Luke handed her the steaming coffee mug, and she eagerly swallowed a mouthful of its bracing contents. "Thanks," she said.

"Right." He stood near her and waited for the color to return to her cheeks. After a minute or so, he broke the pulsating silence. "Aren't you going to call the police?"

"Because he's trying to make me miserable? There's no law against that."

"Jodi, I heard him threaten you."

Jodi guzzled the coffee and set the mug on the desk. Then she got up and walked over to the sofa. From Luke's grim

154

countenance as he sat beside her, she knew he wasn't going to let the matter drop.

"He won't hurt me anymore. Those days are over." Jodi saw the flash of fury in Luke's watchful gaze as he understood what she'd implied. "It's all right," she hastily reassured him. "A couple of weeks ago Quentin asked me to be his agent again, to energize his waning popularity, and I told him no."

Ever since the phone call when Jodi had addressed the man as Quentin, the wheels in Luke's brain had been turning sluggishly, until now when the cogs suddenly meshed. If Jodi had kept her married name, the puzzle pieces fit. Not completely accepting what his logic told him, Luke glowered at Jodi. "You married *Quentin* Turner?" When she nodded, he continued in spite of his better judgment. "That coke-snorting, groupie-scre . . . ah . . . chasing blot on the musical profession?"

Embarrassed and oddly defensive, Jodi uttered a brittle laugh. "That's a good thumbnail description. And yes, I married him."

"Why?" Once more Luke had raised the level of his tone.

"Because I loved him. Or thought I did."

Luke failed to hear the regret or the self-accusation in her softly spoken reply. His reaction centered on the picture her words created in his mind: Jodi making love with that jerk. To help the unwanted scene he conjured up fade to black, Luke moved quickly, jerkily, across the cabin, picked up Jodi's empty mug, and strode with it to the kitchen.

From where she sat, her pleading voice followed him. "Have you never done anything you were sorry for?"

Sure I have, Luke answered silently. *When I cheated on a high school history exam. When I made a pass at Gus's girl. When I kept a secret I maybe should have told. When I loved and trusted Corinne.*

"Well?" Jodi, standing at his elbow, startled him.

Because the mental listing of his major past mistakes had briefly dimmed his present, he'd been unaware of Jodi's approach. Now here she was, watching him expectantly with those lapis-blue eyes, waiting for him to speak.

To lighten her mood—and his—Luke told her, "Yeah. Once I did a bad thing. In the third grade I kissed Mabel Pettigrew during recess. She bopped me."

Jodi understood that Luke's silly remarks were meant to detour her unhappy thoughts, but her musing, set in motion by Quentin's phone call, sped *sans* humor and *sans* brakes along the roadway of her mind.

She wasn't afraid of Quentin.

Was she?

Several strange, danger-suggesting incidents had occurred since the day he'd stormed out of her office. And he'd threatened her then, too.

At the time she'd assumed his departing I'll-get-even shouts to be like his wild ravings during the divorce proceedings. Without substance. Because after the divorce he'd simply stayed out of her life for three years.

But now he was back, and reasonless, upsetting events were happening.

Should she notify the police about Quentin's threat? They could do nothing until he broke the law. A warning to him from the authorities would only exacerbate his anger, his retaliation. No. The best thing would be for her to wait. *If* Quentin contacted her again, she would definitely obtain a court order to keep him away.

The decision made, Jodi felt . . . safer.

Luke, who'd been standing beside her and wondering what she was thinking, noted the easing of tension on her face and the slight relaxing of her shoulders. Her whispery sigh encouraged him to do what he always seemed to be doing where Jodi was concerned. Apologize.

"I'm sorry. Your relationship with your ex is your business." His accompanying smile softened the usual abruptness of his speech pattern.

Jodi threw him a sharp look. "I don't *have* a relationship with my ex! And I don't want one—which is why I can't tell the police about his call."

Luke scowled and shook his head in disagreement, but

remained judiciously silent as he followed her back to the sofa and settled beside her.

"I don't think you understand where I'm coming from." Jodi paused, hesitant to discuss her marriage with someone she hardly knew. But then she remembered Luke's *Only in Texas* story. It wasn't the same, of course; Luke's college band experiences involved no severe emotional problems. She doubted if he'd ever share his hurtful memories with her, but he had shared *something,* and Jodi sensed that in itself was a rare gift. She knew Luke had figured out from her earlier remark that she'd been abused, and he clearly had trouble picturing her and the bad-boy-of-heavy-rock as a couple. She recoiled from the idea that Luke might be considering her a weakling or a fool. That possibility afforded her the reason, as well as the inner strength, to tell Luke the truth.

"Quentin was the first client Sunbelt Images let me handle on my own. In the beginning—five years ago—he was fun to be around, and he absorbed all my advice, and that of the instructors and counselors I sent him to, like a grateful, obedient sponge. I was proud of the changes in him, changes I was responsible for." She paused. "I became infatuated with the person I had created."

"That part's understandable," Luke grudgingly admitted.

"Understandable but unwise. I'd never been in love, and Quentin was . . . different. He affected me in all sorts of new and exciting ways. I was inexperienced and gullible—and much too willing to believe him when he swore he loved and needed me. The needing part was true." Her mouth twisted into a bitter grimace. "I found out later the loving part wasn't. But we were married after a year, and I worked to get him media exposure and build his image as a performer. He appeared on talk shows and as the opening act for several big-name rock and rollers. Then I booked his first concert as a headliner, and his career took off like a missile. Quentin changed again—or maybe he was like that all along and I was too blind to see it."

"Fame changes people." Luke was trying very hard to visualize the situation from Jodi's viewpoint.

"Our lives suddenly revolved around his ego. He seldom came home between concerts, and when he did, he expected me to be his gofer—or a quick lay." Her cheeks flushed, and she refused to meet Luke's eyes. "I knew he was on drugs, and he was drunk a lot of the time."

"He hit you." Fury hoarsened Luke's voice.

"Only twice—and neither blow was a wounding one. Except to my pride."

"The louse!"

"When Irish and Annie found out, they raised all manner of hell. Ordered me to leave him. But I'd never before failed at anything important, and the institution of marriage is important to me. I wasn't ready to give up on my ten-month-old vows."

"Stubborn," Luke accused grumpily.

The corners of Jodi's mouth gentled into a faint smile. "I guess. Anyway, I thought maybe it would help if I spent some time in his public world and less in what he liked to call my ivory-tower office.

"He had a concert scheduled in Houston, and I decided at the last minute to join him there. I arrived too late to see him before he went on stage, so I bought a ticket. I hated every bit of it—the bone-jarring noise, the garish lights, Quentin's gyrations that called forth the ear-piercing screams of his fans. That hour and a half made up my mind. We lived in two different worlds, with two conflicting sets of standards. I went backstage, but there was such a crowd, yelling and shoving, that I gave up. It wasn't the time or the place for us to talk, anyway.

"I had a leisurely dinner at a Tex-Mex restaurant, then took a cab to Quentin's hotel. After checking my identification, the desk clerk gave me a key to Quentin's suite. I told the clerk not to call upstairs, that I wanted to surprise my husband."

For the first time since she'd begun her narrative, visible anguish marked Jodi's facial features. She rose and sauntered aimlessly around the living room area. Her voice cracked as she forced herself to continue. "I surprised him, all right. When I unlocked the door, I stepped into a sexual orgy. Quentin and two teenage girls, naked and so intertwined I couldn't tell whose arm or leg was whose."

"That sleazy bastard!" Luke leaped to his feet, ready and eager to take on Quentin had he been there.

Jodi gave her shoulders a desultory shrug. "At least I'd already stopped loving him. If I ever truly did. So I wasn't heartbroken. But I felt so insulted, so degraded." She sighed. "And so betrayed. He destroyed my trust in everything I'd always believed in. That hurt most of all."

"I know," Luke said brusquely as he came up behind her. With an extreme gentleness, he put both hands on her shoulders and turned her around. So many emotions jockeyed for prominence in his crystal green eyes: sorrow, pain, empathy, tenderness—and longing.

Slowly, deliberately, he bent his head—Jodi numbly watched that unruly curl fall down onto his forehead—and lightly placed his mouth over hers. Before Jodi could react, except for a strange tumbling in the region of her stomach, Luke stopped the kiss and, without another word, walked out of the cabin.

Stunned, confused, Jodi stared at the quietly closing door. One fist pushed against the thudding heartbeat in her chest as the fingers of the other hand feathered across her tingling lips. She felt . . . needy. She yearned for Luke to return and kiss her again. A real kiss, taking and giving, demanding and promising.

Promising what? A chance for her to hope again? A renewed faith in the happily-ever-after? For such a long time she'd put aside her dreams, not daring to trust any man. Could she trust Luke, who had thrown away his music, to keep and to cherish her love?

Suddenly realizing where her thoughts had led, Jodi was awestruck . . . and afraid. . . .

Could she possibly be falling in love with Luke?

Sixteen

Jodi, who disliked loose ends of any sort, took that question apart and put it back together again at least twenty times during the next two pensive days. And restless nights. Around the clock, the raveling, frayed ends of her security blanket, her self-control, dangled in her mind.

Was she falling in love with Luke? Or was the process already a done deal? Even if she still could, did she *want* to call a halt to her escalating emotions? And if she wanted to stop wishing for more from Luke, how did she accomplish that?

Never before had she been so attracted to or affected by a man, and she didn't know how to handle her roller-coaster feelings. And that loss of control over the situation worried her, confused her the most. The minute she thought she'd figured out what she wanted and possibly how to achieve it, she decided that wasn't what she wanted after all. Jodi loathed wishy-washiness, and she'd become the epitome of that loathing. If it weren't so abhorrent, it would be downright laughable. Jodi Klerkton Turner, the I-can-handle-this lady, unable to sleep at night because of unasked-for, seesawing reactions to a *man!*

A man who ran away every time *his* emotions surfaced. Luke certainly wasn't a prime example of someone to be relied upon.

But Jodi had seen Luke's love for and devotion to Becky. Jodi had sensed for herself Luke's concern after her apartment break-in, his comfort during the thunderstorm, and his irate response when he learned the facts about her marriage. Irish, always a good judge of character, had discerned Luke's problem right away. Not a basic weakness, but a plausible flight from being hurt again.

And isn't that what I've been doing? Jodi asked herself. In a shocked effort to be honest, she admitted she, too, had been on the run. From her guilt and grief over Annie's death, and from any relationship with another man that might undermine her monument to independence.

For the hundredth time Jodi relived Luke's "butterfly" kiss and wished he'd *taken* the control she'd been willing at the moment to give him. Perhaps in that willingness, that eagerness to hand the control over to Luke, lay the crux of the matter. She must find out how it was that she felt so connected to a man she met only two weeks ago. That much, her head, her heart, her very soul demanded of her. The not-knowing was unthinkable.

Chances were she would never know who killed Annie or why, but she was determined not to return to her job in Austin and leave behind a passel of *if-only's* where Luke was concerned.

And she certainly wouldn't discover the truth by remaining closed up in this cabin with her vacillating emotions.

On the day of the barbecue, Jodi had noticed a large plastic basket in the storage room, which she now retrieved and filled with her dirty clothes and bed linens. After a brief phone call to verify Becky's presence at home, Jodi walked outside.

From her yard a flock of robins pecking at the grass for bugs and worms flew across the road. Jodi's gaze followed their soaring patterns and noticed that the redbud trees circling Troy's hillside lodge had literally bloomed overnight. She sniffed, hoping to catch the pink blossoms' fragrance, but smelled instead the wood smoke from someone's fireplace.

Trudging along the road's grassy shoulder, Jodi sensed

the ineffable eyes of her *watcher.* She stopped and slowly, furtively, checked around. Squinting against the bright sunlight, she spied Luke turning over the earth in a flower bed alongside his house. Had he been watching her approach, then returned to his task before she saw him? What about the other times? He'd been outdoors on those occasions and could have been watching her then, too.

Well, she didn't like being stared at till goose bumps raised on her arms and chills prickled the back of her neck, and she damn sure intended to tell him so!

Annoyed, Jodi hurried down the curved driveway, kicking at the loose gravel washed up on the concrete by the recent storm. She felt Luke's blatant stare and looked up from the scattered pebbles at her feet, prepared to order him to stop watching her all the time.

But his gaze held a welcoming warmth, completely different from the strange, shivery raking of ghostly fingers along her spine a few moments ago.

" 'Morning." Luke straightened and massaged his back after he stuck the spading fork in the loose, pungent soil. "Need some help?"

"Help? Oh, you mean with the basket."

How could he act so . . . so normal? Evidently, he'd chosen to forget the kiss that had eradicated her slumber the past two nights. Jodi couldn't decide whether to be disappointed or relieved.

"I can manage." She hitched her burden up on one hip. "Thanks anyway."

Luke noted how the shifting weight of the laundry basket pulled Jodi's sweater tight against her breasts, and he cautioned himself not to think about the revelations under her wet T-shirt . . . or about the brief, hungry response of her mouth beneath his. Roughly, he grabbed the garden tool's handle and grunted, "Becky's inside."

"I know. I called." Jodi hesitated while Luke attacked a crusted area of ground with the fork tines. Then she sighed.

Luke was being his usual recalcitrant self. But she was

162

absolutely positive that he was *not* her malevolent watcher! She'd never really believed he was. She'd simply wanted the watcher to be someone she knew . . . so she could make him stop. The stranger's unwanted perusal upset her, but not as much, perhaps, as the fact that he *was* a stranger. An unknown, unmanageable entity.

At some time during the disturbing events of the past week, Jodi had ceased to consider the watcher a possible figment of her imagination. She *knew* he was real! She just had no idea who he was or why he spied on her.

Just as she had no idea why someone had deliberately forced Annie's car off the highway and caused her death.

Oh, Lord! Was there a connection?

Jodi's breathing stopped. And for a moment she feared her heart might follow suit. Feeling as motionless and lifeless as a mannequin, she let the laundry basket drop with a dull thump to the floor. Then returning sensation rushed through her body, flailing her raw nerve ends and wrecking her equilibrium. To keep from falling, she wrapped both arms around one of the columns flanking the steps.

That was how Becky found her when she opened the front door.

"Jodi! I heard a noise, and . . . oh, you dropped your basket."

Jodi relinquished her hold on the post and stepped back.

"Are you all right?" Becky asked. "What happened?"

I lost my mind, that's what happened. I mixed apples and oranges and came up with vegetable soup. The nerve-wrenching happenings of the past couple of weeks had stripped away her logic and left her absurdly paranoid. There was no reason for Annie's murderer to be watching *her.* Jodi gave an embarrassed laugh, then a credible answer to Becky's concerned query. "I stubbed my toe on the edge of the top step and nearly wound up on the floor. I'm okay now."

"Good. Then let's go inside."

Jodi picked up the plastic basket and followed Becky into the house.

While Jodi's clothes washed, the two women talked. Jodi spoke about some of her famous, and infamous, clients. As always, she was careful not to reveal any secrets. Becky told tales she'd heard from Swallows Bluff's longtime residents about the building of Buchanan Dam. Sadly, many people had been compelled to leave homesteads settled by their great-grandparents. One stubborn old man refused to vacate his hilltop property, and when the lake filled to capacity, his self-constructed log cabin perched on a tiny island of high ground. Alone and isolated, he remained there until he died a few years later.

"What about the cabin?" Jodi wanted to know.

"It's still there. The young folks around here go over there sometimes for picnics. And sex." Becky smiled ruefully. "No park police. No streetlights."

Because Jodi knew it was expected of her, she chuckled. But deep inside, beneath her sophisticated veneer, she fantasized about what it would have been like to be young and without the worrisome responsibilities of the adult world. What it would have felt like to experience the thrill of a carefree first love.

Had Luke taken *his* first love over to that island, or to another equally secluded place, to claim her innocence? Jodi felt deprived . . . and jealous of some special girl out there somewhere.

She shook off the surge of envy and nodded her head, she hoped appropriately, in response to whatever Becky had said while she had indulged herself in daydreaming.

Jodi's gaze fell on the old-fashioned piano similar to the upright she and Annie had practiced on. She hadn't played in years, but in retrospect she recalled the hard, smooth feel of the keys as she pressed them down and sounded the scales at the bidding of her fingers.

During the next lull in their conversation, Jodi asked Becky, "Do you play the piano?"

Becky threw her a surprised look, then said, "Heavens,

no," and sighed. "If that one hadn't been in our family for generations, I'd get rid of it."

"Oh, no!" Jodi disagreed. "You'd be sorry. I wish there'd been some way for Annie and me to keep Mother's, but Irish's living room was too small."

"You and your sister both played?"

"Annie was the gifted one. She made a quick, easy transition from piano to guitar. At first I missed banging out a familiar tune now and then, but before long, records and tapes satisfied my yen for music." She paused. "I'd better go check on my laundry."

Jodi spent a few minutes transferring the damp items from one appliance to the other, then set the dryer cycle knob and rejoined Becky. The other woman stood beside the piano, looking wistfully through the floor-to-ceiling window at Luke as he squatted just outside, removing pebbles and sticks from the freshly spaded flower bed.

"I really miss hearing him play." Becky was talking to herself. Jodi understood. If she tried hard enough, sometimes she could still hear Annie singing her own lovely country-and-western ballads to the accompaniment of her guitar.

Becky turned at the muffled sound of Jodi's nearby footsteps on the carpet. "Would you play something for me?"

Jodi, too, watched Luke for a few sorrowing moments. "I couldn't," she murmured.

"You do read music?"

"Yes, but—"

"There's a lot of sheet music in the piano bench. Surely you can find something."

"I meant I can't play because of Luke. He'd hear me."

Becky gave Jodi an ingratiating smile. "He won't expect you to play like a professional."

Impatient with Becky and shocked by her insensitivity, Jodi spoke sharply. "He'll be upset—because *he* can't play. I couldn't do that to him."

Becky looked at her with dawning comprehension. "You're worried about how he'd react. That's so thoughtful. But he won't mind your playing. Honest," she added at Jodi's perplexed frown. "I had a party here last Christmas to introduce Luke to all the neighbors. He'd just moved in with me. One of the ladies played the piano for us to sing carols. I was afraid Luke might feel bad about it, but he took it in stride. Even sang along with us."

"In that case . . ." Jodi walked over and raised the needlepoint-upholstered bench lid. Thumbing through stacks of sheet music, she exclaimed happily over old, old songs her mother had loved. She found one—"It's a Sin to Tell a Lie"—that had been her grandmother's favorite. The slick yellowed pages crackled with age as Jodi spread them open on the music stand.

She sat down, pulled the seat up close to the piano, and picked out the melody with her index finger. Humming at first, then softly singing the familiar sad, pleading lyrics, she began to play hesitantly, using both hands.

With her peripheral vision, Jodi saw Luke straighten and face the window. Because of the deep shade in which he stood, she couldn't make out his expression. What was he thinking? And feeling? Should she stop playing?

With the clarity of a trumpet blast, Jodi's plan was born full blown, daring and a little prankish, but she deemed it worth the gamble. She played with more confidence and tromped on the damper pedal to increase the volume while accentuating the beat. For her maneuver to succeed, Luke had to hear the music through the thick plate glass. Each time an oft-repeated chord appeared in the arrangement, she purposefully chose to press the wrong keys, creating a horrendous discord. Again and again she deliberately played the chord wrong. When out of the corner of her eye she noted Becky's flinching at every loud, dissonant sound, Jodi grinned to herself.

She stole a glance out the window. Luke was nowhere in sight. A minute later she heard the front door open and slam shut, and then Luke's vigorous, rapidly approaching footsteps. Performing the chorus for the third time, Jodi continued the unharmonious notes until Luke sat down and, with his hips, firmly shoved her to one end of the piano bench.

"You're doing it wrong!" he groaned, and with a savage impatience he pulled her hands away from the keyboard. As though in a trance, he painstakingly and awkwardly with his left hand positioned the stiff fingers of his right hand, one at a time, atop the proper keys.

Jodi literally held her breath and expected Becky was doing the same. She dared not turn her head to check lest the movement distract the man sitting beside her.

Luke's forever-damaged hand exerted its clumsy pressure and created the perfect, melodious chord. He inhaled deeply, then slowly blew out an audible sigh.

Jodi's exhalation joined his as she turned sideways to see his face. If she lived to be a century old, she knew she would never forget the pure, distilled glory of that moment. Surprise, pride, and sheer ecstasy glistened in Luke's green eyes and formed the beatific smile that set Jodi's heart to soaring in tandem with his.

"I really did it," Luke whispered as particles of wonder clung like fairy dust to his shaky voice.

Jodi's triumphant laughter bubbled in her throat. "I knew you could play! I just *knew* it!"

Instantly rigid, his thigh muscles bunching against Jodi's legs, Luke glowered at her. The joy, the glow of his small victory, had completely vanished. "You *planned* this?" he snarled.

"I—I— Yes, I did." Bravely, she met his stormy glare. "I wanted to prove to you that you can still play the piano. A little. Maybe enough to compose your own music."

A dark pall of defeat fell across his features, displacing the initial anger. He looked terribly sad and utterly forlorn.

"Luke?" Jodi anxiously searched his face for some hint of why her wonderful help-Luke project had gone wrong.

"What you proved," he said in a low, rasping voice, enunciating each word as though he were a judge instructing a jury, "is that you like to meddle in other people's lives."

He slammed a clenched fist on the keyboard. Ignoring Jodi's wincing at the awful noise, he also failed to see the sudden moisture that pooled in her wide, astonished eyes. He rose and, lingering only a second to lightly stroke his sister's shoulder, stalked out of the house.

The clothes dryer buzzed into the uncomfortable silence and provided Jodi a means of escape from the unfathomable look on Becky's face. After haphazardly stuffing her laundry in the basket, she turned around.

Becky's full figure blocked the doorway to the kitchen as she asked, "Where do you think you're rushing off to?"

"Home," Jodi replied contritely. "Before somebody named Prentiss murders me."

Becky *laughed*.

Stunned, Jodi gaped at her. She dropped the basket on the floor between them.

"You deserve a reward," Becky said, "for making me see what Luke needs. Not an excuse of a job without a future, but a future somehow related to his music."

"He'll never consider that now." Jodi's regret misted her eyes anew. Her intentions, however lofty and bright with hope, had plummeted to the dark, dank cellar of failure.

"Yes, he will." When Jodi fiercely, negatively shook her head, Becky insisted. "He *will*. You saw the look on his face when he touched the piano keys. He won't be able to forget how happy—how complete—he felt."

"But after that he got so angry."

"Not with you. I think with himself, for having shut out the truth all these months. Luke knows now, in his gut, in his soul, that music *is* his life, however he eventually decides to deal with it."

"I hope you're right," Jodi murmured prayerfully. "I don't want him to hate me forever."

With a Cheshire cat smile and a sparkle in her hazel eyes, Becky advised, "Just give him some space, Jodi, and some time."

Seventeen

For a whole week Jodi took Becky's suggestion. She stayed away from the Prentiss house and from the enigmatic man who lived there. Becky visited Jodi twice, once with a warm loaf of potato bread and another time with a mass of yellow, orange, and red nasturtiums floating in a shallow green glass bowl. On both occasions she mentioned that Luke was trying to play the piano. Not regularly, not successfully, and each session, whether short or shorter, had thus far concluded with his pounding discordantly on the keys in frustration.

At first the information delighted Jodi, but then she wished Luke would share his turnaround with her, maybe even thank her for "meddling."

Later, Irish, always her sounding board, caught the brunt of her disappointment when she brought him up to date. Over the phone Jodi heard his unsympathetic impatience. "Before you tricked Luke into touching the piano, didn't you consider what his reaction might be?"

"I didn't trick—!" Jodi halted in mid-sentence, then groaned. "Yes, I guess I did, didn't I?" Her stubbornness surfaced when she reminded herself that Luke was *still* touching the piano. "But it was worth the risk."

"Even if Luke stays angry with you?"

A lengthy silence ensued, one that spoke paragraphs about Jodi's worst, unadmitted fear.

"Jodi, this isn't the first time your Miss Fix-It complex has backfIred. Nor will it be the last. You have a penchant for doing what's best—what *you* think is best—for those you love."

"I don't love Luke!" Jodi snapped.

"No?" Was that a chuckle she heard? "Well, I used the term loosely. I should have said 'those who for one reason or another matter to you.' As a fan, you do want Luke to become involved in music again?"

"Of course. That's why I—"

"Did what's best for him. So . . . why are you complaining?" Now he was frankly laughing at her.

"I hate you, Irish O'Meara." A contradicting fondness— and a surrender to merriment—rollicked through her voice.

A click on the line diluted the mood.

"My call waiting," Irish said. "I'll call you back."

"That's okay. I'm through complaining."

Smiling, feeling more cheerful, Jodi hung up the phone. No more than a dozen seconds later, it rang again. She rushed back across the room and lifted the receiver.

"Irish, I told you not to—" She stopped . . . and waited, absolutely certain her godfather wasn't on the line. She didn't know how she knew, except that she had the same eerie, something-is-not-right sensation as when the unknown watcher raised the hairs on the back of her neck. "Who's there?" Jodi asked breathily.

The quartz clock on the desk tick-ticked into the heavy silence. The phone almost slipped out of her wet palm. "What—" She licked her lips and started over. "What do you want?"

The dead-sounding phone came alive with a faint, tuneless whistling somehow more frightening than the quiet had been.

Jodi tried not to panic. *Think. Whistling. Music. Luke!* Was it possible?

"Is that you, Luke?" she pleaded querulously.

If the caller was Luke paying her back for her gone-awry

scheme a week ago, she could handle that. Better than if it were some crazy—or Quentin—getting his kicks by scaring a woman alone half to death.

Her mysterious whistler broke the connection.

Jodi immediately dialed the Prentisses number. Becky answered.

"This is Jodi. Did Luke call me?"

"He hasn't mentioned it to me."

"I mean just now."

"No. It couldn't have been him. Listen. He's been at it for nearly an hour this time."

Jodi, until that moment coping with the uneasiness and annoyance caused by the stranger on the phone, became aware of piano music in the background. With a joyful, pounding heart she heard the halting, two-fingers harmony of "Love Me Tender."

"That's great," she told Becky.

She could only imagine the determination, the tedium, the patience, followed by the sense of accomplishment, embodied in Luke's rendition of the simple melody. And if he never spoke to her again, she would always treasure this moment and find solace in the knowledge that *she* had reopened the door to Luke's dream. A different dream, to be sure, but a dream encompassing music, the magical Pied Piper that somehow would lead him to happiness and fulfillment.

Jodi shifted her reclining weight on the chaise lounge and watched a cluster of puff ball clouds slide slowly across the Wedgwood blue sky. On the deck floor beside her sat an empty coffee mug and the romance novel she'd just finished reading. Birds twittered everywhere. The spring-fresh perfume of newly mowed grass, wafted from a neighbor's lawn by the soft breeze, pleased Jodi's sleepy senses.

Strange distant sounds awoke her curiosity and brought her up to a sitting position. She glanced around, then located the source of the racket. High, high above her flew a long V of birds, and from their honking calls Jodi assumed they were Canada geese on their northerly migration. She marveled at the precision and stamina of one of nature's spectacles. How remarkable were the leader's instincts. His was the responsibility to direct his flock on the right path through a chartless ocean of air and to find wildlife preserves or last season's as yet unplowed grain fields where his followers could rest and feed. She gazed at the mesmerizing triangle until the honking died away in the distance and the V disappeared behind a towering gray-white thunderhead.

After rubbing more sunscreen lotion on her exposed skin, Jodi lazed in the warm sunshine. A steady knocking at the front door roused her from her nap.

"I'm coming, Becky, I'm coming," Jodi called out as she rushed through the cabin. Becky had informed her that morning that she was baking more potato bread and would put Jodi's name on a loaf.

Jodi pulled the door open and sucked in a startled gasp. Luke, dressed in black denim, leaned against the front railing, a quizzical look on his face and a large, flat rectangular object wrapped in brown butcher's paper under his left arm.

"Will Becky's brother do?" he asked in that abrupt, clipped way of his, as nonchalantly as if they had parted a mere hour ago and on the best of all possible terms.

He never ceased to confuse, astound, and . . . excite her. Jodi's heart raced like that of a schoolgirl welcoming her first prom date. She took a couple of steps backward.

"Becky's brother will do fine." Her cheeks reddened as she mentally owned up to the understated veracity of those words. "Uh . . . come in."

Why was he here? What would they talk about?

While entering the cabin, Luke answered both questions in typical fashion. Thrusting the package into her hands, he announced without preamble, "My turn to meddle."

"Wh—what is this?" Taken aback, she stared at his offering.

"Open it." He waited, so close she could smell his woodsy cologne.

Jodi laid the lightweight package on top of the desk. She ripped off the heavy brown paper and exposed a huge sketch pad of the type used in grammar school art classes.

"Oh," she said for want of something adequately clever.

"From the Millers' store." Luke sounded let down by her reaction.

"I don't understand."

"Here," he said, and pulled from his shirt pocket a box of several bright-colored felt-tip pens. "To draw with."

Jodi accepted the pens and said, "Thank you, Luke. But I don't draw anymore. I haven't for at least ten years."

"You drew squirrels and cats on Becky's manuscript."

Why was Luke so persistent? she wondered.

"That was for fun." She uttered a nervous little laugh. Was he mocking her?

"So are these"—Luke gestured to the sketch pad, then tapped the box of pens in her hand—"for fun." His expression was deadpan, inscrutable. "Like you playing those horrible chords on the piano last week was for fun."

"No. I was serious about— Oh." Jodi gasped as she perceived the motive behind Luke's silly but dear gifts.

His now-you've-got-it grin blockbusted years from the calendar of his face. At his exultant nod, an unruly dark blond curl dipped to the corner of a twinkling light green eye.

She grinned back at him, unable to hide her joy. "That's what you meant by it being your turn to meddle." She loved the way he looked, so thoroughly pleased with himself. She loved *him*.

Unbelievable!

When had it happened? That first day on the wharf? The morning he showed her how to build a fire in the fireplace? While he protected and comforted her during the fearful thunderstorm? Whenever. But now she had the true, forever solution to the puzzle that had bewildered her for days.

"Jodi?" Luke's strident tone indicated that he'd already spoken her name several times. She felt numb; she likely bore the countenance of a dullard.

"Uh . . . yes?"

Now that he had her attention, his tone softened to almost forlorn. "You're angry."

"Angry?" she repeated dully. *Where are my wits? In some long dormant I'm-in-love cranny of my brain, that's where.*

"About the sketch pad and colored pens. About my interfering. I only wanted to help. Honest."

Careful, Jodi, her waking wits warned. *Don't say something stupidly romantic.*

Struggling toward a calm not yet accessible to her whirling emotions, she decided to say something *friendly.* "It was a very thoughtful gesture."

"Thoughtful, hell!" he exploded. "You made me understand I need music in my life. To thank you for that, I bought the best artist's supplies we have at the store. Because I think *you* need to draw. If that makes you angry . . ."

"No, Luke, no." At last Jodi's brainpower functioned on all cells. "I'm not angry. Just surprised that you remember I used to like to draw."

"I remember other things, too. The comeback baseball pitcher in the movie. What you said about your Dad being a quitter. Even then, you were telling me not to give up on myself. I see that now."

"I thought you at least ought to *try.*" She threw him a half-apologetic, half-satisfied grin.

"Right." Once more he motioned toward the gifts, then he said, "Now you." Once more the man of few words made his point with a heart-stopping smile.

"All right," Jodi conceded. *I'll do anything you ask.* "While I'm here at the lake. But I won't have time for a hobby when I go back to work."

It hit Jodi then. She'd found the answer to one question—how did she really feel about Luke?—and in the process had raised new, upsetting ones. When she returned to Austin, would she see him again? If so, would she have to settle for friendship? What if Luke chose to stay out of her life completely? A dread, deeper and more painful than any she'd ever known, stabbed her reawakened heart.

Luke, standing beside her, observed the strain and unhappiness on Jodi's beautiful face—and mentally booted himself in the rear. What a fool he was for giving this wealthy, worldly woman some cheap, childlike tools of an avocation he'd literally forced upon her! No wonder her thoughts were about returning to her fancy, prestigious job and hunting for a polite way to tell him, a has-been musician, to butt out of her life.

Luke turned away from her and started toward the door. *He's running away again.* Why, every time Luke's emotions began to emerge, did he become as on edge as a guerrilla jungle fighter checking for booby traps? For once, Jodi wanted him to exit—later—in a perfectly ordinary manner.

"Wait," she said.

"What for?" He slowed his pace but continued to move, his sullenness negating his interest in her put-aside dream.

"For a Coke?" Jodi suggested hopefully.

At last Luke stopped and turned. He appeared more relaxed. "Thanks, but I drank one just before I left the store. I'll take a rain check, though—for when you have a drawing to show me."

Then he actually *winked* at her and departed the cabin with an exaggerated machismo swagger.

Certainly not the normal leave-taking Jodi had wished for. Much better. Enticing and promising.

"I can handle that," Jodi whispered as she peeled the narrow sealing strip off the box of assorted colored pens.

Eighteen

"Of course I'm sure I can handle a boat," Jodi answered Luke's terse question.

They stood in the boathouse on the platform between the two slips where Becky's boats were berthed.

At Luke's visible skepticism, Jodi continued, "I know I haven't done it in years, but it's like riding a bicycle. You never forget how. Dad taught me everything he knew about boats and water safety."

Luke scowled. *Some safety. He died along with your mother in a boating accident on a lake like this one.* For a moment Luke worried that he'd spoken aloud, because Jodi's expression clouded over. Her reply told him she'd at least read his thoughts.

"He was drunk that day, Luke, and a sudden storm came up." She peeked out from under the boathouse roof. "Today's weather is perfect, and all I've had to drink is cranberry juice and coffee. And this picnic basket"—she raised it from the full extension of her arm and held it between them—"contains a large Thermos of Perrier, in case there's a fresh water shortage on the island."

"I'd go with you if I hadn't promised Herbert I'd drive his pickup in to Burnet this morning for extra cases of beer and cold drinks and junk food. This coming week is spring break, and quite a few college kids come up to the lakeshore woods to hike and camp out."

And have sex. Jodi recalled Becky's earlier comment.

She was going to the island to sketch the historical log cabin, and maybe it was best that Luke had other plans.

During the week since she'd assigned the word *love* to her feelings for him, they hadn't been alone together until now, and Jodi was uncommonly unsure of herself. Luke stood so close she couldn't ignore the fragrance of his after-shave or the fresh-starched scent of his pale green dress shirt—the exact shade of the eyes that gazed at her with candid warmth and desire. If he looked at her like that long enough, and if they were alone on a deserted island, Jodi feared she might rush into his arms and beg him to have sex with . . . No. For her, at least, it would be making love.

"So," Luke was saying as he nodded toward the small wooden fishing boat, "you've decided to take the ancient one."

They had previously discussed the subject, and Jodi had expressed an uneasiness about taking the powerboat. She restated the reason for her choice "I'm familiar with what you call the ancient one. It's like the boats my Dad rented."

"Also like the ones your *grandfather* rented." Luke chuckled.

Jodi loved the sound. Luke laughed more readily these days, and sometimes he even spoke more than three sentences at a time. He seemed less withdrawn into himself, less angry with everything outside himself, more accepting of things the way they were. He worked at the piano every day, Becky confided, and twice, while Jodi sat in Becky's garden to sketch the flowers, she herself heard Luke's struggles to create harmonic chords.

"At least the old boat has a new state-of-the-art motor," Luke told her, "with a self-starter."

"Thank goodness. In my youth the hardest part was winding the cord around that gizmo and yanking my arm off to start the motor." She turned up her nose at the irritating memory.

"In your youth," Luke repeated solemnly. Then he added in a reedy, wavering old-man voice, "Well, Granny, your seaworthy floating carriage awaits. Just don't get your rheumatizz wet."

They laughed as one, and Luke helped Jodi into the boat, then handed her the willow picnic basket and the tote bag containing her art supplies. He watched while she donned a life jacket and started the motor. She gave him a thumbs-up signal and carefully guided the wooden "ancient one" out of its slip.

The boat moved slowly westward through clear blue, glass-smooth water. Following Becky's directions, Jodi crossed the cove where the Prentiss boathouse stood and rounded the tip of a narrow promontory. She saw the island not far ahead, shaped like a big scoop of ice cream, at least two miles from the nearest land. Towering century-old trees, swarming with restless starlings, red-winged blackbirds, and boat-tail grackles, hid the cabin from view.

As she drew closer to shore, Jodi noted that the island's rim where she approached it was littered with small stones, faded to white from years of sun and ceaselessly lapping waves. Cautiously, she ran the prow of the boat up to the pebbly verge and shut off the engine. After removing her life jacket, she stepped out and checked to be sure the craft was far enough aground that it wouldn't drift away.

A path—a barely discernible trail where the weeds and grass were not as tall or thick as on either side—led sharply uphill from the gravel beach. Jodi picked up the picnic basket and tote bag and set out for the cabin.

About halfway up the steep grade, she spied a large flat-topped rock beside the path. Stopping for a breather, she peered through the underbrush and tree trunks at the lake below. Near the shore, where the shallows sloped gradually downward, the water glistened a clear blue-green; but farther out, where the lake was deepest, the color of the water changed to a murky indigo, almost black under the shadows of the drifting clouds.

Jodi shuddered at the mere idea of swimming in those deeply dark waters. Only as long as her feet could touch bottom did she feel safe. Not for the first time, Jodi thought how terrifying, how hopeless must have been her beloved mother's final minutes of life. If only Dad hadn't been drowning his self-pity in alcohol, he might have prevented both of them from drowning in that storm-struck lake.

"Hi," said a voice behind her.

Momentarily startled, Jodi spun in the direction of her visitor. Among the bushes stood a towheaded, skinny, shabbily dressed girl of thirteen or fourteen.

"Hi yourself," Jodi welcomed with a friendly smile.

"My name's Hannah." A toothy grin marked her freckled face.

"I'm Jodi. Do you live on this island?" She knew the answer but deemed her query more tactful than "Why are you here?"

"No, ma'am. I live on the south shore. With my Mom and Gra'ma. I come over here a lot, though."

"By yourself?"

"Sure." Hannah giggled at Jodi's concerned frown. "Since I was ten and Mom showed me how to run the boat. I used to sneak over here—till Gra'ma caught me one day and I got a wallopin'. Then I stopped coming till I was twelve and Mom said I could. I'm near fifteen now," she stated proudly. Obviously delighted to have a captive audience, she added, "Gra'ma don't look after me no more. Me and Mom, we look after Gra'ma now. She broke her hip and has to stay in bed."

"I'm sorry."

"Me too." Hannah screwed up her face as though she were going to cry. But then she dragged the toe of one red sneaker through the dirt and gave Jodi a wan smile. "That's why I come here today. Tomorrow's Gra'ma's birthday, and I come to see if I can find some of them wild white violets she likes that grow over yonder." She pointed a finger to the area beyond the path from where she stood.

179

"I hope you find some." Jodi sensed the family love that embraced the teenager. Obviously poor in schooling and in dollars, Hannah was rich in what counted most.

"Me too," the girl said again. "Well, I gotta go look. Mom goes to work at two, an' we don't like for Gra'ma to be by herself."

"That's a good idea," Jodi approved. She called out, "I'm glad to meet you," as the young girl quickly crossed the trail and disappeared in the dense undergrowth.

When Jodi reached the crest of the hill, she saw the log cabin. Weather-beaten but sturdy, fronted by yew and laurel grown amuck from lack of care, it presented excellent prospects for her sketching. She walked around the twelve-by-twelve-foot structure, considering several angles from which to work. Once she stumbled as she caught her toe on a tough honeysuckle vine lying along the ground. The pesky plant abounded everywhere. It choked other plants to death, but a few weeks later its unmistakable heavenly perfume would permeate the island.

Muscle-tight, breathing hard and hungry after all the unaccustomed exercise, Jodi noticed a low, makeshift bench in the form of a large thick above-ground live oak root. Sitting down with her back against the rough tree trunk, she removed the salami sandwich and deviled egg from the picnic basket, then poured cold Perrier into the thermos cup. Above her, hordes of blackbirds flapped their wings and squawked, reminding her of the classic Hitchcock movie. Their racket almost deafened her, but she wasn't afraid. Only a handful of the creatures ventured close enough to claim the bread crusts she tossed away.

Sated and rested, Jodi lifted her face to the sunshine that filtered through the glossy pinnate leaves. The birds grew quieter; maybe they were tired, too, Jodi mused, or feeling the increasing heat and humidity.

Jodi dozed, then woke with a start. What had disturbed

her sleep? Then she heard it again and, fully awake, identified it as the *putt-putt* of a boat motor. Hannah leaving the island, Jodi assumed, and hoped the young girl had found a bouquet of the rare white violets for her bedridden grandmother.

Loosely holding the fragile violet stems in one hand, Hannah knew she must hurry. Locating the flowers had taken longer than she'd expected, and Gra'ma would worry if she was late getting home. Hannah plowed her way through waist-high weeds and brambles and headed for the path. If she followed it down to the beach, she could then quickly circle the island, or half of it, to where she'd left her mother's boat.

Near the bottom of the hill, she looked down at a man wearing camouflage clothing, who bent over an old wooden fishing boat. His back was toward her, but Hannah could see that he held something shiny, something that flashed in the sunlight when he moved it back and forth. Then the man lifted it over the side of the boat and laid it on the ground.

Curious, Hannah moved closer. The tool was a saw, a short, narrow, needle-nosed one like she'd never seen before. But the ugly jagged teeth positively marked it a saw.

As she approached the man, her shoes scuffed the gravel. He stood and wheeled around at the rattling noise.

"What are you doin', mister?" Hannah asked.

"I'm . . . uh . . . I'm fixing my boat."

"Then you musta come here with Jodi," she reasoned aloud. She'd hiked over most of the island that day and seen no one else.

"Jodi?"

"Yes, sir. Jodi. The pretty dark-haired lady with the picnic basket. I don't know her last name."

"But you . . . uh . . . saw her." The man fidgeted from one foot to the other—like she did when Mom had caught her breaking a rule.

Hannah sensed something amiss but couldn't figure what.

181

She hastened to reassure the nervous man. "Sure I saw her. We talked about Gra'ma's violets." She showed him the wilting flowers.

"They're . . . uh . . . nice. Jodi likes flowers."

The man smiled at her and he sounded friendly and he knew Jodi liked flowers, so he must be okay. Hannah walked over to him. The man stooped and picked up something. Hannah smelled fresh sawdust and glanced down into the old boat, under the triangular front seat.

What she saw astonished her. And alarmed her—for Jodi's sake.

"Why did you put a hole in Jodi's boat?"

The man still smiled but his eyes had turned . . . evil. The object in his hand was a big greasy wrench.

Understanding at last, Hannah turned to run, but the man grabbed her arm and twisted it cruelly behind her back. She felt the awful, death-dealing blow to her head for the barest second—just before the white violets fluttered softly to the ground.

Refreshed by her nap, Jodi made a half-dozen varied drawings of the cabin's exterior. Something about the way the eccentric old hermit had held on to his space kept her from going inside. Respect for his independence, perhaps? Jodi only knew she would have felt like a snoop.

As the afternoon wore on, Jodi noticed a gradual change in the light. Details of the landscape grew dim, less prominent. She looked up from the sketch pad. A gusty wind stirred the highest treetops, full of birds, fussing as though already settling down to roost. Jodi glanced at her wristwatch: 4:06. At least two and a half hours before sunset. How odd. Why were the birds acting so strangely?

She stood, flexed her stiff knees, then walked around until she spotted a break in the trees that offered an unobstructed view of the western sky. A wall of dark gray clouds stretched across the distant horizon and blocked out the lowering sun. The birds had, of course, sensed the storm's proximity.

"Damn!" Jodi spouted.

She wasn't ready to quit sketching but knew she must stop now in order to get home before the storm hit. Immediately, but without undue haste because crossing the lake and cove to the boathouse would require a maximum of twenty minutes, Jodi gathered her belongings and headed downhill.

Once she reached the open beach, she could see that the storm front had advanced faster than anticipated. But if she hurried, she still had ample time to safely cross the water. Forcibly, she shoved the front of the boat. It didn't budge. Darn! She'd pulled it up so far on the shale that now she had to step out into the ankle-deep water and push hard on the gunwale. The boat slid free, and Jodi scrambled inside before it could float away.

Rather than put the tote bag and picnic basket in one of the storage bins, she dropped them at her feet, then reached for the starter. Happily, it turned over on the first try. Quickly, she moved the boat away from the island and gunned the motor. Grateful to be on her way and finally able to relax a bit, she became more uncomfortably aware of her wet feet. She wriggled her toes inside the squishy shoes and glanced down.

The entire bottom of the boat was awash!

Alarmed, puzzled, she looked closer. In her throat, her shocked, gasping breath fought with a sob of denial. Near the prow, a little whirlpool spun, like dishwater going down the sink drain, except in reverse. Water was swirling *into* the boat!

How could that be? Had she somehow damaged the boat when she pushed it across the gravel?

While she stared, still half disbelieving what was happening, the depth rose above her ankles.

Maybe if she slowed down—or stopped altogether—it would help. Jodi shut off the motor . . . and heard the incoming water bubbling like a witch's brew in a boiling cauldron.

The boat was filling rapidly, and a very frightened Jodi finally admitted to herself that it was going to founder. Trying not to panic, she reminded herself that she could swim. A little. A very little. Thank goodness she had the life jacket, which in her blind haste to get away from the island she'd forgotten to put on. Understandably, she'd had other things on her mind.

She reached under the seat but couldn't feel the rough canvas fabric.

The life jacket *had* to be there! She'd stowed it there this morning before leaving the boat, and she'd have seen its bright orange color if it had worked its way out of the storage place. One of the straps had probably caught on something.

Kneeling on the boat's bottom, sucking in her breath at the chill of the water as it came up almost to her waist, Jodi groped beneath and around the seat.

The life jacket wasn't there.

"Oh, God," Jodi whispered.

It wasn't anywhere in the boat.

Nineteen

Terror. Heart-stabbing, muscle-tightening, dizzying terror grabbed hold of her body and fuddled her mind. Kneeling in the boat, Jodi stared wide-eyed at the water rising around her. It was a dirty brownish gray. It smelled of fish. It was icy cold.

A violent shiver contracted her taut muscles and shook her brain into action. In another few minutes the water would engulf the boat. She had to get out before it could suck her under or strike her as it sank.

Leave the boat? Go alone into that *deep* water without a life-preserving device?

She *had* to.

"Oh, God," she moaned.

The boat was no longer the safe, taken-for-granted barrier between her and her worst nightmare. The dying craft would soon be as dead as her hopes for rescue. If she got out of this alive, she had to do it by herself. There was no fitness club coach to swim beside her and speak helpful reassurances in her ear when she faltered.

Think, Jodi, think!

Shoes. She'd read somewhere that swimmers in peril should always remove their shoes. Once she left the boat, she would definitely be in peril. Untying the wet shoe-laces proved impossible for her trembling fingers, so with the toe of one foot she pushed at the heel of the other until each sneaker yielded. One thick sock came off with its shoe, and Jodi quickly toed off the other.

Her clothes? No, no, no! If the slimy creatures that lived in the lake planned to gnaw on her, they'd first have to eat a chunk of her jeans or sweater. Maybe they'd get indigestion and go away. Jodi listened to her silent, bizarre reasoning and, in some sane corner of her mind, realized she was half crazed with fear.

Clearly, as though Annie were beside her, Jodi heard her sister's years-ago plea. *Learn to swim, Jodi. Please. So you won't drown like Mom and Dad did.* How had Annie guessed this day, this dangerous fearsome moment, would come?

Well, Annie, I learned to swim. Now we'll find out just how good I am.

With that, Jodi stood and, after a long prayerful breath, stepped out of the water inside of the boat and into the bottomless water of the lake. She swam a dozen or so feet before she stopped, trod water, and looked back. Becky's terminal "ancient one" expired with a *whoosh* and hardly a ripple. The tote bag and willow basket survived a few seconds more; then they, too, already waterlogged, vanished beneath the surface.

The murky and forbidding water moved gently up and down like the skin of some panting sea monster. Jodi valiantly summoned the small bit of calm she had left. There was no monster, only the lake shifting under the wind outflowing from the approaching clouds.

"Oh, no!" she cried, taking in a mouthful of muddy, brackish water and using up that remaining iota of calm.

She'd completely forgotten the storm!

Hysterical, Jodi began to thrash about, her hands splashing at the water until their frantic movements pulled her under. She swallowed more of the horrid-tasting liquid, then came up choking and flailing her arms. With her insides churning, she spit out water and vomit. Her throat burned with the bitter aftertaste.

Instinct, or the miraculous timely recall of her swimming teacher's instructions, gave her the know-how and the control to thwart her second submergence. But she doubted her ability or her stamina to swim very far.

Which was closer, the island or the boathouse? Using her hands like whirling propellers, she managed to lift herself enough to check her location. The distance to the island presented less than half the swim to where she *wanted* to go. The faraway mainland meant dry clothes, hot food, a comfortable bed and, if summoned, sympathetic friends. But she'd never make it. She'd be damn lucky to find the energy and strength to swim back to the island. And, once there, the log cabin would provide shelter until the thunderstorm passed.

The decision made, Jodi regretfully turned away from the lake's north shore and, hand over hand, stroked through the water. She tired more quickly than she'd expected, and for a brief heartbeat she almost surrendered to helplessness and panic. Until she remembered that her teacher had promised her that *anyone* could survive in a pool—or, please God, in a lake without high waves—by floating on her back. Jodi kicked herself over and tried to relax, catching her breath and resting her aching muscles.

There. That felt better. But she couldn't lie there wasting time. The storm winds were already gusting across her drenched face and roughening the surface of the water.

Gritting her teeth against the agony in her legs, the pain in her arms and the draining of her determination, Jodi forced herself to swim. Until all of her fight washed away. *I can't do this anymore. I have to stop.*

Sad, ashamed, beaten, she let herself go . . . and touched bottom.

Not quite believing her luck, she bounced up and down on her toes, verifying the bottom's existence, until water sloshed into her nose and mouth. She didn't care how awful it tasted; she was so glad to be safe.

Looking heavenward, she murmured, "Thank you, God," then reined in her galloping delight when she saw the next disaster so near. Only a narrow strip of pale clear sky remained, high above the advancing wall of roiling turbulence. Separate black to charcoal gray clouds, ever-changing shapes within the huge mass, bore faint tinges of green, indicating the presence of hail.

Energized by the new dread, Jodi labored through the heavy water to the shore. Pebbles dug unmercifully into the soles of her bare feet. There were no rocks in the trail, but she sustained scratches and cuts from the tough blades of grass. Her frenzied flight up the hill, awkward because of the clinging weight of her wet clothes, took forever. Time after time she stumbled and fell, then compelled herself to get up and run again. Finally, the torture cramping her leg muscles became unendurable. Sobbing, she crumpled to the ground.

The wind grew ominously still. In the eerie silence Jodi heard her rapid, raspy breathing. Lightning flashed, blinding her. Thunder shook the earth. Goaded by sheer terror, Jodi struggled to her feet and staggered the rest of the way to the cabin. She lurched up the single rickety step and across the stoop, flung the door open, and collapsed on the floor.

Lying there, her every sinew and muscle crying out in agony, Jodi gasped for breath. Gradually, she became aware of the smells—dust, straw, mold, all the odors of human neglect and vermin habitation. She struggled to a sitting position, then looked around. The dull gray of daylight filtering through grimy windows at either end of the cabin revealed a plain wood table flanked by two ladder-back straight chairs and, against one wall, a crude bedside stand at the head of an Army cot, with a blob of orange almost hiding a jagged tear in the canvas. Everywhere, she saw empty beer cans and paper trash. Lightning from the doorway provided more illumination, and Jodi noticed the black, gaping fireplace, a welcome stack of dry logs standing beside it.

"Praise be," she said. A feeble smile split her damp, dirt-and-grass-covered face. With a fire she'd at least have some heat and light . . . and a less cheerless place to wait out the fear-filled hours of the stormy night. Jodi stood and walked waveringly across the floor, not permitting herself to think about what besides dust she might be stepping in. Swiping one hand along the mantel, she found plenty of grit and spiderwebs but no matchbox. She checked on the hearth bricks and amongst the tabletop litter, then in the nightstand drawer that slid open only after several minutes of her violent yanking and fierce mutterings.

No matches.

A hissing sigh escaped through her lips as Jodi ran a nervous palm over the top of her head and down the dripping cascade of hair that stuck to her shoulders and chest. Why would anyone have the forethought to leave dry firewood for some needy drop-in guest . . . and fail to leave matches?

"I think," Jodi announced to the gloomy, depressing room, "this has *not* been my day."

The active search for matches, followed by the anger-induced surge of blood through her veins when she found none, had briefly, slightly warmed her. But now the letdown, plus the strengthening attacks of cold wind through the still-open door, set Jodi to shaking uncontrollably. Dragging her feet, she rushed to the door and jerked it shut. Standing there in her soggy clothes, chilled to the bone, wishing for a miracle but certain none was forthcoming, Jodi once more looked all around the cabin.

In the colorless shadows the spot of orange on the rotting, useless cot caught her eye. She walked over and noticed it was a piece of thick cloth. Cautiously, she poked it, prepared to let it be if the movement dislodged any fuzzy, crawly, or scaly creatures. When nothing happened, Jodi dared to slowly, warily lift a corner of the fabric between her thumb and index finger.

The orange object turned out to be a University of Texas stadium blanket. Faded, crusty with dirt and grime, but a blanket to ward off some of the long night's chill.

"My miracle," Jodi whispered as she gave the blanket a couple of shakes.

Lightning lit the cabin's interior like a photographic flash. The immediate, loud crack and boom of thunder terrorized her. Weak-kneed and quivering, Jodi threw the musty-smelling blanket around her shoulders and fled to the nearest corner. She crouched there, tugging the stiff, scratchy wrap up over the back of her head and holding it in place with trembling hands clasped under her chin.

The rain arrived like hundreds of hammers pounding on the roof, bringing with it pitch-blackness. Lightning flashes briefly marked the locations of the small, high windows at either end of the cabin but afforded no comfort to Jodi. In her head she *was* the frightened, out-of-control girl who hid in Irish's dark closet to escape the scary thunderstorms.

The lonely darkness magnified the sounds. The battering of the rain. The wind howling and scraping tree limbs along the outside of the cabin. The gusts shrieking and moaning down the chimney. Raindrops slapping the window glass. The door rattling in its frame until Jodi thought surely it must give way.

Thinking she should prop a chair under the doorknob but afraid to forsake her nook of refuge even for a few moments, Jodi huddled inside the stadium blanket and worriedly stared at the vibrating door.

After a while it flew open. Wind and rain rushed in.

So did a man.

Jodi screamed.

Twenty

"What are you doing?" Becky demanded of Luke as she walked into the laundry/utility room.

"What does it look like?" Luke grumbled as he stepped into the yellow plastic trousers.

"But why?"

"Jodi's not back from the island."

"Are you sure?"

"I'm sure. The boat's still out."

"Oh, dear. There's a storm coming." At the first distant rumble of thunder, Becky had unplugged her computer and gone in search of her brother to ask what he'd like for dinner.

"I know. I'm going over there."

"Jodi's an intelligent woman. She won't start home in a storm. She'll wait it out in the old man's cabin." Worry crept into her voice. "If you go out on the lake now, you'll be in more danger than she is."

"You know she's scared of storms." Luke's mouth tightened into a stubborn line.

"But I'm sure she's more frightened of drowning. Like her parents did. She knows she'll be safer inside."

"Becky, I remember that last storm, under Umbrella Rock. And I'm responsible for her being over there on the island." At his sister's denying look, he added, "I practically pushed her into sketching."

191

"Today?" Becky was becoming more impatient with her headstrong brother by the minute.

"No. I tried to talk her out of going alone. She's not used to handling a boat. I've been a little worried about her all day."

"Luke, she's a grown woman, with a sensible head on her shoulders," Becky argued. "More sensible than yours, by the way, if you take off across the lake with a storm so close."

"Maybe." Unsuccessfully, he tried to grin. "But I can't get out of my non-sensible head that story you told me."

"What story?"

"About the murderer who escaped from prison in Huntsville and hid out on the island for a month. Till some local deputy remembered the convict was raised in Swallows Bluff and would have known about the island."

"Oh." Now Becky looked as upset as he. "You don't think—?"

"I think there are all kinds of crummy men hanging out in the Highland Lakes area these days. I think Jodi shouldn't have gone over there alone. And I think it's my job to make sure she's okay."

Becky sighed. "All right. What can I do to help?"

"Do you have any sleeping bags?"

"I have two." She paused. "One's a roomy *double.*" Seeing that he was in no mood for her teasing, she added, "You know how I hate tight, confining places."

For a millisecond, both recalled those first days in the psychiatric hospital when Becky had been kept in restraints—and then the endless but healing months when she had slept in that dim, ugly cell of a room.

"Right." Luke swallowed hard as he slid his green shirted arms into the sleeves of the knee-length yellow plastic coat.

"Your wading boots?" Becky asked as she started for the sleeping bags.

"In the boathouse. I'll put them on over my sneakers."

"Take a flashlight," she reminded him. "And the First Aid/Survival kit."

"Right." Luke tried not to think about Jodi, alone and in the dark, confronted by her own special terror.

He'd given her those darn art pens and that sketch pad. He'd challenged her, goaded her. And he'd let her go off by herself in that ancient boat.

A dozen times that day he'd thought about her, hoped she was enjoying herself. He'd also had a strong, unexplainable feeling that something was wrong. But then he'd told himself to be sensible. Jodi was an independent, capable woman. Nothing could happen to her on a tiny uninhabited, nameless island.

The lake crossing, although not pleasant, was fast. The roaring high-powered boat hit the crests of the wind-pushed waves with such force that the bouncing jarred Luke's backbone; but he refused to reduce his speed. As he neared the island, even in the deepening gloom he noticed Becky's boat was not where Jodi had been instructed to beach it. Had he and she literally been two boats that passed in the near-night? He hoped so. The alternative—that something bad had happened to her—made his heart falter, then race like a wild mustang fleeing a cowhand's lasso.

But wait. Maybe she'd beached the boat slightly off track, around a bend in the shoreline, in which case he wouldn't be able to see it from his vantage point. Yes, that must be the answer, Luke attempted to reassure himself as he dropped anchor, waded to the shore, and knotted the prow line around the base of the nearest big tree. After he returned to the boat for the sleeping bags and First Aid kit, he hurried up the steep path.

The rain began, coming down not in drops but in a solid curtain he pushed his way through. Without the flashlight, he could easily have missed the trail and lost a lot of time. Footing was slippery, and Luke barely managed to stay upright, but slowing down was unthinkable. Jodi needed someone. Jodi needed him.

As Luke clambered up the rotting cabin step, he caught the toe of one rubber wading boot on a loose plank.

Anxiously, he called Jodi's name. No answer. He tried again.

"Jodi! Are you in there?"

Silence again . . . except for the deafening wind and rain. She *had* to be here!

Luke dropped the sleeping bags on the stoop, grabbed the doorknob, and yanked the door open.

He was certain that never during the rest of his life would he hear any music as beautiful as Jodi's scream.

"It's okay, Jodi. It's me," he shouted above the bedlam of the elements. As he rushed across the chilly, musty-smelling room to the corner from which her outcry had come, he knew he was laughing with relief. He couldn't hear his laughter but he felt it rolling in his chest.

"I'm so glad you're here," he said as he knelt in front of her and laid down the flashlight. In its glow he met Jodi's panic-dazed stare. She didn't know him. He reached out and touched her—touched some sort of wool-like wrap around her shoulders—and she flinched as if he'd struck her.

"Jodi, don't be afraid. It's me. Luke." He hated having to yell. It probably augmented her fright.

"Luke?"

He barely heard her hope-filled question but felt the breath of it on his wet face.

"That's right. Luke." One finger lightly touched her cheek. This time she didn't wince, and he thought she momentarily leaned into his touch. "Wait here. I'll be right back."

He hurried outside, brought in the sleeping bags, and closed the door. With the wind and rain shut out, the noise level abated somewhat. Quickly, he removed his plastic rainsuit and wading boots, then returned to Jodi's side. He took her hands and slowly tugged her to her feet. Her wrap slithered to the floor, and he reached for her shoulders, thinking to give her a friendly hug.

"You're all wet," he said, surprised.

With the blanket gone, Jodi started to shiver violently. "And so c—cold."

Luke stooped, picked up the damp cloth, and re-draped it around her. As he did so, he pulled her against him for a moment and held her shaking body tight and close.

"Stay here. I'll build a fire," he said in her ear to be sure she understood.

"N—no matches," she told him.

"I brought some." He watched her sink with a sigh of relief to the dirty floor. Then he walked over to where he'd set the First Aid kit. After he located the tin box of matches, he busied himself with starting a fire in the fireplace, which took up most of the wall opposite the door. Since kindling was unavailable, Luke used a few of the old newspapers scattered about the room, stuffing them under logs taken from the stack near the hearth. He struck a match and jumped sharply when the crumpled papers flared. Stepping back, he waited the few moments until flames curled around the logs.

The storm was blowing itself out, so Luke could hear his footsteps when he crossed the floor to sit beside Jodi.

"Now," he said, "can you hear me okay?"

She nodded her head but refused to look at him. He had to lean closer to hear her faint reply.

"I'm s—sorry. I—I lost the boat." Part of her trembling was due to the temperature inside the cabin, and part of it resulted from her guilt over the loss of Becky's boat. But the major part of it, she knew, came from the fact that she was alone on a deserted island with the man she loved. A situation she wasn't ready for.

"Why didn't you just stay here in the dry?" Luke demanded harshly.

She wasn't ready for Luke's explosive anger, either.

Raising her eyes to his, she felt her own anger heating,

195

like iron turning red-hot in a blacksmith's forge. Jodi stiffened her shoulders and shifted a few inches away from him. "I had plenty of time to get home safely," she said, "but the boat sank."

"The boat *sank?*" Incredulous, Luke stared at her. When she had said she "lost" the boat, he'd thought she'd forgotten where she left it and had traipsed out in the rain to locate it.

"The boat sank," Jodi repeated crossly. "I'll pay for it."

"Forget the damn boat! I shouldn't have let you use it. It was a worthless piece of junk."

He sounded so frustrated, so furious with himself, that Jodi caught herself smiling a secret little smile. She suspected Luke's fierceness was generated by his concern. Her temper—and her heart—softened like butter under a July sun.

"It wasn't a collector's item?" she coyly teased.

"Don't be cute," Luke snapped.

"I'm okay now, Luke. Really." Her voice was lively and, amazingly, she did feel better. Because a caring Luke was here with her.

He had detected the amusement in Jodi's tone, which only served to refuel the fires of his outrage. "Your boat sank. I find you alone and scared, in the dark, soaking wet and half frozen. And you're *okay?* The *hell* you are!"

The wind and rain stopped as suddenly as they'd begun.

"You're yelling at me." In the eerie quiet, Jodi spoke softly.

"I'm *not—*" He lowered his voice to a normal volume, "yelling."

A log in the fireplace, burning through, tumbled onto the edge of the stone hearth with a shower of sparks. Quickly, Luke approached the fireplace and, after an interval of staring at the danger, squared his shoulders and kicked the two chunks of red-hot wood under the grate.

Having just endured her own phobic purgatory, Jodi sensed how much it had cost Luke to touch those fiery coals. Even with his shoe.

To distract him, she said, "I hope those are blankets." She gestured toward the bundles near the door. "The fire helps, but I'm still cold."

"*Not* okay, huh?" Luke grinned an I-told-you-so grin.

Jodi thought he'd never looked more lovable—and the stunning warmth of her desire briefly burned away her chill.

"They're sleeping bags," Luke informed her as he walked over, picked them up, and approached her corner. "But before you crawl into one, you have to take off all those wet, clammy clothes."

"All of them?" Jodi squeaked. There was no bathroom, not even the tiniest closet where she could undress in privacy. No robe to cover herself. No escape from Luke's curious eyes.

"I'll turn off the flashlight." He did, as humor rippled through his response. "And I won't peek. I promise."

"Go stand across the room," Jodi commanded with a nervous hitch in her voice. Then she sneezed.

Luke laughed uproariously, then, still chuckling, said, "Seems to me *you* better go stand across the room. By the fire."

"Don't be cute," she muttered. She sneezed again.

"I'm serious, Jodi." And the lack of levity in his tone conveyed his message. "Get out of those wet clothes and into one of the warm, dry sleeping bags."

"Yes, *sir!*" Jodi carried one of the bedrolls close to the hearth, where she laid it out flat. Then, her words loud with tension, she said, "Turn around."

"Yes, *ma'am.*" As he complied, Luke wondered how the scene would play in a movie—funny or suspenseful. He voted for the latter, because he himself was definitely tense and uneasy. Very shortly now, Jodi would be completely nude and less than ten feet away. It had been a year and a half since he'd been with a woman. Never with one as lovely, as evocative, as Jodi Turner. But he'd made her a promise and he intended to keep it.

The waiting stillness gave way to soft thuds as Jodi's sodden jeans and sweater plopped on the floor. Luke held his breath, then released it with a muted hiss when, with tantalizing whispers, her bra and panties joined the puddle of her outer clothes.

Another log chose the next instant to separate with a loud crack and a shower of sparks that lit the room with a brief glow.

Jodi squealed.

Afraid she'd been burned by the displaced log, Luke whirled around.

Jodi was all right. Far better than all right.

He was the one on fire. Hot blood flowed through his every vein, searing his wildly pumping heart. Entranced, mesmerized, he gazed at Jodi, her statuesque body painted ivory and gold by the flickering firelight. She was perfection, from the swell of her breasts to the triangle of black curls below her flat stomach. Although her astonished face, her slender arms, and her long, trim legs bore dirt-streaked traces of her struggle up the path, Luke saw only the clean, pure beauty of a glowing Venus.

It took the fraction of a second for his hungry eyes to gather and file the vision away in his memory-log.

It took slightly longer than that fraction of a second for Jodi to spin and face the fire. She shrieked, "You promised!"

"You screamed," Luke replied, still unable to breathe normally. "I thought you'd been burned by the log."

Jodi could tell from the direction of his voice that he was once again facing away from her.

"Well, I wasn't," she announced gruffly. "I'm okay."

"I could see that," he muttered, and knew immediately he'd said the wrong thing. Well, *this* time he refused to apologize. He was tired of apologizing, tired of running from the emotions Jodi compelled him to confront. Luke noisily cleared his throat and said, "You are so beautiful."

Jodi offered no reply. Luke heard the *zzzzz* of the sleeping bag zipper, a soft rustling as she crawled inside, and then the closing zipper accompanied by Jodi's faint, blissful sigh.

It was safe for him to turn around. He did, and said in a firm voice, "You *are* beautiful," as if he expected her to argue with him.

Jodi didn't disappoint him.

For the past few minutes, her feelings had ricocheted from mortification and anger that he had broken his promise, to gladness that he'd worried lest the broken log had harmed her, and back to embarrassment because he'd stared at her nakedness. And now he had the egotistical male effrontery to sound pleased about his gawking.

The man was insufferable.

Cozy and dry at last, Jodi felt her strength, like the chill, fast draining out of her weary joints and muscles. If she was going to dredge up the proverbial last word in this verbal fray, it had to be done quickly—before she surrendered to the foolish longing to believe what he'd said about her being beautiful. He didn't believe that; he'd said it merely to ease his conscience. Well, his ploy wasn't going to work, for she remembered another time . . .

"You said I was *skinny!*"

Luke heard the softly spoken accusation . . . and smiled. Jodi was one hell of a woman. Exhausted by the dangers and terrors she'd encountered, she still had the gumption to fight back.

Slowly, he turned and walked to the sleeping bag where she lay. Squatting down, prepared to apologize one more time, he looked down at her pale, lovely face . . . and smiled again.

Jodi was fast asleep.

Twice during the night Jodi awoke when Luke stirred the fire and added fresh logs. Silently, sleepily, she watched him shift her clothes around on the backs of the two chairs placed directly in front of the fireplace. Before he returned to his sleeping bag alongside hers, she closed her eyes and succumbed to the lure of more slumber.

"Jodi. Wake up."

She lifted her heavy eyelids. Luke, towering six-feet-plus above her, brought to mind Paul Bunyan or, perhaps because of those incredible green eyes, the Jolly Green Giant. She smiled a sleepy smile. Luke's whisker-shadowed jaw, his uncombed curly hair, his soiled and wrinkled green shirt, made him appear much more human than the food-hawking leviathan.

Luke saw her smile. "You're awake. Good. We should get going. Becky will be worried."

"All right." Jodi reached for her sleeping bag zipper. She started to throw off the cover, then remembered her state of undress. She blushed and gazed questioningly up at Luke. *What do I do now?*

"I'm going out to find some firewood to replace what we used last night," he told her. "Your clothes are almost dry."

As soon as Luke closed the door, she slid stiffly out of her warm bed. "Ow!" The bottoms of her feet were sore. Gritting her teeth at each step, she moved the chairs aside for space to dress as close to the dying fire as possible. She discovered her pale blue lingerie was dry. So were the sweater and jeans except for the slightly damp seams and waistband. Grimacing as she dressed, placing her full weight on first one foot and then the other, she devoutly wished she hadn't assigned her shoes to a watery grave. Jodi shuddered as those awful minutes in the sinking boat freshened in her memory. Determined not to let the recollections mar the knowledge that she was safe, alive, she rolled up her sleeping bag. Then she pulled one of the chairs to the edge of the hearth and sat down, propping her feet on her heels in the hope that heat would ease her throbbing soles.

Luke found her in that position when he returned with an armload of wet logs. Quickly, Jodi stood and shoved her chair aside to make room for him to unload his burden.

"Thanks," he muttered.

"Welcome."

He began to put on the yellow plastic pants and coat.

"Is it still raining?" Jodi plaintively asked.

"No, but it's easier to wear them than carry them, with the sleeping bags and First Aid kit."

"Oh." Arguing was no longer on her morning agenda. She simply wanted to go home—and she dreaded the trip down the trail.

Before Luke donned the wading boots, Jodi asked, "May I wear those?"

"Huh?" Had all the strain of yesterday made her a little crazy?

Jodi noted the amazement brushing his features. Caustically, she explained. "Floppy rubber boots are better than nothing."

Luke glanced at her bare feet and groaned. "I didn't realize. How could I have been so blind?" Because last night he hadn't been looking at her *feet*. Mentally writhing under Jodi's readable, accusing gaze, he commanded, "Sit." He motioned to one of the chairs.

"Bow-wow," she muttered as she obeyed.

"Don't be cute," he responded.

All of a sudden they were both heartily laughing, venting the pressures of the past few hours.

Jodi knuckled the tears of laughter out of her eyes while Luke examined her feet.

"Yipes!" The one-word diagnosis substituted for a shelf of medical tomes. "Cuts and scrapes and bruises already turning blue." He raised his compassionate eyes to hers. "Hurts like the devil, I bet."

"Then let me borrow your boots."

As it turned out, Luke suggested a better solution. He wore the boots *sans* thick cushion-sole socks and sneakers, which he tenderly placed on Jodi's sensitive feet.

They negotiated the tedious downhill journey without conversation and without incident. Reaching the beach a few steps ahead of Jodi, Luke stopped and asked, "What's this?"

Jodi looked where he pointed. Strewn over a small area of the gravel she saw the tiny, near-white wilted flowers.

"Hannah's violets," she said.

"Who's Hannah?"

Briefly, Jodi told of her meeting with the teenager. "She wouldn't have just thrown away her Gra'ma's birthday violets." Apprehensively, she inquired, "You didn't see them yesterday?"

"No, but it was almost dark, and I was in a hurry."

It had been the same for her.

Jodi caught the surprise, the wariness on Luke's face as he looked over her shoulder. She whirled—and immediately noticed the single red sneaker lying at the edge of the path. Some of the tall weeds and grass had been disturbed, mashed down as though something had been dragged over them.

"Oh, no!" she whispered.

Moving rapidly even in Luke's oversize shoes, she followed the streak of flattened vegetation.

"Stop!" Luke called out as he followed her. "Wait for me!"

Jodi stopped only when she reached what she feared, what all her instincts had warned her she would find.

Hannah. Limp, rain-soaked, grotesquely dead. Wearing one red sneaker.

Twenty-one

All the way across the lake, Jodi kept remembering Hannah's sweet face, her friendly manner, her eagerness to please her grandmother. The bedridden grandmother who on her birthday would be informed of Hannah's tragic death. Hannah's murder, for it obviously was no accident. Huddled inside Luke's yellow plastic coat, Jodi furtively brushed at the tears in her eyes. Luke would consider her too sentimental, bawling over someone with whom she'd shared less than fifteen minutes. Or maybe not. It was Luke who had gently, almost reverently, covered Hannah with one of the sleeping bags.

Sad himself, Luke watched Jodi's efforts to hide her sorrow and wondered what he could say to cheer her. The discovery of the girl's body, the gruesome scene immediately confirming foul play, would have been traumatic even if Jodi hadn't met and liked the victim. And ahead loomed their dealing with the authorities, which Luke knew was bound to revive Jodi's memories of her parents' and sister's deaths.

Luke guided the boat under the boathouse roof and into the slip, stepped out, then offered a steadying hand to Jodi as she disembarked.

"Are you both all right?" Becky called as she hurried along the pier. "Why didn't you bring both boats?"

"The fishing boat sank," Luke answered quickly. "Jodi

had to"—he made a valiant attempt at humor—"abandon ship."

"Oh, my goodness! You must have been scared half to death." Reaching them, Becky gave Jodi a hug.

"Scared three-quarters to death was more like it." Jodi decided to use the protection of Luke's levity. "But I guess the lake monsters were even more frightened of me, because they let me swim safely back to the island." She paused and grew serious. "I'm sorry about your boat. I'm afraid pulling it across the beach knocked a hole in it."

"There aren't any rocks there big enough or sharp enough to do that," Luke pointed out. "It must have sprung a leak where one of the ribs was caulked."

"No. It had a hole in the *bottom*. The water came in like a little whirlpool." Jodi saw the strangest look, both pensive and fierce, flash across Luke's face, and he wouldn't meet her eyes.

"Yuk," Becky responded, shivering her shoulders in sympathy. "But don't worry about the boat. It came with the house, or I'd never have owned such an old one." She glanced at her brother. "Is there something else you haven't told me?" Both boaters looked well, although tired and disheveled, and in Jodi's case oddly attired in oversize shoes; but Becky sensed something was wrong.

"There's been a murder on the island," Luke said. Seeing Becky's alarm, he hastened to reassure her. "Neither of us was involved. We found a young girl's body this morning as we were leaving. I have to call the sheriff's office right away."

While the trio walked across the upsloping lawn to Becky's house, Luke explained to her about Jodi's brief encounter with the victim and how the violets on the beach and the red sneaker had led them to their grisly discovery.

After Luke phoned the sheriff, Jodi went to her cabin to shower and put on clean clothes . . . and her own shoes. When she returned to Becky's, for that was where the authorities would come, she found breakfast waiting. For once she was delighted with bacon, scrambled eggs, and hot buttered biscuits instead of her customary bowl of cereal.

The three ate in hurried silence, each dreading for a different reason the arrival of the Burnet County sheriff. Becky hoped to keep hidden her former identity; Jodi hated the prospect of retelling what she saw and felt on the island; Luke shrank from putting into words his theory regarding the damage to the fishing boat.

Sheriff Sutton introduced himself and said, "I sent a couple of deputies over to the island, but I wanted to talk to you myself." Fiftyish, with a slight paunch, sun-streaked hair, and leather-tough skin, he fit Jodi's mental picture of a typical rancher—until she saw his eyes. His were the angry, steel-hard eyes of a man who'd seen the gut-wrenching aftermath of every crime imaginable and was driven by a pitiless resolve to bring each wrongdoer to justice.

He politely declined Becky's offer of coffee and chose the chair that afforded him a straight-on view of his witnesses. People's faces, especially in times of stress, oftentimes revealed unstated information.

"Now," he said, "tell me what happened."

Luke did the talking. It was only right, Jodi thought, since this was his home and his boat that had been lost. The sheriff listened intently as Luke told how Jodi had gone to the island to sketch, how he went to check on her, how they spent the stormy night in the cabin, how they found Hannah's body. Then he turned to Jodi.

"Ma'am, Ms. Turner, you recognized the victim?"

"We spoke for a few minutes yesterday morning. She told me her name was Hannah. Not her last name."

"Could she have been there to meet some young man?"

"I'm sure not, Sheriff. She said she was fourteen. She looked younger, and she spoke so openly and naturally about hunting white violets for her grandmother's birthday." Jodi paused when her voice cracked. "The moment I saw the wilted flowers lying beside the path right at the edge of the gravel, I feared something was wrong. And then Luke—Mr.

Prentiss—pointed out the red sneaker, and I knew." Recalling the horrifying sight of Hannah's body, her frail arms and legs twisted at crazy angles like those of a ragdoll thrown down in a little girl's fit of temper, Jodi looked away from the sheriff to hide the moisture rising in her eyes.

The sheriff saw it, and he asked his next question in a less authoritative tone. "Did . . . er . . . Hannah say how she got on the island?"

"Yes, sir. In her mother's boat—with her mother's permission, by the way." She'd hate for the sheriff to think ill of that friendly, freckle-faced child. "I heard her . . ." Jodi stopped and turned as white as tissue paper.

The sheriff waited patiently for her to speak again, and after a couple of deep, restorative breaths, she did.

"I was going to say I heard her boat leave. But she didn't leave, did she?" Jodi shuddered as she watched the mounting interest in the sheriff's eyes, and out of the corner of her own she caught the quick jerk of Luke's head as he turned toward her.

"You heard a boat?" Luke asked. He sounded worried. And shouldn't that have been the sheriff's question?

"Yes, I did." Jodi threw Luke a scathing look. Being interrogated by one man was sufficient. "After Hannah left, I ate lunch. Then I dozed off. I don't know for how long. I didn't check my watch, but it couldn't have been much more than a half-hour. I woke up when I heard a boat motor. I supposed it was Hannah, heading home. She said her mother went to work at two and they didn't like for her grandmother to be alone."

"And you didn't see or hear anything or anyone else?" the sheriff prompted.

"No, sir. Nothing but the storm—and then Luke when he came."

"Fine." For the first time since declining the coffee, he turned to Becky. "Ms. Prentiss, would you mind if I went down to the boathouse and took a look at both of your boats?" He stood and started toward the door.

206

"Not at all, Sheriff," Becky replied, "but there's only one boat left."

"I forgot to tell you." Luke spoke hurriedly when the sheriff's eyebrows jumped up, wrinkling his sun-bronzed forehead. "The fishing boat sank. The one Jodi took over to the island." He had risen and was practically herding the sheriff toward the terrazzo vestibule.

"You forgot?" The older man's tone clearly conveyed his doubt.

"Can we talk about this outside?" Luke's murmured-aside request received a slight, curious nod. Louder, for the benefit of the two women still seated in the living room, Luke volunteered, "I'll walk around the house and down to the boathouse with you."

Once outside the door, Sheriff Sutton halted under the arcade. His eyes piercing and his mouth tight, he turned to Luke and said, "All right, Prentiss. What's this about a boat sinking?"

"Jodi—Ms. Turner—left the island yesterday in plenty of time to get home before the storm. But she'd gone only a short distance when the boat started to fill. After a few minutes she stopped and saw the water swirling in through a hole in the bottom. Like a whirlpool, she said. She thought she'd damaged the boat when she pulled it up onto or off of the beach."

"Not possible. That beach is all gravel. No big rocks, no sharp stones."

"Right." Dismay and anger vied for primary place in that single curt word.

"You think . . ." The sheriff stopped. Watching Luke's scowl, he thought he knew what Luke would say. Careful and fair lawman that he was, he allowed Luke to present his idea. Also, he wanted to be certain they theorized along the same logic.

"I think someone put a hole in Jodi's boat. It was old but perfectly shipshape, or I'd never have let her use it."

"Obviously." Sheriff Sutton smiled faintly at the transparency of the other man's feelings. "And you think maybe the girl—Hannah—saw someone do whatever he did to the boat . . . and got herself killed for being at the wrong place at the wrong time."

"Could be. The boat Jodi heard wasn't Hannah's, so someone else was boating close to the island early yesterday afternoon. Maybe fishing. Maybe not."

"Hmmm. Next question: Who would want to harm Ms. Turner?"

Luke tensed and avoided the lawman's gimlet gaze. "You'd have to ask Jodi about that."

"I will. Meantime, I'll check to see what my deputies find on the island. And what the coroner has to say."

"And raise the boat?" Luke suggested with respectful, caution. "Shouldn't be hard to locate. Jodi says it went down less than one third the distance from the island straight across to the mainland."

"I'm the sheriff, and I'll make that decision," the lawman reminded him.

"Right." Luke capitulated with a shrug he hoped came off as nonchalant. But he didn't feel the least bit nonchalant. Jodi could have perished out there in that lake, and reluctant as he was to admit it, the loss would have left a hole in his life much larger than any hole the authorities would discover in Becky's "ancient one."

As soon as the sheriff drove away, Jodi returned to her cabin, built a fire, kicked off her shoes, and stretched out on the bed. The telephone roused her, but she felt too lazy and groggy to move. Peering at her watch with sleep-hazed eyes, she saw it was 4:57. Had she slept that long? Then her brain clicked in, and she remembered her watch had drowned even if she hadn't—at 4:57 P.M. yesterday.

Groaning, Jodi left the soft comfort of her bed and half staggered to the persistently ringing phone. Irritated, she lifted the receiver and hoarsely said, "Hello?"

"It's Becky. Were you asleep?"

"Yes, but I needed to get up." The desk clock registered 6:10, so she'd been asleep even longer than she thought. Justifiably, she excused herself, because the past twenty-four hours had been traumatic and energy draining.

"The sheriff is here again and wants to speak with you and Luke."

"I'm on my way." The laid-back vacationing Jodi metamorphosed into the harried woman with an urgent purpose. Eager to complete her business with the law, she ran a comb through her long dark hair, put on makeup and shoes, and hurried next door.

The Prentiss living room reeked of tension, and the solemn faces of those waiting for her magnified her alarm.

"Good evening, Ms. Turner," the sheriff said as Jodi settled on the sofa between Luke and Becky.

"Sheriff." Jodi threw Luke an anxious, questioning glance. He ignored her, but she felt him shift nervously on the seat beside her.

"First of all," Sheriff Sutton began, "we've identified the victim as Hannah Lowry. Her widowed mother's a waitress at the Lakeshore Diner. According to the coroner, the girl was killed by the blow of a blunt instrument to the head. She was not sexually assaulted."

"Thank heaven," Jodi whispered, and Becky reached over to squeeze her hand in agreeing relief. At least the mother and grandmother wouldn't have to live with that heartrending knowledge.

The sheriff continued. "We located her boat on the other side of the island. We also raised Ms. Prentiss's boat"—both surprised women gasped in unison—"and we did discover a hole about three inches square in the bottom under the bow seat, a spot that would have been accessible while the boat was pulled up on the beach. I figure, after Ms. Turner left the shore, her speed, together with the weight of the motor, caused the boat to fill quite rapidly."

"You said a square hole." Recognizing the significance of that fact, Becky squeezed Jodi's hand even tighter.

"Yes, ma'am. Cut with some kind of a saw. We could see the fresh sawtooth marks on the raw wood." Then he looked straight at Jodi, who sat stiff and still and blankly staring. His tone softened. "I'm sorry, Ms. Turner, but someone deliberately damaged your boat."

"No," Jodi whispered. "No, no, no." The sheriff was wrong. Her fingernails carved fiery red crescents in Becky's palm.

"Do you have any idea who might want to harm you?" the sheriff queried softly.

Another whisper: "No." Then louder, *"No!"* The possibility that someone—anyone—hated her enough to scuttle her boat nauseated her.

"Some revengeful client, perhaps?" After a beat and an indignant gasp from Jodi, he explained. "Ms. Prentiss told me about your job at Sunbelt Images. You must know a lot of secrets."

At his insinuation, Jodi's self-defense kicked in. And a semblance of control. "I would never use any of that information, and my clients trust me."

"All right. Then how about a vindictive ex-lover?"

"I don't *have* any ex-lovers!" Jodi snapped.

Luke permitted himself a moment to savor the import of Jodi's spunky denial. At least, unlike Corinne, Jodi didn't use sex as a career bargaining chip.

Surprisingly, the sheriff smiled. "A beautiful woman like you? No sweetheart, no fiancé, no . . . ah . . . I believe 'significant other' is the current term?"

Jodi stiffened again. "I . . . had a husband. We're divorced."

"Was it a friendly divorce?"

Luke felt Jodi flinch. He made a move to clasp her hand, the one not holding Becky's, but he thought better of it. His sympathetic touch might weaken Jodi, and she needed all

210

the inner strength she could muster to sustain her through the rest of the interrogation.

Sheriff Sutton's keen trained eyes noticed Jodi's negative reaction to his query. He also watched Luke's almost unobtrusive, uncompleted gesture of . . . Support? Warning? Relentlessly, he pushed his advantage. "Ms. Turner, why did you divorce your husband?"

Engrossed in disturbing memories of her marriage, Jodi failed to wonder how the sheriff knew she instead of Quentin had instigated the divorce.

"Because he was unfaithful. And because"—she inhaled deeply—"he was physically abusive."

This time Becky did the hand squeezing.

"I see." The sheriff, who despised battering males, managed to maintain an outward calm. "Have you seen him recently? Had any communication with him?"

Jodi understood the man was doing his job, but illogically, she felt as if she were parading naked in front of him.

"He's been asking me to take him on as a client again."

"And you refused?"

"Of course."

The sheriff removed a small notebook and pen from his uniform shirt pocket. "His name?"

"Quentin Turner."

"The rock-and-roll singer." He recognized the name because he'd moonlighted as a security guard at one of the man's god-awful concerts. "I could check for myself, but do you by any chance have his address?"

"No, but I believe he lives in a condo on the opposite shore of the lake." She heard Luke's hissing intake of air.

"That close." The lawman frowned.

Suddenly, Jodi understood where this was leading. "Oh, no, Sheriff. Quentin didn't put that hole in Becky's boat. He wants me alive. To create a publicity campaign that will boost his sagging popularity."

"You told me you refused. Didn't that make him mad?"

"Yes, but he'd never—"

"He threatened to kill you, Jodi. I heard him." Without forethought, Luke had interrupted Jodi's defense of her ex-husband. At the sheriff's raised eyebrows, Luke added, "When he shouted at you over the phone."

The room vibrated with shock and tension and fury. The fury emanated from Jodi.

"That's *my* business!" She jerked the upper portion of her body around to confront Luke. Her blue eyes, almost black with anger, stood out in her colorless face like two ink spots on a sheet of white paper.

"And mine." Sheriff Sutton's stern, quiet voice sounded an attention-getting contrast to Jodi's outburst of temper.

Ignoring the lawman's remark and presence, Jodi's irate stare never left Luke's stubborn face. "If Quentin wanted to . . . kill me, he'd need to *see* me die. He would have marched up the hill to the old man's cabin and tormented me before he—before he— Quentin got his kicks out of watching me cry and grovel." Jodi's spurt of anger had depleted her energy. She finished so softly, so hesitantly, that the others had to strain to hear. "He'd never be satisfied with putting a hole in my boat and—and leaving."

Her eyes, awash with tears of humiliation and shame, looked from Luke to Becky to the sheriff, pleading with each in turn to let the matter drop. The Prentiss siblings, feeling and sharing her distress, were willing to comply, but not the man whose motivation was to solve a terrible murder.

"He would," Sheriff Sutton insisted, "if he wanted your death to look like an accident. That way, his name would never come up. And his plan probably would have worked, too, except for the girl and the fact that you were able to swim to safety. I think Hannah Lowry happened to see him on the island and therefore could have identified him. She may even have witnessed him sabotaging your boat. So he dragged her body 'way off the path into the underbrush, where she might not have been discovered for days; and by then, he hoped, no one would have connected the killing of a local . . . ah . . . nobody—in the media's view—with the accidental drowning of a vacationing well-known Austin businesswoman."

Jodi, whose analytical mind considered the sheriff's scenario plausible, still decried the conclusion he'd reached. In all fairness, despite her antipathy toward Quentin, she felt compelled, obligated to voice her opinion.

"I still don't think Quentin would do all that—plan for me to drown, kill Hannah—just because I won't help rebuild his career. Ending a bad situation with one quick act of violence is not his style." She paused and took a shaky breath. "He'd stretch it out. His retaliation would much more likely involve harassment—spreading my worry, my fear, over weeks . . . months. Like the watcher."

The instant the last three words passed her lips, Jodi knew, as if she'd swatted a hornet's nest, she'd stirred up a whole swarm of new cross-examinations. They flew at her simultaneously, buzzing in her ears, barely distinguishable, all stinging her emotional privacy.

"What watcher?" the sheriff wanted to know.

"Someone's been watching you?" Becky asked worriedly.

"What the hell!" Luke, completely blown away, reverted back to the angry man of few words.

"Please," Jodi said. "I don't *know* anybody has been watching me. It's just a feeling I've had. Like the feeling you get sometimes in a crowd, and you turn around and see someone you know staring at you. Except when I looked, there was no one there."

"Ms. Turner, this could be important. When did it happen? More than once? And where were you at the time?"

"All right, Sheriff, I'll tell you," Jodi conceded with a sigh, "but you'll think I'm certifiable."

"Intuition, gut instinct, paranormal factors, all have been known to aid in crime solving." The sheriff smiled encouragingly at Jodi. "I've learned never to discount a person's 'feeling, as you call it."

So, with her three companions digesting every unprovable word, Jodi, with bemused self-disdain, explained about her watcher, concluding with, "Right now I don't feel watched. I just feel foolish."

Becky mumbled little disagreeing sounds.

Luke's silence was undecipherable.

The lawman dourly admonished, "Don't. What you've told me is one more point in Quentin Turner's disfavor. I'll have him brought in for questioning. May be able to charge him with suspicion of murder."

"Oh, no! Please, Sheriff, no!"

Seeing the stark terror on Jodi's face, everyone in the room understood she hadn't leaped to her ex-husband's defense.

"I have to." The sheriff spoke sympathetically but with an undertone of determination. He offered Jodi slight comfort when he promised, "But he won't bother you again, Ms. Turner, whatever my investigation discloses."

"Thank you," Jodi murmured, her eyes still reflecting the remembered pain and Quentin's wild-eyed, face-contorting rage. "Can you . . . will you let me know what happens?"

"Sure. And I'd best be going."

After Luke excused himself to answer the phone, Becky and Jodi accompanied the sheriff outside. A man, tall and fair and wearing fancy western duds, leaned against the fender of a black Cadillac parked on the shoulder of the road. He approached them while they walked to the Sheriff Department van.

"Hello, Troy." Jodi greeted him with a smile, wondering offhandedly why he was there.

"Hi, Jodi. At the Millers' store, everyone was talking about the little girl's . . . uh . . . murder and the . . . uh . . . damaged boat the deputies found. I stopped at your place, but you weren't home. Then I noticed the county car and figured you must be over here. I hope it's okay that I . . . uh . . . waited outside to be sure you're all right."

"Of course it is," Jodi told him. Designating him an old friend, she introduced Troy to Becky and the sheriff.

Becky recognized the name at once. "You're the Troy

Morrell who won the Country Music Association awards last year."

"Yes, ma'am," he answered proudly. "Jodi, as they say, knew me 'way back when."

"Then perhaps you know her ex-husband." The sheriff's remark sounded casual enough, but Troy readily picked up on Jodi's sudden nervousness.

"He and Jodi were divorced before I met Jodi, so no, I don't know Quentin personally. But I do know he's a lush and a wife-beater."

"Troy was engaged to my sister." Jodi hastily added "for a while," in the desperate hope that Annie's demise wouldn't become a topic of conversation. She'd had all the talk about death and dying she could handle for one day.

Troy, bless him, allowed the partially true explanation to stand. Then he upset her anew by expressing her concern along a different tack. "Is Quentin threatening you again?"

Before Jodi could reply, the sheriff, alert and curious, interceded. "You've heard him threaten Ms. Turner?"

"No, sir, but Annie . . . uh . . . Jodi's sister told me Quentin made several nasty threats at the time of the divorce. I just thought, since you brought up Quentin's name . . ." Troy stopped, turning to Jodi as shock registered on his face. "Do you think Quentin is responsible for what happened to you and . . . uh . . . that girl on the island?"

"I don't know," Jodi answered, her torn emotions evident in her voice and in her eyes. She heard Luke's footsteps on the driveway behind her. "Sheriff Sutton thinks it's possible. I don't know, but *someone* sawed a hole in Becky's boat so it would sink."

"And Quentin knows you can't swim."

Twenty-two

Troy's statement created a tableau of paralyzed silence equal to that generated by the old television commercial, "My broker is E.F. Hutton, and E.F. Hutton says . . ." The frozen hush lasted a full ten seconds—until Jodi gasped, "Oh, God! I forgot about that!"

Then the sheriff sufficiently recovered from astonishment to demand, "What's this about Ms. Turner not being able to swim?"

Troubled by the overall reaction to his remark, Troy skittishly explained. "Everyone who knows Jodi or has ever known her knows she's absolutely terrified of the water. I guess because her folks drowned. Anyhow, she never learned to swim."

Luke stepped around Jodi, grabbing her arm as he did so and turning her to face him. His eyes blazed with hot green anger. "Why the hell didn't you tell me?" Some of his rage thrust inward at himself, for sending her out in that boat after making a false and dangerous assumption that she could swim.

Jodi, her eyes shooting sparks of their own, jerked loose from Luke's painful grip. "I *can* swim! Or did you think some big good-fairy catfish let me ride on his back from the boat to the island?"

Luke's fury fizzled as though Jodi had doused it with a bucket of chipped ice. "I didn't think," he told her with a guilty look that carried an underlying concern, emphasized by his next words, "I just reacted."

"Hah!" Jodi's indignant snort clarified her opinion on his constant "reacting."

Observing and listening to the dialogue with amusement, Sheriff Sutton decreed the propitious moment had arrived for his intercession. "Ms. Turner, when did you learn to swim?"

"Last winter." Jodi answered the sheriff but still fixed her intense gaze on Luke.

"Who knows you can swim?"

"The five of us standing here. And Dr. Dennis O'Meara, my godfather."

"Not your ex-husband."

"No. Oh, I forgot. The swimming coach at the Northside Fitness Club in Austin knows."

"So your swimming coach obviously wouldn't expect you to drown if your boat sank." Not very subtly, the lawman had made his frightening point.

Jodi was compelled to accept the terrifying truth: Quentin wanted her dead. He hated her *that* much. She'd denied him another rising career. She'd defeated his every attempt to regain control over her. The only recourse left to a vindictive, ruthless man like Quentin was the total obliteration of his subjugator.

Rocked by the knowledge that someone she'd once cared for despised her enough to plan her "accidental" drowning, Jodi felt cold frissons of sheer horror crawl along her spine. To be sure she didn't scream, she covered her mouth with trembling hands.

Above her cupped hands, her fear-glazed eyes, dark as a midnight starless sky, met Luke's green ones, whose sharing hurt almost did her in. Jodi smothered a sob and turned her frantic, pleading eyes on the sheriff's grim visage.

"I'll bring him in for questioning," he told her.

This time Jodi offered no protest, only a muffled "Thank you."

After brief farewell nods at the others, Sheriff Sutton climbed in the van and drove away.

Another silence ensued—not of surprise and shock, like the earlier one, but an uneasy, hesitant silence, with Luke, Becky, and Troy waiting for one or the other to speak first. As for Jodi, she stood motionless except for intermittent shudders and shallow breaths.

Finally, Troy lightly touched Jodi's arm to capture her attention. "You need a break from all this. Let's drive into town for *fajitas* and margaritas."

Jodi emphatically shook her head, then vainly tried to smile to remove any sting from her refusal.

"I won't keep you out late, I promise," Troy insisted.

"It's already dinnertime," Jodi pointed out, "and the restaurant's two hours from here."

"Not the way I drive." Troy favored her with one of his impish boy-next-door grins that Annie had loved.

Jodi wished she weren't too upset, too drained, to accept his invitation. Any other evening, she would have enjoyed his company.

"Speaking of dinner, Mr. Morrell, why don't you join us?" Becky suggested. "I made a big pan of lasagna before the sheriff came and I've been keeping it warm." She smiled in Jodi's direction. "I'd already planned for Jodi to eat with us."

"I really should go home," Jodi said. She still hadn't broken entirely free of the cage of disappointment and fear the sheriff's interrogation had built around her.

"Nonsense," Becky argued. "It's all settled. Lasagna for four coming up."

She and Jodi headed for the arcade, illuminated by four time-switch-activated Spanish lanterns along the white stucco wall.

A startled look flitted across Troy's face when his proffered hand was shaken by Luke's scarred one. "I'm Troy Morrell, and I've been a fan of *Only in Texas,* and of yours, for a long time." He paused, then decided not to ignore the obvious. "I'm sorry about your hand. I'd wondered why you weren't with the band anymore."

"Now you know," Luke replied brusquely.

Who was this man to show up out of the blue and assume Jodi would dash off with him for a night on the town? Luke was aware that Troy Morrell was the top country-western singer/composer, because Becky had watched the awards show while he'd found it necessary to leave the house and drive around in a near-freezing rain to avoid the television screen. But what place did Troy Morrell hold or fill in Jodi's life? They shared a friendship; that much was apparent. What else they might have shared, Luke did not care to think about as he silently preceded the man up the driveway.

After welcoming her guests inside the house, Becky drafted Luke to help make the salad and set the table. Disgruntled, he listened to the laughter and cheerful sounds coming from the living room. From time to time, when he passed the doorway, he saw Troy reach out and touch Jodi— on the hand, on the arm, on the cheek—and he grumbled under his breath.

At first Jodi felt uncomfortable when Troy touched her. But soon she understood the touches were casual, born of a reflexive habit, and she relaxed. The pair of friends spoke of Troy's soon-to-be-released album, of Jodi's work and the job-stress malaise that had brought about her vacation. With a surprisingly merry nostalgia they even shared a few memories of Annie.

"Which reminds me," Jodi said. "Do you ever see Ginger?"

"Not since . . . uh . . . Annie . . . uh . . . Why do you ask?"

"I just wondered." Jodi looked pensive, a little sad. "I haven't seen her, either, and she was my sister's best friend in the whole world, for heaven's sake. Lately, I've been feeling bad about cutting myself off from the people who knew and loved Annie. I'm at the point now where I think it would be good for us—certainly for me and possibly for Ginger—to have a long talk."

"Maybe not. Has *she* contacted *you?*" Troy reached out and softly patted her cheek as though warning her against seeking out a hurtful, unneeded rejection.

"She sent me the dearest note and a thank-you bouquet after I had Annie's guitars boxed and shipped to her." Jodi sighed regretfully. "I should have delivered them myself."

"You were too upset," Troy commiserated. "I'm sure Ginger understood."

"Maybe. But I'm going to call her as soon as I get back to my cabin and see if we can meet for lunch tomorrow. I need to go into the city anyway—for some different clothes and for my other watch. The one I brought with me wasn't . . . lake-proof." Remembering her helplessness as the deep, murky water closed over her when she'd nearly given up, Jodi jerkily picked at the shiny fabric on the chair arm.

Troy seized and steadied her hand just as Becky summoned them to dinner.

By the time the delicious meal was enjoyed and each of the diners had taken his or her dishes to the kitchen, rinsed them, and stacked them in the dishwasher, the four were on a first-name basis. Almost. Luke avoided calling the other man Troy; in fact, he avoided speaking to him at all if possible. He'd watched the easy congeniality between Troy and Jodi . . . and glowered at his plate whenever Jodi happened to catch his eye.

Once in the living room, the usual incidental topics comprised the conversation, until one of the those sudden lulls occurred that make some people fidget. Becky, who up till then had handled all the social amenities by herself because Luke sat sullen and withdrawn in one corner, fidgeted.

Abruptly, too abruptly, she addressed her male guest.

"Troy, would you play and sing your award-winning song for us?"

Jodi sensed the immediate throbbing, pulsating tension around her. What had possessed Becky to make such a request? Luke started to stand, as if to leave the room, then sat back down, every muscle taut and probably every nerve end twanging. Jodi could only guess what the decision to stay had cost him.

Troy's agitation showed in his eyes as, filled with doubt, they met Jodi's. *What do I do?* he seemed to be asking her. She commended his sensitivity to Luke's predicament but had no answer for him.

While Jodi's mind floundered around like a flapping fish out of the net, Becky realized what her hasty, thoughtless effort to play the gracious hostess had engendered. She blushed, directed an I'm-sorry glance in her brother's direction, and bravely slogged through the muddy mess she'd created. "I'm sure we'd all like to hear it. I must confess your work isn't familiar to me. We . . . uh . . . haven't had much music in this house recently." She pulled in a hitching breath. Was her nervous chattering helping the situation? Oh, Lord. If she got through this night without Luke happily slitting her throat . . ." Please, Troy. I'd like to hear it." *Even if Luke wouldn't,* her embarrassed tone implied.

Although exasperated with Becky, Jodi jumped in to assist her discombobulated friend. She smiled encouragingly at Troy. "I've only heard your song a couple of times myself, so I'd appreciate a personal performance."

Some of the strain faded from Troy's face. He rose and walked over to the piano, sat on the bench, shifted its position, then, after a heartbeat's hesitation, began to play the introduction. He wasn't the gifted pianist Luke had been, but he played an adequate accompaniment for his far-better-than-adequate tenor voice. Like many country-western songs, the ballad's lyrics mourned a lost love. When the last clear, plaintive note died away and Troy's fingers rested motionless on the keyboard, he sat stiffly, anxiously awaiting their reactions.

The two women's applause didn't completely hide Luke's sigh of relief. Everyone, for various reasons, appeared glad the entertainment was over.

Jodi threw Troy a puzzled, introspective look, then asked, "Where have I heard that before?"

Still facing the piano, Troy uttered a chuckle that sounded forced. Jodi's question obviously nonplussed him. His reply carried a twinge of impatience. "A few minutes ago you said you'd heard it a couple of times."

"No, you misunderstand. I've heard your *record*, sure, but I have a strange feeling I've heard your song played like you just did it—without other instruments in the background." Her memory groped ineffectually back into the past for the solution to her bewilderment.

Then Troy, with another chuckle, this one more natural, turned to face her and supplied the answer. "You probably heard me playing the melody—or pieces of it—on the piano in Annie's apartment. Sometime during the period when I was composing it."

"Of course, that's it," Jodi agreed, satisfied with Troy's explanation. She'd trained her mind to collect, catalog, and recall details, and she absolutely hated it if some one of them refused to surface when called upon. Leaning comfortably back in her chair, Jodi yawned.

"That's my exit cue," Troy said, a teasing lilt in his voice.

Five minutes later he had thanked Becky for her hospitality, expressed his pleasure at meeting Luke, bestowed a kiss on Jodi's forehead, hugged her, and departed.

Jodi said to Becky, "I'm leaving, too, before I fall asleep right here. I took a long nap this afternoon, but I guess the events of the past two days have zapped me good, as the kids say." She moved toward the door, making no attempt to cover a second yawn.

Suddenly energized, Luke hurried past her, held the door

open, then stepped back. With a glance over his shoulder at Becky, he said, "I'll walk Jodi home."

"I know the way," Jodi objected, "and I'm not afraid of goblins, ghosts, or gremlins."

"What about your watcher?" Luke gruffly reminded her as he sidled around her to block her departure.

For a brief instant Jodi, brushed by apprehensions, hesitated, then declared, "He can't see me in the dark." She felt triumphant. She'd won another word skirmish. Why on earth did this handsome, exciting, lovable man manage to push her temper button so easily and so often?

"I'm walking you home," he growled. He walked through the doorway, reaching back to grasp her arm and tug her, not too gently, out onto the arcade.

Jodi and Luke strolled down the center of the dirt road. Lighting their way, a full moon hung high in the sky, a gleaming silver ball against a blue-black, star-sprinkled velvet backdrop, with thin, wispy clouds, like spiderwebs, floating across the brilliant sphere in ever-changing patterns. A slight breeze wafted the garden plot's fragrances through the not-quite-chilly night air. Most detectable to Jodi was the delicate perfume of the tiny, pale orchid blooms of the three chinaberry trees planted along the property line.

She broke the silence with an audible sniff and "Smells heavenly."

"The new-mown grass?"

"That, too." Which she hadn't noticed until Luke pointed it out. "I was referring to the chinaberry trees."

"Not many folks know how good they smell every spring."

"We had one in our front yard. Annie and I used to play beneath it all summer. So shady and cool."

"Good memories."

Jodi heard the smile in his voice. It surprised her—and pleased her—so accustomed was she to his grumpy retorts. To his mercurial moods, too, so she shouldn't have been surprised or displeased by his next words.

"Why did you let Morrell paw you all evening?"

Jodi was outraged. "Paw me? That's a gross overstatement. In fact, it's just plain gross!"

"He punctuated every damn sentence with a pat on your arm or a grab of your hand or a . . . caress of your cheek." The last phase he uttered scarcely above a whisper.

Beneath his accusation and annoyance Jodi suddenly sensed Luke's . . . misery. He was *jealous!* Her heart did a crazy little skip-hitch before it took off at an Indianapolis-500 pace. Quickly, she turned away from him because she knew her joy danced in her eyes and grinned all over her face. She forgot she'd been angry with him a few minutes before.

Sighing loudly, Jodi said, "That's just Troy's way. He's always been a tactile person."

"Always?"

Did she hear a cautious curiosity in Luke's query?

"All the time I've known him." Smiling in the dark, she waited, mischievously hoping Luke would, according to his own description, "react."

He did. "All of what time?" He slowed to a halt.

Stopping beside him, Jodi looked up into his moonlit, scowling face. She decided to set him straight about Troy before he exploded.

"I met Troy about three years ago. Right after my divorce," she added, unable to resist testing him one more time. Her ploy worked. Even standing a foot away, she felt Luke tense up. She smiled to herself, then continued her explanation. "Troy was Annie's . . . ah . . . significant other."

Luke's noisy exhalation of the breath he'd been holding delighted Jodi, convincing her he really had been upset by a presumed romantic relationship between her and Troy.

"He's conceited and boastful and too full of himself," Luke declared. He felt free to speak his mind, now that Jodi wouldn't think his opinion was based on jealousy. On the gut-gripping jealousy he'd deny until his last breath.

"Perhaps. But if that's true, he has a right to be proud. His mother was an alcoholic and a prostitute. She didn't know who Troy's father was. Troy grew up in squalor, taunted by his school friends, ashamed of who he was. He left home when he was fourteen and lived on the streets for four or five years. Never in trouble with the law, which is a lot to be said in his favor, considering he often had to scrabble for food from garbage cans in the alleys behind cafes and restaurants."

"He looks well fed now."

Jodi laughed aloud at Luke's reluctance to give Troy credit for anything, simply because he disapproved of the other man's demeanor. As she walked toward the cabin, Luke came up alongside her, shortening his stride to match hers. She took up Troy's story where she'd left off.

"Somehow Troy caught the attention of the owner of a small music store. The man was old and a bachelor, with no living kin. He hired Troy to clerk in the store and to handle chores he was too feeble to do. Gradually, he became the father Troy had always wished for. Troy lived with him, and when the store owner passed away, Troy discovered the man had willed him his store, his house, and a sizable bank account. So, before he was twenty-five, Troy inherited what to him was a fortune."

"Lucky son of a . . . gun," Luke muttered.

"Except that Troy still felt like a nobody because of his background. During the years, he'd learned how to play several instruments and how to put down on paper the tunes he had in his head. Several musical friends, customers of the store, tried in vain to help him locate a song publisher or a record company that believed in him. Then he met Annie at a concert, and his life—and Annie's—changed practically overnight. They fell in love, and Annie's contacts and influence were just beginning to pay off for him when— when she died."

"Too bad she didn't live to share his success," Luke said, sounding for all the world as though he meant it.

"Yes," Jodi agreed, her heart aching for the young lovers.

Having reached the cabin, Luke took Jodi's keys, unlocked the door, and pushed it ajar. Jodi reached inside to flip the porch light on. In the sudden brightness, she noted the strain around Luke's mouth and the uncertainty narrowing his eyes.

"Life is damn unfair," he told her, and before she could reply, he wheeled and marched across the lawn, a rapidly disappearing silhouette.

What unfairness had Luke had in mind? Annie's untimely death? Troy's only half-enjoyed fame? Or his own lost dream? She could do nothing about the first two. But maybe she could give Luke a new dream to replace the old one.

Twenty-three

Jodi sat in her favorite Tex-Mex restaurant, munching on corn chips and salsa, expectantly watching the double front door, half of which was propped open to let in the warm spring air. The exhaust-polluted warm spring air. Strange, she mused, how only a few weeks at the lake had conditioned her to take for granted the crisp, clean air laden with the smell of green growing things and with the quiet, restful country sounds.

The continuous din of traffic out in the street affronted her ears. Honking horns, squealing tires, revved-up motors, and a shrill, passing siren. Jodi hated sirens. Even as a child, when she heard one, she had worried about who might be hurt. Since Annie's death, a siren sound never failed to remind Jodi of her loss. She hadn't heard that particular siren on that cold, rainy New Year's Eve, but her imagination heard it . . . and agonized over what Annie's final minutes must have been like. The nearby traffic noises finally obliterated the siren's fading wail, and Jodi felt the muscles in her neck and shoulders relax.

Her lunch guest flounced through the open doorway, and waving to attract her attention, Jodi laughed softly. Many things changed, but Ginger Tillman remained the same: a petite package of perpetual motion, decorated with flyaway bright auburn tresses, laughing brown eyes, and an intriguing row of copper-colored freckles across her pert nose.

227

"Howdy, sweet thing." Ginger's unaffected drawl matched her blue denim jacket and jeans and high-heeled red leather boots. She plopped down on the booth seat opposite Jodi, put her fingers to her smiling mouth, and threw the other woman a kiss. "What do you think? I've been practicin' that. For onstage at the end of my next concert." Her saucy grin was infectious.

As though they had been together yesterday, Jodi grinned back. "Looks good to me."

It felt wonderful to see and hear Ginger again. With Ginger there were no frills; what you saw was what you got. Annie used to say you could always depend on Ginger to call a spade a spade—even if the spade dug a hole in your ego. The girls had been friends since grammar school, and after both became professional musicians, their relationship strengthened. While Annie's talent had lain in playing the guitar and composing, Ginger's sprang from her throaty voice that many compared favorably to Patsy Cline's. They had performed together countless times, including the last day of Annie's life.

"This is great!" Ginger's delight sparkled in her eyes.

"I know!" Jodi relished the other woman's enthusiasm. She reached across the table and touched Ginger's hand. Like magnets, their fingers intertwined, and the merriment drifted away as quickly as smoke in the wind. "I should have called you sooner," Jodi told her.

"Last night was just fine." Ginger gave Jodi's hand a tight squeeze, then released it and grabbed the menu. "I'm famished. Let's order, and then if we're still in the mood, we can cry on each other's shoulder."

That was Ginger—optimistic, trusting, non-judgmental.

After a waitress took their order and departed, Jodi said, "I want to hear everything that happened in Dallas."

Ginger didn't pretend not to know what Jodi was talking about. "I told the police when they interrogated me two days later. Didn't help then. And won't help you, Jodi, to relive that awful time. Let it go."

"I will. I can—*after* I find out what I want to know." She took a sip of water to moisten her cotton-dry mouth. "When Annie left that morning, she was so angry with me. Because I wouldn't go with her. Did she tell you that?"

"Not that she was angry. She just said you were busy with a new client. Hey! It was all right with her. Annie never stayed mad more than five minutes, and she didn't carry a grudge more than five feet. You know that." She caught a flicker of doubt in Jodi's eyes. "Surely you haven't been blaming yourself all these months?"

"I knew she hated to drive at night. I knew the weather might worsen, even turn to ice on the highway."

"The weather didn't kill her, Jodi." Ginger saw her friend wince at the bluntness, but it was time somebody knocked the notion of blame out of Jodi's mind . . . and heart. "Who did? you ask. *I* think it was some wacko creep out for a power ride. Maybe strung out on dope or booze."

"Maybe."

More than anything, she wanted to believe Ginger's theory. Better a stranger drunk or on drugs than a person who knew Annie and for some unimaginable reason wished her dead. Jodi knew hit-and-run accidents—murders—frequently went unsolved. Especially when no witness came forward. If only someone had identified the car that had pushed—no, knocked—Annie's compact car off the road. The day after Annie's funeral, Detective Hanley had come to Jodi's apartment and told her that a pickup driver had been following some distance behind her sister's vehicle but was certain of nothing except that the incident had unquestionably been intentional.

"Maybe," Jodi repeated. "But I still need to know about Annie's last day. What she did. Who she talked to. How she spent the hours. For me, it will be a kind of . . . closure, you know?"

Ginger made no comment while the waitress set the oval-shaped, oven-hot plates of *fajita* makings in front of them and poured their coffee. When they were alone again, she said, "I can understand that." She folded a *tortilla* around the aromatic strips of beef and onion, took a bite, chewed, and swallowed. "Yum," she approved. "Okay, I'll tell you everything I can remember about that day. I drove down to Dallas from a gig in Oklahoma City and as planned met Annie at Reunion Arena around two o'clock. We spent most of the time together, but of course we did wander apart to speak to different friends. The Columbia Records rep came over to us and asked to speak to Annie privately. They probably talked ten minutes, and she looked upset when the rep walked off. I asked Annie what was wrong, and she said it was just a misunderstanding about one of her songs."

"That's all she told you?"

"That's all."

They ate for a few minutes, then Jodi asked, "Besides you and Annie, who else was on the program?"

"Clint Black, Troy Morrell, the *Roadrunners, Only in Texas*—"

"Do you know Luke Prentiss?" Jodi realized as soon as the words left her mouth that she'd overreacted.

A very perceptive Ginger replied, "Yeah. And so do you, I gather."

"He's my . . . neighbor up at the lake."

"You're kidding." Ginger didn't miss the way Jodi became quite busy making another *fajita.* "You're *not* kidding! Luke's a nice man. Besides being handsome and talented and sexy and . . . Jodi Turner, I do believe you're blushing." Ginger laughed delightedly. "How *close* a neighbor *is* he?" The teasing innuendo heightened the color in Jodi's cheeks still further. "Jodi, sweet thing, talk to me."

"There's nothing to tell," Jodi denied, meeting Ginger's glance head-on. "Luke lives with his sister, who owns the house next door to Irish's place. I met them both three weeks ago. We're friends."

"Uh-huh. Do you happen to know why Luke isn't with *Only in Texas* anymore? There's a rumor going around that he's terribly ill. I hope that's not true."

"No. He's all right." Jodi paused. "Ginger, I want your cross-my-heart-and-hope-to-die promise that you'll keep this between me and you."

"You got it. I promise."

"Luke wouldn't approve of my telling you, but since I brought up his name myself—"

"Hey! I promise." Ginger was, Jodi knew, as trustworthy as she was trusting.

"He can't perform because his right hand was severely burned in some kind of a gasoline explosion."

Ginger stared at Jodi in speechless horror, and the freckles appeared more prominent on her paling face. After a long moment, she spoke, her words husky and uneven. "If I . . . ever lost my—my voice, I think I'd want to . . . die."

"I'm sure Luke felt like that at first," Jodi told her, "but he'll muddle through. As would you, my friend. Because you both have a lot of intestinal fortitude—and because neither of you can ever close your ears, or your hearts, to music." Jodi inhaled a long, noisy breath, then exhaled a nervous laugh. "And that's your philosophy lecture for the day."

While finishing the meal, the two women talked about other mutual acquaintances who had attended the New Year's Eve concert in Dallas.

"Annie told me Troy went up a day early to help Clint's people set up the time slots for all the bands and singers." A shadow crossed Jodi's face as she continued. "If only they had gone together."

"Qué será será." Ginger shrugged her shoulders. "I imagine Troy has an 'if only' of his own."

"What do you mean?"

"I have a hunch that he, like you, regrets his last words with Annie. She and I had just finished our burgers and fries when Troy motioned to her from across the floor. She flew to him like a homing pigeon. They kissed and then started to argue right away. They argued a lot, you know. They loved each other, but both of them had mulish streaks a mile wide.

231

Anyway, afterward Annie seemed kinda sad, quiet, jittery, too. But when I asked her what was the matter, she just shook her head and complained about Troy being so damn stubborn. There wasn't anything for me to worry about, she said. They'd settle everything next time they saw each other."

"No wonder Troy still feels bad about losing Annie," Jodi murmured. "Nobody likes unfinished business or loose ends."

"Speaking of loose ends, Quentin was at the concert, too."

Jodi couldn't breathe. The earth quaked. The sun eclipsed. A silent wind roared in her ears.

Quentin attended the concert? Afterwards, he would have driven south along the same route Annie took. He'd never been fond of Annie, and after she testified against him during the divorce hearing, she'd received her own share of Quentin's threats. On the way home, had Quentin recognized Annie's old car and, just inside the Austin city limits, seized the opportunity to get even with her?

The dreadful possibility whooshed through Jodi's mind in a tornadic millisecond.

"Jodi! Jodi, sweet thing!" Ginger's concerned cries summoned Jodi back from the edge of the abyss that had opened up at her feet. "Does Quentin's name still do that to you? If I'd had any idea . . ."

"Why was he there? Did you speak to him? Did he know Annie was there?"

"Hey! One question at a time," Ginger chided, giving her friend a puzzled look. "Yeah, we talked for a couple of minutes. Quentin said he was there hoping to make a deal with the Columbia Records rep. If he'd seen or heard any of the concert promos, he knew Annie would be there. But she wasn't anywhere around when Quentin ran into me backstage, and he didn't mention her."

Jodi's throat almost closed over her next question. "Did he mention me?"

"No." Ginger sounded surprised. "Why should he? That was two years after your divorce."

"I know, but—" Jodi stopped, loath to tell her companion about Quentin's storming into her office or about the boat mishap. Ginger's insatiable curiosity, however loving, would dredge up too many details Jodi didn't want to refresh in her own mind.

"But what?" Ginger insisted.

Jodi lifted one shoulder in a no-big-deal shrug. "But I suppose I'm still a little paranoid where Quentin's involved."

"Hey, you've got a right." Ginger willingly excused Jodi's overreaction.

However, Jodi's uneasiness lingered, boiling and building underneath their catching-up conversation, until the pressure escaped with an abrupt, "Ginger, I have an appointment." Jodi fumbled in her purse for her wallet, then dropped a twenty and a five-dollar bill on the table. "Here. This'll cover the bill. I'll phone you soon."

Before Ginger could do more than gasp and voice a stunned " 'Bye," Jodi slid across the seat, rose, and headed for the door.

She had to see a detective about a murder.

Twenty-four

Hurry up and wait, Jodi moaned to herself as she tried to get comfortable in the molded plastic chair in Detective Hanley's office. She'd sped her blue Saturn to the police department's northside station and at the sergeant's desk breathlessly demanded to see the detective at once. After being calmly informed that Detective Hanley was in a staff meeting and asked if she'd like to wait a few minutes, she spat out a harsh "Yes" and was escorted by a young officer to the enclosed cubbyhole.

In there, at least, she wasn't subjected to the odors of the bullpen area—cigarette smoke, sweat, the cheap perfume worn by the prostitutes, and the smell of fear exuding from the other suspects brought in. The glass walls, while affording a view of the hectic activities outside, shut out most of the noise. Ringing phones, officers shouting information and orders and jibes back and forth across the room, the curses and angry protests of those being booked—all blended into an unignorable hum, preferable to the cacophony of individual sounds that had blasted her ears when she first entered the one-story brick building.

For the tenth or eleventh time Jodi glanced impatiently at her watch, the one she'd picked up this morning at her apartment. The desk sergeant's "few minutes" had crawled to thirty, and the hard chair had numbed her derriere. Jodi stood and strolled the half-dozen feet to the rear wall where four award plaques hung.

"I wish one of those was for success with hit-and-runs," Detective Hanley said as he entered his office.

"So do I." Jodi threw him a feeble smile.

"Good afternoon, Ms. Turner. The sergeant tells me you're anxious to see me." He motioned to the chair across from his desk, to which Jodi returned.

"I am. Detective Hanley, did you interrogate my ex-husband?"

"Regarding your sister's death?" Following Jodi's nod, he pondered a few moments, then said, "I spoke to several of her friends but, as I recall, none identified himself as your former husband."

"Quentin was not Annie's friend."

The sharp, belligerent tone of Jodi's statement quickened the detective's interest. "Are you saying there was some evidence I overlooked?"

"I don't know!" Jodi answered, half hopeful, half reluctant to chance another of the man's we've-done-all-we-can speeches.

Hanley walked briskly to the door, opened it, and called to the young officer standing nearby, "Hopkins, bring me the Klerkton file. Suzanne Klerkton. Open hit-and-run."

"You remember her name," Jodi said, amazed and pleased.

"I remember all the unsolved ones," he solemnly informed Jodi. "They show up in my nightmares." He accepted the file and thanked the departing Hopkins. When the door closed again, offering them privacy and reasonable quiet, the detective sat at his desk, opened the folder, and sorted through its contents. "Quentin, you said. His last name?"

"Turner. We were only married a year." From the man's raised eyebrow, she guessed what his next question would be, so she answered it. "I kept his name because by then all my clients at Sunbelt Images knew me as Jodi Turner, and that's how my name appeared on the company stationery and records. You know the drill."

"Yes, ma'am. Less painful than making a lot of explanations."

He read aloud from the pages he sought in Annie's file. " 'Ginger Tillman. Best friend. With subject at concert. Furnished names of interviewed people below:

"Troy Morrell. Subject's lover. Drove to Dallas previous day. Quarreled with subject at concert re her driving home alone. Owns red Mustang. Checked it. No dents or scrapes on passenger side. Only visible damage: Paint nicks on hood, probably caused by stones thrown by other vehicles.' "

For several minutes Hanley continued to quote from the information obtained from musicians and friends of Annie's. Then he spoke a name unfamiliar to Jodi. " 'Wayne Kidd, Columbia Record Company representative from Nashville. Personal friend of subject and Morrell.' Says he and Klerkton discussed a problem with one of her songs, which she promised to take care of. That's the lot," the detective stated as he laid the page down. "No Quentin Turner."

The final entry proved to Jodi that the Austin Police Department had done a thorough job of contacting the people whose names Ginger had given them. She'd simply forgotten to list Quentin.

The man behind the scarred wooden desk waited for Jodi to explain the reason for her visit.

"Quentin was there," she said. "At the concert. I just found out today when I had lunch with Ginger Tillman. It was the first time I'd spoken with her since—since—you know."

"I wonder why she didn't give us his name."

"Probably because he and I had been divorced for two years and because, when she talked very briefly with him, neither my name nor Annie's came up. Quentin told her he was there to see the man from Columbia Records. Mr. Kidd, I believe your report said."

"Could Miss Tillman have been protecting Turner?"

"Heavens, no! She knew about his . . . abuse and his in-fidelity. She couldn't stand him. And anyway, she was one hundred percent loyal to Annie, and Annie despised Quentin."

"And Quentin despised Annie. Is that what you're telling me?"

"They never got along. And at my divorce hearing, Quentin made some ugly threats."

"Against your sister?"

"Yes, sir, and against me." Jodi breathed deeply and plunged past the decision of no return. "He would have taken the same highway back here that night as Annie. He probably would've recognized her old car, the same white Volkswagen she'd had for at least five years."

"You think he hated her—and you—enough to kill her?"

"Maybe. It could have been a spur-of-the-moment thing. When he's angry, he strikes out without considering the consequences. And he holds grudges like crazy. I'd never have thought of him as a suspect, though, except for what's been happening to me. Sheriff Sutton thinks Quentin may be to blame for that. And now I have to admit Quentin may have a motive: to keep me from figuring out someday that he killed Annie."

"You've lost me, Ms. Turner. What's been happening to you, and why does Sheriff Sutton feel your ex-husband is involved?"

Jodi proceeded to recount the details of her near drowning and of the discovery of Hannah Lowry's body. Then she explained the basis for the sheriff's suspicions: Quentin's several threats, his belief that she couldn't swim, and his living across the lake, close enough to commit the crimes and then disappear, so to speak, into the woodwork.

"Could Turner be responsible for the break-in at your apartment?"

"It fits his vindictive personality—making a horrible mess because he knew how it would upset me."

"Did you tell the sheriff about that?"

"No. I've had so much else on my mind, I didn't remember the break-in until just now when you brought it up."

"I'll tell him. We've worked together on a few cases. Dave Sutton's a good man, a good sheriff, and if he believes Turner may be guilty, he'll keep at it till he learns the truth, one way or another. Now you can supply a possible motive for the events at the lake. I'll call Dave tomorrow, and we'll compare notes." For the first time since he'd greeted Jodi, his face broke into a smile. "It's possible we may solve three crimes with one leaky boat."

Even under the grim circumstances, Jodi laughed at Hanley's bad joke. She knew full well his purpose had been to lighten her mood, and she didn't want to disappoint the kind man sitting across from her.

"Is there anything else I can help you with?" Detective Hanley asked.

Jodi hesitated, then replied, "I'd like to ask you one question."

"Shoot."

"When you were reading from the list of people interviewed, there was something about Troy Morrell's car. He wasn't a suspect, was he? That's not possible. He loved Annie very much."

"That was just routine. The witness—or the almost witness, I should say—reported both vehicles were red, so when we learned Morrell owned a red Mustang, we checked it out as a matter of course."

"Both vehicles? There were two?" Utterly bewildered, Jodi stared at him.

"You didn't know about that? Oh, no, I remember. I didn't mention that when I came to see you after the . . . memorial service. I saw no need to prolong or add to your grief by dwelling on something that might turn out to be a weird coincidence. I was right. It led us nowhere."

"May I see the accident report?"

"I don't see why not." Hanley handed Jodi the complete file. "It's the top sheet."

Jodi carefully read every word on the page. Officer T. Jamison, who signed the report, had obviously quoted Joe Bob Perkins verbatim. The pickup driver's plain-talk Texanese would have been amusing but for the sorrowful fact that it described the final minutes of Annie's life.

When Jodi finished, she laid that page down and perused the next couple of pages, which contained Hanley's findings. Annie's body had been covered with a man's unlined tan nylon raincoat, generic style and make, no labels. The position of her body—flat on her back, limbs perfectly straight—indicated she'd been pulled, not thrown, from the car. According to the coroner, Annie died instantly of a broken neck when the car rolled over. Her body sustained no burns despite the fact that her VW almost totally burned up, till the rain quenched the fire.

"I'm glad Annie didn't suffer," Jodi murmured. "She was probably . . . dead before—before—"

"The coroner said there's no doubt."

"Why did you let the public assume Annie's death was accidental? And what about that man who asked the pickup driver, Mr. Perkins, to call in the accident? He must have dragged Annie's bo—Annie out of her car. Why didn't you put that in the newspaper?"

"I knew you'd raise those questions after you read your sister's file. You see, we hoped the . . . ah . . . Good Samaritan would come forward and maybe provide us with some viable evidence. Since he didn't, we figured he was the one who caused the accident. In that event, we wanted him to think he was home free. We didn't want him to know we had proof the hit-and-run was deliberate. You see, the fire destroyed your sister's vehicle but didn't hide the dents and scrapes and gashes all along the whole left side—damage that couldn't possibly have been done by a roll-over in a rain-filled grassy ditch." He paused. "Ms. Turner, what kind of a car was your ex-husband driving at that time?"

Immediately, Jodi followed his train of thought. "I wish

I could tell you, but I can't. When we were married, Quentin drove a black Corvette."

"The day after the accident, we sent notices to every body shop and garage within a hundred-mile radius of Austin to be on the lookout for any car with a badly banged-up front and right side. Especially red ones. No responses. I figured the perpetrator kept on driving, probably into another state. But with the information you've brought me today, especially in view of the recent occurrences up at Lake Buchanan, I believe Quentin Turner is a logical hit-and-run suspect."

"I just want Annie's murderer found and punished." Jodi rose. As Hanley walked ahead of her to the door, she said, "Thank you for letting me see Annie's file. I understand better now what happened."

"Good."

When he held the door open for her, the deafening bedlam made her cringe and frown. She hurried through the large desk-cluttered room.

The detective's loud, resonant warning followed her outside. "Be careful, Ms. Turner."

On the return trip home—odd, how she thought of Irish's cabin as home now—Jodi mulled over the new information gleaned at the police station. Some of it depressed her; some of it surprised her. Some encouraged her, because now she knew for certain that Detective Hanley had never set Annie's case on the back burner and forgotten it. He'd simply let it simmer until new ingredients could be added that would create a complete dish of arrest and indictment. If her experiences during the past forty-eight hours helped to make the recipe complete, Jodi would consider her terrors palatable.

When she parked in Irish's graveled driveway, Luke rose from the cabin porch steps, where he'd been sitting, and hurried toward her car. She alighted before he reached her door and, observing the grim expression on his face, anxiously asked, "What's wrong?"

"Where have you been?" Luke demanded.

"I went to my apartment for some things," she responded tartly. "And I'm here now, so you don't have to shout."

"I'm not shouting!"

"Yes, you are!"

An unwanted mistiness blurred her vision. Seeing Ginger and talking with the detective had stirred unhappy memories and taxed her control. Now, at home, where she had expected to find peace of mind, Luke's bad-tempered attitude had exacerbated her vulnerability.

Jodi rapidly blinked her eyes dry and swallowed around the tightness in her throat. "I don't like to be yelled at."

"You deserved it. With all that's gone on around here lately, I don't like your traipsing off alone to God-knows-where."

"God knew." Jodi waited a beat for her deadpan remark to sink in.

Luke emitted a long drawn-out moan at her unholy humor as they walked along side by side.

"Why were you waiting here on my front porch?" she asked.

"To give you some information I knew you'd want to have the minute you got here."

"What information?"

She took a seat on the steps and motioned for Luke to join her. It was so good to smell fresh air and have no tall, jammed-together buildings blocking out the view of a spectacular gold and peach and mauve sunset. As a special treat, a brilliant red cardinal flew in a pattern of sweeping up-and-down scallops as he sped low over the bluebonnets that carpeted the sloping field across the road.

"Sheriff Sutton phoned," Luke said, leaning against the post and stretching out his long legs. "Said he'd called the cabin a half-dozen times, then thought you might be at our house. I asked if there was a problem, and he said yes."

"Yes?" Jodi straightened her spine and gave him a sideways distressful look.

"Well, not a problem exactly. A setback. He had to leave at four on an overnight campout with his grandson's Boy Scout troop. He thought you'd want to know today, so he gave his report to me."

"Which was?" The way Luke had already held back the news nudged Jodi's intuition into apprehension.

"Your ex denied everything. Claims he never threatened you. Says he doesn't own and hasn't rented or borrowed a boat. Swears he'd never heard of Hannah Lowry until he read about her murder in this morning's paper."

"Of course he denied it!" Jodi exclaimed, clenching her fists in her lap. "To hear him tell it, he was never, ever to blame for anything. It was always *my* fault!" She stopped; realizing she was speaking not about recent events but about long-ago days of anguish and betrayal.

Luke's hand tenderly covered hers. "It's all right, Jodi." His eyes smiled down into hers, and she felt a calming warmth embrace her. Almost as though he'd wrapped his arms around her. Then his next words recycled her disappointment. "Turner has an alibi for day before yesterday, all day. He was . . . entertaining a friend in his condo."

"A female friend," Jodi sneered. At Luke's amazed glance, she said, "I don't care who he . . . entertains. He's just so damn . . . charming when he wants to be. That woman, whoever or whatever she is, probably couldn't wait to tell the sheriff she spent the day with Quentin. Whether she did or not."

"That's what Sheriff Sutton intimated. He promised he wouldn't give up."

Detective Hanley had assured Jodi the sheriff would find whatever proof was there to be found. So maybe the sheriff wasn't willing to accept Quentin's word, or that of his alibiing bedmate, as gospel.

"Then we're not quite back to square one, after all," Jodi murmured, a wistful smile touching her lips.

She stood, walked across the porch, and lifted the jingling keys from her purse. Luke took them, his hand brushing hers, lingering a second longer than necessary and stop-starting Jodi's pulse beat.

After he unlocked the door, pushed it open, and reached inside to switch on the porch and inside lights, he said, "I have to go. Becky'll want to know you're home safe." When he'd crossed the yard and reached the road, he stopped, looked back, and called out, "Be careful, Jodi."

The same parting words the detective had used. *Be careful.* Be careful of whom? Of what? When? Where? How?

Determined to leave the scary, unanswerable questions outside her safe haven, Jodi shuddered once to shake them off, then stepped over the threshold.

Into another nightmare.

Twenty-five

Oh, God, he's been here again!

Jodi smelled him. That faint musky odor that somehow hinted at danger and made her want to vomit. The heavy air, disturbed by his movements, was still eerily unsettled.

Her skin prickled. She gagged; her hand covered her mouth and nose in an attempt to block out the sensory proof of the stranger's intrusion.

He was gone. The same sixth sense that alerted her to his sneaking into her cabin while she was away told her she was alone now. There was no sensible explanation. She just *knew*. The same way she had known, the instant she stepped inside, that he'd been there.

Panicked, she ran to the bedroom alcove and yanked open the top dresser drawer. Her quick shallow breathing blew away the silence. Every item of lingerie remained as she'd placed it, folded neatly and in its proper stack.

So . . . this time he hadn't left behind shuffled underwear as the hallmark of his sick presence.

What *had* he done?

Jodi spent the next ten minutes frenziedly checking every foot of the cabin's interior. She discovered nothing broken, vandalized, or stolen. Two of the high bentwood stools were shoved together near the open end of the bar. One rocked unsteadily on three legs. She remembered moving the stool aside, as usual, so she could conveniently reach the cereal box in the upper cabinet. Ordinarily, she repositioned the stool but probably hadn't done so this morning because she was harried and running late.

Her initial horror and the frantic search that followed had siphoned off her energy and her strength. Jodi wilted into the nearest armchair and leaned her head against the uphol-stered back. Mindlessly, she sucked in deep, quivering breaths until she could no longer feel her heart slam against her ribs.

Finally able to think coherently, she considered phoning the sheriff. But as certain as she was that someone had come uninvited into the cabin, she was also certain the authorities would find no proof, no fingerprints. Her intruder might be crazy but he wasn't stupid. Intuition suggested the interloper and her watcher were one and the same; logic confirmed it. He came on her property only when he was sure she was gone. Why? If he wanted to harm her, he could have done so at any time since her arrival at the lake. She had no inkling why he continued to watch her, and she desperately hoped he'd soon tire of his game-playing with her and choose another "partner."

In the meantime, she had a more important agenda than allowing some neighborhood weirdo to turn her into a para-noid weakling. She needed to talk to Troy about Annie's last day. She should have done so months ago.

Troy's answering machine informed her he was unavail-able but would return her call as soon as possible. Frustrated, Jodi replaced the receiver, but the phone rang before she could remove her hand.

"Hello? Troy?"

"No," replied another male voice. "Were you expecting Troy to call?"

"Irish. Hello. Yes, I just left a message and he might have picked up a second too late."

"Then you've seen Troy since you met on the road the day after your vacation started."

"Not until yesterday. He stopped at Becky's when the sheriff—"

"Something wrong at Becky's?"

"Don't sound so worried, *Dennis*. It gives you away." Jodi chuckled fondly.

"Don't you sound so pleased. I'll handle my own public—and private—relations."

"Yes, *sir*," Jodi vocally saluted.

"What happened at Becky's?" Irish solemnly insisted.

"On the island. Luke and I discovered Han—a girl's body there and—"

"I read the account in this morning's paper. No mention of names. No details. Something about a boating accident."

"I've been meaning to thank you. For making me learn how to swim."

Jodi had tried to keep her remarks light but knew she'd failed when, after a long vibrating silence, Irish hoarsely, almost angrily, asked, "Jodi, were you in that boat?"

"I'm afraid so."

"Good Lord! Are you all right?"

"Obviously."

"Is that why you called the office this morning?"

"Partly. I forgot it was your day to do monthly examinations and treatments at Safe Harbor. While I was in town to have lunch with Ginger, I thought I'd come by and bring you up to date on all that's been happening around here."

"Bring me up to date now." Irish, his tone calm and caring, striving for patience, reminded Jodi of their adolescent, what-have-you-done-this-time sessions.

"Not on long distance. I'm perfectly fine, and the police have everything under control. I'll explain it all when I see you."

"That, my dear," he stated firmly, "will be early in the morning."

"You don't have to—"

"Yes, I do. I'll be there. Early. For now, you get some

rest. You sound stressed out. Tired. Hell, I sent you up there to rest, not to find dead bodies and—"

"Good *night,* Irish," Jodi warned just before she slowly hung up on him.

Glaring at the silent phone, she envisioned Irish glaring at his. She forced the oxygen out of her lungs until her chest hurt; then she refilled them with a wide, noisy yawn.

She *was* tired. The strange, exhausting day had taken its toll. Jodi luxuriated under a warm, soothing shower and, yawning again, slipped between the fresh lemon-scented sheets.

Sunlight danced between the breeze-tossed leaves of the tall pecan tree outside her window, flicking gold and shaded designs across her face. Instantly wide awake, Jodi scrambled out of bed and glanced at her watch lying on the dresser top. Nine o'clock! Had she really slept fourteen hours? Irish would be here before she had breakfast. Dressing quickly, she hurried to the kitchen.

"Darn!" she groaned as she pulled open the cabinet door. She'd eaten the last of her cereal yesterday morning and forgotten to buy more when she was in town.

Then she spied a box of flakes at the back of the shelf. Not her brand but they'd do in a pinch. Lifting the box down, she noticed it had been opened. She parted the folded cellophane liner, smelled and tasted a couple of flakes. They appeared fresh enough, so she shook a liberal amount into her bowl, added three spoonfuls of sugar, and poured milk over them.

The phone rang. Rushing to the desk, Jodi mumbled, "Forgot my cereal. Forgot my cordless phone too." At the phone's third ring, she picked it up. "Hello?"

"Troy here. Good morning. I found your message when I got home last evening around ten. When I looked out and . . . uh . . . saw your cabin was completely dark, I de-

247

cided to wait until this morning to call. I figured your trip to the city . . . uh . . . tired you out."

"You were right. But it was a nice day. Part of it at least. I had lunch with Ginger, a wonderful visit. She said to give you her best when I saw you."

"Thanks. I guess you two enjoyed reminiscing about . . . uh . . . the good old days."

"Yes, we did. And we talked about that day in Dallas." When Troy offered no comment, Jodi went on. "Ginger told me you and Annie quarreled about something."

"Oh, that. Yeah, we did. And I've . . . uh . . . always been sorry."

"Ginger thought Annie seemed unusually quiet afterwards."

"Well, I . . . uh . . . chewed her out pretty good. About driving back by herself at night . . . and in the rain besides. She was supposed to bring—" He stopped, sounding embarrassed.

"Me," Jodi filled in for him, her own tone regretful.

"Yeah. Well, anyway, I wanted her to . . . uh . . . leave her car and ride home with me. I could've asked one of the . . . uh . . . band members to drive her car back."

"Why didn't she do that? She hated driving long stretches at night alone."

"She was . . . uh . . . bullheaded and contrary. Told me I wasn't her boss—yet—and until I was, she'd drive where and when she pleased." His soft, nervous chuckle rumbled in Jodi's ear.

"That sounds like Annie, all right. Thanks for telling me. The police report merely states that you argued."

After a moment of silence, Troy asked, "You saw the police report?"

"Yesterday, when I went to see the detective who handled Annie's case. I had something else to tell him, and he let me read the complete file."

"I see. Is there some . . . uh . . . new evidence in the hit-and-run?"

"Not really." Jodi didn't want to elaborate on Quentin's possible involvement in the crime until the authorities could substantiate it. It would only give Troy false hope.

"Oh. Well, if and when the cops learn anything new, let me know. I want them to catch that . . . uh . . . creep."

"So do I. Troy, I'd like to chat, but I slept late and I haven't had breakfast yet."

"That's okay. We'll talk later."

After she hung up the phone, Jodi returned to her cereal. "Yuk!" The limp flakes had soaked up half of the milk. She despised soggy cereal.

Carrying the bowl outside, she dumped its contents over the deck railing for the birds, always waiting for table scraps.

Before refilling the cereal bowl, Jodi decided to take a few minutes to check her stock of fresh vegetables. Potatoes, onions, carrots, celery. Good. She'd prepare Irish's favorite pot roast for dinner. While taking the meat out of the freezer, she heard an unusual commotion coming from the rear of the cabin.

Stepping out on the deck, she stared in disbelief at the scene below. A dozen or more wildly screeching sparrows were flopping crazily around, dragging their wings in the dirt, jerking their heads. What was happening to the poor little creatures? The only word that came to Jodi's horrified mind was *convulsions*. Even as she watched, a couple of the small birds tumbled over and, their legs in the air, grew utterly still. They were dead!

Suddenly, Jodi understood. There was something awfully wrong with the cereal. But she'd eaten a few flakes, and she felt okay. So far. Alarmed, she dashed inside, wondering whether she should call next door. She might black out.

At that moment Irish marched through the front door. He gave her one of his normal bear-hug greetings, and she clung tenaciously to his torso. He stepped back. "You look awful! I thought you told me you were all right with the boat incident and—"

Ghostly pale, Jodi grabbed his hand and half dragged him

out onto the deck. "The birds," she croaked, pointing to the ground. "The cereal."

"Good heavens!" Irish exclaimed, dismayed by the group of dead and dying sparrows. Then his doctor's brain clicked in. "The cereal, you said. Down there? Killing those birds? Jodi, how much did you eat?"

Jodi gazed up into her godfather's fright-struck eyes. Now that he was here, she felt calmer.

"Only a bite. And that was at least twenty minutes ago, and I still feel fine."

"Honey, let's not panic," he said, for himself as much as for her. "Show me the cereal."

She did. Fumbling, Irish separated the cellophane liner, then sniffed noisily. "Smells okay."

"I smelled it, too, before I poured it. Maybe it absorbed some kind of odorless roach poison you sprayed on the shelves. The box was here when I moved in. Already opened."

"I've never put poison in my cabinets, spray or otherwise. What made you throw the cereal out in the first place?"

"It turned soggy in the milk while I was talking on the phone."

Irish looked extremely thoughtful. "Then you'd already added the sugar."

Jodi had to grin; he recalled all of her habitual routines so well. "Sure I had."

Irish refused to grin back. "Show me the sugar," he urged.

"The sugar? It's just everyday, ordinary sugar. Here." She picked up the sugar bowl and held it toward him.

Irish accepted it, then smelled and violently shook its contents. Under the kitchen light, they both watched the tiny white granules shift. Some sparkled brightly; strangely, some didn't. Irish's lengthy, teeth-clenched hiss reminded Jodi of an angry snake she'd heard once in a zoo. He slammed the sugar bowl on the counter and said, "Get me the sheriff on the phone."

Totally confused, Jodi asked, "What for? I still feel okay. Besides, you're here and you're a doctor."

"Don't argue, Jodi. Just do it."

He hadn't spoken to her that harshly since she used to balk at performing some onerous chore he'd assigned her. Today, however, Jodi sensed it was he who faced the unpleasant task.

When Sheriff Sutton came on the line, Jodi handed the receiver to the grim-faced man beside her.

"Sheriff, this is Dr. O'Meara. Please come to Jodi Turner's cabin or send a deputy as soon as you can arrange it. Someone has tried to poison her."

"Why was I holding my—" Her querulous question
faded into the frowniness, something, "Oh." She saw that, ROY,
around

Twenty-six

Vaguely aware of Irish's reassurances to the sheriff that
she was all right—physically—Jodi felt a smothering, as
though someone had dropped a plastic garbage bag over her
head and tightened it around her neck. Airless; as hot as an
oven, and as dark. No light. No oxygen. No strength in her
knees.

"Jodi?"

Along with Irish's worried outcry came his fingers, grabbing and bruising her arms. He led—no, dragged—her
through the black gloom engulfing her and, with his strong
hands gripping her shoulders, pushed her down on something soft and smooth and cool.

His voice sounded faraway. "Jodi. Breathe."

I can't breathe, she wanted to tell him, but there was no
air left in her lungs.

"Breathe!" he repeated and slapped her cheek—hard.

How dare he hit me! Like Quentin.

Furious, Jodi sucked a slow, painful breath through her tight
throat, and her vision cleared. "That hurt," she complained.

"I know, honey. I'm sorry." Irish, his eyes misty, sat beside her on the glove-leather sofa. With one arm he encircled
her waist. His other hand held her wrist, his finger checking
her pulse. "I had to do it. You were holding your breath,
and you almost blacked out."

"Why was I holding my——?" Her querulous question faded into sudden, horrifying remembrance. "Oh," she whispered.

If she'd eaten that bowl of cereal—if Troy, bless him, hadn't phoned when he did—she'd be dead. Considering how rapidly the poison affected the sparrows, she probably wouldn't have lasted until Irish arrived. Jodi knew she'd be afraid later for herself—frightened that someone had very nearly succeeded in killing her—but at the moment she was livid. The imagined scenario infuriated her. Irish, dear gentle, unselfish Irish, discovering the last person he loved on this earth lying lifeless in the very place he'd sent her to be happy and safe. How ghastly for him.

Monitoring Jodi's every heartbeat, Irish thankfully watched her face change from ashen to flushed. Her darkening blue eyes flashed sparks, a manifestation of her temper barely held in check. As long as she was reacting, he didn't mind that the emotion was anger because he had struck her.

"I'm sorry," he apologized again. He stuck out his chin. "Here. Slug me as hard as you want."

Astonishingly, Jodi laughed. Irish, mouth agape, stared at her. Was she hysterical?

"I'm not mad at you," she told him as she bestowed a kiss on his jutting jaw. "But I'd sure enjoy slugging the person or persons who's"—she reached for humor—"killing my birds."

Irish wasn't amused. "Persons? More than one? You suspect somebody?"

"The watcher. Or Quentin. Or both, because I think Quentin *is* the watcher."

"What watcher?"

Her gaze skittered away from his, and her body language said "Oops!"

Irish grew very still, and his blue gaze, no longer compassionate, pierced Jodi's conscience like pointed steel through plywood. "I think it's time you stopped keeping secrets. Tell me everything that's been happening up here. And I mean everything."

For the next fifteen minutes or so, Jodi complied, with Irish asking pertinent, insightful questions. Without reservation, he believed that her sensations of being spied upon and her feelings that a stranger had been in the cabin were based on actuality, not on a reasonless paranoia. Incontrovertible proof lay in Jodi's sugar bowl. The sweetener had been harmless when Jodi used it yesterday morning; today she would have died if she'd eaten the sweetened soggy flakes. Some person watched until she drove away, then slipped into the cabin and mixed the poison with the sugar.

Someone who knew about Jodi's habit of using an excessive amount of sugar on her preferred daily breakfast.

"Quentin." The single misery-connoting name exited Irish's mouth, bearing all the venom of the vilest curse.

Jodi, who'd been uneasily awaiting Irish's response to her having withheld important information from him, sat bolt upright and gave her godfather a befuddled look. "Quentin?"

"Quentin. Who else knows you take three spoonfuls of sugar on your cereal every morning?" Fury roughened his quavering indictment.

"Oh . . . my . . . God," Jodi whispered.

The emotions that had hovered around her since her near-blackout finally pounced. Shock. Revulsion. Despair. And a terror that dug deep into her spirit like the talons of an attacking hawk. From the wound bled the last drop of her doubt. Quentin wanted her dead. Jodi wasn't exactly sure why, but she *was* sure that when Quentin wanted something, he usually made it happen. One way or another. Sooner or later. If the police couldn't break his alibi for the island/ boating incident or prove he'd planted the poison or discover other irrefutable incriminating evidence, Quentin would continue to harass, persecute, and imperil her until one of his dastardly schemes succeeded.

Smarting from that awful, frightening, menacing truth,

Jodi remained slumped against the sofa back while Irish opened the door for Sheriff Sutton.

Neither man bothered with small talk, so in thirty minutes each had shared what he knew, or suspected, about Quentin. The deputy who accompanied the sheriff had done as instructed—cleaned up the lethal mess on the ground below the deck, placed a couple of dead birds in a small plastic bag, and collected samples of the dry cereal, milk, and sugar, both from the bowl on the counter and from the canister in the cabinet.

"I don't know much about poisons," Sheriff Sutton admitted. "Any ideas, doctor?"

"There are only a few that are odorless, tasteless, and colorless and kill as rapidly as this one. You might suggest to your lab that they check for sodium fluoroacetate. It's a fast-acting rodent poison, available to anyone with the cash to bribe a greedy, unprincipled exterminator."

"Thanks, Dr. O'Meara. I'll tell the lab to start there." He walked over to the sofa and looked down at Jodi, still shaken and unnaturally quiet. "Thank heaven that phone call interrupted your breakfast," he said with a gentle smile. Then his mouth hardened into a stern, no-nonsense line. "Once the tests on the poison are complete, I can obtain a probable-cause search warrant and pay another visit to the rock-and-roll singer. So far, all the evidence is circumstantial. Let's hope a thorough going-over of Turner's condo turns up something solid. Meanwhile, don't eat or drink anything that isn't canned or safely sealed. Someone out there . . . doesn't . . . love you," he parodied.

"I'll take care of her," Irish gravely assured the lawman.

Even as the departing county vehicle's wheels crunched on the driveway gravel, Irish said to Jodi, "You're going back to town and staying with me until this is settled."

"No, I'm not."

Irish's promise to "take care of" her had reignited Jodi's independence like a bellows pumping smoldering coals into

255

a fiery blaze. "I'm not running away. I'll be as safe here as anywhere."

"But . . ." Irish cut off his protest to answer the phone. "Hello. This is Dr. O'Meara."

"Hello, Irish," Becky greeted him. "I saw the sheriff's car. Is everything all right over there?"

"No, Becky, it's not. Something else has happened."

Jodi stepped up and spoke softly in his ear. "Go tell her about it. I'm going to find something to eat that's canned or safely sealed. I missed breakfast." She smiled at her godfather, took the phone from his hand, and gently but firmly pushed him toward the door. "He's on his way," she said into the receiver, then hung up before Becky plied her with questions.

Jodi cheered when Irish finally gave up trying to tease or coax her into moving home with him. He left before dinner, the uncooked pot roast ingredients having been returned to the freezer and vegetable bins, awaiting word from the police lab.

Twilight had barely brushed the sunset-painted horizon when Jodi switched on every lamp and ceiling light in the cabin. She told herself it was because she'd had a nagging headache for hours and her vision was slightly out of focus. For crossing and recrossing the floor to check each lock twice, she had no excuse. She was afraid.

A tap on the front door sent her scurrying to the kitchen for the butcher knife, the only weapon in the cabin, until she realized the enemy wouldn't announce his presence. Nevertheless, her voice quavered when she called out, "Who's there?"

"Luke. Open up. Before I drop this stuff."

Jodi hurriedly unlocked the door and met Luke's laughing green eyes above a stack of vari-sized plastic dishes precariously balanced on his crossed arms.

"What on earth?" Completely surprised, she moved out of his way.

Luke rushed past her and set the containers on the bar. "Dinner for two," he told her, watching her eyes dance with delight as one by one he removed the lids. "Baked chicken and dressing, candied yams, green beans, lettuce and tomato salad, hot buttered rolls, and one slice of pecan pie. The pie's for me. You don't like sweets."

Jodi gasped, and his last words resounded in Luke's head.

"Damn!" The pie-slice-shaped lid tumbled unnoticed to the floor as Luke reached out and pulled Jodi into his arms. "I didn't mean it like that," he murmured unhappily. "I was thinking about dessert, not about—about sugar."

Inexplicably, Jodi felt safe, protected. She nestled closer in his embrace.

"I'm an insensitive cad," Luke told her. Well, maybe not entirely insensitive, he mused. Some of his senses—or his hormones—proved to be in excellent working order.

"Not insensitive," she objected, her words muffled against his chest. "You care."

"I care," he agreed gruffly. His fingers beneath her chin raised her head so he was able to look in her eyes. The honest desire in those midnight-blue orbs heated his blood. Slowly, he traced the shape of her mouth by running the tip of his tongue along the outer edges of her lips. She sighed, then touched his tongue with hers and opened for his kiss. Tasting the soft, sweet moistness, Luke slipped one hand down her back until he cupped her bottom, pulling the juncture of her thighs against the throbbing bulge inside his jeans.

"Luke," Jodi whispered when he allowed her to breathe. "Oh, Luke." She burned. Her blood, her skin, her whole body.

Luke's other hand crept inside her blouse. He hesitated for a heartbeat when his fingertips met the soft lower swell of her breast. Then, slowly, his finger-steps crawled upward.

Hurry, hurry, Jodi silently pleaded. She couldn't have spoken aloud if she'd tried. Luke's hot, hungry mouth totally possessed hers, and her pulse jumped in tandem with the wild movements of his marauding tongue.

At last Luke's fingers found the treasure he sought. Jodi's nipple hardened at his tender, exploring touch.

"Touch me," she whimpered against his mouth. "Don't tease me. Touch me."

Luke's hand greedily enveloped her breast. He squeezed and stroked, lifting its weight in his palm, while Jodi uttered little moans at each caress.

Suddenly, Luke jerked his hand from beneath her blouse, broke the kiss, and stepped back. "No more." His growl emerged from deep in his chest.

Jodi stared at him with passion-hazed eyes. "Why?" She felt discarded. Luke had made her ache for him. Having him stand so close, no longer holding her, was unbelievable torture. How could he be so cruel? "Why?" she repeated.

"Because I want you." Luke's eyes darkened with a burning desire that eliminated Jodi's pain of deprivation. "Since that stormy day under Umbrella Rock. Maybe even before then." He swallowed the lump in his throat. One finger, in spite of his intention to give her emotional space, feathered down her cheek and brushed the corner of her mouth, wet and swollen from his kisses. "And the other night, with the firelight turning your body to gold . . ."

Jodi buried both hands in his thick, curly hair and roughly pulled his mouth down to hers. "I want you, too, Luke."

Gently but firmly, he enfolded her hands in his and stepped away again. "You're scared, Jodi, and upset and reaching out for comfort."

"No," she refuted his save-her-from-herself gallantry. "I'm reaching out for you. *You,* Luke. Not because I'm scared or upset. Because I love you."

She hadn't planned to vocalize those three committing words, but when she beheld the joy on Luke's face, the shimmer in his eyes, she felt no regret.

No regret, either, as she took his scarred hand and, with

secret smile of anticipation, led him to her bed, delaying only long enough to turn off each and every light along the way.

Later, much later, Jodi and Luke ate their warmed-over dinner. At first Jodi was embarrassed, unsure, because she was unaccustomed to the soul-deep happiness of her after-the-loving glow. She'd made love with a wantonness she would never have believed possible. Luke's lovemaking, so different from Quentin's hurried, selfish sexual gratification, evoked feelings Jodi had only imagined or dreamed about. And by dropping his cloak of mistrust and exposing his innermost longing and need, Luke proved his love for her. Even if he didn't gift her with the three special words she gave him earlier.

During the meal Luke showed her how they could continue to make love. By touching fingertips, by feeding each other, by drinking from the same spot on the same coffee cup, by exchanging naughty heated glances while they laughed and talked. Jodi's nervousness vanished before the astonishing discovery that loving did not have to stop when she left the bed.

After the dishes were rinsed and stacked in the dishwasher and the safe-to-eat leftovers stored in the refrigerator, Luke took Jodi's hand and led her back to bed.

Twenty-seven

When Jodi awoke, Luke was gone. She barely remembered a featherlike kiss and a whispered "Have to go to work." Toasty warm in the sunshine, Jodi stretched like a lazy, pleased-with-herself cat. Some unused muscles, as well as other places, were sore, but she'd never felt happier or more complete. She didn't even mind her strange hatched-up breakfast—a heated leftover roll spread with jam from a newly opened jar. The practical side of her brain understood that yesterday Quentin had almost murdered her. But the fanciful side, predominant after last night, promised her nothing bad could happen to her now that she'd found the love, and the lover, of her dreams.

All morning, while she did her chores, a foolish grin kept popping up on her lips. The lips Luke had worshiped—and made his own, for always.

By mid-afternoon, Jodi, restless and missing Luke, decided the next best thing to being with him would be visiting his sister. So she gathered Becky's half-dozen plastic dishes, put them in a grocery bag, and went next door.

"Thanks for the dinner," she told Becky as soon as she stepped inside the entranceway. "Everything was delicious."

"I'm glad." Accepting the paper sack, Becky led the way to the living room. "Luke said you both enjoyed it."

A sudden discomfiture struck Jodi.

Becky momentarily put her at ease. "I'm glad he stayed over. After what you went through yesterday, you shouldn't have been alone." Then she paused, and a twinkle in her hazel eyes accompanied her devilish grin. "When Luke came home to change clothes and eat breakfast, he looked . . . different. Pleased with himself. Content."

Inexperienced in proper morning-after behavior, Jodi flushed and stared at the carpet.

Becky touched her arm and said, "It's all right, Jodi. Don't be ashamed."

"Ashamed?" Jodi's head came up, indignation written all over her face. "I'm not ashamed. I'm just not used to handling . . . a situation like this."

"I know that," Becky assured her as they sat down. "I just felt like teasing you a little. Irish says you like to be teased."

"Well, yes, but maybe not about something as special as . . ." She stopped. And blushed again.

When after a few seconds she dared to look at Becky, the other woman's expression was serious but her eyes still smiled. "You love him," Becky said.

"Yes," Jodi proudly admitted. "I love him."

Becky's smile shimmered in her eyes. "I hope you know how pleased I am. And happy for you both."

Slightly uncomfortable, Jodi hastened to nullify Becky's premature assumption. "We're not engaged or anything like that. I'm not sure how Luke feels, exactly."

"I am," Becky declared. "He wouldn't risk his heart or his trust on a casual relationship."

"I hope that's true." Jodi's soul-deep conviction that Luke loved her was not proof of his wish to be a permanent part of the rest of her life.

"He'd never use you, Jodi, or any woman. Not after the way Corinne treated him."

"So that was her name," Jodi murmured. She'd wondered. When Becky volunteered no more information regarding Corinne, Jodi asked her friend about another matter that had been bothering her for weeks. "Can you tell me, without violating a confidence, how Luke's hand was burned?"

"I thought I told you. It was a gasoline fire."

"Yes, you did say that. The day I met you."

"Have you asked Luke?"

Jodi sensed that Becky had withdrawn into the emotional closet where she and her brother stored their unhappy pasts, but she wasn't willing to accept defeat. "Last night. When we were . . . He promised to tell me later, when he felt more like talking about it." She gave Becky a sober, stubborn look. "But I feel like talking about it now. I want to know how and why it happened, so I can understand him better. Help me out here, Becky. I love him, and I want no secrets between us."

Becky gazed at Jodi's determined, entreating face. She had no qualms regarding Jodi's love for her brother, and since Luke planned to tell her the whole story, she could save him a lot of anguish by complying with Jodi's request. Finally, she said, "All right. But you must tell Luke I told you—and why. If I tell him, he'll only be angry with both of us."

"I'll discuss it with him the first chance I have."

Becky fisted her hands in her lap. "Luke was on his way home from a concert. Just on the outskirts of Austin, while he was pulling a young woman from a wrecked car, the gasoline tank exploded." She paused and added, with a poignant bitterness, "The accident victim was already dead, so Luke's good deed went for naught. He was a concerned passerby whose involvement was rewarded with the destruction of a promising career."

"Wh—when?" Jodi almost choked on the word.

"And that's another irony for you. It happened on a holiday, so Luke will never forget to remember. A year ago last New Year's Eve."

Oh, God! Please, God, no! Jodi silently shrieked the useless denial. For one agonizing moment she thought she might faint. The stabbing torment in her heart. The cut-off

262

of air from her lungs. The black spots jittering around in her blurred field of vision. She gave her head a violent, sight-clearing shake and leaped from the chair.

"I—I have to—to think about this," she harshly proclaimed, then ran—stumbled—out of the Prentiss house.

It couldn't be true! Jodi thought as she rushed toward the sanctuary of her cabin. But two similar accidents on the same date in the same locale defied every possible happenstance. Luke had to be the stranger who had stopped to rescue Annie on that cold, rainy night. Detective Hanley's Good Samaritan.

Why hadn't Luke come forward to tell the police what he knew? Was *he* responsible for the hit-and-run, deliberately forcing Annie's car off the highway and causing her death? No! Jodi refused to believe that. She recalled from the detective's notes how someone had covered Annie with a man's raincoat. Her murderer wouldn't have bothered. She flashed back to the island when Luke had so carefully spread the sleeping bag over Hannah. No, Luke wasn't the killer.

Once inside the cabin, Jodi practiced a make-believe chat with Luke, thanking him for his efforts on Annie's behalf. A new awareness assailed her, knocking her to her symbolic knees.

While attempting to rescue *her* sister, Luke had been horribly burned and as a consequence lost his dream career. Dear Lord, would her guilt never end? If she'd gone to the concert with Annie, the accident wouldn't have happened, and today Luke would be physically whole and well on his way to fame and fortune as a country-western musician.

How could she tell Luke she was partly to blame for the tragedy that had forever altered his life? How could she begin to make it up to him? By loving him. That was all she had to offer. Plus the truth. As difficult as the telling would be, she owed him that. If Luke didn't forgive her, at least he could be sure she, unlike Corinne, was worthy of his trust.

Jodi's eyes felt dry and gritty as sand. Tom-toms thrummed

behind her temples and at the base of her skull. What would she say to Luke? No, she knew *what*. It was the *how* that worried her. Quickly she swallowed a Tylenol, kicked off her shoes, and stretched out on the couch.

She was still there an hour later when the phone roused her. The grogginess vanished with a single apprehensive gulp the instant she heard Luke's voice. She wasn't ready to face him.

"Hello, Jodi. I'm calling from the store. I have to drive the Millers to Burnet, to the emergency room."

"What happened?"

"Maggie dropped a case of canned beans on her foot. Broke it, we think."

"I'm sorry."

"Me, too. I intended to see you tonight, but it'll be late when I get home. And I'll be helping Herbert tomorrow. Saturdays are his busiest days."

"Of course. I hope Mrs. Miller feels better. 'Bye." Jodi cradled the phone, thinking it was too bad about Mrs. Miller's mishap but glad to have her talk with Luke postponed.

Sheriff Dave Sutton phoned Jodi when she was nibbling an early dinner of yesterday's leftovers.

"Good news, Ms. Turner. The poison, the one Dr. O'Meara suspected, showed up only in the sugar bowl, so your other food is not contaminated. We searched Turner's condo and found the poison in a mayonnaise jar in the broom closet, along with detergent, disinfectant, and insect spray."

A relief rushed over Jodi like the tide cleaning a public beach of its ugly litter. "You arrested him?"

"Yes, ma'am, and booked him for attempted murder. All the way in to the station he kept screaming he hadn't done anything. And cursing you."

"I'm not surprised." Jodi sighed.

"No, ma'am. But this time we've got the indisputable evidence against him. Maybe when we bring him back in for interrogation—"

"He's not in jail?" A frisson of fear snaked along her spine.

"Out on bond," the sheriff told her regretfully. "But he won't bother you. I promised him that if he goes anywhere near you or your cabin, I'll personally lock him up and drop the only key in the deepest part of Lake Buchanan."

The picture he painted brought a faint smile to Jodi's lips.

"As I was saying," he continued, "we hope we can trick Turner into giving himself away regarding the Lowry girl's murder and the sabotaging of your boat." He paused. "Rex Hanley got in touch with me yesterday, told me about your sister's death. I'm real sorry."

"Thank you, Sheriff."

"We're going to try to tie Turner in with that, too, but Hanley says the Fairmont Hotel confirms Turner's alibi, that he spent the whole New Year's weekend in Dallas. Of course, he could have followed your sister, pushed her car off the road, and returned to the hotel. But the trail is pretty cold."

"I understand." Jodi didn't want this kind man to feel inefficient. "Even if no one proves Quentin killed Annie, I'll always believe he did. Why else would he be so determined to—to kill me, too? I think not because I refused to be his public relations rep again. He's afraid I'll remember something. I can't imagine what."

"Well, if you do remember, you be sure to notify Detective Hanley."

"I will, and thanks for letting me know about Quentin's arrest."

Surprisingly, Jodi's headache, the one that had been tapping at her temples for two days, had disappeared, along with the tension that had danced along her nerves. She felt like celebrating. At long last, after so many months of grief and guilt and frustration, she knew the identity of Annie's murderer. Quentin would pay for that and for all the other

265

wrongs he'd done her, although the latter wouldn't appear on the bill of indictment.

This was the time, Jodi sensed, to celebrate Annie's life and to close off the final phase of her own mourning. The time to sort through the keepsakes and unfinished songs she'd removed from Annie's apartment the day after she died.

Taking a slow, deep breath, as if nudging herself to jump into cold, dark, dreaded water, Jodi took her car keys from the desk drawer. In minutes she'd unlocked the trunk, which hadn't been opened since the morning after her arrival at the lake. The large lidless cardboard carton was heavy, and the shuffling about of its contents as she carried it made it difficult to handle, but she managed to get it as far as the porch without dropping it. From there she slid it inside and across the floor to the end of the bar.

On top lay the dusty discolored white scrapbook with embossed black notes spelling out the musical phrase "Happy birthday to you," Annie's sixteenth-birthday present from Irish. Jodi had skimped for months to pay for Annie's first expensive guitar, and the photo stuck on the front page depicted the three of them hugging, grinning, and holding up the gifts.

From there Jodi leafed through six years of memories, beginning with a flyer announcing Annie's first solo appearance at Irish's hospital Christmas gala, through clippings announcing awards and concerts, to the final entry, Annie's obituary notice. Jodi, dry-eyed and self-punishing, had glued it to the center of the blank page, then closed the scrapbook and laid it on top of the other mementos.

As Jodi slid off the bar stool to switch the overhead kitchen light on, her heart felt lighter. Slightly bruised by the nudging blows of days forever gone, but no longer weighed down by a crushing sorrow.

Luke knocked on the door and called her name. She swiped the back of her hand across her misty eyes as she went to welcome him. In the illumination spilling out of the cabin onto the steps, Jodi saw he'd come directly from the store. His shirt bore sweat stains under the arms, and his jeans were darker on the hips where he'd wiped his soiled hands.

"Hi," Jodi said, suddenly nervous. She was a divorced, almost-twenty-nine-year-old woman; yet she felt as flustered as a young girl greeting her first date.

"Hi," Luke said, suddenly nervous. One look at Jodi's frankly adoring face, and he forgot his promise to himself to ignore what had happened between them the other night. The fullness, the ache in his loins, reminded him. His head said he wasn't ready for a serious relationship, but his heart refused to listen. He could trust this caring, giving woman, so he must now trust his own feelings for her. He lowered his head until his mouth, tantalizingly close to hers, blew little puffs across her lips as he spoke. "I stopped by to ask if you've heard anything from the sheriff."

Jodi moistened her tingling lips with the tip of her tongue. "He arrested Quentin."

"Great! Do you have time to tell me about it?"

That was when Jodi looked over Luke's shoulder and noticed the odd shape of her night-shadowed car. The trunk lid was still up. She'd neglected to go back outside once she began to read the clippings in Annie's scrapbook. She jingled the car keys, still in her pocket, as she answered Luke. "Sure, I'll tell you everything." And she did mean everything, because she was eager for Luke to know her beloved sister was the person he had tried to save on that fateful night. She wanted to thank him. "First, though," she said, "I'd better lock my trunk before I forget it again. Go on in. Cokes in the fridge. Help yourself."

Luke stepped across the threshold and thumbed the porch light on so Jodi wouldn't be out there alone in the dark. Then he walked toward the kitchen, where he tripped over the carton lying in his path at the open end of the bar. He caught himself by bracing his palm on the counter. Actually, on a large open book, its thickness cushiony beneath his hand. Curious, he looked down and saw the small newspaper item centering the otherwise empty page. *Strange,* he thought. Then he moved closer and read the first two words that appeared in large, bold type: *Suzanne Klerkton.* He remembered the name. From the hit-and-run account in the newspaper a nurse's aide had left on his bed the morning after his admission to the hospital. A name he'd never forget as long as he drew breath. The woman who, together with the help of fate, had unintentionally ruined his life.

With a host of wordless questions fogging his mind, Luke scanned the brief obituary notice:

Suzanne Klerkton, age 22. Died in auto accident.
Survived by one sister, Jodi Turner, of this city.

Luke's thought processes failed to function beyond the names in the article. Suzanne Klerkton. Jodi Turner. Suzanne. *Annie!*

Holy . . . Mother . . . of . . . ! He'd done it again. Trusted a woman . . . loved a woman . . . who'd made a complete fool of him.

Jodi had deceived him. And it hurt! Worse than the awakening fire in his hand and arm when he drove like a crazy man to Emergency. Worse than the excruciating debridement of dead skin from his raw flesh. Worse than the endless, agonizing therapy to loosen his constricted tendons.

Luke raised his shaking hand from the bar, and with his support gone, for a second he feared his knees would buckle. Spreading his feet apart to maintain balance, he squarely faced the front door.

Hurrying inside, Jodi asked, "Did you find a Coke?"

"No, but I found something else." A cold fury roughened his voice, and his eyes flashed with anger.

Stunned and bewildered by the change in him, Jodi halted her rush across the floor. Alarm raked her intuition.

Luke stabbed the open scrapbook with a scarred finger and hoarsely demanded, "How much longer did you intend to lie?"

Suddenly, Jodi understood. She breathed a little easier. As soon as Luke understood, everything would be all right. "I didn't lie," she answered.

"You damn sure didn't tell the truth."

"I know you're upset, but—"

"Upset? *Upset!* I'm mad as hell and so disgusted I could puke."

"Disgusted?" Jodi asked weakly. This was not going at all as she'd hoped.

"With you, for playing me for a sucker. And with myself, for taking the bait." He stopped to catch his breath, then mocked her. "Annie this. Annie that. Poor sweet Annie died in a car accident." He uttered a humorless chuckle. "You neglected to tell me your Annie is why I'll carry this"—he thrust his scarred hand close to her ghostly pale face—"to my grave."

Shocked, Jodi staggered backward. But she was still determined to make him understand.

"I didn't know," she protested vehemently. "Not until Becky told me, and I haven't seen you since then."

"Right." Luke snorted his disbelief. "You've known since the day we met. You felt sorry for me, and to make it up to me for Annie's part in my . . . injury, you worked like mad to get me to play again. That way, you could be my agent, and we'd both wind up filthy rich."

"No," Jodi whispered.

"I've already had one agent who pretended to care . . . and dumped me when I was no more use to her." Bitterness ravaged his face.

Numbly, Jodi realized that Luke was referring to Corinne. She'd been his fiancée *and* his agent. No wonder he despised agents.

"I never wanted to be your agent," she murmured.

He appeared not to have heard. "And when that little plan didn't work," Luke ranted on, "you decided the only other way to pay your family debt was to take me into your bed."

Jodi recoiled as though he'd struck her. "No, Luke! No!

269

I love you. I did it all . . . because . . . I—I love you. You *have* to believe me!" Her plea broke off with a dry sob.

Suddenly, Luke's outrage ran down like the broken spring of an old-fashioned wind-up clock. With a quiet calm that frightened Jodi more than any of his angry shouts ever had, he answered her. "What I have to do is make damn sure you stay the hell out of my life." The implacability on his haggard face and the irrefutable disdain in his eyes told Jodi their time together, like the hours already marked off by the clock, had run out.

Twenty-eight

Stunned, Jodi watched Luke slowly cross the room. At the open doorway he paused and, fixing his accusing and pain-filled eyes on hers, said, "Goodbye, Jodi." Silent tears blurred Jodi's vision as she weakly made her way to the desk. She lifted the phone, then put it down. Her first instinct was to call Irish; he could fix anything. But no, neither a doctor's medication nor a godfather's wisdom could halt the breaking of a heart.

"I—I have to h—handle this m—myself," Jodi sobbed aloud.

Collapsing on the lounge chair, she mentally went back over her conversation with Luke. She'd tried to tell him the truth. He hadn't believed her. Instead, he had jumped to harsh, unfair conclusions and refused to listen to her disavowals. She had done nothing wrong, and she'd be damned if she'd sit here weeping and wailing and *feeling guilty*. Not this time. She loved Luke, would always love him—Jodi dabbed at a renegade tear with the hem of her blouse—but she'd had a life before she met him, and somehow she'd manage to exist without the love he didn't trust her enough to give.

One thing was obvious, however. Staying here in the cabin would be like prodding a fresh, open wound with a scalpel without anesthesia.

When the phone rang, hope spewed adrenaline through

Jodi's whole body. She leaped to her feet and ran to pick up the receiver.

"Luke?" The word split into two syllables as it exited her Sahara-dry mouth.

"No," Troy said. "Sorry. I heard over the music grapevine that . . . uh . . . Quentin has been arrested. I just wanted to let you know how glad I am."

Jodi shook off her disappointment. "Thanks. I feel a lot safer. But I'm moving back into my apartment tomorrow anyway."

"You are? Too bad we haven't been able to . . . uh . . . spend more time together."

"Yes, it is." Suddenly, Jodi knew how to remedy that. "I've finally started going through the box of Annie's music stuff, and I promised you a memento. If you're not busy, why don't you come down off your mountain"—she forced a chuckle—"and choose what you'd like to keep?"

"Tonight?" He sounded pleased, even excited.

"Sure. It's early yet. And I should start getting used to night-owl hours again." The prospect of the same old socio-business merry-go-round appalled her, but she had no alternative.

"I'll be there in . . . uh . . . about thirty minutes, and . . . uh . . . thank you."

Jodi splashed cold water on her tear-streaked face, freshened up her makeup, and retackled Annie's carton. Every tape and every sheet of staff paper was identified with the initials "A.K." and a date. Annie had begun the habit when, at fourteen, she read about the plagiarizing of a composer's song; and although Irish often teased her about it, from then on she had marked every scrap of her work even if it was bad and she expected to destroy it later. Some of those unfinished tunes were still in the box. Sadly, Jodi wondered how many might have wound up on the country-western charts if Annie had lived.

When Jodi started to remove the rubber band from a sheaf of staff paper, the band broke and stung her hand, startling her into dropping the pages on the floor. Stooping to retrieve them, she noticed they all seemed to be completed songs. Some had titles; some didn't. Some even had lyrics written in Annie's tiny, almost illegible script. Jodi recognized three as Annie's award winners. *Maybe Troy will appreciate one of these,* Jodi speculated as she checked the date on each sheet and arranged them chronologically.

The chore completed, she saw the top sheet had been initialed and dated only a month before Annie's death. *This one,* Jodi selfishly promised herself, *is mine,* and she started to hum the melody. Tentatively at first, then with more confidence as the tune became familiar. Jodi recalled the time Annie had proudly played it for her, bouncing all over her living room declaring she had another winner.

A winner.

Jodi gasped. She'd just hummed *Troy's* award-winning song. The one he played at Becky's. He'd *stolen* Annie's melody!

Unbelievable outrage assailed Jodi. How *dare* Troy claim Annie's song as his? Well, he sure as hell wasn't going to get away with it! She'd see to it that his awards were rescinded and his theft made public.

"Hello, Jodi."

Troy's greeting from across the room shut down Jodi's mind. She couldn't think what to say, how to act, what to do, except to reflexively stuff the telltale evidence in her jeans pocket.

"The door was open," Troy told her, bestowing her with his boy-next-door smile. "Sorry if I . . . uh . . . startled you."

"Startled me?" She stalled for time to collect her wits. "A little, but that's okay." She asked herself why she returned his smile when she really felt like choking the man. But she knew why; she needed to catch her emotional breath. Jodi motioned to the cardboard box and the clutter strewn over the counter. "This is everything I brought from Annie's apartment."

273

After reading the labels on the practice tapes, Troy set them all aside. Next, he rifled through the piecemeal tunes.

"These are all . . . uh . . . unfinished." Troy scowled and tapped his fingers on the bar.

Jodi picked up the chronologically arranged stack and handed it to him. "Then maybe you'd like to choose one of these."

Greedily, Troy reached for the pages and fanned them out like a deck of cards, muttering some of the dates. After checking and rechecking, he exhaled a long, noisy sigh.

Beginning to enjoy herself, Jodi shrewdly responded to his obvious relief. "But you haven't picked one."

"No. I thought—" He stopped and paled as Jodi pulled the song page from her pocket.

"Were you perhaps looking for this?" Fury blazed in her eyes as she held the winning song close enough for him to recognize it even without its title.

Like a deflated balloon, Troy slumped onto the bar stool next to Jodi's. "You know," he murmured.

"Yes, damn you, I know!" Jodi answered hotly. "And I plan to shout from the housetops that you're a cheat and a liar and a thief!"

"You can't do that, Jodi."

Did he actually believe pleading would stop her?

"Yes, I can, and I will."

Troy grabbed for Annie's song, but Jodi was too fast for him and slid it back in her hip pocket.

"But then everything will have been for nothing." He sounded sad. Not worried, not guilty, just sad. When Jodi made no comment, Troy continued. "All the things I did to *be* somebody."

Anxious for Troy to leave so she could report his thievery to the sheriff, Jodi feigned an interest in his last self-centered remark by asking politely, "What things?"

"Tom Harrigan."

Jodi recognized the name of the elderly music store owner

who had befriended Troy. Had he stolen something from his benefactor, too?

"And Annie," Troy added in a singsong fashion. "And that girl."

"What girl?"

"The girl with the violets."

For one benumbed millisecond, Jodi simply stared at Troy. The violets, per the sheriff's orders, hadn't been mentioned in any media accounts of Hannah's death.

Then with all the force . . . and the horror . . . of a bomb, the truth exploded in Jodi's head. Troy hadn't *stolen* from the three persons he named. *He had murdered them.* Like debris from the bomb burst, shock and bitterness and grief littered Jodi's emotional space.

Before she could stop herself, she reacted. "Y—you killed Annie."

"I didn't intend to at first." Unbelievably, Troy spoke in a normal conversational manner. "That day in Dallas, Wayne Kidd told Annie I must be catching her style—like measles or something—because the song I sent him sounded so much like one she might've written. And then the dumb ox mentioned the title. Annie ripped me up and down about it, said she hadn't told Wayne but she would tell a lawyer soon as she got home. I just wanted her to stop and talk to me first."

"She *knew* it was you banging into her car?" The idea horrified Jodi.

"Sure she did. I just wanted to explain. You see, Annie had won all kinds of awards. It was my turn. I did help her a little bit with the lyrics, so I felt okay about using the song to make a name for myself."

Jodi missed the nervous "uh's" in his usual speech pattern and realized that Troy, probably for the first time in his life, felt totally self-confident. Weird. And frightening. She had only begun to fathom his insane, twisted logic, but she sensed that until she could outwit him and escape, her safety lay in feeding his ego. She took a deep breath and pasted a smile on her lips. "So when Annie wouldn't stop and let you explain, you . . . very cleverly f—forced her car off the road."

"Yeah. Cleverly." He beamed.

Inwardly, Jodi winced, but with a colossal effort she maintained an admiring attitude. "You were smart to get your car repaired so quickly," she said, recalling the police department had checked it two days after the accident and found no damage.

"The next morning I rented a car exactly like mine, exchanged the license plates, and stored my car. After about three months, I drove mine to Louisiana to some little burg and had it fixed, then turned in the rental. Worked out fine."

"It certainly did." Jodi paused, wondering how she could get him to tell her about Tom Harrigan. Detective Hanley could use every scrap of information against Troy, who deserved the severest punishment the courts could mete out. Then the solution came to her; in Troy's warped mind, it would be a natural progression. "And if Tom hadn't left you all his money, renting that car for such a long time wouldn't have been feasible."

"That's right." The pleased tone in his voice made Jodi ill. "I got tired of working for room and board, so when Tom told me about his will, I just hurried things along. You see, I needed some cash and a business . . . to make people notice me. Tom was in his eighties and had heart trouble, so smothering him with a pillow was easy. Nobody ever suspected. I was okay for a while, until I decided I wanted to be *somebody* in the music world—like Randy Travis or George Strait."

"So you used Annie." Jodi's icy accusation had no effect on Troy's self-fulfilling revelations.

"Yeah. She was cute and talented and asking for love. I loved her . . . I guess . . . at least for a while."

Jodi would never have believed it possible she'd want to kill anyone, but at that instant Troy was fortunate there wasn't a loaded gun within her reach.

"Annie wanted to help me," Troy continued, "but she kept telling me to be patient. Finally, I got tired of waiting. I copied Annie's song from that sheet you have."

For the first time since he began his evil confession, Troy appeared upset. He took a step toward her, and she sidled around the corner, putting the bar between them. Troy shrugged, smiled again, and said proudly, "I just *knew* that song was a winner, and all my fans everywhere proved it. But then you told me you'd kept Annie's music. I was afraid that song was still in the box. I couldn't let you find it. I looked in your apartment, everywhere it might be." He laughed at her evident surprise. "You hadn't figured that out yet, had you?"

"No, I hadn't," Jodi admitted, clenching her pocketed fist.

"I watched the cabin from my house—with binoculars— so I'd know if you were home. The day you went to town, I came in here and hunted for Annie's stuff."

And fondled my lingerie. Jodi shuddered, and her heart jackhammered against her ribs.

"How did you get in?" She knew her ignorance would augment his hateful boasting, but she needed the answer.

"I used the key Irish gave Annie right after he bought this place." He scowled when Jodi failed to praise his ingenuity. "I couldn't find the song, and I was getting scared you'd find it first. When I watched you go out to the island, I borrowed a boat and followed you. I didn't want them to find you shot. They might suspect me, so I planned for you to drown. And then that girl caught me sawing a hole in your boat. Still, I figured they couldn't connect that girl to you—or me." Momentary anger flared in his voice and eyes. "But you learned to swim."

Jodi remained silent and inched away, putting distance between them. Once she reached the middle of the cabin, Troy swiftly moved between her and the door. His expression, sickeningly friendly, made his obstructing maneuver doubly menacing. Jodi gazed longingly at the dark opening in the wall—and understood how a mouse felt when a grinning tomcat sat between it and the escape hole in the base-board.

The cat decided to taunt the mouse. "But I bet you hadn't stopped putting all that sugar on your cereal. I remembered how Annie used to tease you about it. So I got the poison and waited for a chance to mix it with your sugar."

Jodi yearned to tell him *his* phone call had saved her life, but she dared not. Only in cartoons did the mice taunt the cats. Jodi clamped her mouth shut and said nothing.

"Stashing the poison in Quentin's condo was no problem. And it got him arrested." Troy frowned. "Except you didn't eat the sugar. So"—he pulled a small handgun from beneath his untucked shirttail—"now I have to shoot you."

Staring at the pointing weapon, Jodi felt a blinding terror and a suffocating hopelessness, but even more acutely, a soul-deep regret that she would never be able to convince Luke how truly, honestly she loved him. A bullet from Troy's pistol would forever deprive her of that second chance.

But Jodi Turner was the independent, take-charge woman who *never* gave up.

Jodi lunged at Troy, sharply striking his gun arm karate-style with the edge of her hand. Completely surprised by her offensive action, Troy loosened his grip on the weapon, and it fell undischarged, from his grasp. Cursing, Troy scurried to retrieve it, but Jodi's shoe sent it skidding across the uncarpeted floor. Troy brutally seized her shoulder and turned her around with her back to him, his free hand groping for the song sheet in her hip pocket. Bending her knee and raising her foot as high as possible, Jodi kicked up and back with all the strength her anger and fright could muster. Troy grunted with pain and crouched over, clutching his groin.

Slightly disoriented by the scuffle, Jodi headed for the open doorway and freedom. But Troy, not wholly incapacitated by Jodi's desperation blow, managed to stagger far and fast enough to catch her ankle. With a mighty jerk he halted her escape, and as she fell she saw the approaching sharp corner of the lamp table.

Shit! I screwed up again. I couldn't drown her. I couldn't poison her. And tonight I didn't shoot her . . . But hold on. This is even better. Nobody's heard a gunshot, and she's knocked out real good. I can set fire to the cabin and walk back up the hill to my house while Jodi burns or inhales enough smoke to kill her. Quentin's out on bail. They'll suspect him . . . Let's see. I need something flammable. Ah! Here's a can of lighter fluid under the sink. I'll just sprinkle it around on the furniture and drapes, like so. . . . Now I take the box of Annie's stuff outside, then I strike a match and toss it inside . . . and poof! Jodi's history.

Twenty-nine

After he said goodbye to Jodi and robotlike negotiated
the cabin steps, Luke began to run, his mind on nothing
except putting one foot in front of the other. Along the road,
across the garden, through the woods. He slowed only when
he collided with a tree trunk unseen in the moonless night.
Out of breath, he trudged back to the garden, where he
plopped down on the stone bench. Sitting quietly, inhaling
the mingling fragrances, hearing the splash of the fountain
and the distant hoot of an owl, Luke realized he'd become
a classic example of you-don't-know-what-you-had-until-
you've-lost-it. Maybe if he'd admitted to himself how much
he loved Jodi and told her, he wouldn't be here alone in the
dark, feeling his heart shatter like a smashed light bulb
whose life is spent. The break-up with Corinne was a pin-
prick compared to the knife-in-the-gut pain overwhelming
him now.

In his aching head he replayed the conversation with Jodi.
Her frantic denials, her pleading declaration of love. He remembered how two nights ago she'd given herself to him
passionately . . . and selflessly. Was that the behavior of a
liar, a deceiver, a user?

Had his knee-jerk reaction been too hasty, his judgment
unfair? Lord, if that were so, he had displayed a cruelty
more hurtful than any of Quentin's blows. Would—could—

Jodi ever forgive him? For a long time he sat and contemplated a way to make amends for his callousness. He owed her—and himself—an opportunity to talk, to sort out their misunderstandings. He'd see her tomorrow.

Luke stood, stretched his tight leg muscles, and took a deep breath. And smelled wood smoke. Maybe Jodi was still awake and lonely and had built a fire for company. Smiling at the memory of her being afraid she'd burn down the cabin, he glanced in her direction—and saw the telltale orange glow. Oh, dear God!

Forgetting his tired, aching muscles, Luke ran down the road, praying with every footfall that he wasn't too late.

By the time he reached the cabin, it was already engulfed in flames. Noting the open door, Luke leaped over the steps and rushed inside. The heat was intense, the oxygen rapidly depleting. Luke closed his mouth and forced himself to take shallow breaths. Flames crackled perilously close to him and licked hungrily at the walls. Where was Jodi? In the bedroom? The thick, swirling gray smoke made his eyes water, and he could hardly see. Stumbling over something, he stooped down to touch it. Fabric. Jodi's T-shirt. Thank heaven, he'd found her!

Picking her up in his arms, he staggered outside and gently laid her on the night-dampened grass. Squatting beside her, he suddenly felt helpless—and scared to death. Tears rolled down his smoke-blotched cheeks as he checked her throat for a pulse. It was there! Unbelievably, miraculously, strong and steady.

"Oh, Jodi," he murmured thankfully. "Oh, Jodi."

At that moment Becky, wearing her robe and slippers, came dashing across the lawn. "Luke! Jodi! Are you all right? I called 911. Firetrucks and an ambulance will be here right away." She knelt beside her brother and her friend.

Jodi opened her eyes, and Luke leaned over to kiss her cheek. "You're going to be all right," he told her.

"He . . . set . . . fire," she whispered huskily.

For her, Luke again felt the heat and flames as if they were real.

"I could kill Quentin for this." Now Luke understood how a heretofore law-abiding citizen could be driven to commit murder.

"Not . . . Quentin," Jodi croaked. The crisp, clean air felt good to her aching, smoke-filled lungs. She coughed. "Troy. Troy did . . . sugar . . . boat. Oh! My head . . . hurts." She was so tired.

In the glow of the towering orange flames, Becky caught the alarm in Luke's eyes. "It's all right," she reassured him. "Jodi just fainted."

They exchanged relieved, loving smiles as sirens wailed in the distance.

Becky phoned Irish from the hospital, and he arrived an hour later, in a near panic until he was able to confirm the diagnosis of Jodi's doctor of record: a slight concussion and mild smoke inhalation. Jodi would spend the remainder of the night under observation, and if no new symptoms developed, she'd be discharged the next morning—if she promised to take it easy for a few days.

With Jodi out of danger, Becky returned home, but Luke insisted upon staying close to Jodi's bedside.

Upon Irish's assurance that such concern wasn't necessary, Luke adamantly replied, "It is, to me. I want to be there when she awakens." Irish nodded in agreement and settled on one of the waiting room armchairs.

Luke watched as from time to time a nurse came into Jodi's room, roused her and asked, "What's your name?" received the anticipated response, and left. After a half-dozen such checkups, usually prescribed for concussed patients, Jodi opened her eyes clear and wide, glared at the nurse, and said in a strong, irritated voice, "I'm getting tired of telling you this, so please don't ask me again. My name is Jodi Turner."

Luke laughed under his breath. Jodi was back to normal, stubborn and assertive. The moment the rubber soles of the nurse's sturdy white shoes squeaked her departure, Luke walked over to the edge of Jodi's bed.

"Hi," he said softly as he lightly touched her hand. He gave her a nervous grin, and her eyes, reddened by the smoke, smiled back.

Jodi was glad he was there but cautioned herself not to expect too much; he'd simply reverted to his role of friendly neighbor. Maybe, she hoped, they could be friends, for Becky's sake if for no other reason.

"So you're tired of telling the nurse your name is Jodi Turner." Luke's expression turned serious. Not accusatory serious. Warm and caring serious.

"You heard."

"How about, next time she comes in to check, if you tell her your name will soon be Jodi Prentiss?"

The tears in Jodi's dark eyes shimmered like raindrops. Luke had to bend over to hear her. "Don't tease me."

"I'm not teasing," he vehemently denied as he grasped her trembling hand and caressed her palm with his thumb. "I was an idiot not to believe you or trust you or listen to what you said. I'd already decided to tell you this tomorrow—today now—and when I realized you were in that burning cabin, I was sure of only one thing. I don't want to live my life without you. I knew that when I ran into the cabin."

"Oh, Luke, you rescued me?" Jodi read the answer in his fabulous green eyes. "You, the man who quakes with fear when he strikes a match, deliberately ran into those hot, horrible flames to save me?"

"Well, I—" Luke's hesitancy revealed an adorable shy modesty.

Irish tiptoed into the room. Seeing Jodi wide awake, he hurried to her bedside and kissed her forehead. "Hello, honey," he said.

"I'm sorry about the cabin."

"You're safe. That's all that matters." He cleared his throat. "Are you up to another visitor?"

"Becky?"

"No. She went home several hours ago. As soon as she found out you'd be all right. No, the person waiting to speak to you is Sheriff Sutton."

"Oh." Why was he here at this hour, with dawn barely graying the dark square of her room's window? Whatever it was, she might as well get it over with. "Tell him to come in."

From the doorway Irish motioned to the lawman, and the two men approached her bedside.

"Good morning, Ms. Turner," the sheriff said. "I'm glad you're going to be okay. You look surprisingly well, considering."

"Thanks."

Sheriff Sutton, on the other hand, appeared exhausted, his eyes red and bleary, his jaws bewhiskered, his uniform smudged with black embers and soot.

"The Doc here tells me you'll be going back to Austin today"—Jodi stubbornly glowered at Irish, who just as stubbornly nodded his head—"so I wanted to bring you up to date while you're still in my jurisdiction." He paused. "Do you remember telling Prentiss that Troy Morrell was to blame for everything that happened to you up here at the lake?"

"I remember."

"Well, ma'am, when my deputies went to his house to arrest him, he went into the den, ostensibly for his jacket, but instead he took his gun from the desk drawer and . . . shot himself in the head."

"I see." Jodi knew she sounded cold, almost glad, and in a way she was. She'd be spared the hassle and publicity of a trial. She hadn't forgotten what the news media had done to Becky. In fact, that had been on her mind since that awful argument, or whatever, between her and Luke. The three men were waiting for her to say more. "Troy always needed to be somebody important, and winning the country-western awards was for him the pinnacle of success. But in order to make that happen, he had to steal *Annie's* song"—her companions evidenced disbelief, then disgust—"and then had to—to kill to keep the world from finding out his fame was based on a lie." She sighed. "I think he shot himself not to avoid punishment for his crimes, but to avoid disgrace and the scorn of his musical peers."

"Perhaps," the sheriff agreed tersely. "The deputies found a box of tapes and other items with your sister's initials on them in Morrell's den. They're in my office."

"Oh, I'm so glad they weren't in the fire," Jodi said. And Annie's last song was still in the pocket of her jeans, probably hanging in the hospital room closet.

"I called Detective Hanley about the fire," Sheriff Sutton told her, "and he said to tell you he may never know for sure who killed your sister."

"I know," Jodi said, her eyes shining through their sudden moistness. "Troy did it. He told me. He killed Hannah, too."

"Well, I'll be damned," the lawman said. "Guess that ties it all up then. No. One other thing. The charges against Quentin Turner have been dropped. But he knows if he ever bothers you again, my threat still applies. I'll be going now. Good luck to you."

Irish volunteered to walk the sheriff to his van, and as soon as Luke and Jodi were alone, Luke said, "There's one more thread to disentangle. Why I left Annie that night and never went to the police."

"You wanted immediate care for your hand, and if you'd waited for the ambulance, it would have delayed that by at least thirty minutes. As for identifying yourself to the authorities, I think you were concerned that if the news media played you up as a hero, they might connect your name with Becky's and rehash her tragedy."

"Damn, woman, you're too smart for me." Luke gazed at her with merry, worshipful amazement. Then he looked somber. "One thing you maybe *don't* know. I love you, Jodi, and I always will, with all my heart. Could you possibly spend the rest of your life with this stubborn, ill-mannered

285

grocery clerk who promises to be a piano player again some-day?"

"I can handle that," she breathed ecstatically just before Luke's sexy mouth claimed hers.

Epilogue

Fourteen Months Later

The week's featured guests on *Austin City Limits,* the prestigious country-western public broadcasting program, were Ginger Tillman and *Only in Texas.* Jodi and Luke, now living in their large A-frame home built on Irish's old lot, which he gave them as a wedding gift, occupied the center front row seats. Beside them sat Irish and Becky, the latter having been coaxed by the doctor to come out of seclusion for the event.

During her stint on stage, Ginger, vivacious and western-togged as always, sang two of Annie's award-winning ballads and was well received. But the majority of the huge crowd had attended because of an announcement that *Only in Texas* would play for the first time a song composed by Luke Prentiss, their former and still fondly remembered piano player.

Mavis, Jodi's secretary at Sunbelt Images, stopped by their seats to say hello. Upon Jodi's recommendation, Mavis had been promoted to her employer's old job when Jodi resigned to work full-time in the artist studio incorporated in the lake house, along with a soundproof music room for Luke.

Only in Texas played several songs, and then Gus, the spokesman, came to the footlights with the microphone and said, "Ladies and gentlemen, you will witness musical history tonight. You came here expecting us to perform Luke Prentiss's song. What we didn't tell you is . . . *he* will play it himself."

Surprised into speechlessness, Jodi threw a worried, questioning look at her husband, who was already on his feet. He patted her hand, climbed the steps to the stage, and took his seat on the piano bench.

When he began to play, the audience gasped in astonishment, then listened in rapt, pin-drop silence. Luke performed the slow, bluesy melody and two-part harmony on the bass keys with his left hand, and he struck what would normally have been the bass chords on the treble keys with his burn-impaired right hand. After he finished, a magical hush hovered over the auditorium, followed by thunderous applause that went on and on.

Finally, Luke stepped up to the microphone, his green eyes frankly moist. Jodi swallowed, wondering if it were possible for one's heart to burst with happiness. Only she understood the incredible triumph embodied in Luke's performance. She was so proud!

The cheering quieted as he began to speak. "Usually this is the place where the musician does an encore. I have none for you." A collective groan spread throughout the crowd. "I'll continue to write songs, but this is a one-time-only performance—a wedding anniversary gift to my wife, who not only has made me happy, but who made me dream and gave me the courage to be the piano player I promised her I would be someday. Jodi, this night . . . and this song . . . are for you."

Wild applause broke out anew, and Luke beamed from the stage. Jodi felt the unashamed tears of joy cascading down her cheeks as she smiled up at her husband and lovingly ran her hand over the swell of their unborn child, who in three months would make their family complete and their life together absolutely perfect.